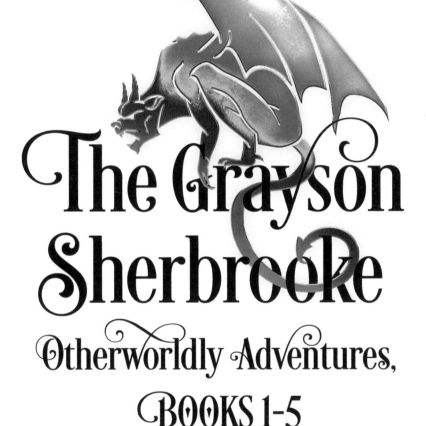

The Grayson Sherbrooke

Otherworldly Adventures,

BOOKS 1-5

BOOKS BY CATHERINE COULTER

HISTORICAL SERIES

THE SHERBROOKE SERIES
The Sherbrooke Bride
The Hellion Bride
The Heiress Bride
Mad Jack
The Courtship
The Scottish Bride
Pendragon
The Sherbrooke Twins
Lyon's Gate
Wizard's Daughter
The Prince of Ravenscar

THE REGENCY SERIES
The Countess
The Rebel Bride
The Heir
The Duke
Lord Harry

THE BARON SERIES
The Wild Baron
The Offer
The Deception

THE NIGHT TRILOGY
Night Fire
Night Shadow
Night Storm

THE MAGIC TRILOGY
Midsummer Magic
Calypso Magic
Moonspun Magic

THE LEGACY TRILOGY
The Wyndham Legacy
The Nightingale Legacy
The Valentine Legacy

THE DEVIL'S DUOLOGY
Devil's Embrace
Devil's Daughter

THE STAR SERIES
Evening Star
Midnight Star
Wild Star
Jade Star

THE MEDIEVAL SERIES
Warrior's Song
Fire Song
Earth Song
Secret Song
Rosehaven
The Penwyth Curse
The Valcourt Heiress

THE VIKING SERIES
Season of the Sun
Lord of Hawkfell Island
Lord of Raven's Peak
Lord of Falcon Ridge

CONTEMPORARY ROMANCE SERIES

THE "A" TRILOGY
Aftershocks
Afterglow
The Aristocrat

CONTEMPORARY ROMANTIC THRILLERS
False Pretenses
Impulse
Beyond Eden
Born to be Wild

THRILLER SERIES

THE FBI SERIES
The Cove
The Maze
The Target
The Edge
Riptide
Hemlock Bay
Eleventh Hour
Blindside
Blowout
Point Blank
Double Take
TailSpin
KnockOut
Whiplash
Split Second
Backfire
Bombshell
Power Play
Nemesis
Insidious
Enigma
Paradox
Labyrinth
Deadlock
Vortex

A BRIT IN THE FBI SERIES
The Final Cut
The Lost Key
The End Game
The Devil's Triangle
The Sixth Day
The Last Second

#1 *NEW YORK TIMES*
BESTSELLING AUTHOR

CATHERINE COULTER

The Grayson Sherbrooke

Otherworldly Adventures, BOOKS 1-5

**BLACK
STONE**
PUBLISHING

Published in 2022 by Blackstone Publishing
Cover and book design by Alenka Vdovič Linaschke

The characters and events in this book are fictitious.
Any similarity to real persons, living or dead, is coincidental
and not intended by the author.

Printed in the United States of America

First edition: 2022
ISBN 979-8-200-74927-0
Fiction / Mystery & Detective / Collections & Anthologies

Version 1

CIP data for this book is available
from the Library of Congress

Blackstone Publishing
31 Mistletoe Rd.
Ashland, OR 97520

www.BlackstonePublishing.com

To my brilliant and very nearly perfect personal assistant/ secretary/right brain, Karen Evans. Thank you for your excellent input on *The Virgin Bride of Northcliffe Hall*.

To Jessica Fogleman who has edited the four novellas. Thank you for your continued excellent commitments to Grayson and his cohorts. I'm so pleased you enjoyed this one so very much.

My ongoing thanks to Nicole Robson and Cailtin O'Beirne for their humorous and very wise counsel and hard work.

,

TABLE OF CONTENTS

The Strange Visitation at Wolffe Hall

THE FIRST NOVELLA
IN THE GRAYSON SHERBROOKE OTHERWORLDLY
ADVENTURES SERIES

CHAPTER ONE

She jerked up in bed, wide awake, breathing hard and fast. The dream—this was the second time she'd had the identical dream. She was herself in the dream, and she was surrounded by a hazy sort of pale light that kept her from seeing anything clearly. It was as if she were in the middle of a long, foggy tunnel with a low humming all around her that slowly changed to a low voice that spoke quietly at first, all around her, then the voice became gradually harsher and louder, yelling at her. Then she came awake, sweating, terrified, and still not understanding what it was all about. The same sounds were in both dreams, and she realized this time the sounds were words, only they were garbled and distorted as if coming from a long way away, and she couldn't make them out.

She pinched her arm—yes, she was awake. She was still breathing hard, her heart pounding. Had P.C. had the same dream again? She had to go to her, but suddenly, she was so afraid she couldn't get spit in her mouth because the once-warm scented air was turning icy cold. She would swear she could see the air shimmering in the dim light cast by the half-moon from her window. What was going on?

She felt the first tremor, only a slight shuddering, and she saw her small writing desk slide across the floor.

What was going on here? She had to get to her daughter.

Miranda lit a candle, threw on her bed-robe and her slippers, and ran into the wide corridor, yelling her daughter's name. She threw open P.C.'s door, but P.C. wasn't in her bedchamber. Miranda ran back into the corridor and skidded to a stop when, suddenly, her candle went out, as if an invisible hand had pinched the wick, throwing the hallway into impenetrable darkness.

"P.C.!"

No answer. There didn't seem to be another living person in Wolffe Hall, as if she were completely alone, but how could that be? It made no sense. She called out for the Great, her mama-in-law, the servants. No answer. And always as she made her way in the dark, feeling along the wall, she called out as she went, "P.C.!"

"Mama! I'm here. Where are you?"

Miranda got herself together. "I'm here, love, walking toward the top of the stairs. I yelled your name—where were you?"

"I was trying to find you. Then I heard you shouting my name. Didn't you hear me?"

She shook her head. She hadn't heard a thing. Her daughter ran into her, and she hugged her against her side. "The dream came again, but now it's more."

P.C. had her arms tight around her mother's waist. "It's scary, Mama, really scary. Did your candle go out too?"

"Yes. I couldn't find you, and it simply went out."

"Mama, it's coming. Listen."

Miranda felt something in the air itself, something black and cold, and it was building and building. She and P.C. heard a low growl of the voice, that same voice, so far away, but screaming the same words over and over.

"Mama, can you understand the words?"

Miranda got herself together. "No, I can't, but it will be all right, P.C., because we're going to leave. We'll be able to see the moon through the downstairs front windows. Be careful. Come slowly, all right?"

"It's like we're the only ones in the house, but you know we aren't."

P.C. panted out the words, pressing closer to her mother. "Mama, what about the Great and Grandmama?"

Miranda looked back up the stairs. With no light, the stairs quickly disappeared into inky blackness. "We have to try another candle." Miranda ran into the library and fetched one of the Great's candles. The flame flickered, but held. The air was so cold both of them were shivering violently as they walked back up the stairs, Miranda cupping the candle.

When they reached her mother-in-law's bedchamber, Miranda turned the doorknob, but nothing happened. She twisted, but still, nothing. She pounded on the door, but there was no answer.

P.C. whispered, "Mama, where is she? Why is the door locked?"

Miranda pounded on the door again, threw back her head, and yelled, "Mama-in-law! Where are you?" And there it came, the voice from their dreams, not screaming, but low, a whispery faraway voice, muffled, as inside a tunnel, blurred, unintelligible. The same sounds over and over and it was coming from everywhere, closer and closer, like a circle drawing in tighter and tighter, swirling around them. It was becoming louder again, but they still couldn't understand. Now the voice was shouting, but it was all confused, deep, guttural sounds.

Then silence, utter silence.

They ran to the Great's door. It was locked too, but Miranda yelled, "Sir! Lord Great!"

But there was no answer.

Mother and daughter huddled in the dark hallway, wondering about the servants, when they felt a small tremor as if from an earthquake, something neither of them had ever experienced, but instinctively recognized. Then the house began to shudder and shake around them. "Mama, we've got to get out of the house, now."

Miranda knew she was right, but what about the servants? She took P.C.'s hand, and they raced to the bottom of the third-floor stairs. Both of them shouted, "Suggs! Mrs. Crandle! Marigold!"

No answer.

Again, Miranda felt like they were alone. It was terrifying because it made no sense.

The air was colder now than it had been an instant before, and the slight tremors were coming more frequently. No hope for it. Miranda grabbed P.C.'s hand. "We're getting out of this cursed house, away from that cursed voice."

She clasped her daughter's hand as they ran back down the hall to the main staircase. They paused, listened, but there was no sound of another person, nothing, only silence, dead silence, and the cold air and the growing tremors.

It felt like the hall would be ripped from the ground itself so violent was the shuddering. They had to get out, now. This was real, and it was terrifying.

Once again they heard the voice, and yet again it was low and blurred, enfolding them. "Ignore it." Miranda pinched out the candle when they reached the head of the stairs, afraid the tremors would make her drop it. The thought of a fire was more frightening than the infernal shaking. They stepped off the bottom step into the entry hall and nearly fell into a gaping hole in the middle of the black-and-white squares, and it was spinning around and around. From where they stood, they could see no bottom.

Miranda whispered, "An abyss."

She grabbed P.C.'s hand and ran around the black swirling hole to the front door. Both of them felt its pull, trying to jerk them in and go— where? To hell, Miranda thought, that black gaping hole went directly to hell. She unfastened the three locks and tugged. The massive door didn't budge. Miranda pulled, and P.C. added all her weight, but the big lion's paw knob wouldn't move. The voice came again, behind them. No more gentle whispers, now it was loud, angry, but still they couldn't understand what it was saying. Miranda looked over her shoulder. Was the voice coming from deep in that black hole?

Miranda pulled P.C. to the large window beside the front door and unlatched it. It wouldn't push outward. It wouldn't do anything at all.

"It doesn't want us to leave, Mama," P.C. whispered, so afraid, and the voice kept coming, so loud now their ears hurt.

Miranda screamed, "What do you want? What are you saying? We cannot understand you!"

Louder and louder, the same words or sounds over and over again, belching out of the abyss. Then the voice simply stopped and the tremors became great shudders and the black hole suddenly disappeared. Miranda grabbed the gilt Louis XVth chair in the entryway and slammed it against the window. There was a grunting sound, like she'd struck someone in the belly, then the window shattered, not outward, but insanely the shards flew inward, showering them with glass, and something hurtled them back, and Miranda would swear she felt breathing on her face, fast and harsh, and then a whisper, right in her ear, and she knew it was the same words, only she didn't understand them.

Miranda couldn't move, couldn't think. She felt the pricks of glass shards, but ignored them. "P.C., are you all right?"

"Yes, Mama, maybe a small cut on my arm—I think that's all. Whatever it is, it's really mad at us."

Miranda felt the welling of blood from a cut on her own cheek and wiped it away. The house seemed to tilt upward, throwing them back. Miranda grabbed P.C., pulled her tightly against her, trying to protect her, but the shaking hurled them into a table leg, and the vase of roses atop it went flying, striking the tiles, sending water and flowers everywhere.

"Hold on!" Miranda shouted. She buried P.C.'s face against her chest and closed her arms around her head. The mad convulsions went on and on. Miranda would swear she heard the voice shriek out a low moan and a part of a word—it sounded like *hoos*. What was a hoos? Or who was a hoos? No more, she simply couldn't stand any more. She grabbed her daughter and staggered across the wildly swaying floor. She managed to lift her out the open window, climbed out after her, and they ran as fast as they could away from the shuddering house.

CHAPTER TWO

Lightning slashed through the black sky and thunder rolled, so loud it shook the ground, sending rocks tumbling down the cliff in front of him. The wind whipped his hair about his head, and the rain pelted down on his black cloak, but he didn't move, only stared off at the huge, dark castle bathed in clear, cold white light by yet another burst of lightning. Raven's Peak—so old it should have crumbled long ago, but it hadn't. It still jutted out proudly at the end of the distant promontory into the North Sea, the centuries-old sentinel to ward off enemies. It had festered with ancient mysteries and deadly secrets over the centuries, and too many deaths to be explained by the rational mind. But now at least one of those mysteries was solved, its secrets revealed.

Lightning burst wide, bathing Raven's Peak yet again in daylight brightness. Only one final death tonight. He'd delivered the final blow himself, and the ancient evil was gone, hurled back into the depths of hell. The Ballinger family was now safe, at least in this generation. But the next? Who knew when evil would once again slither up from the deep crevices in the earth?

Grayson Sherbrooke laid down his pen, rubbed the ink off his fingers, and stretched his hands. He smiled. *The Evil Within* was done, and he was pleased. Thomas Straithmore had once again vanquished unspeakable evil, this time a demon from the bowels of hell unleashed accidentally by the small son in the Ballinger household. Grayson's publisher, Benjamin Hawkes, would be pleased with Grayson's latest manuscript since he liked nothing more, he told Grayson, than a cup of hot brandy while Grayson scared him to his toes. *The Evil Within*, starring Grayson's demon-killer Thomas Straithmore, should freeze all the blood in his toes at the gut-cramping scenes he'd written.

"Papa?" Tap, tap, tap on the library door. "Papa? Are you awake?"

Grayson wasn't surprised. Pip always had perfect timing. Pip's nurse, naturally, had no idea her four-year-old charge was wandering around Belhaven in the middle of the night since she slept the sleep of the angels. Grayson rose, stretched, and opened the library door to see his son looking up at him with his heart-melting smile, his small feet peeking out from beneath his white nightshirt, his arms held up. Grayson scooped him up, spun him around, and drew him close to his heart. "It's midnight, you imp. Why are you awake?"

Pip pulled back in his father's arms, studied his face, and lightly patted his cheek with damp fingers. Pip still sucked his thumb. He whispered against Grayson's ear, "I heard my Mary Beth telling Mr. Haddock that you were finishing your next scary book tonight, so when I went to bed I told myself to wake up and I did. Mary Beth shivered when Mr. Haddock said that, Papa, and she knew it would frighten her right out of her stockings. Mr. Haddock said he wanted to see that. She called him saucy and hit him in the arm."

So Mary Beth had called Haddock saucy, had she? Haddock was his butler and valet, since he'd confided in Grayson in a low, vibrating voice three months before that valeting was in his blood, his grandfather having taken care of the Duke of Devonshire way back in the olden days. Grayson had to admit Haddock had a fine way with ironing shirts. He'd also been giving Mary Beth, Pip's nanny, interested looks for nearly three months now, but she was having none of it. He was too short, she said, too old for her. Both were true, Grayson thought, but Haddock was determined. Interestingly enough, Haddock's hair had turned stark white when he was twenty-three. At thirty, he looked like Moses.

He looked down at Pip. "The book's done, not two minutes ago."

"What is the title, Papa?"

"The Evil Within."

"At the end you saved everyone, didn't you? You smashed the evil hard?"

"Thomas Straithmore saved the day again, and yes, the evil got smashed."

"Grandmama said you always kicked evil in the dirt, and that buoyed her spirits. Grandpa laughed, said you were always a hero, even when you were as little as me. I told him that couldn't be true since I'm not little now, Papa, I'm nearly five."

"Four and a half." His father believed he was a hero, did he? Grayson hugged Pip close, kissed his small ear, and breathed in that sweet child smell. He didn't want fear or unhappiness to touch his young life. Thankfully, Pip had been too young when death had first knocked on their door. His mother, Lorelei, had been dead three years now, come next week. Grayson felt the familiar punch of pain, felt it recede into the past again. "It's time for you to be in your bed, Pip. No, no arguments. That's where I'm headed myself."

"But you always have a glass of champagne when you finish a book, Papa."

Pip was right. No matter what time of the day or night he wrote the last line, he toasted himself with champagne. "We can't wake up Haddock—"

Pip pulled his thumb out of his mouth. "Mr. Haddock says he has to sleep eight hours to grow his hair."

Since Haddock was blessed with more hair than he deserved, Grayson couldn't argue with the eight hours a night. "Maybe Mrs. Elvan left a bottle of champagne in the icebox. I told her about my champagne tradition, and she knew I was getting close to the end of the book. Let's go to the kitchen and see."

Grayson carried the candle branch in one hand, Pip pressed against his shoulder with the other. *The house groaned with its night sounds as he walked along the wide corridor, boards creaking beneath his booted feet, and the air hung quiet as a crypt, musty, choking—but wait, he heard something. Something close, too close, maybe in the wall, a muffled moan, not a human moan, no—*

Grayson shook his head at himself. His mind always went to the macabre, to the potentially terrifying. Hmmm, *Thomas was carrying the small son—or daughter—of the house to safety, not knowing what lay waiting ahead, but the sounds he'd heard were deep in the wall, or perhaps behind the wall, trying to punch through—*

The Belhaven House kitchen sported a brand-new icebox, an experimental invention by Mr. Hubalto Custer of York, who'd asked Grayson to give it a try, which he'd agreed to even though Mrs. Elvin believed the monstrosity to be the work of Satan. *Imagine, a box with a huge block of ice in it that melted all over everything and dripped on the floor and made a body slip and slide—no Christian would be responsible for that.*

He unlatched the wooden box door and raised the candle. The once-big block of ice was melting, true, but it was a slow drip, most of it caught in a pan set in the bottom. And because Mr. Custer had stuffed sawdust in the inside doors, the interior remained cold. Mrs. Elvan hadn't complained about that. It was an amazing invention. Yet another remarkable invention by a man named Fox-Talbot was photography, not a painting or drawing, it was a recording of what you actually saw. One of Grayson's good friends, Murdoch Tynes, said it was time someone finally developed a cure for baldness. And train cars were becoming more widespread, and, of course, his icebox. Grayson leaned in and saw the two lower shelves of the icebox held three covered dishes and a single bottle of Legrandier's finest champagne. The bottle was cold to the touch. Should he give Pip a sip? He could see Lorelei smiling, and so he did, a very small sip after they toasted his completion of *The Evil Within.*

He heard a noise, not a house sound, something else entirely, and it wasn't from his imagination. "Pip," he whispered against his son's ear. "Don't say a word. I'm putting you down. Don't move."

The sound came again, a scraping sound. Someone was trying to open the locked door at the back of the kitchen.

Grayson lightly squeezed his son's arm, said again, "Don't move."

Grayson left the candle on a tabletop and carried the champagne bottle by its neck toward the back door.

CHAPTER THREE

Grayson silently unfastened the lock, turned the knob, and jerked the door open. A boy no more than ten tumbled in headfirst, squealing as he hit the floor. He rolled onto his back and stared up at Grayson. "Lawks, don't ye kill me, yer lordship! I only be 'ere because me mistress be in a revoltin' way."

Grayson set the champagne bottle on the floor and came down beside the boy. "Are you hurt?"

"Me buttocks took a fair knock."

"Knocks are good for buttocks, especially young boys' buttocks. Any place else on your person that took a knock?"

There was thought about this, then a shaggy head shake.

Grayson took in his small intruder. He was as skinny as a walking stick, with dark-red hair curling all over his head atop a pale face with a small scattering of freckles. Grayson looked directly into very nearly Sherbrooke blue eyes. He saw no pain. "Who are you?"

"Barnaby, yer lordship."

Pip crowded in behind his father. "It's late, Barnaby, you should be at home in bed."

"See 'ere now, nipper, so should ye. I'm an old man compared to ye. Besides, I'm on a mission, I am, to 'elp me mistress."

"And your mistress would be?"

"P.C., yer lordship."

Grayson cudgeled his brain for a neighbor with the initials P.C. but couldn't come up with a single name. "What does P.C. stand for, Barnaby? And I'm not a lordship."

"I can't tell ye, ah—yer grace, she'd pull my innards out through my nose. But P.C. said she really needed ye, had me repeat yer name three times so's I wouldn't forgets, and I 'eard her say, *I really need Thomas Straithmore or next time it will come and everything will fall off the earth into the abyss.*' Aye, that's exactly what she said. I don't know what this abyss is, but I figure it's gots to be really bad. She said to tell ye she needed ye to come right away so she can tell ye what happened and ye can fix things like ye always do, Mr. Straithmore, yer grace."

"I'm not a grace either, Barnaby. If I hadn't been in the kitchen, what would you have done if you'd managed to break the door open? Searched out my bedchamber and tapped me on the shoulder?"

"I 'ad to light me candle first, yer chancellorship—I ain't no idjut." Barnaby pulled a stub of a candle from his jacket pocket, a nicely made jacket, Grayson saw. "I needs me a Lucifer. I sees a box of 'em over there on the counter."

"Then you would have found the stairs and climbed up and begun your search for me?"

Pip leaned close. "I know where Papa's room is, Barnaby. I could take you to him so he could be a hero for P.C. Papa's not a chancel-ship. I never heard of that sort of boat."

"Yer a smart nipper, ain't ye?" Barnaby gave Pip an approving look, then sat up, wrapped his arms around his bent knees, and looked up at Grayson. "But yer right 'ere, so I don't gots to do no lookin' around for ye. Will ye come wit' me now, yer worship?"

Grayson started to tell the boy Thomas Straithmore was a fictional hero, but he realized the boy's eyes were no longer on his face, rather focused on the bottle of champagne on the floor not three feet away.

"Ye be drinking the bubbly? Wit' the nipper? Fer shame, yer worship.

If ye wants a drinking companion, me mistress likes to tip the bubbly. She stole some once, fair to set her ma's hair on fire."

"Only a tiny sip for the nipper. How far away is your mistress? I'm not a worship."

"She's down by the 'ollow, jest where yer land leaves off, all crouched down behind a willow tree by the edge of the little lake the Great built back in the time of Noah, she told me, said she'd wait there fer ye. Will ye come now, yer princeship?"

Was Barnaby talking about Colonel Lord Josiah Wolffe, Baron Cudlow? The old curmudgeon who reputedly hated all his neighbors and sat in his library polishing his Waterloo medals? Grayson had heard his wife had passed on some twenty years ago, but his widowed daughter-in-law lived with him. He'd also heard a widowed granddaughter-in-law lived there now, but he knew nothing about her. Grayson had lived at Belhaven House for only four months, and all his neighbors had visited to welcome him, invited him to dinner and to small parties, but not the Wolffes of Wolffe Hall. The vicar, Mr. Elijah Harkness, had told him in a lowered voice that he and Mrs. Harkness were invited to dinner once a quarter when the baron paid his employees' wages because he wanted a witness, a man of God, to attest to his probity.

Was Barnaby's P.C. the widowed granddaughter-in-law's daughter? Hard to sort through that. Grayson asked Barnaby, "Is P.C.'s last name Wolffe?"

Barnaby looked distressed. "Sorry, yer guvnorship, I can't tell ye else P.C.'d burn off me toes and stick 'em in me ears since she told me to fetch ye and keep me clapper shut."

An abyss? Not a child's word, an adult's word. His interest and curiosity were near to brimming over. He knew he wanted to know what was going on, and so he said, "Barnaby, give me a moment. Pip, it's time you were in bed. Barnaby, wait here, I'll be right back."

"What be that big wooden thing?"

"It's called an icebox. And no, do not even think of opening the handle. You never know what might jump out at you. Stay right where you are or I won't go with you to P.C."

Barnaby's attention turned back to the champagne, so Grayson picked up the bottle in one hand, Pip in the other, and went upstairs to the nursery. "Papa, I want to help save P.C."

"Not this time, Pip."

"But I'm nearly five, Papa, well, maybe four and a half, but I'm tall, way past your knees, I could—"

And on and on. How had Pip learned so many words? Grayson would have gray hair by the time his son ran out of arguments, and P.C. would have fallen off the earth into the abyss. Bribery, no hope for it. "I'll take you into York to Mr. Hebbert's Viking Marvels, but only if you get into bed now and sleep."

Finally, a nod. Visions of brutal Viking axes and shields and helmets won out, this time. "When?"

The second-most-asked question. "As soon as I take care of P.C.'s trouble." Grayson wasn't surprised to see Pip's nanny, Mary Beth, sound asleep.

He tiptoed to Pip's bed, settled him under the covers, kissed him, and heard his son whisper, "Save P.C., Papa. Take her the champagne, to calm her lady's nerves."

Grayson, now warm in his greatcoat, followed Barnaby, a lantern in one hand, his dueling pistol stuck in his belt. He said to the boy leading him, "How did you find your way to Belhaven House without any light?"

Barnaby turned to grin up at him, showing a mouthful of very nice white teeth. "I gots me superior eyesight, yer—" He stopped, blinked, and shook his head. "I can't think of another title, guv, can ye help me out?"

"I could be His Holiness."

"Oh niver, me ma'd skin me alive iffen she were still here on our worldly plane, which she ain't. Ye can't be no 'oliness, that's against the law."

"Very well, you may call me—" Grayson paused, then smiled. "You may call me Mr. Straithmore."

And so they continued in the cold, calm night, a three-quarter moon overhead, clouds scattering in front of it to very nearly obliterate the narrow path. "Barnaby, it's time you told me P.C.'s last name. After all, we're going directly to Colonel Wolffe's property. Is she P.C. Wolffe?"

"Sorry, yer amazingness, but me mistress also told me to keep mum since ye might 'ave over'eard stories about Lord Great and might not want to get yerself near him. I don't mean he ain't a nice old codger, 'cause he is, but I don't want to take no chances. Iffen ye didn't like 'im, then ye wouldn't want to come save P.C. from the abyss, whatever that be."

"Lord Great? This is Colonel Wolffe, Baron Cudlow?"

Barnaby nodded. "The Great—that's what me mistress calls him, her ma too. He likes it, she told me. He thinks it fits since he thwacked Napoleon but good way back in the time of the Crusades."

Barnaby turned back to the path and jogged forward, whistling a very graphic ditty written years before by the Duchess of Wyndham. Barnaby did indeed have fine night vision. After ten minutes they reached the edge of Sherbrooke land and the small pond that divided the two properties.

Grayson automatically began looking about for a willow tree with a female named P.C. sitting beneath it. He heard an owl hoot.

Barnaby stopped in his tracks, raised his head, and hooted back. It wasn't badly done, if the owl were in severe distress.

Grayson didn't know what to expect, but when he saw the small figure run from tree to tree, then finally emerge to look about, then trot up to him, he knew this wasn't it. He supposed he should have expected another child, but this one—she looked younger than Barnaby. This was P.C.? This infant tipped the bubbly? She'd pull Barnaby's innards out through his nose? She was worried about falling into the abyss?

She stopped three feet from him and said in a proper little lady's well-bred voice, "Please, sir, hold up the lantern so I can see your face clearly. I must know you are indeed Thomas Straithmore. His picture is on the back of my favorite book, you see, so I can't be fooled." She was right about his picture. His publisher, Benjamin Hawkes, knowing Grayson Sherbrooke was very well connected—his uncle, after all, was the Earl of Northcliffe—had a drawing of Grayson's likeness put on the back of one of his novels, knowing every influential person would recognize him and most likely buy the book. Beneath the drawing was the name Thomas Straithmore. From that book on, Grayson remembered, Thomas Straithmore fast became a household name.

"I am he," Grayson said.

CHAPTER FOUR

The little girl walked up to him and stuck out her hand. He leaned over, took the small hand in his, and shook it. "And you are P.C.? What might P.C. stand for?"

She leaned close. "A revolting name, sir—I will never say it aloud until I am breathing my final breath, and then I'll speak it aloud and horrify my great-great-grandchildren because they'll doubtless deserve it."

All that out of the mouth of a what? Eight-year-old? "Why did your parents give you a revolting name?"

"It was Papa, not Mama. She said he had fire in his eyes when he said it, impassioned fire, she said, so what could she do?"

"Are you Baron Cudlow's great-granddaughter?"

She nodded. "I call him the Great, but he prefers Lord Great, which sounds quite silly to me. He says he's so old his gout's forgotten how to flare up. He doesn't mind that I'm a girl and not a boy and his heir. But he tells me it isn't my fault. I think he believes it's my mama's fault, but he doesn't say that out loud. I pour his tea and he pats my head and has me sit at his feet, and he talks about his glory days, whatever those are. He talks about Waterloo when men were men, and young, and earned medals, and died for glory, not like all the fops today. He has a lot of medals. He saw me pick up one of his medals once and I thought he would expire, but he didn't, of course."

"I can understand your great-grandfather would be very fond of his medals, not at all surprising since he was a hero at the Battle of Waterloo, so the vicar told me. Why are you going to fall off the earth and into the abyss, P.C.?"

"Mr. Straithmore, sir." She leaned close and Grayson obligingly bent over so she could whisper in his ear, and she told him about the two dreams that had come to both her and her mother, and the voice, always the voice, whispering, yelling, but you couldn't understand it, and then the horrible earthquake. And how they'd jumped out of the front window and run to the barn. And there was Barnaby—she poked him in the arm—sound asleep with Musgrave Jr., and he didn't wake up until she nearly shook him to death.

Grayson asked questions until he thought he had the gist of the fantastical tale. It was beyond believable, he thought, surely the child was exaggerating, but something deep inside him sparked.

"You said that no one else in the house—not the Great or Lord Great, not your grandmother, not the servants—heard or felt a thing."

"We banged on their doors, but no one seemed to be there. Even the servants, we yelled up at them, but nothing. It was like we were alone. But how could that be, Mr. Straithmore? It was a horrible racket, and the house nearly lifted off the ground." She began shaking from the memory of it, and Grayson brought her up close, gave her comfort and his warmth. "It sounds like both you and your mama were very brave and very resourceful. You escaped from the house."

"Mama threw a chair through the window. I didn't know she was so strong. And then both Mama and me recognized a bit of what the voice said. It sounded like *hoos*."

"Like *house*, you mean?"

P.C. shook her head. "No, like *whooss*, that's closer. Mama didn't make that out, so I can't be sure."

Barnaby patted P.C.'s shoulder. "'Ere now, P.C., yer bein' a waterin' pot. Ain't like you to be a girl."

P.C. gulped and pulled away from Grayson. "You're right, Barnaby. I'm sorry."

Grayson marveled at both of them. "I can't imagine your mother wants to remain at Wolffe Hall."

"She wants to leave right now, but she says we need to know what the Great thinks about this first, and depending on what he says—" P.C. shrugged. "She kept saying over and over she couldn't take a chance on this thing, whatever it is, could hurt me. And then she'd say bad words and look toward the Great's locked library door. She thinks the Great knows what this is all about. I heard her mutter to herself that he was so bloody old, he knew about everything both good and rotten that happened on this earth. Then she said 'the abyss' out loud and started to shake until she saw me. I looked up *abyss* in the dictionary, and it took me a long time because it's spelled funny. I asked her why she didn't call it the voice, but she said it was worse than that, what with that black whirling hole in the floor, and she thought it was angry at us because we couldn't understand."

"Me, I niver seen nothin'."

P.C. gave Barnaby a good shove. "That's because you were snoring and didn't wake up."

"Nobody else woke up either, P.C."

"I know. To be honest, sir, only Mama and I have heard it in dreams, and then it came and shook the house and nearly killed us. Only us. I asked Mama how the Great could know anything—it didn't shake him out of his bed."

"Maybe it did and he just didn't tell you. Now, you said you went to the barn. And all was calm?"

She nodded. "This morning when we went back to the house, we heard the Great yelling about who broke the bloody window and broke his favorite bloody vase from China. Mama says when she told the Great the voice came again and it could have killed us, he turned pale and had to lean on the desk so he wouldn't fall onto the floor. He told her he hadn't heard a thing, didn't know a thing, and she and I had to leave Wolffe Hall, that she had to take me to Scarborough where his younger sister lives. That's Great-Aunt Clorinda. He said we'd be safe there until he could figure this out.

"Safe from what exactly I don't know since he didn't know anything, but he only shook his head and patted her cheek. She told me she wasn't about to take any chances with me, so we have to go.

"Mr. Straithmore, Great-Aunt Clorinda is so old she doesn't have any eyebrows. She said they'd fallen to her upper lip so now she had a mustache." P.C. shuddered, then her thin shoulders squared and she looked him right in the eye. "Sir, when I saw you in the village this morning and I recognized you from your picture on your books, I knew you could help us. I remember Grandmama telling the Great he should read your books because you lived here now, and it was only polite. She said he snorted, said who cares if you live here now since you spend your life stringing words together, so long as you aren't an imbiber and fall off a cliff?

"My mama and grandmama love your books too. She reads them to me, and then I read them to her, to practice my speech. Mr. Straithmore, Mama and I don't want to go to Scarborough.

"And what would become of Grandmama and Barnaby and all the servants? You've got to fix what is wrong. You've got to speak to the voice and tell it to be clear in what it wants, or I know it's the abyss for Mama and me, or worse, Great-Aunt Clorinda."

"Why does your mama believe the Great knows about this?"

"She said when he tries to hide anything, his left eye twitches something fierce and he rubs his hands together, like Lady Macbeth, but I don't know who she is. Mama said he was already writing a letter to Great-Aunt Clorinda telling her of her joy in having us live with her."

Barnaby said, "Nobody wants Miz Miranda or P.C. to go to the great-aunt. Suggs is muttering and telling Mrs. Crandle to do something. Marigold, she's the upstairs maid, and Meg, she sees to Miz Elaine and Miz Miranda, they don't want them to leave even though Mrs. Crandle said it sounded like P.C. and Miz Miranda had rust in their upper-works. As for Suggs, he thinks it's a lovely enigma, whatever that is, his words exactly."

P.C. said, "Suggs is older than the Great. He'd look like God if he had any hair."

CHAPTER FIVE

"Aye, the old blighter is bald as a river rock," Barnaby said. "Ah, Old Suggs is the butler. A rheumy eye has Old Suggs, catches me whenever I sneak a pie from the kitchen."

P.C. turned on him. "You don't even know what *rheumy* means, Barnaby. You're copying what you heard Mama say." P.C. smacked him in the arm.

"Yeow!"

"You sounded like Musgrave—he was my cat before he died of old age," she said to Grayson. "Mama said a mouse could ride around on Musgrave's back and Musgrave wouldn't even notice, he was just that stupid."

"Well, now ye've got Musgrave Jr., and he's as stupid as his ma."

Grayson wanted to laugh, but he didn't, not with those two young, worried faces staring up at him like he was their savior. He looked around and spotted a smooth grassy spot. He took off his greatcoat and, despite the chill, spread it on the ground. "Both of you, sit down." They collapsed onto his coat, boneless, like Pip, like he himself had when he'd been a child, he supposed. He saw P.C. was wearing disreputable boys' clothes, probably Barnaby's castoffs. He couldn't tell about her hair; it was tucked under a dirty black wool cap. "That's right. Now, let's get back to the problem at hand. You said the voice brought the abyss last night. Describe the abyss for me again."

"It was this whirling black hole right there in the middle of the entryway. The last time we heard the voice it was coming from that black hole. We slept together with Barnaby, and today Mama wouldn't let me out of her sight. Mr. Tubbs, he's the head stable lad, he woke us up."

"You're here," Grayson said. "Your mama isn't."

The little girl looked down at her feet. "Well, she was tired from packing all our things and was sleeping, and I slipped out. This was important, sir, surely you see that. I don't want to leave Wolffe Hall." She looked at Barnaby. "I don't want to leave him either. He'd wither away without me, Mr. Straithmore. And I'm afraid the voice and shudders will come while I'm gone and Mama's all alone."

"I think yer ma'll be all right, P.C. I been considerin', yer inkpotness, that maybe the voice has to rest up afore it puts on another show for P.C. and her mama."

"Interesting, Barnaby. The voice, the shudders and quaking, the black hole—it would all require great energy, great power." Grayson again felt that spark, now more a flame, he realized, burning bright now, making his blood heat, his heart speed up. "I'm not an inkpotness."

"Well, ye don't sing yer stories, do ye? Ye write 'em down. Ye use ink, don't ye? Ye don't try to use spit, do ye?"

"He can't spit down the words, Barnaby," P.C. said. "They'd dry and disappear, and then where would he be?"

"Well, that's why the sirness 'ere is an inkpotness, not a spitpotness. And I ain't gonna wither, P.C. I'm a boy and boys grow up to be big strong trees."

Again, Grayson wanted to laugh, but P.C.'s bright blue eyes were once more fixed on his face like he was the only possible savior of her world. He realized too that he liked Barnaby's newest title for him. "You said your grandmama's bedchamber door was locked?"

P.C. nodded. "Grandmama told Mama she hadn't locked it and that she was asleep, probably dreaming about Alphonse. She really likes Alphonse."

Who was this Alphonse? Not important—he'd find that out later.

"All the servants are worried, sir. They don't want to think we're nutters, but they don't know. I think they're afraid too."

"P.C. says if ye don't help, then we'll all be swept away into this abyss or they're leaving for Scarborough on Saturday."

"Mama doesn't want to leave her garden, sir. It's really quite amazing. You do believe me, don't you? You don't think I'm just a little kid and I'm making this up? Or that I'm a nutter?"

"If you're making this up, you're far better at storytelling than I am. Who else lives at Wolffe Hall?"

"Besides the Great, only Grandmama—she's my daddy's mama. Her name's Elaine. She's a floater, like a fairy whose feet don't really touch the ground. She spends most of her time in the portrait gallery, standing in front of Alphonse, talking to him. I don't know what she says, but she never tires of standing there, looking up at him, and talking. I brought her a chair once, but she had Suggs take it away. Mama said Alphonse lived back in Queen Elizabeth's court and that was about forever ago, and that's why he's wearing funny clothes, like a ruff, that's the name Mama told me for the fancy collar. And he has on green tight pants. Grandmama calls him her darling Alphonse. He's got a pointed beard and I think his eyes are sly, but Grandmama doesn't agree.

"Mr. Straithmore, Mama knows how to shoot, and she put her little gun under her pillow, said she'd shoot into the abyss because who knew what was hiding down there?"

"Your mama knows how to shoot?"

P.C. nodded. "She told me since my papa—he died a long time ago when I was little—since he was sometimes involved in fisticuffs, she wanted to learn how to protect him. She fences too."

He said, "Your mama sounds fierce."

Barnaby snorted and looked disgusted. "If I was Miz Miranda, I'd beat the wickedness out of P.C., but all she ever does is stroke 'er 'air and kiss 'er."

"She kissed you once, frog-face, something I'll never understand. You liked it so much I saw your back teeth you were grinning so wide." She added to Grayson, "Barnaby is like our barn cat—he doesn't have a family except for us. He needs us; we can't leave." A pause, then, "If it weren't for Mama, I'd like to be a barn cat too."

Even though the lantern light wasn't all that bright, Grayson could tell P.C. was looking thoughtful. "What is it, P.C.? You've remembered something else?"

"I was thinking about Barnaby, Mr. Straithmore. I hadn't realized it until now. His grammar is very bad."

Well, he's a barn cat.

She snapped her fingers. "I know, after you've taken care of everything, Mr. Straithmore, I'll ask Mama if she can teach Barnaby too. Otherwise, what will he make of himself when he grows up?"

"I expects I'll still be a barn cat," Barnaby said. He pulled up a piece of grass and began to chew on it.

"Mama and the Great wouldn't ever let me marry a barn cat. That means you will learn to speak properly."

Barnaby looked horrified.

P.C. patted his bony knee. "I wish we had some bubbly. Sir, you'll come over tomorrow and fix everything?"

Grayson said, "Do you know, I wonder why only you and your mother have dreamed anything or heard anything or felt anything? Who is this voice? That's the key. And what word is *whooss* a part of?"

CHAPTER SIX

A storm blew in heavy, cold rain off the North Sea after midnight and dashed against the windows until dawn. To Grayson's surprise, the sun came out right after breakfast and was now shining brightly on this glorious spring day. Grayson rode Albert, his gray gelding from the Rothermere stud, who, unfortunately, stopped without fail if he spotted a patch of strawberries. Luckily, there were few strawberries about Belhaven. Grayson breathed in the rich, briny smell of the North Sea only a half mile to the east.

Ten minutes later, he gently pulled Albert up in the middle of the long drive leading to the hall. Pip was bouncing up and down, pointing. "It's bigger than our house, Papa, but it's not like the pictures Mary Beth showed me. There were lots of columns. This one doesn't have any."

"No, it's not in the Palladian style." Wolffe Hall stood tall and proud atop a small hillock surrounded by acres of chestnuts, oaks, and larches. The three-story rectangular stone house had aged to a soft gray over the past three hundred years, a handsome property, a dozen well-run tenant farms supporting it nicely. The prosperity, however, wasn't due to Baron Cudlow, he was told in confidence by the vicar, but rather to his steward, Max Carstairs, the second son of an impoverished knight from Kent, endowed with the patience of Job, more important than brains, it was said in the village.

Belhaven House was a mere hundred years old. When he'd purchased the property, his parents were surprised he didn't change the name of his new home, but he admitted to them that the name—*Belhaven House*—sang on his tongue and tasted sweeter than green grapes from his uncle's succession house in Sussex. They'd rolled their eyes.

"Let's see what's happening here," Grayson said and click-clicked Albert forward until they reached the front of the entrance with its romantic ivy framing the portico and a dozen deep-set stone steps. The front door immediately flew open and out ran P.C., wearing a white dress with a bright green sash around her small waist, holding up the skirts as she raced down the steps, showing her white stockings and slippers. "Sir! Mr. Straithmore! You're here!" She skidded to a stop, pointing. "Who is the little boy? He can't be a barn cat like Barnaby, he looks too clean."

"Hello, P.C. Pip, are you a barn cat?"

Pip said, "A barn cat—that sounds like fun. Would I have to eat mouses, Papa?"

"Mice," P.C. said, frowning at him.

"I could eat them too. Are they better?"

"You're too young to make jests," P.C. said, rolling her eyes. "Your brain isn't leavened enough."

Pip looked her over. "You're a little girl. How can you be Barnaby's mistress?"

P.C. drew up her full height, threw back her skinny shoulders. "I am the daughter of the house—I'm everyone's mistress. You may call me P.C."

"I'm Pip. This is my papa, and he's famous."

"P.C. and I are old friends, Pip." Grayson looked around again for a stable boy. "Remember, I told you I met her last night."

"Where's Barnaby?" Pip asked.

"He's probably chewing straw and playing with Musgrave Jr." P.C. eyed Pip, nodding slowly. "Oh, I see, sir. You brought him so the Great would be distracted and more likely to spill his innards to you. You must be careful, though, or Bickle—he's the Great's valet—he is always wanting to please the Great, and since the Great is very sad he doesn't have an heir, Bickle might try to steal him." She put her fingers in her mouth and whistled, eardrum-shatteringly loud, probably as far as the distant seaweed-strewn North Sea beach.

Pip was amazed. "I want to whistle like that. P.C., can you teach me?"

"Your mouth isn't big enough yet." She shot Grayson a disappointed look. "I thought you were an *unmarried* hero." She added hopefully, "Or perhaps the little boy is your nephew? Maybe a stray neighbor's boy?"

Pip said, "My mama lives in heaven. I was little when she moved there." Pip looked up at the white clouds dotting the blue sky.

"I'm sorry. You're still so little I can barely see you."

Barnaby came running around the side of the house. "Lawks, it's yer 'eaven-sentness, come after all. Welcome, sir, welcome. Ah, and who is this sweet boy?"

Since Barnaby had already met Pip, Grayson assumed he was talking about his horse. "Good morning, Barnaby. This is Albert. You remember Pip."

"Beautiful big boy." He pulled an ancient, wrinkled carrot out of his pocket and gave it to Albert, who nibbled it gracefully out of his hand. Barnaby wiped his hand on his baggy pants. "Hullo to ye, nipper. I knows ye smuggled the bubbly into yer bed when yer pa weren't looking last night, didn't ye, nipper?"

Pip cocked his head at his father. "I never thought of that," he said, and Grayson groaned.

"You're four and a half years old, Pip."

"Nearly five, Papa, well, four and a half. Maybe we can have bubbly for my birthday?"

"That was funny for someone with as small a brain as you have," P.C. said to Pip, and she walked to Albert, patted his nose. To Grayson's surprise, Albert whinnied softly and nudged P.C.'s shoulder, nearly sending her over backward. She kissed the perfect white star on his nose, then held up her arms. "If you will give the nipper to me, Mr. Straithmore, I will carry him into the house." She didn't have to add that it would make him look more manly and heroic not carrying a little boy, but Grayson well understood, and grinned at her. He looked at those skinny little arms, felt the weight of his son, shook his head, and dismounted, Pip pressed against his shoulder. "Barnaby, you'll take care of Albert?"

"Aye, come along, purty boy, I'll give ye more carrots from Miz Miranda's very own garden." And Barnaby led Albert away, whistling.

P.C. shaded her eyes as she watched him saunter away. "Surely you agree with me, Mr. Straithmore. I can't very well marry him if he doesn't learn to speak Queen Victoria's English, now can I?"

"Probably not," Grayson said, and then he frowned, staring after Barnaby. He realized Barnaby looked familiar to him. He'd probably seen him in the village. No, that wasn't it, it was something else.

P.C. nodded. "I will have to see to it. I told my mother you were coming, sir. She wanted to know how I'd met you and I lied, said you'd bought me an ice in the village and thought I was a cute little button. The Great knows you're coming. I told him. He raised a really thick white eyebrow at me, but didn't say anything. My grandmama is hovering about the portrait gallery, as usual, talking to Alphonse. My mama's out pulling up weeds from her garden, one eye on the lookout for the abyss. She said we're leaving in the morning. She said the Great wouldn't tell her anything, blast his eyes, because he believed that females were helpless and he was protecting us by sending us to Great-Aunt Clorinda. Mama told him she could shoot better than he could, and he patted her cheek and said he'd shot at least a dozen Frenchies off their horses at Waterloo, and she told him that was all well and good but he couldn't see beyond his own nose now.

"Mr. Straithmore, in case you don't remember, I don't want to leave, I really don't. I was born here." And she looked at Barnaby's retreating back.

"I will do my best," Grayson said.

That earned him a brilliant smile. "Give me your hand, Pip, you don't want your papa to carry you now, do you? I mean, you're almost five years old." Pip immediately pulled away from his father and tucked his hand into hers. "You'll never be as old as I am, so you can forget it. I'm nearly eight, so that means I'll be a grown-up long before you."

Grayson noticed P.C. slowed considerably when climbing the deep stone steps beside his small son.

She didn't look like a ragamuffin this morning, what with the pretty white dress that was a bit on the short side. She had a mop of honey-colored hair, bouncing curls all over her head, threaded through with a silver ribbon. She had amazing blue eyes, nearly the same shade as Sherbrooke blue eyes, nearly the same blue as Barnaby the barn cat's eyes, and her face was already turning a summer gold. He wondered about her mother. Miranda. Shakespeare's Miranda?

He saw a huge calico ribboning around her ankles. She dropped Pip's hand, leaned down, and hefted the cat into her arms. "This is Musgrave Jr.," she said, and kissed the cat until he yowled and leapt away, tail straight up, hopping like a rabbit back into the house.

And Grayson wondered what he'd gotten himself into. What did P.C. stand for?

CHAPTER SEVEN

Grayson eyed the Great—Colonel Lord Josiah Wolffe, Baron Cudlow—from six feet away in an ancient Louis XVth chair that creaked with his weight. He rose slowly when P.C. brought Grayson and Pip into the room. He was still a large man, shoulders squared, not stooped at all.

P.C. opened her mouth to introduce him, but the Great said, "I know who he is, P.C. He's that nearly noble fellow who writes ghost stories to terrify every adult in England."

Grayson nodded, hoping it was so. "Grayson Sherbrooke, sir. And this is my son, Pip."

The Great had a full head of wildly curling white hair, an equally white curly beard, sharp old eyes the color of pewter, and the look of a man who was on the edge. At the moment, though, he looked more obstinate than Grayson's Uncle Douglas when he didn't get his way. He knew he'd been ambushed by his great-granddaughter, and he wasn't very happy about it. But he was a gentleman, and that meant he would be civil.

The Great nodded and smiled down at Pip. "You're a great big boy, now, aren't you?"

"Yes, sir, I'm nearly to my papa's waist."

"A great height for one so young. Do be seated, both of you."

They sat on a green-and-white striped sofa opposite from a huge wing chair where the Great now sat.

Grayson said, "Sir, I understand you were an excellent leader and served throughout the Napoleonic wars."

"Aye, that's true enough. I was even at the signing of that blasted silly Treaty of Amiens back in '02." The old man called out, "Suggs, where are Mrs. Crandle's blessedly wonderful seed cakes? We have a little boy here who needs to grow up strong." He beamed at Pip. "I had a son once too, you know. He was full of promise like you are, at least I think he was, but it's hard to remember it was such a long time ago. But then he turned into a rotter, and that smashes a father's heart. As for the son he managed to bring into this wonderful world, well, he was a crusader."

"What's a crusader, sir?"

"Well, I'll tell you. Crusaders were a lot who should have died out a very long time ago, but didn't. They changed from being brave soldiers into morons who get stabbed because they join all the good-for-nothings who are making Big Trouble in our factories." The old man sighed and rested his bearded chin on his hand. He roused himself when he saw Pip. "I say, little fellow, best keep close to your papa else my valet— Bickle is his name—might try to nab you for me."

Pip eyed the man who looked so old maybe he was God on High, or one of God's friends, in which case, was he asking Pip if he wanted to come to heaven? Now? Pip knew heaven was a fine place, but not yet, he knew that too. Pip had to be careful. "Why would Mr. Bickle want to nab me for you, sir?"

"He frets, Bickle does, because I don't have an heir. You see, my third cousin and my only heir died a year ago. The fool was a hunting man and got himself knocked off his horse by a tree branch—killed him on the spot. Since I don't have an heir, my title will become extinct upon my death."

"Couldn't P.C. be your heir, sir? Or her mama?"

"Alas, no, Pip. In our country, only males can inherit titles. It's called the law of primogeniture. Poor Bickle doesn't want my title to go extinct. He's very proud of it, you see. So he is always trying to find me an heir."

"I'm sorry, sir, but I can't be your heir. I'm Papa's heir."

"And you speak well for such a little tyke," the Great said. "You're a smart young'un, aren't you?"

Pip didn't know what to say to that, so he smiled and nodded. He knew adults did this all the time and it got them by.

"Mind my word, Pip, keep an eye out for Bickle. He's sly and he's fast." The Great turned piercing eyes on P.C. "Why did you invite Mr. Sherbrooke to visit me, Palonia Chiara?"

Palonia? Chiara? Why had P.C.'s parents bestowed these two curious Italian names on her? At least it was unique, bless her heart. Grayson cleared his throat. "Sir, Palonia and I have met before. Ah, in the village. She invited me to meet you and the family."

The Great ruminated over this for a moment, then said, "She invited you to talk me out of sending her away. But you must listen, my child. I know you don't want to leave, but it is for the best. You and your mama must trust me."

P.C. said, "Why, sir?"

"Because you are my responsibility. I've told your mother this, but she continues to believe she can be of assistance. She cannot for there is simply nothing for her to do, and you're a little girl. I want you both safe. Now, I don't know what you've told Mr. Sherbrooke—"

"Sir, his name is Thomas Straithmore."

"Hmm, very well, it isn't all that important, now, is it? Ah, our seed cakes. Set 'em down on the table, Suggs. Palonia Chiara can pour the tea. Go burrow in your cave, Suggs. I'll call if I need you."

Suggs was indeed bald. Grayson found himself mesmerized, watching sunlight from the wide front window stream down on the old man's head, making it glisten.

"Is Bickle nearby, Suggs?"

"I have not seen him, my lord. It is likely he is beneath the stairs devising a strategy." Suggs looked at Pip, turned on his heel, and walked slowly from the huge drafty drawing room. He turned back at the doorway. "My lord, no new medals have arrived as yet today."

For an instant, there was stark fear on the old man's face, and Grayson saw it. Medals? Then the baron waved a veiny hand. "Thank you, Suggs."

Once Suggs was out of the drawing room, the Great said to Grayson, "Suggs has always wanted to be a Bedouin in the Bulgar and live in a cave with wizards, so he polishes the silver in the basement, keeps it nice and dark down there.

"Palonia Chiara, don't forget, three spoonfuls of sugar for me, aye, that's right, and don't forget the milk. Same for the little lad here."

Pip liked a spoonful of honey in his tea, but he manfully didn't say anything. P.C. gave him a very small cup. "Don't spill it on the carpet, Pip, else Grandmama might chance to look down and see it, though that isn't likely. She probably won't even see you."

"That tiny cup was a wedding present," the Great said, his voice sounding far away. "Too small for anything useful except for visiting little boys." He was reaching for a second seed cake as he spoke when a sharp female voice from the doorway stopped him in mid-flight.

"Mrs. Crandle told me if you eat that second cake, your skin will fall off your face." She flitted over to a chair and sat, arranging her dark-green skirts around her. So this must be Palonia's grandmother, Elaine Wolffe, who hummed and spoke to Alphonse's portrait and had been the wife of the rotter, the Great's only son. The Great's skin would fall off his face?

Grayson had to admit Palonia Chiara's grandmother had seemed to float maybe an inch off the floor when she'd walked ever so gracefully into the room. She was still beautiful at what—sixty? Which put her father-in-law well north of eighty. When she'd been young, she'd probably had every man within a hundred miles slavering over her hand. Her hair was dark brown with a single thick white swatch starting at her forehead and going straight back, all of it piled haphazardly on top of her head with thick hanks falling beside her face to her shoulders. She had the greenest eyes he'd ever seen, sharp, intelligent eyes, no matter she was a floater. He rose immediately.

"My dear," the Great said, "this is our neighbor, Mr. Sherbrooke, and his son, Pip."

Elaine Wolffe rose slowly and floated over to stand in front of him. Grayson bowed and lightly kissed her wrist. As for Pip, he eyed her with awe. He scrambled off the chair, and the teacup shook in his small hand.

P.C., so fast she was nearly a blur, grabbed the cup before it spilled. Pip gave P.C.'s grandmother a formal bow, practiced with his nanny Mary Beth for nearly a year now.

Elaine reached out a white hand to lightly touch Pip's shoulder. "That is well done. Aren't you a handsome little lad? My Benedict was a handsome little lad as well." Then she sighed.

"I'm nearly five," said Pip, chin up, shoulders back. "Who's Benedict?"

"He was my son and, I agree, he was a crusader."

Pip didn't know what to make of that, and so he took his small cup back from P.C. and reseated himself.

Elaine turned to Grayson. "Mr. Sherbrooke, it is a pleasure."

He nodded and smiled toward P.C. "Or Thomas Straithmore."

The Great sat back, his hands over his vest. "This is the boy who writes the spirit stories you and Miranda like to read. Now since he has visited, I must needs read one for myself. But before I do—" The Great ate another seed cake, swallowed, and laughed. "All my skin's still there, so what does Mrs. Crandle know? Did Mrs. Crandle really say that, or are you making it up, Elaine, to make me feel guilty?"

"You will never know," she said and reseated herself.

CHAPTER EIGHT

P.C. came to stand beside Grayson. "Grandmama, you must call him Mr. Straithmore. He wrote *Deadening Shadows*. Mama read it to you, and you nearly screamed three times."

"Of course," Elaine Wolffe said. "A spirit was trapped in the body of a villain who wanted to kill his wife and the spirit wouldn't let him. It was a fine tale." She gave him a beautiful white-toothed smile.

"Grandmama, may I serve you tea?"

Elaine nodded her graceful neck. "And tea for your mama, if you please."

"Mama isn't here, Grandmama."

Miranda Wolffe appeared in the doorway within the next three seconds. P.C. didn't seem surprised, merely smiled at her mother and held out her teacup.

Grayson, still standing, eyed Miranda Wolffe. She looked skinny in the baggy brown gown at least half a decade out of date. She wasn't all that young—well, perhaps in her late twenties, two or three years younger than he. Her hair was glorious, the same honey shade as her daughter's, and she wore it in a thick braid down her back. Hunks of the rich stuff had worked free of the braid to curl around her face. He thought her eyes were also as blue as her daughter's, but he couldn't be certain because she wore glasses. He wanted her to eat—perhaps the rest of the seed cakes would be a good start. Why was she wearing that ugly old dress?

Miranda nodded to Grayson. "I know who you are, sir, and now that I see my daughter's face, I know what you are doing here."

"Mama, how did you know Mr. Straithmore was here?"

"Mr. Straithmore? Barnaby fetched me from my garden. He told me I'd best hurry so Bickle didn't sneak in and try to steal the little boy who came with you. Pray be seated again, sir. Ah, I see Bickle peering in through the window. Keep the little boy close to you."

Grayson smiled at her as he pulled Pip close against his leg. "Mrs. Wolffe, it is a pleasure to meet you. Your daughter invited me for tea. And the little boy I'm protecting from the valet Bickle is my son, Pip. Your daughter knows me by my other name, ma'am, Thomas Straithmore."

P.C. leaped to her feet. "Sir, a man cannot be two men. You cannot be this Sherbrooke man since you're Mr. Straithmore. You solve frightening otherworldly mysteries that bedevil families, and you write about them. You are a hero, sir. This other man clearly cannot intrude."

Grayson smiled at an outraged P.C. "I'm sorry, P.C. I am both men. You've told me bedevilment is going on in this family." He looked at the Great. "I will try to stop it if you, sir, will explain it to me."

The Great rose, and Grayson saw his glorious white hair giving him another three inches in height, haloing curls around his head. "What have you told this young gentleman, Palonia Chiara?"

"I told him about the voice coming to both me and Mama two times in dreams, and then Wednesday night it was shrieking those same words we can't understand, heaving and shuddering the house, and it made the abyss in the entryway. He's here to help—please let him."

The Great shook his head and turned back to Grayson. "Listen, Mr. Sherbrooke, this is a family matter, at least I hope that it is."

P.C. stepped forward. "Sir, if you would please think about consulting Mr. Straithmore. Please. I don't want to leave you or Grandmama or Barnaby."

Grayson said, "You could consider me an objective other, sir. It's possible I could help you figure this out."

The Great looked undecided. No, Grayson thought, it was more than that. He didn't want to tell anyone because there was something he wanted to keep hidden. This was interesting.

The Great flicked a look toward Miranda and P.C. "I really do not wish them to leave. I mean, my sister, Clorinda, she is such a fussy old biddy, but still vigorous, I'll give her that. I think it's all the hair that's growing out of her ears. Hair of that sort comes from a healthy brain, and that's why she's still vigorous."

P.C. said, "But sir, you don't have any hair in your ears."

The Great frowned over that.

Pip said, "Perhaps it's only true for ladies, sir."

"Ah, what a smart little nit you are," the Great said.

P.C. said, "Sir, if you promise to consider consulting with Mr. Straithmore, Mama and I will take Pip to her garden. We will keep a lookout for Bickle. Please, sir."

The Great considered this, but Grayson saw that same expression, the desire to keep something hidden. Why? Did it embarrass him? But why? Or was it pride? The obvious fact that Grayson was a complete stranger?

It was then Grayson saw the huge basket filled to the brim with medals, scores of them. He'd thought P.C. was speaking only of the Great's medals, but no. His medals were finely displayed behind glass on the wall. What were these medals in the basket? Grayson said, "My lord, I will accompany P.C. and Miranda to her garden, protect Pip, and return in say twenty minutes?"

The Great looked over to Pip, now holding Grayson's hand. "Pip, when you next visit, I will show you something to make your hair as curly as mine."

Pip took a step toward him. "Would it make me taller than my papa's waist?"

"If we brush it straight up, you'll be nearly to his armpit."

Elaine called out as the four of them left the library, "Do not prick yourselves on the rose thorns. I will tell my papa-in-law all about

Alphonse's prized stallion, Cuspis. I read about him in an ancient history of our family."

When they were out the front door, P.C. said to Grayson, "Sir, I think the Great is about ready to tell you what he knows about the voice." She rubbed her hands together. "Do check your watch—we'll time exactly twenty minutes before you go back." She said to Pip, "Keep hold of my hand until we are in Mama's garden. Even though it is fenced in, you still must pay attention and keep watch for Bickle—he well might be lurking about." She sighed. "I've heard the Great reassure him endlessly that he will find him a fine post, but Bickle won't be swayed. It is a pity the Great obviously likes you, Pip, that will bring Bickle, fast. Ah, here's Barnaby. He can help guard you too."

They came to a gated garden, large and surrounded with a lovely white wooden fence, freshly painted. Grayson watched Miranda Wolffe unlatch the gate and stand aside to let them all in. It was charming, well planned, and beautifully tended. Graveled pathways cut between sections of flowers, many of them beginning to bloom. In high summer, it would be stunning. There was a stone seat, an arbor overhead with jasmine twined through the slats.

"It's lovely, Mrs. Wolffe."

Miranda merely nodded and waved them toward the stone bench.

She stood in front of Grayson, her hands on her hips, her eyes going from him to her daughter. "He knows, which means you told him, which means you sneaked out of the house last night, didn't you, P.C.?"

"Yes, Mama. I had to. Mr. Straithmore is here to help us." She drew in a big breath and spit it out. "I told him everything."

Miranda paused and turned to face Grayson, squinting to see his face in the bright sunlight. "And do you believe her, sir?"

"Yes, ma'am, I most certainly do."

"That's all well and good, but you are still a stranger despite the fact I feel like I know you since I read one of your novels. Sir, listen to me. Besides tending my garden, I read and I ponder and I consider things. I am smart and competent. However, the Great doesn't believe a female person can do things to save the day, and thus I am at an impasse. I fear we must leave on the morrow, although I'm more afraid of what the night could bring. I must protect P.C." She gave him a dispassionate look. "I have always resented the Great's dismissal of my brain. But for you, a man, he will doubtless come around and spill his secrets."

"I know it must be galling, ma'am, but what's important here, what you must keep your eye on, is getting him to tell us what is happening. If he will only speak to me, a man, well, so be it. You and P.C. and I will solve the problem once he tells me what it is."

"Nicely said, sir. You are a great sopper."

"Sopper?"

She nodded. "Yes, as in placating me quite nicely."

Grayson was charmed. She took off her glasses and cleaned them on her sleeve. He saw her eyes were indeed as blue as her daughter's, beautiful, clear, and yes, brimming with intelligence. But her face was too thin. Understandable with a huge swirling black hole in the middle of the entrance hall. "Thank you, ma'am. Since I am here, you might as well make use of me. I smell roses. Won't you show them to me? And your vegetable patch where Barnaby got the carrots for Albert?"

Miranda nodded as she eyed her daughter. P.C. had doubtless knocked on the poor man's door and invited herself and her problems in. "I have always admired Belhaven House, Mr. Sherbrooke."

"Please call him Mr. Straithmore, Mama," P.C. said, crowding in. "His other name isn't the one that will help us."

"Very well, then. Mr. Straithmore, come and admire my roses and carrots."

"Mama, please call him Thomas. And he can call you Miranda since you're grown-ups."

"Grown-ups don't immediately leap to familiar names, P.C., they are more careful, more formal. Isn't that right, Mr. Sherbrooke—Mr. Straithmore?"

"In some dire, possibly dangerous situations, I'd have to say that formality tends to fall by the wayside."

"What does that mean?" Barnaby asked.

"It means, bacon-brain, that he wants Mama to call him Thomas. Now, be quiet and watch out for Bickle."

Miranda chewed on her lower lip. "Why did you move to Belhaven House, Mr. Sher—Mr. Straithmore?"

He shrugged. "I fell in love at first sight. I moved myself and Pip here from London four months ago."

"His wife didn't come with him," P.C. said. "She's in heaven, but he has Pip. Mama, I feel it, the Great is on the edge. He's afraid, and not just for us. Mr. Straithmore will make him pop right open. We only have fifteen minutes before he goes back into the hall and wrings out the Great." She patted her mother's arm. "It's all right that he's a man, Mama. Like he said, we can make use of him."

"Actually, twelve and a half minutes," Grayson said.

Miranda was fingering a velvet rose petal, a particularly vibrant shade of pink. She straightened. "P.C., you have told everything to Mr. Sher—ah, Mr. Straithmore?"

"Yes'm, she did that," Barnaby said, "but ma'am, don't lock her up with bread and water. She didn't know what to do and she doesn't want to leave, so she asked me and I agreed, so I'll take the bread and water. She wants his smartness to save us all from the abyss. Not that yer not smart yerself, ma'am, but he's an extra smartness with lots of experience with strange sorts of otherworldly things."

"That is an interesting way of explaining it, Barnaby." Grayson turned to Miranda. "What or who do you think this voice is, Mrs. Wolffe?"

"I don't like melodrama, sir, but it seems to me the voice has to be a malignant spirit, but as P.C. told you, we can't understand what it's saying. Well, P.C. said she clearly heard *hoos*, but it does sound more like *whooss*. When we got downstairs, there was this giant maw, black and deep, swirling around and around, trying to suck us in, and I know there was no bottom. The abyss."

She should write novels.

CHAPTER NINE

There was a moment of stark silence, then Pip said with no hesitation, "This sounds very scary, ma'am, but my papa is a hero. He will beat up this bad spirit, he will hurl him back into this abyss. He will protect both you and P.C." And his precious son patted Miranda's hand.

She looked down at the beautiful little boy and gave him a shaky smile. "Thank you, Pip. Now, let's all sit down."

"Nine minutes," P.C. said.

It was really eight minutes.

Grayson asked, "Is there anything you know that P.C. doesn't know, ma'am, that would assist me?"

Miranda said slowly, "Mama-in-law doesn't want us to leave. She was very upset that she didn't hear a thing last night, but what she admitted to me this morning made me absolutely certain the Great knows what's going on here." She shot a look at the children. "It's disturbing."

"Go ahead, Mama, we can take it."

"Very well. About a month ago, your grandmother was in the library with the Great, trying to speak to him about restoring some portraits in the gallery. This is very difficult to believe, but here is what she told me. A huge black funnel burst through the open window and roared right at him, twisted and turned around him, then went straight through him, she said, at least a part of it did. It blasted all his medals from the wall, made them fly out of the frames, shattering the glass covering them, and then went flying. Then those medals the Great collects and polishes, the ones in the big basket—the basket itself was thrown into the air, scattering the medals everywhere. Then, Mama-in-law said, the black funnel whooshed back out the window again and was gone. Nothing more happened, she said. She said she nearly fainted, but the Great only stood there, his mouth working, but he didn't say anything. He told her to keep her mouth shut because no one would believe her, and so she had.

"She said she eventually convinced herself that it had been a shared hallucination. She said to think anything else would give her a heart seizure. But after what I told her happened last night, she knew she had to warn me."

"A month ago," Grayson said. "When did you and P.C. have the dream?"

"The first dream came two weeks later." She paused, cocked her head in thought. "This is the final proof for me that what is going on here involves the medals. I mean, why else would the funnel hurl them about like that? I've come to think the black funnel was trying to communicate to the Great, but he didn't understand and the voice became angry and thus came after P.C. and me. But why?"

Grayson said simply, "Because the Great loves the two of you more than anyone else in the world."

"Oh," P.C. said. "Perhaps that is true. Do you think so, Mama?"

"Perhaps," Miranda said. "Mr. Straithmore, the Great has collected medals for many years now, all of them Waterloo medals. Since Max Carstairs came, he's the one who buys them from pawn shops, and the Great polishes them up and returns them to the soldiers or the soldiers' families if they were killed at Waterloo. I asked him why he did this. He said so much was owed to all these brave men, it was the least he could do since after Waterloo times were hard and so many soldiers had to pawn their medals."

Barnaby shouted, "I see ye, Mr. Bickle! Ye keep yer distance from the sprat!"

Grayson looked over to see a small man dressed all in black slink from one oak tree to the next. Then he crept to stand behind a sapling, and he was so thin Grayson couldn't see him. He pulled Pip closer. Since Pip was still holding Barnaby's hand, the three of them ended up huddled together on the bench.

P.C. said, "He's not moving now, but you know he's listening." She lowered her voice. "This funnel—the voice—do you think it wants a particular medal? Maybe the spirit wants its medal returned to its family? And it wants the Great to find it?"

Miranda said, "I think that must be it. But who or what is *hoos*?"

Barnaby said, "I agrees, it's got to be a dead soldier from the Battle of Waterloo, and 'e wants 'is medal back."

Grayson nodded. It sounded right to him.

Miranda slowly nodded. "But why would the spirit come now? Waterloo was years ago. Why begin this reign of terror now? Why not right after the battle? And the Great is looking for the spirit's medal."

Grayson said, "But it appears the voice couldn't get the name through to the Great. So it tried you and P.C. Still no luck, so it's taken the next step." He sent Pip a worried look, but of course Pip wasn't afraid. He'd been raised with talk of spirits and malignant creatures. His eyes glowed with excitement.

P.C. whispered, "Barnaby, Bickle slipped behind that maple tree. He's only twelve yards from Pip."

Pip looked over at the strange little man dressed in a shiny black coat, and waved to him. Bickle looked aghast and dived behind a yew bush.

Grayson said, "What about the servants? Do they know about the funnel? About the two dreams? About you and P.C. running from the house?"

Miranda said, "Oh yes, servants always know everything that happens. They're nervous, on edge. But not Suggs."

P.C. called out, "Bickle, we see you. You will not steal Pip. Go away."

From behind the oak tree came a squeaky voice. "You know I must continue stalking my prey, Miss P.C., else his lordship will not eat properly and I worry."

"This is all very strange, Papa," Pip said, never taking his eyes off Bickle.

When Grayson returned to the Great's study with one minute to go, Suggs informed him that his lordship had left to pay visits to his tenants. It was just as well. Grayson had some reading to do. He and Pip took their leave of Miranda and P.C. Grayson found himself looking down at Miranda Wolffe, and he was smiling. "Don't worry, we will figure all this out. And soon."

CHAPTER TEN

Grayson awoke from a dream struggling with a banshee who looked remarkably like the Great. He was trying to grab up Pip and run out the door when he snapped awake at the yelling and banging on the front door.

He threw on his dressing gown, grabbed his pistol off the shelf in his dressing room, and ran downstairs. He threw open the door to see Miranda and P.C., both in their nightclothes, hair bedraggled, huddled together on the front step.

He quickly herded them inside and without a thought brought them both against him. They were trembling, but he didn't think it was from cold. No, it was from fear. What had happened? He heard another shout.

It was Barnaby, and he had Musgrave Jr. tucked inside his jacket. Musgrave was not a happy cat. He bounded out, a calico blur, and skidded across the entrance hall. The four of them watched him fetch up against a table leg. He turned to look at them, tail swishing, and he proceeded to wash himself.

"Come here," Grayson said, and in the next moment, he was trying to hold all three of them against him, his hands stroking backs, saying over and over that it would be all right now. Musgrave meowed, tail high, and walked into the drawing room.

"Well, Musgrave's all right," P.C. said. "That's good. Why did you bring him, Barnaby?"

"'E were outside, yowlin' 'is fur off, P.C., so what could I do?"

"You did the right thing," Miranda said, then looked at Grayson. "Oh dear, I hope you do not mind Musgrave making himself at home in your drawing room?"

"Not at all."

Grayson heard Haddock's deep voice and turned to see him holding a candle high, Mrs. Elvan behind him, her hair wound around in tight little rags all over her head, holding up her own candle.

"Sir, may I ask why we have visitors at this hour?"

"I don't know as yet, Haddock," Grayson said. "Mrs. Elvan, if you would give me your candle and accompany Haddock to the kitchen and prepare some tea?" He looked at Barnaby and P.C. "Mrs. Elvan, may we also have some of your delicious walnut cake left over from dinner? A saucer of milk too, if you please, for Musgrave Jr."

Haddock and Mrs. Elvan eyed the three refugees, the little girl hugging a big cat to her chest, Mrs. Miranda hugging both children against her, looking a bit on edge herself. Grayson knew both of them were bursting their seams with curiosity. However, since they both knew they'd find out every detail by morning, they nodded and disappeared into the nether regions of the house.

Grayson turned and gave a reassuring smile to his unexpected guests. He saw Miranda wasn't wearing her glasses, and her hair hung loose in deep, heavy waves tangled around a face as white as the banshee's face in his dream. But unlike the banshee's fierce, bony face, hers was fine-boned, looked soft as silk, and was, he realized, a really quite lovely face.

P.C., bless her heart, now that she knew she was safe, looked more excited than afraid, her eyes sparkling. As for Barnaby, unlike mother and daughter, he was fully dressed.

"All that runnin'," Barnaby said, "fair to made me stomach hollow. I'm ready to gnaw my elbow. Walnut cake, ye said, yer savior-hood?"

Now *savior-hood* had a ring to it, but Grayson liked *yer inkpot-ness* best. "Yes, walnut cake, Barnaby. Mrs. Elvan's is the best. It will fill in all the cracks in your stomach. Let's go into the drawing room and you can tell me what's happened."

"Papa! P.C.! Did the abyss come again?"

No hope for it, Grayson thought, when he saw Mary Beth running down the stairs after Pip. He scooped up his son and nodded to Mary Beth. "All right. We're all here now. Come along into the drawing room."

P.C. was out of breath, so Grayson took Musgrave Jr. from her, sat down in his big winged chair and placed the cat across his thighs. "All of you take a deep breath and calm yourselves. Everything is all right now. That's right. Now, Miranda, tell me what happened."

Miranda drew in a deep, calming breath and got herself together, watching Grayson stroke his hand down Musgrave Jr.'s back, the cat purring so loudly she could hear him. She looked down at her bed-robe, at her slippered feet. "I didn't even think to change—everything happened too fast. We're all very glad you were home, Grayson. What happened— it was very frightening, and I knew we had to leave the manor." She paused. "All right." She drew another deep breath. "I was worried and couldn't sleep. It wasn't yet all that late, so I decided I wanted to speak to the Great. He didn't come back for dinner after he escaped you this afternoon. I wanted to tell him neither P.C. nor I would leave Wolffe Hall. I was determined I wouldn't let him shake his head and seam his lips at me anymore because I was a helpless female who had to be protected and kept ignorant.

"He wasn't in his bedchamber. I went downstairs and saw a light beneath the library door." She looked over at the sprawled purring cat, at Pip, who'd moved closer to his father and was now petting the cat. "I knocked on the door, but there was no answer. I knocked again. Finally I opened the door.

"I fully expected to see the Great in his ancient blue brocade dressing gown polishing a medal, ignoring any interruptions. But he was standing in front of his desk, his hands out in front of him, as if he would ward something off. It was then I saw it."

Mrs. Elvan appeared in the doorway, a covered silver tray in her arms, Haddock behind her, bringing tea. Miranda stopped talking until they left, steps slow. Grayson, however, knew they'd be listening outside the door, and that was all right. They were part of the family.

P.C. poured the tea. Grayson set Musgrave Jr. on the floor and cut the cake, giving a big slice of walnut cake to Barnaby, who immediately stuffed it into his mouth. Grayson handed P.C. a healthy slice, then looked at Miranda. She shook her head. Musgrave Jr. put his paws on Grayson's knee and meowed.

"He loves cake," P.C. said. And so Grayson gave him a sliver and nodded once again to Miranda.

Haddock appeared in the doorway with a saucer of milk for Musgrave Jr. "Sir, for the feline after he's finished the walnut cake."

"Thank you, Haddock," Grayson said and set the saucer on the rug. "Now, Miranda, tell me."

She drew in a deep breath, pictured her grandpapa-in-law clearly. "I think he was looking at something I couldn't see. His lips were moving, but I couldn't make out what he was saying. Then it was there—the black funnel. It was coming through the closed windows—how I don't know—and the curtains billowed, and the funnel whooshed right at him and stopped. Then it started whirling around him, then it went into him, through him, like Mama-in-law said it had a month ago, and I heard him say over and over, loud, nearly shouting, 'I have it, you cursed spirit. I have it and surely you know I have it. What else do you want from me? Do you want me to tell you again that I'm sorry? You know that if I could change what happened, I would! What else do you want? I promised you I would send it to your family—leave! Go away! I've done what you asked! Leave my family alone.'

"And then the black funnel backed up a bit and hovered right in front of him. I couldn't move, I was too scared, disbelieving, really, and then it was as if it saw me standing there frozen, and in the next instant it seemed to leap toward me. The Great yelled, 'No! Leave her alone!' I dropped my candle and ran as fast as I could. I heard the Great shouting after me, but I kept running. I grabbed P.C., and we ran to the barn. Barnaby helped us saddle horses, and we came here. There wasn't another horse for Barnaby, so he ran here. With Musgrave Jr."

Miranda's hands were shaking. She quickly took a drink of tea and closed her eyes a moment. She brought P.C. closer to her side. Grayson watched her calm herself again. He admired her a great deal in that moment. She had guts.

She looked over at him. "That's all of it, Mr. Sherbrooke—Grayson. What are we going to do?"

Grayson rose. "Obviously the Great was sorry. He would change what happened if he could. Do you know what he means, Miranda?"

She shook her head.

Grayson stood. "I'm going to dress now, then ride over to Wolffe Hall. This time the Great will not escape me. You will all remain here."

P.C. jumped to her feet. "But Mr. Straithmore, the funnel might attack you!"

"No," Grayson said slowly. "You see, it has no reason to attack me. I can't help it get what it wants."

"But we can't either," Miranda said.

Mrs. Elvan said in her comfortable voice from the doorway, "Yes, Master Grayson, you should go back to Wolffe Hall and take care of things once and for all." She set a new pot of tea on the table, then leaned over to pat Miranda's shoulder. "Do not worry yourself, Mrs. Wolffe. The master will make everything right. Young Master Pip, you will stay here with me, as will all the rest of you." She saw Pip open his mouth, and being a very smart woman with six children and eight grandchildren, she said quickly, "I will read you the master's new manuscript."

But Grayson knew this offered treat wouldn't do the trick. He saw his son was marshaling his arguments, so he said quickly, "I really need you to remain here and take care of Mrs. Wolffe, P.C., and Barnaby. You're now the master of the house, all right?"

He believed he'd been inspired with that reasoning, but Pip said quickly, "But, Papa, what if Bickle tries to sneak in and take me?"

"We'll all protect you, Pip," Mary Beth said, rushing over to him to hug him. "We can all sleep together if you would feel safer."

Pip reconsidered, stood straight. "Papa said I was to be the master of the house. I will protect all of you. If Bickle comes, I'll kick him in the shins."

"Thank you, Pip," Grayson said.

Miranda rose, frowned, and shoved her hair out of her face. Yes, here she was, a lady, and she was wearing only her bedclothes in a gentleman's drawing room and it was past midnight and the gentleman was looking at her. No, she was absurd, he wasn't looking at her like that, and it didn't matter. What mattered was that he would take care of things.

"What's the matter, Mrs. Wolffe—Miranda?" Grayson asked her.

She wanted to tell him that of course she was returning with him, she didn't have any clothes, for heaven's sake, but what came out of her mouth was, "This room doesn't have any color."

He stared at her.

Miranda shook herself. "How stupid of me. It's not important. I really should come back with you." She swatted her bed-robe. "I need clothes, P.C. needs clothes. Besides, you need me." She saw he would argue, so she stuck up her chin. "If you don't take me, sir, neither I nor P.C. will leave Wolffe Hall." *And because you're so honorable, you will believe yourself responsible if anything happens to us.*

He didn't want her to go back to that house, but then again, she was smart, and she'd used the perfect leverage. He would be there to protect her. He smiled at her. "All right. No, P.C., Barnaby, you will stay here. Mrs. Wolffe and I will be back when we can. P.C., everything will be all right, I promise you. Now take care of Musgrave Jr." Grayson's last view of the big calico was on his back, all four paws up, two feet from the sluggishly burning fire.

Ten minutes later, Miranda, dressed in one of Mary Beth's gowns, rode beside Grayson back to Wolffe Hall. He wanted to hear the story again, ask her more questions, but what came out of his mouth was, "Why do you believe I'm a man who loves color?"

"Your books," she said simply. "Even though you fill them with spirits and frightful and strange creatures from other mysterious realms, you always place them in vibrant settings, colorful settings. Am I wrong?"

"No, you're not wrong."

"I used to be a woman of color," she said more to herself than to him, "but it's been a very long time now."

He said, "You will wallow in color again, not too long from now."

"How could you possibly know that?"

He grinned at her. "It's all a matter of how you see the world around you, and soon your world will be a very different place."

"Does that mean you will fix everything, like P.C. assures me you will?"

"Yes, I will fix everything."

Miranda realized as she looked at him, listened to his calm, certain voice, the awful fear lessened. Would she really see color again?

They continued toward Wolffe Hall, saying nothing more.

But when they arrived at the manor, all the windows were dark. Suggs, wearing a sleeping cap and a shiny dressing gown, finally opened the door and gaped.

Grayson said, "Suggs, I know our unexpected presence alarms you, but everything is all right. We must speak to his lordship."

"But, Mr. Sherbrooke, his lordship took himself off to bed nearly an hour ago."

Grayson nodded. "You will return to your bed, Suggs," he said over his shoulder as he and Miranda hurried up the stairs, "we will see if his lordship is asleep."

There was no answer to their knock. The door handle didn't turn. The Great had locked his bedchamber door and wouldn't come out. He yelled out, "I know it's you, Mr. Sherbrooke. I don't want you here. I told you I will deal with this." A pause, then, "Miranda, when you and Palonia Chiara leave in the morning, do you mind leaving Musgrave Jr. here? No harm will come to him."

Miranda rolled her eyes. "He adores that wretched cat. Musgrave Jr. sleeps with him, you know. Warms his ancient bones, he says."

CHAPTER ELEVEN

Miranda showed him to the guest room next to her mama-in-law's, a good-sized room, but filled with a great deal of pink—wallpaper, counterpane, even the bed was canopied with frothy pink silk. A single big window overlooked the side gardens, framed with pink draperies. Grayson could make out the home woods that stretched out beyond, pines and oaks and larches pressed together in the night. It was a lovely prospect. At least the bed was firm, the way he liked it. Still, Grayson didn't sleep well, probably because the Great wouldn't speak to him, he thought when he was coming downstairs the next morning, not because of the pink. He wondered if the Great was still locked in his bedchamber.

Suggs stood in the entrance hall, dressed immaculately, his bald head shining, staring up at him. He cleared his throat. "I did not tell his lordship that you remained, that you made yourself quite at home in the Pink Room, usually reserved for the fairer sex with questionable taste."

"Have you seen Mrs. Wolffe, Suggs?"

"Which one, sir?"

"Miranda Wolffe." Of course Suggs knew well which Mrs. Wolffe

Grayson was asking about. He was trying to protect the Great, but the time for that was over.

"I have not yet had that pleasure, sir. But doubtless she will come to breakfast. Follow me, sir."

Grayson stepped into the small dining room to see the Great sipping a cup of strong Indian tea, reading the *London Gazette*. The day was overcast, on the cool side, but the windows were open, a stiff breeze sending the light draperies blowing into the room. The Great looked up. He didn't look at all surprised. He waved toward a chair. "Do you know at my age, my boy, if you wake up and discover you are able to take two steps without falling over, you know it will be a good day.

"I suppose Miranda is with you? And you had the brains to leave Palonia Chiara at Belhaven?"

Grayson nodded.

The Great sighed. "Well, sit down, sit down. The two of you shouldn't have come back. You two should leave immediately after breakfast. Really, sir, this is none of your affair."

Grayson pulled out a dining chair, turned it to face the Great, and straddled it. He said, "The Battle of Waterloo will go down in history as a pivotal battle that changed the course of history. It removed Napoleon once and for all, and finally brought peace. The medals are historic as well, Colonel. What makes them extraordinary is that every man who fought at the Battle of Waterloo received one.

"For the remainder of the man's life he'd be known as a Waterloo Man, and he would wear his medal with pride and distinction, since his name is impressed around the edge. They are silver, not all that valuable, but if a family were in need, they would pawn it, and so many have."

"You know a lot for a man who was a boy in short coats at the time of the Great Battle."

"I did a great deal of reading and thinking yesterday, sir."

The Great started to eat some kippers, then set down his fork. "Our duke was responsible, of course, for getting the Prince Regent to agree to the expenditure. Wellington wanted to recognize and thank every single man who fought not only at Waterloo, but in all three bloody battles—Quatre Bras, Ligny, and of course Waterloo on the third day, June 18, 1815."

"Did you find the medal the spirit demanded you find, sir?"

The Great gave him a look of acute dislike. "I see the women in my household can't keep their mouths shut." He sighed. "Yes, as luck would have it, yes I did. Last week a dozen or so medals arrived from Norwich.

"Listen, young gentleman, I have decided this is my problem and mine alone. Miranda and Palonia Chiara are leaving this morning."

"What about your daughter-in-law, Mrs. Elaine?"

"What about her? She didn't dream anything."

"No, but she saw the black funnel come into your study and hurl all the Waterloo medals around and go through you. Did it communicate with you, sir? Or couldn't you understand what it was saying, any more than Miranda and P.C.?"

The Great leaned back and laced his gnarled hands over his belly. "I will say this again. I will deal with this, sir, not you, an outsider, a man who is too young to know anything."

"The funnel—the spirit—it gave you a name, didn't it?"

The Great started shaking his head, then stopped. Finally, "Yes, at first it felt it to me, I suppose you could say, as unbelievable as it sounds. But I couldn't understand what it said. Then, to my astonishment, the funnel, or whatever was in it, screamed right in my face, '*Find Major Houston.*'"

So that was the whooss.

"I screamed back that I'd found his medal, that I would return it personally to his family, but that didn't placate the spirit or whatever strange sort of being or thing it is. In any case, it gave up on me and dreamed himself to Miranda and Palonia Chiara.

"Don't you understand? My finding Major Houston's medal has made no difference. The black funnel, the abyss, as Miranda calls it, attacked them, and only them, to scare them, to make me do what it wanted. But don't you see, I can't do what it wants. I can't find Major Houston."

"You believed since you couldn't find Major Houston, if you found his medal, the spirit would leave you alone?"

The Great stared some more at the kippers. Finally, he said slowly, "I reasoned there was nothing else he could want. I mean, when he first came to me, he scattered the Waterloo medals everywhere. Rather a huge clue, don't you think?

"But the fact is, I really couldn't believe I actually found Major Houston's medal. There were so many struck, upward to forty thousand, and yet at last I found the right one and I told him over and over that I had it. Surely the spirit knows it. But it didn't help."

Grayson said, "It seems to me, sir, the spirit was very clear. It wants you to find Major Houston, not his medal."

They looked up to see Suggs hovering by the door. He arched a thick white eyebrow.

Suggs executed a splendid bow. "My lord, like Mr. Sherbrooke, I wish to know what you are supposed to do with the spirit as well since it is my responsibility to keep the house safe. I can assist Mr. Sherbrooke, your lordship. None of us wish Mrs. Wolffe and Miss P.C. to leave. And Musgrave Jr., of course. You know too that Barnaby would go with them. Our family would be broken up. It would be a disaster, my lord."

Miranda appeared in the doorway, hands on her hips, her glasses sliding down her nose, her hair back in its thick braid, wearing a yellow gown, so old it was faded nearly to white.

"Come in and eat your breakfast, Miranda," the Great said. "How can Mr. Sherbrooke possibly want to marry you when you're so thin?"

Grayson stood frozen in place, his mouth open, but Miranda was made of stern stuff. She leaned forward, planting her hands on the table. "I'm thin because you brought this malignant spirit into the house, sir. Who could eat with gusto when a black funnel could whirl in at any moment and go into you? Or make the house shake off its foundation and open up a black hole to swallow P.C. and me?

"Sir, listen to me. No more running away, locking yourself in your bedroom, no more of your clever distractions. I wish to hear the answer as well as Suggs. This is our home. We have the right to know. Why does the spirit want you to find this Major Houston? As luck would have it, you did find the medal, amazing since there were so many made. You had to know you'd have a better chance of finding the man."

The Great chewed on his knuckles, then sighed. "It's been so many years. I suppose it really doesn't matter any longer. Very well, Miranda, sit down. Suggs, come closer."

The Great waited until Suggs was standing at the other end of the dining table, tall, shoulders back, like one of the Great's soldiers back in the old days.

Grayson said, "Sir, I realize you believe you cannot find Major Houston because he died at Waterloo."

That brought Miranda to her feet. "Major Houston is dead? But that makes no sense, Grayson, why would the spirit of a dead man come to the Great and demand that he find him? He's dead, so that's impossible. The black funnel hurled all the medals into the air. That's why you believed Major Houston wanted his medal returned to his family, isn't it, sir?"

Before the Great could respond, Grayson raised a hand. "Sir, what I do not understand, however, is why you wouldn't want to tell Mrs. Wolffe, all of us, immediately. Why the secrecy?"

The Great looked from face to face, then down at the congealed eggs on his plate. "Very well, I will tell you. Major Houston served under me in the Third Battalion, Fourteenth Regiment of Foot. He saved my life, slammed the sword out of the French soldier's hand, knocked him off his horse. I had no time to thank him, and he was gone again. An hour later, I was in the middle of the bloodbath, fighting two French infantrymen, when I sensed another coming up behind me. I turned and slashed out with my sword, killed him. Then I realized it was Major Houston coming to help me and I'd killed him. I'd killed the man who'd saved my life. When I realized he wasn't an enemy soldier and I'd killed my own man, I nearly fell apart, but you see, my men needed me.

"There was no choice but to leave him lying there since there were more French infantry surrounding me. On and on it went, until finally, it was over and I still lived, and I stood in that field of blood holding my arm." He laughed, shaking his head. "All the dead men surrounding me, the wounded, and I had only a minor slash in my forearm. I began searching for Major Houston, but a messenger came upon me, told me the duke wanted me to come to him, and so I had no choice but to leave the field.

"The first chance I got, I went back to search more for Major Houston, but I couldn't find his body. There were so many bodies, so many men whose lives were gone. Simply gone."

There was silence in the breakfast room.

"This is difficult, Miranda—this is why I didn't want to tell you. It is my guilt to bear because I killed my own man, the man who saved my life. I killed Major Houston.

"After I returned to England, I traveled to Sussex to meet the major's family—his father and mother, his younger sister. They were devastated, of course. I expressed my gratitude at their son's bravery and my condolences. I told them he had saved my life. But in the end, I was a coward. I did not tell them I had killed their son. Can you imagine the horror they would feel?

"I spoke to the duke when I found out about the medals, and asked him if I could myself present the major's medal to his family, and he agreed. But there was some sort of mistake and his medal never got to me. I wrote the family, asked them if they'd received his medal. They said they hadn't.

"I suppose I put it out of my mind—there was so much to be done here at Wolffe Hall since I had been absent far too long.

"Major Houston's mother wrote me three years ago to tell me her husband, Major Houston's father, had died. It was about that time I learned that many Waterloo medals had been pawned and sold, so I began collecting all the medals I could find, polishing them and returning them, to expiate my guilt, that was certainly part of it. I was also hoping to find the major's medal for his mother and sister, to honor him, and of course, praying that finding his medal and returning it would also help lessen my guilt.

"I believe it is Major Houston's spirit that has come to me. He must have realized I was searching for his medal—I can't imagine how—I've never believed in such things as spirits and ghosts—and that's when the funnel came into me. I swear, after all the indistinct mumbling, he shouted right in my face, '*Find Major Houston!*' Of course I assumed the spirit meant he wanted me to find Major Houston's medal and that's why it hurled all the medals around the library.

"Then a miracle happened. I found the medal—I actually found it in a pile Max had purchased from a pawn shop in a small town in Sussex. I was pleased because at least I could do something. I was ready to return it to his family, but he came to me again, more mumbling, more whirling around me, then shouted in my face, '*Find Major Houston!*' and I shouted back that there was no question of finding the major, he was long dead, bones and dust now, but I had found his medal and I would take it to his family. I even called the spirit Major Houston. I told him he could stop his spirit visitations, but he didn't stop." The Great looked at each of them again. "There, you now know my awful secret. I carry the guilt around on my shoulders every single day. Yes, I am convinced the spirit is Major Houston—there can be no other.

"But I cannot understand why he continues with this harassment and why he keeps telling me to find him! It makes no sense. It's got to be about his medal. What I do not understand is that although Major Houston was a very young man, he was honorable, straight-thinking, he was brave. He wouldn't have ever threatened another, and in such a horrific manner."

"Last night, he screamed at you again?" Miranda asked.

The Great nodded. "I kept reassuring him, swore to him yet again that I would take the medal to his family." The Great fell silent and stared down at his plate. "There, I have told you the lot of it. There is no more." He looked suddenly tired, at the end of his tether. "It is all my fault. I killed him and now I must pay. With my life? I suppose it is fair. After all, I have had more years given me than that poor young man did. But it is not right that I pay with your lives as well.

"Miranda, I do not know what will happen now, so tomorrow morning I believe it best that you take Palonia Chiara and leave this place. I cannot and will not take a chance with your safety." He turned to Grayson. "I ask that you take my granddaughter-in-law and Palonia Chiara to Belhaven tonight and protect them. I don't wish any harm to come to them."

CHAPTER TWELVE

Grayson nodded. "Of course. But, sir, first I would appreciate your telling me more about the major's family."

The Great raised an eyebrow, but he said readily enough, "His father was the vicar in the town of Witchery-Tyne. Evarard Houston was his name, serving for more than thirty years. I have kept in touch with Mrs. Houston, but I have not informed her of her dead son's visits to me, his attacks on Miranda and Palonia Chiara. I doubt they would believe me, in any case."

"And Major Houston?"

"Major Houston's first name was Charles, and he was made a major at the age of twenty at the battle of Badajoz for his outstanding bravery. When he died at Waterloo, he was only twenty-three. He was a young man to admire, to trust.

"But now his spirit—he's changed, he's different, he has turned spiteful and violent. As I told you, he wasn't like that in life."

Grayson said, "Sir, why did the major's spirit wait nearly twenty-five years to come to you?"

"I have wondered the same thing, Mr. Sherbrooke. I have no answer. You say, sir, you know about otherworldly beings, so how do you explain what his spirit is now doing? Why he has changed so much?"

Grayson said, "There is only one logical conclusion, sir. Major Houston isn't dead. It isn't his spirit."

The house shuddered.

Miranda jumped to her feet. "Who are you?"

There was one more shudder, then it stopped. Everything was quiet.

"Oh my," Suggs said, but didn't move.

"No!" Miranda ran toward the window where the curtains were billowing madly. The black funnel was slowly forming, whipping itself up—turning toward Grayson. Miranda ran directly at the black funnel. Grayson lifted her out of its path and moved to stand in front of it. He felt warmth coming from that madly whirling funnel, and something else— what? An urgency, he felt that, and a plea. He relaxed, opened himself, and felt the warmth settle around him, felt it moving into him, slowly, as if exploring, uncertain. Then he was one with it. He heard the Great's voice, heard Miranda yelling at him, even Suggs bellowed once. Grayson wished they'd all be quiet. He wasn't afraid. And he made out one word—*heir.*

The funnel whirled back outside. The curtains settled. The house was calm. The silence was deafening.

Grayson looked down at Miranda. She'd run in front of him, to save him. He saw her face was white, her eyes dilated. She stared up at him and came up on her tiptoes, her warm breath feathering against his ear. "It is very odd, Grayson. You smell like lemons."

It wasn't only Grayson—the lemon scent filled the dining room.

The Great said suddenly, his voice far away, "There was an orchard of lemon trees off the battlefield. You could smell the lemons when the wind changed. It lessened the stench of blood and death. For a moment. You are wrong, Grayson, it is Major Houston's spirit, it has to be, and he brought the smell with him."

"No, sir, it is an entirely different spirit, but the visitations are about Major Houston." Grayson smiled. Finally, everything came together. Simple, really, but still, best to be sure. He said, "Sir, do you have genealogy records of the Wolffe family?"

"Of course, but why?"

"I believe they may reveal the answer."

Miranda looked at the smile, saw the gleam of knowledge in his eyes. "You know what this is all about, don't you, Grayson?"

"Yes, I think I do."

An hour later in the Great's library, Grayson was slowly making his way through the faded, nearly indecipherable handwriting that stretched back to the sixteenth century.

And there was a family tree, shown in full detail.

"You've never studied this, sir?"

The Great shook his head. "No, I have no interest in such things."

"A pity," Grayson said.

"Why?" Miranda was nearly hanging over his shoulder, and then she saw it. "Good heavens, sir, would you look at this!"

"Yes," Grayson said. "There, I believe, is our spirit. He visited you, told you to find Major Houston."

Miranda said, "But if Major Houston isn't dead, then why didn't the spirit contact him? Send him here?"

"I hope that he has," the Great said, "since we have no idea where to find him. Imagine, Charles Houston is alive, but what happened to him?"

CHAPTER THIRTEEN

When Grayson and Pip came into the Great's study, he was grinning wildly, showing his six remaining teeth, waving a letter. "It's from Charles—Major Houston. Grayson, he found me!" And the Great read:

My dear Colonel Lord Wolffe:

How the years fall away when I write your name, when I picture your face in my mind. So many years since that fateful day at Waterloo.

Let me hasten to tell you that I never blamed you for wounding me. It was I who was at fault. Of course you would believe me an enemy the way I came up behind you. I lay there, the sword slice through my side, knocked unconscious because I evidently hit a rock when I fell. A young man from a nearby village, Jacco Hobbs, found me and pulled me to safety. I survived, but strangely, my brain was perfectly blank. Jacco nursed me back to health, but still I could remember nothing, who I was, who my family was, and poor Jacco had no idea either. So the two of us set sail to Boston, where we've lived for the past twenty-five years, Jacco as my valet.

I married, went into my father-in-law's shipping business, but still, I had no memory. My poor wife and my small daughter both died in a cholera outbreak that left many dead.

The years passed, and still I had no memory until I took a fall from my horse, hit my head, and when I came awake, I remembered everything. This was about four months ago.

Then something very strange happened. I hesitate to lay it down in writing for fear you will believe me unbalanced, but here is the truth as I experienced it. I will call it a spirit for want of a better word. This spirit visited me in a dream and told me to find Colonel Wolffe. I believed it only a strange dream, but I had the same dream three more times. And then, forgive me for stretching your beliefs, sir, but a black funnel came upon me when I was alone in my countinghouse. It swirled all over the room, pulling accounting books from their shelves, and then it came into me, and I heard it clearly, yelling at me to find you.

I do not understand this, sir, but I hope that you will. I will arrive to see you as soon as I am able to leave Boston. Naturally, I will visit my family before I come to you.

All of this is very strange, and I have no notion why this happened. Incidentally, the spirit hasn't visited me again. I hope you will be able to tell me what is the meaning of all this—

> *Yr. Faithful Servant,*
> *Charles Houston*

Grayson and Miranda walked to the portrait gallery to see Elaine staring up at Alphonse. They heard her say, "The Great now has his heir, Alphonse, and that means the Barons of Cudlow will continue into the future. But this young man who has lived so many years in the Colonies, what if he despises us? What if he makes us leave Wolffe Hall?"

Grayson and Miranda joined her. Grayson stared up at the handsome face, pale as snow, the thin pointed beard on his chin black as night.

A man in his prime, probably a wicked man, given the devil-may-care look in his eyes, the arrogant tilt of his head. He fancied he could see the resemblance to the Great. Or perhaps it was his imagination, perhaps it was what he wanted to see. He took both Elaine's and Miranda's hands. He said, "Major Houston does not even know he is the Great's heir. I fancy he will be surprised and very pleased to have a new family. I predict he will wear a smile on his face for a very long time to come. I'm sure Alphonse would agree."

Elaine said, "Oh dear, Mr. Sherbrooke, I fear we are beset yet again— like the Great, Charles Houston does not have an heir. All right. It can be done, and I will do it. I will find him a sweet young girl. We will all go to London, open the house on Portman Square. Can he look higher than a baron's daughter? Hmm, we will see. Alphonse, you and I will discuss this."

Elaine fell silent, deep in thought. Grayson said to Alphonse's portrait, "Alphonse de Marcy, we have read all about you, sir. You were the original owner and builder of Marcy Hall in 1587. Five of your sons survived into adulthood, and they produced many males to seed the direct line.

"But the de Marcy descendants died out and your property went to your great-granddaughter and her husband, a military man named Wolffe. And Marcy Hall became Wolffe Hall in the early eighteenth century, and the first Baron Cudlow came into the picture. And there it becomes complicated. All I know so far is that Charles Houston is related through your maternal line that goes back to the original younger sister of your great-great-granddaughter.

"Alphonse de Marcy, you must have realized Major Houston wasn't dead on the day he regained his memory. You have done well. Your descendant is on his way here, and you will see him very soon. The Great accepts that you are a Wolffe Hall ancestor, and he wishes to learn more about you, who you were and what you did during your lifetime. He thanks you, sir."

Grayson and Miranda left Elaine alone with Alphonse. Of course, only Elaine saw that Alphonse's eyes twinkled.

EPILOGUE

"A toast," the Great said. "To you, Mr. Sherbrooke." And he raised his glass.

"Hear, hear."

"To Mr. Straithmore!" P.C. called out.

There were some smiles. Grayson sipped his wine. He felt better than he had when he'd finished the third chapter of his new novel, a gnarly tale of twin sisters, both evil to the bone, but perhaps one could be saved. This time he'd actually done something that mattered, something real, something not between the pages of one of his novels. He'd helped to bring a man lost for nearly twenty-five years home again. He couldn't wait to meet Charles Houston. He saw Miranda was smiling at him.

"And to my heir, Major Charles Houston."

"Hear, hear."

Miranda set down her glass. "I have drunk so many toasts God will surely punish me for being a tippler. Now, I want all of you to listen. I have an announcement. I am going to give Barnaby speech lessons."

Stark silence.

She said, more forcefully this time, "Listen to me, all Barnaby needs is a little polish."

The Great cocked his head. "Our stable boy? Miranda, he's a bastard, brought to us by Vicar Harkness when he found the babe on the steps of the church. We feed him and clothe him and he tends the horses nicely. Why do you wish to make him into a young gentleman?"

"Barnaby's smart, sir, very smart," P.C. said, sitting forward. "He was the one who took me to Mr. Straithmore. He deserves a chance." She added after a moment, "He needs a lot of polish, Mama."

The Great slowly grinned. "Perhaps I shall tell Bickle that Barnaby is my spare heir—might keep the bugger from grinning all the time." He rubbed his hands together. "Imagine, I now have my heir. Imagine."

Miranda leaned toward Grayson. "You never said what you thought about my educating Barnaby."

"So P.C. can marry him when they grow up?"

She rolled her eyes. "P.C. is very smart. I think she said that to push me into doing something, but the fact is, Barnaby deserves it. He's very bright, very good-hearted."

Grayson frowned. "You know, I swear he looks familiar to me. Perhaps when he speaks the Queen's English, I'll figure it out."

When they were in the drawing room later, drinking tea, Suggs appeared in the dining room doorway. He was trembling with excitement. "My lord, Major Houston and his mother are here to see you."

It was nearly midnight when Grayson rode away from Wolffe Hall. There was a full moon overhead, and a stiff breeze from the sea stirred against his cheek, but his cloak was warm. As Albert cantered back to his warm stable at Belhaven, Grayson wondered idly if the Wolffes would mind having this amazing adventure written into a novel. Perhaps Alphonse could communicate with the hero, Thomas Straithmore, or Thomas could find old journals from the sixteenth century that Alphonse had penned, but still it wouldn't be enough, and enraged, Alphonse would suck him into the abyss. And what was the abyss?

Or possibly the truth: Alphonse would send a funnel into Thomas with only one word, *heir*, and trust it was enough so Thomas would figure it out.

The truth, Grayson thought, as he looked between Albert's ears, was stranger in this instance than in any fiction he'd ever written. He also realized he'd quite enjoyed himself. And there was Miranda, beautiful bright Miranda, and who knew what would happen?

The Resident Evil at Blackthorn Manor

THE SECOND NOVELLA
IN THE GRAYSON SHERBROOKE OTHERWORLDLY
ADVENTURES SERIES

CHAPTER ONE

Grayson Sherbrooke awoke to stabbing pain in his head. He didn't want to open his eyes, he knew it would make the pain worse. He lay still in the absolute silence until he heard scratching close by. His eyes flew open. He saw only blackness. He felt a moment of terror. No, he wasn't blind; he saw a shadowy gray light coming through a high slit window cut into a stone wall about twelve feet from where he lay. Stone wall? Where was he? He heard the scratching again, came up on his elbows, and saw a rat sitting a foot in front of him, chewing on what looked like a bone, studying him. He realized the rat didn't look like any rat he'd ever seen. Its size was right, but it had long, curling whiskers and a large head. He shook his head. A peculiar rat, but still only a rat.

He pulled himself to a sitting position and didn't move until the pain in his head stopped its mad drumbeat. He breathed in ancient smells he didn't recognize and the stench of mold growing in the shadowed corners.

The morning sun speared a stream of light through the window, and he saw now he was sitting against a stone wall in a circular room. A dungeon? But how could he be in a dungeon? And where was he? He felt another slash of pain and dropped his head into his hands until the pain slowly eased.

Where? Some castle of bygone days? Why didn't he know? He felt panic. He leaned his head back against the cold wall, calmed, and thought. He clearly remembered leaving Edinburgh to ride to Vere Castle on the Fife Peninsula to visit Aunt Sinjun and Uncle Colin after he'd received her letter asking him to come. There was trouble at Vere Castle and they needed him. He hadn't wanted to leave his young son, Pip, or beautiful Miranda, so new to his life, but there'd been no choice. If Aunt Sinjun was right about trouble, that meant he couldn't take Pip with him, despite all his wailing and whining. He remembered he'd left Pip at Wolffe Hall to be spoiled rotten by all the denizens.

Obviously Grayson hadn't made it to Vere Castle. He clearly remembered leaving the Ashburnham townhouse in Edinburgh that morning, the weather blustery and bone-cold. At least it hadn't been raining, and both he and his horse Astor had taken that as an excellent portent. He'd booked passage on the barge from Edinburgh over the Firth of Forth to the Fife Peninsula. Yes, he remembered more now—how before he'd left, Pip was doing a daily countdown to his fifth birthday when he would be grown up enough to write ghost novels with terrifying mysteries, just like his papa. And Miranda— ah yes, he remembered the night before he'd left for Edinburgh, he'd been kissing her, his hands gliding down her back, feeling the long line of the buttons he was desperate to unfasten—and Grayson remembered he was jerked back from his pleasant memories at the sound of a carriage horn. He'd guided Astor off the rutted path to let it pass. But the carriage hadn't continued on the road. The driver had pulled the two horses to a stop directly across from him. A face appeared in the window, covered by a silver veil, and a young voice called to him in English, but he couldn't make out her words. The coachman never looked at him, remained staring straight ahead.

Grayson clearly remembered walking to the old ornate carriage, like a French nobleman's carriage from the last century, pulled by two pure-white geldings, now tossing their beautiful heads, blowing, turning to look at him. The driver still didn't move. Grayson dismounted and walked to the carriage. As he neared, he became aware of a strong violet scent. It perfumed the air, filled his nostrils, and he breathed in. A woman extended her hand through the window, a beautiful white hand with long, tapering fingers, and he saw himself stretching out his own hand, touching her fingers—then there was nothing.

Try as he might, Grayson couldn't remember anything more. Until now, waking up with a splitting head in a dungeon with a rat that wasn't really a rat sitting across the stone floor from him, still eyeing him, ready to attack if the two-legged rodent tried to steal his bone.

Grayson got slowly to his feet, stretched, and looked around. No, he wasn't in a dungeon, rather, it was like a circular tower room, only it wasn't perfectly round, it was tilted a bit to one side even though the floor stayed even. Looking closely made him dizzy. He saw a small table in the middle of the room, two chairs pulled up to it, an unlit candle on its scarred surface, a box of lucifers beside it.

He saw a chamber pot propped up against the wall, an elaborate affair painted deep blue with tiny white flowers. Nothing else except that strange rat staring at him.

Grayson rubbed his hands up and down his arms for warmth. He moved to stand in the shaft of light and began to feel better. He saw an old wooden door, a slit opening at eye level. Why hadn't he noticed that door before now? The door—like the room—seemed slightly slanted to the left. He felt a moment of nausea. He looked through the slit. A stone wall was facing him, maybe three feet away, nothing else. He pulled on the iron handle shaped like a sharp-pointed hook. It didn't turn. The door was locked. Still, he shook that strange hook handle, pushed against the door, stepped back, and sent his foot next to the hook handle. No give. He called out. Nothing. He stood back and considered. Could he be dreaming? He drew in several deep breaths, slowly let them out. No, this was real—crooked room, crooked door, and the peculiar rat.

He was a prisoner in a circular tower room. Why didn't he remember how he'd gotten here?

He heard footsteps and quickly eased to the side of the door, readied himself. A key turned in the lock, and the door slowly pushed inward. A girl's voice—nearly a whisper. "Sir, are you awake?"

He grabbed her arm and jerked her inside and against him. She was strong and fought him until finally he clamped her arms to her sides and brought her back hard against his chest. She had no leverage now. She was tall, coming nearly to his nose. He whispered against her ear, "Where am I? Who are you?"

"I am Queen Maeve."

She smelled like violets. It was the same smell—was she the young lady in the carriage? "I have never heard of you."

"How could you? You have never been here before."

"Queen of what?"

"I am the hereditary queen of Border. You are hurting me, Mr. Sherbrooke. I beg you, loosen your hold on me."

He did, and she immediately kicked back, her toe connecting with his shin. The lick of pain was greater than the pain in his head. Well, that hadn't been very smart of him. He jerked her hard back against him again, said against her ear, "That was rude, Queen Maeve. You do that again and I will make you very sorry. What is Border? Better yet, where is this Border? And how do you know my name?"

"Well, I suppose you could try to make me sorry. You are in my castle, Mr. Sherbrooke, filled with people to protect me and so many soldiers, more than I can count. However, you are not my prisoner. I am here to save you so you may continue on your journey to Vere Castle in the land of Scotland." Her voice fell to a whisper. "But she is so very strong, and she sees everything. We must hurry."

She'd spoken with no Scottish lilt, but rather clipped, very fine English. She knew the name of his Aunt Sinjun's castle near Loch Leven. He felt another bolt of pain in his head, nearly knocking him off his feet, then it passed. What was going on here? Where was here? "Why do you need to save me? And who is 'she'?"

"Belzaria took you and brought you here. Usually she is content to play her games with our local folk—she calls them her *dollies*—but I know she likes to visit your land, more so than others. I don't know why. What happens is never good."

She became stock-still when they heard a woman's voice. "Where are you, Maeve? Come out immediately. Do you hear me, you wicked girl?"

"You must let me go, you must. If she finds me here, she'll know I was trying to rescue you."

"Is that Belzaria? She is responsible for bringing me here?"

"Yes, yes, let me go, you must, or—" She began jerking against him.

"Does she smell like violets?"

She stopped. "What? Violets? No, she smells like roses, always roses." She began jerking and heaving against him. "Please, please, let me go, you must."

"Then you were the one in the carriage, not Belzaria."

The door opened, pushed by a strong hand. He saw those white fingers coming around the door. Grayson felt a wicked hot pain tear through his head and saw a light so bright it blinded him.

"No," he whispered, and then he was falling, falling, and he heard her voice calling to him. He didn't know if it was Maeve or Belzaria, but he was no longer there to answer her.

CHAPTER TWO

Day One

Grayson whistled as he rode Astor along the rutted road circling the southern side of Loch Leven, a magical place he'd always believed, with its sweet heather-scented air and billowing white clouds racing across a stark blue sky. And he remembered the boy who loved to lie on his back in a field of white heather and look up at those clouds, not to find dragons but to find hovering ghosts up to no good.

Unlike the crags and barren hills to the west in the Highlands, this protected tongue of land resembled, to Grayson's mind, the gently rolling green hills and magnificent forests in southern England.

He and Astor had taken the *Backoxer* ferry from Edinburgh across the narrowest point of the Firth of Forth to Queensferry Narrows on the Fife Peninsula. Astor had been none too happy about sharing his space with valises, boxes, and packages of all sizes stacked together with people and animals, but thankfully, he'd not raised a ruckus, only pressed his nose in Grayson's armpit and let himself be stroked and reassured and fed three apples.

They'd ridden north from Queensferry Narrows to Loch Leven, the sun remaining bright overhead, a light breeze ruffling his hair. He pulled up when he saw Vere Castle in the distance, half medieval castle with turrets and crenellated walls, and half stolid Tudor. Then he turned Astor toward the castle, on a road well maintained by his aunt and uncle so there were no ruts that could trip up his horse, and he'd swear Astor's steps were lighter.

As a child he'd never tired of hearing about the marriage of the impoverished Earl of Ashburnham to Grayson's heiress aunt, Sinjun Sherbrooke, and how their union had brought about the expected prosperity, since the new earl wasn't a nitwit and had pledged to both restore his lands and treat his heiress wife like a queen. In short order the crofts were in excellent repair, and were kept that way, the crofters working their barley and potato fields, just as they were today, and all had flourished. And the earl, according to his parents, indeed treated his wife like a queen, and had thus remained golden.

He remembered the boy again, how he'd always felt like he was riding into a magical kingdom—the castle out of a medieval storybook and the shimmering loch lying before it.

It wasn't Border.

Border? What border? Where had that come from? It sounded like a name. Grayson felt a sharp pain over his right temple, then it was gone.

He decided to blame it on the haggis he'd had for lunch at the Plucked Goose in Cowdenbeath, a village at the base of the black basalt hills. Those same hills had inspired a very young Grayson to terrify his cousins with a tale of the murdering highwayman who'd seen the glitter of gems against the black basalt rock and pressed against it, only to be thrown through a hidden door into the basalt hill itself. He'd been doomed to spend the remainder of his days wandering the thick black basalt corridors, always seeing the glitter of gems just ahead.

Grayson smiled as he leaned forward to pat Astor's neck. He thought about writing a book set in a place like this, but not in the present, no, a book set long ago with powerful bearded men in heavy shining helmets, wearing colorful kilts and wielding claymores. He heard their laughter, their jests, saw their bare butts when they lifted their kilts, and then he saw flitting above them the shadow of an evil magician. Did the evil magician want to steal the magic from this magnificent land? Grayson's writer's brain began to work. What if the magician wasn't a man? What if the magician was an evil sorceress, a beautiful woman who lusted after her brother's crown, a plain gold circlet that pulsed with magic once set upon his head, and he did amazing things, like making corn grow from barren rock. The sorceress sister made her plans to destroy her brother and claim his gold circlet. What was her name?

Belzaria.

Why had that name popped into his head? He felt no shock of pain this time. He'd never heard that name before, he was sure of it. He fancied he saw a stout wooden door in his mind, saw it slam shut in his face. He shook his head. It had to be the haggis.

When the land began to rise as they neared the castle, the bright sunlight fell into shadows cast by the thick oak branches nearly meeting overhead, in full summer plumage. He once again thought of that strange name: *Belzaria.*

Forget the name Belzaria—it meant nothing. He thought instead of seeing Dahling, Uncle Colin's daughter by his first marriage, now married to the future MacPherson laird, sworn enemies of the Kinross clan until Aunt Sinjun had intervened many years before. And Philip, his uncle's heir, who traveled the world mapping remote areas, one of the leading cartographers in England. Philip's wife, Elise, claimed he was only home sufficient periods of time to beget a boy and a girl child. Last Grayson had heard, Philip was off mapping the Bulgar plains.

He looked up to see his aunt Sinjun waving at him from the eastern turret. She yelled something he couldn't understand, then disappeared. He pictured her picking up her skirts, racing down the ancient stone steps and into the old main hall, and throwing open the thick oak doors to dance out onto the ancient stone steps to welcome him.

On such a beautiful, peaceful day, what trouble could there possibly be at Vere Castle? That's what Sinjun had called it in her letter to him. *Trouble.*

CHAPTER THREE

The moment the three of them were seated at the massive mahogany dining table, Sinjun said, "I don't wish to speak of what is troubling us over our delicious salmon because it involves Pearlin' Jane. My dearest Colin would sneer and roll his eyes, and I would be compelled to throw the bowl of peas at him. No, we will have peace at the dinner table. Tell us about your trip here, Grayson, and why you were late. We expected you yesterday."

Grayson frowned as he drank a sip of the light white wine. "Yesterday? But I left Edinburgh this morning, early, as I told you I would. I rode here immediately." He looked blankly between his aunt and uncle, felt the pull of blackness in his mind, shook his head, and there it was, the slight hit of pain. He said slowly, "What day is it?"

Colin said, "Monday."

"Monday? But how is that possible? I didn't even take the time to visit Major McHugh at Edinburgh Castle. I spent the night at Kinross House, then first thing this morning, Astor and I were on the ferry across the Firth of Forth. I rode directly here."

His aunt and uncle exchanged looks. Sinjun said, her voice bright, "Did you meet up with some villains on your way here to put in a future novel?"

"Or a pretty young lass?"

"Nothing happened. No villains, no lasses." But somehow he knew it wasn't true. He saw a young girl in his mind—tall, thick hair the color of rich honey spilling about a face that wasn't beautiful, exactly, but very riveting, a dimple beside her mouth. He felt a lick of pain, and her face was gone and with it the memory of what she looked like. He said, "Maeve. Queen Maeve."

"Queen Maeve? Who is she, Grayson?"

Grayson stared at his aunt, saw her Sherbrooke blue eyes were filled with questions and growing alarm. She reached over and closed her hand over his. "What happened, my dear?"

He continued to look at her lovely face, at her thick blond hair, lighter than his, now laced with strands of gray, woven in braids atop her head. He realized she and Uncle Colin were getting older, the age of his own parents, and that made him realize how very precious time was. How fleeting, how uncertain, and unexpected things could happen. He smiled at both of them. "Forget Queen Maeve. I have no idea who she is—her name simply popped out of my mouth. Maybe she's the character in a new book."

Like Belzaria.

"It is so good to see both of you. It reminds me I haven't visited my parents in nearly six months. Too long. You both look splendid."

Sinjun laughed. "Thank you. It's all the haggis Colin forces down my gullet. My innards have to stay strong to digest that horr—ah—that is to say that most special of Scottish dishes. Haggis. The very word rolls off your tongue," and she gave her husband a fat smile. Colin grinned back at her, and Grayson was struck at how the earl was dark as a pirate, and had the look of one—tall and lean, like Grayson's uncle Douglas, the head of the far-flung Sherbrooke family and the Earl of Northcliffe. Like Aunt Sinjun, there were strands of silver threaded through Colin's dark hair, and Grayson said aloud, "Time is a very strange thing, don't you think?"

Sinjun cocked her head at him. "I never used to think of time, but now I've come to realize time is no longer a constant, to be depended upon to behave in a rational manner. I believe time has become fickle—it races faster and faster the older I become. Do you agree, Colin?"

He looked thoughtful as he took a sip of his wine. "There have been moments in my life when I believed my time had run out, that it was all over for me, and I would swear time slowed to a crawl, maybe to give me time to figure a way out of my difficulties or to ask forgiveness for all the sins I've committed. Then when you and I are dallying pleasantly in the afternoon, sweet Sinjun, time flies out the window. Ah, perhaps we'd best speak of that at another time."

"You are wicked, sir," his wife said.

And Grayson imagined he was indeed. Colin turned to Grayson, leaned toward him. "Grayson, we are not jesting. You are missing a day. Twenty-four hours. What happened? Who is Queen Maeve?"

Grayson slowly shook his head. "I don't know. Really, I don't know." He tried to shrug it off, but couldn't. "I saw a flash of her a moment ago—her face. I remember thinking she was scared. Then a pain sliced through my head and her face was gone and with it the memory of what she looked like." He fanned his hands out in front of him. "I'm not exaggerating. All I know is that I'm missing a day."

"If you had a flash of this girl's face and her name, then it will come back, don't you think?"

"I don't know if I want it to, Uncle Colin, I really don't know."

His aunt and uncle said nothing more.

For the remainder of his first evening at Vere Castle, they spoke of Grayson's son, Pip, and Grayson's cousins and their families.

CHAPTER FOUR

They were treating him gently, Grayson realized with something of a shock as he climbed the stairs to his bedchamber, a lit candle guiding him, like a man who'd been wounded. He appreciated it.

"Grayson, do you have a moment?"

He turned to see Aunt Sinjun, her own candle lit and held high. He wasn't at all surprised to see her. He opened his bedchamber door and waved her in. The room was lit with soft candlelight and a glowing fire in the fireplace. It was warm and cozy, welcoming and familiar. It had always been his room since he'd been a boy.

He set down their two candles on the table beside the sofa. "Please sit down, Aunt Sinjun, and tell me about this trouble. I gather Uncle Colin believes you're making too much of whatever is going on with Pearlin' Jane?"

Sinjun sat on a schoolboy's desk chair, smoothed her skirts. "You know Colin. He's just like your uncle Douglas with the Virgin Bride."

"I am not," came Colin's voice from the doorway. He strode into the bedchamber. "Listen, I am not stubborn like Douglas. I am a reasonable man in all things. But Pearlin' Jane in a dither, my dear? Really?"

She jumped up. "Colin! I thought you were going to your tower room to read romantic poetry to Andrew."

He gave her a crooked grin, said to Grayson, "Andrew is one of the cats. I knew you wanted to speak to Grayson about the trouble Pearlin' Jane communicated to you. I want to hear this myself, but without the drama, if you please."

"Drama!" Sinjun looked ready to explode, but she managed to calm herself as she turned to Grayson. "This is why I don't speak to him about Pearlin' Jane. He knows she and I are close, just as the Virgin Bride at Northcliffe is the protector of all the ladies in the house. As for Douglas, I know he has communicated with the Virgin Bride over the years, but naturally he won't admit it, calls it female hysteria. If you can't see it, touch it, eat a lovely meal with it, then it doesn't exist. He's just like my precious husband here, despite his claim to reasonableness. You, not stubborn, Colin? You're stubborn as a stoat.

"You know Pearlin' Jane is alive and happy—I should say she's dead and happy—and she resides here at Vere Castle." She said to Grayson, "She saved Vere Castle for Colin—" She broke off, shook her head at herself. "No, forget that. But she's with me and we are close."

Colin said, "What do you mean she saved Vere Castle for me?"

"It was a slip of the tongue. If you love me, Colin, you will never bring it up again, all right? As I said, you know very well she's here, yet you refuse to accept it."

He frowned at her, opened his mouth.

"I mean it, Colin."

Grayson could tell his uncle didn't believe she would be able to hold out against him, but Grayson had the feeling it was something she would never speak about, ever. As for the Virgin Bride, a young lady who'd died in the sixteenth century, supposedly before her groom could visit her on their wedding night, he said matter-of-factly, "Since my youngest years, whenever I visit Northcliffe Hall, the Virgin Bride comes for a visit. She simply appears at the foot of my bed and sort of floats there. Sometimes I speak to her of the book I'm currently writing. She looks interested even though her face doesn't change. Sometimes I swear she's able to communicate with me when I tell her about a problem I'm having with a plot. She doesn't speak, but I hear her clearly in my mind. I can also tell you she's very young, not more than fifteen." He paused. "Once I asked her if she was at last with her new husband. I'd swear she paled. You'd think that would be impossible since you can practically see through her, but then she told me he didn't make it to where she was, and she was glad about that. The question obviously upset her, and she was gone in the next instant. When I saw her again, I asked her about the afterlife."

"What did she tell you?" Sinjun was sitting so close to the edge of the chair, Grayson was afraid she might fall off onto her face.

Colin looked the picture of a tolerant parent, the model of patience, with two feeble-brained children. A dark eyebrow went up. "Ah, the afterlife. Did she assure you she was at peace and surrounded by light? Was she surrounded by her loved ones and her pets and everyone was deliriously happy?"

"Actually, no," Grayson said before Sinjun could turn her cannon on her husband. "She told me she missed almond candies, her mother, and her doll named Bess, after the queen. Evidently her mother wasn't where she was either. She said everything smelled like ragweed and she wanted to sneeze all the time, but she couldn't because she had no body. She didn't say any more about where she was."

"You made that up, Grayson Sherbrooke."

"No, that's exactly what happened, Aunt Sinjun. I'd hardly forget."

Colin said, "I've read your books, Grayson. You have an incredible imagination and you're clever. It's obvious you're always thinking of all sorts of otherworldly things, including ghosts."

Grayson was well used to hearing ghosts couldn't exist in this modern world. He should introduce them to Alphonse at Wolffe Hall back home. He smiled at his handsome uncle. "I remember one visit to Northcliffe Hall I woke up to see the Virgin Bride floating at the end of my bed. I told her I'd heard about a Spanish treasure ship that had wrecked off the Cornish coast in 1588 in the violent storm that also sent dozens of ships in the Spanish Armada to the bottom of the Channel or crashing into the coastline. I asked her if it was true, and if it was true, then where was the ship."

Now Colin was sitting forward, his eyes locked on Grayson's face. "What did she say?"

This from Colin, the unbeliever, now fairly bristling with interest.

"She disappeared, but only for a moment or two. Then she came back and I'd swear she was smiling as she thought to me that the Spanish ship was the *Santo Christo De Costello* from the sixteen-strong Squadron of Castile. She told me the ship sank in Mullion Cove and its sailors' bones lay in amongst the gold bars."

Colin sat back, crossed his arms over his chest. "You draw people into a world you yourself have fashioned and make them believe what you put in front of them. Admit it, Grayson, you made that up."

Grayson shook his head. "I wrote to my cousin, Leo, who, as you know, lives in Cornwall, in Fowey. He mounted a salvage operation. They found the wreck in thirty feet of water at the edge of Mullion Cove."

"And the gold?"

"They found bones and gold. They managed to recover three bars before the ship fell into a deep canyon they couldn't reach."

Sinjun said, "I never heard a word of it, never. When did this happen?"

"Three years ago," Grayson said.

"I didn't hear anything about it either," Colin said, "and you know I would have."

"After they were duly authenticated, Leo loaned the three bars to the British Museum. He asked they keep it and not give him the credit because he was afraid treasure hunters would invade Fowey. The museum directors weren't about to attribute the find to a ghost named the Virgin Bride, so they gave the credit to 'Anonymous,' a decision Leo hated but understood. A pity we don't know the Virgin Bride's real name. She could have gotten the credit." He paused. "I've asked her many times what her name is—was—but she's never told me."

"Somehow she communicates with Pearlin' Jane," Sinjun said. "I'll see if Pearlin' Jane knows what her name is."

This was Colin's cue. He rolled his eyes. "Tell me, Sinjun, do they perhaps meet for the yearly ghost holiday in the Hebrides? Or maybe the two of them visit a tea shop on Bond Street in London during the ghost Season on All Hallows' Eve?" Colin topped it off with a snort, but to Grayson's ears the snort sounded halfhearted.

Grayson said easily, "Yes, ask her, Aunt Sinjun. It would be nice to call the Virgin Bride by her Christian name. Now, don't you think it is time to tell me about the trouble Pearlin' Jane warned you was coming?"

Sinjun sent a look to her husband that promised retribution if he opened his mouth. "I didn't want to worry you overly, so that's why I wrote *trouble*, and such a tepid word that is. When Pearlin' Jane warned me she didn't say *trouble* was coming—she said *evil* was coming."

Colin remained silent. He didn't roll his eyes this time. Maybe he was thinking about those three bars of gold.

Grayson said, "The last time I visited you, Pearlin' Jane woke me up. She was whistling, a very old song. Like the Virgin Bride, she didn't actually speak, but I heard her voice clearly in my mind. She's a flirt, that one, and that pearl necklace looped six times around her neck, it's amazing. It's got to weigh more than she does—did. But that's not important. What's going on, Aunt Sinjun?"

Sinjun said, "Actually, Pearlin' Jane hasn't spoken to me for two weeks now. I know she's hiding."

"Why?"

"Two weeks ago I was walking in the apple orchard, and I again asked her to come to me. She didn't, but she did send two names to me: yours, over and over again, and I knew she believed you were the only one to help, and then another name, something like Belatrix or Bellazana. I don't know—it simply wasn't clear. I questioned her, but then she told me over and over, *Evil is coming, Grayson, get Grayson.* She felt such panic, Grayson, and then she was simply gone, and I haven't heard from her since. Two weeks now."

Belzaria. Yet again it was crystal clear in Grayson's mind.

CHAPTER FIVE

Grayson lay on his back, staring up at the beautiful beamed ceiling, lit by the wavering light of a single candle nearly gutted now. A notebook filled with pages of his new novel lay open on the table beside the bed. He felt fatigue pull at him, but he didn't want to fall asleep just yet. First, he wanted to see Pearlin' Jane.

She came like a thief in the night, slowly, quietly, as if she didn't really want him to see her. As if she was too afraid the other would catch her. Belzaria?

"Jane," he said very quietly. "It will be all right. I'm here. Tell me what is happening."

The air became warmer than it had been the minute before, but still she didn't show herself.

"Jane, whatever evil is coming, I will deal with it. I swear to you." And wasn't that a tall order, given he'd lost an entire day on his way to Vere Castle?

He felt a slight movement in the air, as if a gentle breeze had wafted through the open window.

"The evil you warned Sinjun about—is her name Belzaria?"

The air turned icy cold.

"All right, you're frightened, but you have to pull yourself together. If I'm to help, you must tell me what to expect. It isn't fair to leave me helpless."

He waited.

"I lost a day, Jane, an entire day. I have no memory of what happened to me. Three names have popped into my head—Queen Maeve, Belzaria, and Border. I think Border is a place. Is that right?"

Silence and still air.

"Who is Belzaria, Jane? That's the name you told Sinjun, only she didn't hear you clearly. She's the one you're scared of? Tell me why you're frightened of her." He smiled into the empty space at the bottom of his bed. "You could choke her with all those pearls looped around your neck."

The air shimmered.

"Aunt Sinjun told me how you showed imagination and determination when you got your revenge on your murdering husband. You won. I saw the victory in your face in your portrait downstairs in the salon. So why are you afraid of this Belzaria? You believe she is stronger than you?"

A slash of lightning speared through the window. And there she was, her pearls showing first, so many, at least a hundred, he guessed, pure-white pearls, all perfectly matched. And there was her face, like her portrait, but not really. It was as if there were veils, and they were shimmering along with the rest of her. She'd been pretty in life, and young, and her life had ended so badly.

He heard her voice in his mind, surprisingly strong and deep, and he heard the slick of fear.

Belzaria is coming, and she will destroy my painting because she knows what I am and that I live here and I protect Sinjun. She is filled with ill will. She is a malicious evil.

She was filled with hatred and malice? "Who is Queen Maeve?"

I think she is a young lassie, more a prisoner, doweless, a pawn. She is ruled by Belzaria. She would look bonnie wearing some of my pearls. But I could be wrong about her.

"What does doweless mean?"

The air shivered with impatience. Jane looked ready to throw some pearls at him. *She's daftie laddie—she canna do anythin'. Belzaria holds her by her snotterbox.*

Helpless, Grayson thought, doweless meant she was helpless. And snotterbox? Her nose, Grayson realized

"Jane, where is Border?"

Only a slight shudder in the air, then Jane's voice, low, frightened. *Border is a place beyond this place. It is a place outside of our time, a place beyond what a mortal can see or imagine or ken. It churns and heaves, but withal, all are doweless. Belzaria holds the power, and she is coorse—cruel. There is sometimes hope, but it wanes quickly.*

"It is a kingdom?"

A kingdom? Mayhap. It is ruled by monstrous evil.

"And she is here, in Scotland? Is Belzaria a demon escaped from this Border into our time?"

The shimmering air seemed to freeze, and the bedchamber plunged into bone-shattering cold. He wouldn't be surprised to see icicles hanging off the posts of his bed. All he saw were the loops and loops of luminescent pearls. They seemed to encircle the air itself. Jane wasn't there.

His candle went out, as if the flickering flame was pinched between two fingers.

He lay in the darkness, feeling the air slowly warm again. He knew Jane wouldn't come back, not tonight. But Grayson was optimistic. He said into the still darkness, "Sleep well, Jane. Don't be afraid. Together, you and I will deal with Belzaria."

Did ghosts sleep? He'd never thought about it before. Since there was no corporeal self that needed rest, surely there was no need. Grayson's corporeal self was soon asleep. He fell into a place where acres of grass grew tall and thick, and there were paths through the grass, covered with beautifully cut black stones. The sky was blue, but it wasn't a blue he'd ever seen before. One moment it was turbulent and dark, and then it shifted to a pale blue. Thick billowing white clouds filled the sky. Then, oddly, as he watched, the clouds seemed to move quickly across the sky and disappear. As he watched, the same clouds reappeared on the opposite horizon and began their journey again. How could that be possible?

The sky was filled with light, but he saw no sun. There were strange animals milling about in the tall grass, some like unicorns with horns in their foreheads but their faces were long and pointed. Others were like sheep, with thick shaggy hair that grew longer than their legs. In the distance, beneath those journeying clouds, he saw a large city, like London, but not really like London, not exactly. The buildings were taller, and if his eyes weren't deceiving him, they weren't straight. Some were curved, others leaned one way or another, but they all glistened in the bright light that came from where he knew not. He saw a flash of a circular stone circle chamber and saw how those walls leaned in a bit. Then the vision was gone. He walked toward the city on the immaculate stone roads, blacker than a sinner's dreams, and as he drew nearer, he saw stone walkways connected the buildings. The most spectacular building looked a bit like Warwick Castle with its massive walls and its huge stone towers, only he would swear this building was taller, its walls thicker. He saw Saint Paul's Cathedral, only the round dome was elongated and a glittering silver, not marble.

As he stood just outside the city, staring at something he couldn't have imagined, something a mortal couldn't imagine, he realized he was utterly alone. There were no people hurrying about, no carriages or wagons, no horses or drays, only himself. As if all the people had simply left.

He heard a woman's laugh, deep and rich and terrifying because he knew the laugh wasn't really a laugh, it was a promise of great violence and death and pleasure. He heard screams, and they were coming closer, and he knew, deep down, that soon he would be screaming too.

Grayson fell off the walkway onto his back in the thick tall grass. The grass rose above him, like waving arms all around him. He breathed in and began to choke. He couldn't breathe, yet he tried and tried to suck in air. He was dying.

CHAPTER SIX

"Grayson! Wake up! You're having a nightmare. Wake up! Grayson!"

He was gasping, choking. Was that Sinjun's voice? She was shaking him, but still he couldn't breathe. His chest was on fire, and he knew he was dying.

Sinjun slapped his face. "Grayson, open your eyes! Look at me. Can you understand me?"

Dying, dying, he was dying.

She slapped his face again, hard. He grabbed her wrist, pulled it down. He managed to open his eyes, blink up at her. He saw Colin running toward the bed, a scared maid behind him.

He thought his heart would pound right out of his chest. He whispered, his chest heaving, "I couldn't breathe. I don't know why, but I knew I was dying. My throat hurts."

She immediately placed her palm on his forehead. "Are you ill?"

"No, no, it was something in the grass, I think, something that is poison to mortals." He stopped cold, stared up at her.

Sinjun sat beside him and handed him a glass of water from the carafe. At first it hurt his throat to drink, and then it felt like he was being given life. When he handed back the empty glass, Sinjun took his hand between her two warm ones. Colin stood at her shoulder, looking down at him. "Your dream took you to a strange place?"

Grayson realized Colin had chosen his words very carefully. He nodded. "It was Border." He realized it was early morning.

Colin said, "Alene said you were moaning and screaming, that she couldn't awaken you."

Grayson looked beyond Colin to the very young Alene, the daughter of the Kinross cook, and said simply, "Thank you."

"Border?" Sinjun leaned closer. "Tell us about Border."

Grayson told them about Pearlin' Jane's visit, her fear of Belzaria—yes, that was her name. Was she a demon escaped from this other realm, both in time and in place? He didn't know. Jane had left him in a panic, leaving, oddly, her pearls hanging looped in the air. And then, in his dreams, he'd been whisked to Border. "I saw a city, like London, only it wasn't." He told them how the buildings were huge, that they leaned or curved oddly, described the animals he'd seen, and the tall grass. "And I heard her laughing from the tallest point of a castle that looked something like Warwick, but it wasn't a laugh, Sinjun, it was a promise of violence and destruction."

Sinjun said, "Do you think Jane brought you the dream?"

"I don't think so. The woman laughing, I think it was Belzaria."

"You never saw her?"

"No. You know what was truly terrifying? There were no people. This huge city with its massive buildings, but I saw no people."

Colin said, "Do you remember anything more about your lost day?"

"Not yet."

Colin didn't like this otherworldly talk, didn't like the gooseflesh raised on his arms, didn't like the thought of curving buildings and no people, and a demon bent on no good. Pearlin' Jane—surely she didn't really exist, surely it was Sinjun's imagination. And yet. He sighed, not knowing what to do, and the feeling of impotence drove him mad. He wanted to kick something.

He chanced to look down, and his heart seized. He stared, not wanting to believe what he saw, but there it was, sitting in the middle of the Aubusson carpet—a single large white pearl. His breathing hitched. He picked up the pearl and silently handed it to Sinjun.

Sinjun held the pearl in her palm, very real, that pearl, not a ghostly pearl with no substance, and it was warm. And where was the sense in that? She looked from Grayson to Colin. "This pearl must belong to Jane, but it's a real pearl. How can a ghost wear a real pearl? Jane has never before lost one of her pearls. She's very proud of each and every one of them. She told me once there were one hundred and eight pearls and she wore them all the time and thought of her revenge on that murdering wastrel."

Grayson smiled. "A fitting revenge, forcing him to give her pearls to make her stop tormenting him."

Colin said, "Supposedly he ran her over with his carriage nearly a hundred years ago. She should move along with her life—or her death— don't you think?"

Grayson said, "Perhaps, but the Virgin Bride hasn't moved along either. I asked her once why she stayed at Northcliffe Hall, but she had no answer, only shook her head. I don't think she knew, only that she was meant to be there. I've researched it, and there are no records of her in our family history. So why is Pearlin' Jane here? You told me records show that she was murdered near Inverness, yet Vere Castle is her home."

"Yes, but whenever I've asked her in the past, she'd toss her head and tell me about the mischief Rory was causing at Oxford or how tightly Dahling pulls her corset."

Sinjun gently laid the pearl atop one of Grayson's handkerchiefs on the bedside table. "You know she will come for it. I hope she will see it here."

And you expect this ghost to pick it up and restring it? But Colin didn't say it aloud. Pearlin' Jane couldn't exist, she couldn't, yet his heart was still pounding. That wretched pearl—where had it come from? He knew Sinjun didn't own any pearls like that one. He'd held that pearl in his hand, felt its pulsing warmth. He looked from his wife to her nephew. They both treated this entire ghost business so matter-of-factly. It was enough to drive a sane, eminently reasonable, and intelligent man, daft.

Yet Grayson had believed he was choking to death, dying? Naught but a dream, he thought, naught but a powerful dream.

CHAPTER SEVEN

Day Two

To Grayson, breakfast in Scotland at Vere Castle meant a huge bowl of porridge with berries and the special heather honey from Sinjun's bees, with a big knob of rich butter and a basket of scones set in the middle of the table, covered with a heavy linen napkin to keep them warm. He wasn't disappointed.

He was spooning down his porridge, listening to his uncle Colin tell him about the new bell tower in the local church. He saw Sinjun was tapping her fingers. When Colin paused to take a bite of his own porridge, Sinjun said quickly, "I shan't ask you again how you are feeling, Grayson—I do not wish you to throw your tea at me."

He was grateful. The dream was still vivid in his mind, and when he swallowed, it still occasionally hurt.

She said, "I received a note a few minutes ago from our new neighbor, Lady Felicity Blackthorn. The MacNab boy, dressed in gold-and-dark-blue livery—her colors, he proudly told me—delivered it." She added to Grayson, "She has purchased the MacKellar property, which is of great interest hereabouts since it is said to be cursed or haunted or both. Everyone has avoided the ruined manor house until she suddenly appeared on the scene and bought it.

"Colin, you were raised on tales of the MacKellars. Tell Grayson what supposedly happened there."

Colin forked down a bite of haddock, grilled just the way he liked it. "Ah yes, a tale to keep children on a righteous path. It goes back much farther than even Pearlin' Jane. Donnan MacKeller, a Campbell, built MacKellar Manor in 1720. But he ran out of money and was forced to wed a Macleod clan heiress.

"Donnan and his heiress wife had eight boys and two girls. Seven of the eight boys were killed in the rebellion in 1746, three of them at Culloden. As you know, the English retaliation under Cumberland was brutal. Entire families were butchered, people starved, crofts were razed, and the chieftains were all killed, their castles, if not destroyed, given over to King George II. It was a grim time all over Scotland.

"I tell you this because, oddly enough, the English army didn't touch the MacKeller property. Nor was the property turned over to the English throne. It was kept in the MacKeller family. No one could call Donnan MacKeller a traitor when seven of his sons had lost their lives to the English. And so it remained a mystery.

"Calum MacKeller, the eldest and only surviving son, succeeded to the property ten years later when Donnan passed to the hereafter. He wedded well and prospered. One fateful night his young son fell off a balcony to his death. The wife blamed the husband for not making the appropriate repairs, though it was said that no repairs were needed. Calum was found dead one morning, stabbed twelve times. The wife disappeared, never to be seen again.

"The property was inherited by the eldest daughter, who never married. She sold the property some twenty years later. The new owners remained only a year. The children, three boys, were found dead at the base of the same second-floor balcony. It appeared all of them had simply climbed over the stone railing and jumped. There was no explanation, though people like to speculate that the ghost of the MacKeller son had lured them over the balcony to their deaths. The parents, devastated, simply left the manor, never to return.

"The manor was sold a decade later to an Englishman, a Colonel

Farland. He and his wife had five strapping boys. All was well for five years. Then one morning, all five sons were found at the base of the balcony, dead, again, as if they'd all simply climbed over the stone railing and jumped. And the haunting curse went wild—all the dead children's ghosts luring these five sons out to join them. The Farlands left, never to return. They did not sell the house."

Grayson said, "Why did Farland ever buy the property? Surely he knew about the other children's deaths, the rumors of the dead children drawing the living children to jump and join them?"

"It is said he laughed, called it nonsense. In any case, after the Farlands left, the house stood vacant for nearly thirty years, falling into ruin.

"A Lady Blackthorn bought the place seven months ago, and every available man in the district has been working to rebuild the manor to its former glory. Old Clyde, our local smithy, told me the cost could feed every crofter family for a year."

Grayson said, "Perhaps she doesn't know the tales about the house."

Colin shook his head. "That would be the very first thing she'd hear, believe me. Everyone in these parts has dined out on MacKeller tales for years. Parents still threaten their boy children with a good hiding if they go anywhere near the manor house."

Sinjun set down her teacup and leaned forward. "Lady Blackthorn has no children, nor is she married. So she must feel she is safe. I met her only once, two months ago, in Kinross. She's not in her first youth, but she is still quite beautiful and ever so stylish, all the latest London fashions, incredible diamonds and rubies at her neck and ears. When I asked her why she'd come to Loch Leven, she laughed, said she fell in love with a painting of a manor house she'd seen in the Royal Academy in London and was told it was the MacKeller property here at Loch Leven. Then something rather strange happened." Sinjun, a master of storytelling, paused, making both Colin and Grayson forget their porridge and lean toward her. "Our vicar, Charles Gordon, waved to me from across the main street at the draper's shop. He was halfway across the road when out of nowhere came a carriage, going very fast. I nearly expired on the spot when Colin suddenly raced to him and managed to jerk him out of the way at the last minute. It was very frightening. Screams, yells, people running to help. I turned to see Lady Blackthorn staring at you, Colin.

"She nodded to me and said in a very pleasant voice, 'Well, it was a close thing, but he managed it,' and then she smiled and walked away to her own carriage. Colin, the look she sent you—if I'm not mistaken, and I never am about things like that—there was lust in her eyes. I didn't realize that until later since I was too frightened for you at the time."

Colin was shaking his head. "Forget that, Sinjun, she couldn't have seen me clearly enough to even consider lust. Poor Vicar Gordon, he was stuttering he was so distressed. It was a very close thing, she was right about that. Thankfully, I did make it in time. As for the carriage, young Thomas Lamont was driving. He was babbling that he didn't know what happened, the horses simply bolted and there was nothing he could do about it. No one believed him. His father, I believe, took a strap to him."

"'Well, it was a close thing, but he managed it,'" Grayson repeated. "Aunt Sinjun, Lady Blackthorn said that exactly?"

"Yes indeed," Sinjun said, then looked thoughtful. "Looking back on it, I don't think Lady Blackthorn was at all concerned. I know it sounds strange, but I would swear she looked like it was some sort of test."

Colin waved his coffee cup at her. "Test? My dear, you really want to believe that Lady Blackthorn somehow whipped those horses up to run down the vicar? To see what would happen? To see if I would try to save the vicar? Come now, you always want to explain the simplest things as magical intervention."

Sinjun wanted to tell him magic was all around them, but she only smiled. "I think she did it to see what you would do, Colin, to see if you were a hero."

Grayson said, "Uncle Colin, how was it that you were close enough to the vicar to pull him out of the way of the horses?"

Colin frowned, drummed his long fingers on the white tablecloth. "I saw those horses, knew they'd crush the vicar, and I moved faster than I have in my life. Looking back on it, I'm surprised I got to him in time. For a moment, it didn't seem possible."

"But you managed it, didn't you?" *And you could have died*, she thought, but she didn't say it. Sinjun waved the letter. "The lady in question has invited us to a party tonight—to celebrate the rejuvenation of the MacKeller property, now to be known as Blackthorn Manor, so she writes to me. Tonight! And she is sending out her invitations this late? It's very odd." Sinjun shrugged. "Of course we must go. I imagine everyone in the neighborhood will be mad to go as well."

Grayson said, "Blackthorn. I've never heard of any Blackthorn. I wonder who her antecedents are."

Colin said, "Well, there was the prelate, name of Blackthorn. He founded Aberdeen University back in the fifteenth century. Maybe she hails from that Blackthorn. But the title? I don't know. Why didn't you tell me about Lady Blackthorn before?"

"I didn't tell you, Colin, because I knew you'd laugh at me, but you must believe me." She drew a deep breath. "There is something else. I remember you were staring back at her, just before the horses came around the corner."

Colin looked at her blankly, then threw up his hands. "Come now, Sinjun, I never even noticed her. I have never met her. I have only seen her from a distance in Kinross."

Sinjun and Grayson exchanged a look. She said, "Well, she certainly appears to remember you, my dear. In her very nice invitation, she specifically asks you to be present. It's as if I'm invited only because I have to be, as your wife."

Grayson took a final bite of his porridge and carefully laid his spoon beside the bowl. "Aunt Sinjun, when you reply, please tell her your nephew is visiting and would like to attend as well."

"Oh, she mentions you are to come too, Grayson. She even wrote your name. She begs the honor of receiving a renowned author, namely yourself."

Colin said, "It appears word travels very fast hereabouts."

"*Something* travels very fast indeed," Grayson said.

CHAPTER EIGHT

Colin and Grayson were in Colin's estate room, Colin telling him about the success of the new farming implements now used by his crofters, when they leaped to their feet at Sinjun's shout. They ran to the drawing room to see Sinjun standing stock-still in the middle of the Aubusson carpet staring at the fireplace.

Colin was at her side in a moment, nearly stepping on the wreckage. "The portrait—what happened, Sinjun?"

Grayson couldn't believe it. From his youngest years, he'd looked up at Pearlin' Jane's portrait hung above the grand fireplace in the salon. Now it lay on the floor, three huge tears in it, as if ripped by an animal's claws. Pearlin' Jane had told him the previous night that Belzaria would destroy her portrait.

Sinjun was shaking. "I hung that portrait there when I was eighteen, newly married to you. To thank Jane. That was what she wanted, to have her portrait hung next to her husband's, that horrible man who'd murdered her. He'd taken her portrait down when he remarried. She said she wanted him to know she was back in her rightful place."

Colin took her hands in his. "I thought you were in the lady's parlor writing our acceptance to Lady Blackthorn."

"I was," Sinjun said. She stopped, shook her head. "I needed something from the marquetry table and—" She stopped cold, said in a whisper, "I can't remember what it was, only that I needed it urgently, so I came in here to fetch whatever it was, and saw that."

They watched in stunned silence as the portrait of Jane's erstwhile murdering husband toppled to the floor to land on top of Jane's.

Grayson said, matter-of-factly, "It appears Jane's concerns weren't imaginary. Is this Belzaria's work, do you think?"

Colin stared down at the portraits, shaking his head. "Listen, there has to be a logical, reasoned explanation. There is no fiend named Belzaria. The plaster was probably loose—the pictures have hung there for decades. Maybe an animal got in here and tore the portrait after it fell, then escaped." He turned to Sinjun, gave her a brooding look. "And that brings up a question I've asked you over the years that you always refuse to answer. Why did you insist that Pearlin' Jane's portrait be hung here next to the husband who murdered her? I never wanted either of them here. You told me once, when I got you tipsy, that you owed it to her for what she'd done. But you refused to tell me what it was. Tell me now, Sinjun."

She lightly laid her fingers against his cheek. "She asked me not to, Colin. It was important to her, and so I never shall. There's nothing more."

He knew there was a lot more, knew she was an excellent liar, something he admired. "Will you tell me once we're in the afterlife, looking down at Philip and Rory and Dahling and all our grandchildren?"

"I might tell you when we're looking down on our great-grandchildren," she said.

Colin gave her a quick kiss and sighed. "I'll commission an artist in Edinburgh to come and paint another portrait of Jane, all right? As for this idiot husband of hers, we'll throw his portrait in the dustbin. Finally."

"You're a splendid husband," she said, and leaned up to kiss him again. "I don't think Jane will mind."

Grayson wondered, watching them, if his wife Lorelei had lived and they survived together thirty years like Uncle Colin and Aunt Sinjun had, if there would still be such love between them. And secrets too, at least on Aunt Sinjun's side. What had Pearlin' Jane done for her that she couldn't or wouldn't tell Colin? He looked down at the ripped portrait. He fully expected Pearlin' Jane to pay him another visit that night.

But Pearlin' Jane didn't wait that long.

Mrs. Flood, the Kinross housekeeper of twenty-two years, planted herself in the doorway, looking both scared and determined. Mrs. Flood was solid, unimaginative, and believed her mistress daft when she spoke of their resident *doolie*—ghost—as if she were a member of the household, though naturally she never said anything. She looked down at the two portraits on the floor and cleared her throat. "Mr. Hobbs refused to tell ye, my lady, he said I was all aboot in my upper works. A right feardie he is. Mrs. Hobbs tells me if it weren't for the six lovely bairns he gave her, she'd be right sorry she married him thirty years ago."

"What is the problem, Mrs. Flood?"

"My lady, Pearlin' Jane is causing a ruckus in the *kitchie*, even though I know she canna be—any devout Christian would know it's impossible for a *doolie* to do much of anything except flitter aboot. Please, ye must hurry."

As they all ran down the long corridor to the nether regions, they heard screams and yells. When Grayson stepped into the vast Kinross kitchen, it was to see flour raining down, turning the air white, apples rolling out of a big bowl on the wooden table across the floor, and the door on the new Cumberside oven slamming shut, opening, then slamming shut again.

Sinjun put her hands on her hips and yelled, "Jane, that is quite enough! You have made a mess. Stop it. Tell me what you want, and I will do my best to get it done."

The oven door continued its banging.

"I'm having your portrait painted anew," Colin said.

The oven door snapped shut one final time.

There was immediate blessed silence except for the crying hiccups from Brenda, the scullery maid, and the occasional whimper from Teddy, the nine-year-old castle errand boy.

Jane evidently didn't want to speak to Sinjun. She wanted Grayson. *Come to the apple orchard, NOW.*

Grayson said quietly, "Please, no more dramatics, Jane. I'm coming."

The cook, Mrs. Keith, smoothed down her apron, tucked back in a strand of stone-gray hair, and curtsied to Colin. "Thank ye, my lord. Ye stopped the hurricane. I have never afore experienced a hurricane in my *kitchie*, but I suppose it could happen, what wi' the planets hoppin' aboot so close to each either this month." She turned to her terrified staff and clapped her hands. "Let's get back to work here. What a *guddle*, wi' all the flour swirlin' aboot, making the air white. Teddy, I will *vreet* ye a note, and ye will go to Mr. Gunn and buy us more flour."

Mrs. Keith gave a small curtsy to Sinjun and Colin, then turned back to begin picking up the scattered apples on the flagstone floor.

Sinjun said, "Mrs. Flood, would you please ask Elspeth and Ina to come and assist Mrs. Keith?"

She turned on her husband. "Why ever is she thanking you? You did nothing except stand there and look lordly and in charge." She said to Grayson, "It is too bad—she has always treated him like a god. And now this—Jane talked to you, didn't she? Not me, to you, Grayson."

Colin took his wife's arm and led her out of the kitchen. He said over his shoulder, "So she wants you, does she, Grayson?"

"Yes," Grayson said, "in the apple orchard, now."

CHAPTER NINE

As Grayson made his way through the wildly colorful gardens, he clearly remembered one summer playing here with his cousins, James and Jason, climbing the trees, swinging from the thicker branches, throwing apples at each other, taking archery lessons from Aunt Sinjun, getting yelled at by their parents when Jason accidentally shot an arrow that narrowly missed Hobbs the butler, come to give them sweet buns from Mrs. Keith.

So many years had passed. Now his cousins were married and there was a new batch of cousins playing here. He prayed it would continue far into the future. He smiled. No cousins to throw apples at today. Now he was an adult, thirty-one years old, and he was meeting with a ghost. Fancy that. He wondered if Jane liked being called a hurricane.

Life, he'd thought many times, was strange and infinitely interesting. He thought of the last time he and Pip had visited. Pip had loved the apple orchard as well, had spoken endlessly about the adventures he'd shared with his cousins here the year before.

Without pause, Grayson walked directly to the oldest apple tree, King Fergus he and his cousins had always called it. The tree stood in isolated splendor, baby apples thick on its leaved branches. He stood beside the tree and waited.

Silence, then the air around him began to churn and quiver. "Calm down, Jane, no more drama. I had a hard night with strange dreams Belzaria sent me."

Everything stilled, quieted. It was as if all the animals, all the birds and insects, knew there was something here that didn't belong in their world, and they wanted no part of it.

They were smart. Grayson said, "Jane, all you had to do was come talk to me or to Sinjun. You didn't have to destroy Mrs. Keith's kitchen. Why did you do that?"

The air heaved and twisted around him.

"I know you're frightened of Belzaria. You need to calm yourself and tell me about her."

I lost one of my pearls!

"No, no, it's beside my bed. Colin saw it lying on the rug in my bedchamber." He thought a minute. "Why didn't you know where the pearl was, Jane? You seem to know about everything else."

He'd swear her thoughts to him sounded defensive. *I did ken, I did. Canna ye see I'm all pit aboot, my brains jibblin' outta my heid? Did ye see what she did to my painting? An' then she pulled down the bastart's pitur an' made it cover mine. She kens she has to kill me afore she can take Colin—she kens I'd protect him with my dyin' breath.*

You're already dead, Jane, but it's a nice thought. He said aloud, "Why on earth would she want to take Colin? Where would she take him?"

She wants him, powerful bad. Colin has counted many human years, but to a demon it only makes him more desirable. She would change him.

"And he would be doweless?"

Aye, that's it, he wouldna be his own man. He'd be helpless—he'd be her slave.

Grayson remembered Sinjun telling him about the new Lady Blackthorn eyeing Colin. He'd believed she was jealous, nothing more. Was it possible Lady Blackthorn was Belzaria, or was his imagination running amok? Something he had to admit occasionally happened. Then it came right out of his mouth. "Is Lady Blackthorn the demon Belzaria, Jane?"

The air shimmered, and the temperature plummeted.

"Why aren't you showing yourself to me?"

I dinna have all my pearls! How can I be aboot without all my pearls?

"It's only one pearl you don't have, Jane. No one would notice. I see, you're afraid to show yourself, aren't you? You're afraid Belzaria will see you? But what could she do even if she did see you? Run you through with a sword? Be reasonable, Jane. You have no corporeal body to be run through. So what could she do to you?"

She could curse me an' make me explode! She could throw me into Border, aye, and make me watch what she does to Colin. I ken she wants to sneck all my pearls, kinch 'em around her own scrawny neck.

Explode? Now that would be a sight. "No, she can't do any of those things. I wouldn't let her. She did slash your portrait, but Colin told you he is bringing an artist from Edinburgh to paint a new one, an exact copy. Jane, is Belzaria a demon? Is she from Border? Is she Lady Blackthorn?"

Och, aye, I think she is. My world shudders with tales aboot her and how she's taken human form, somethin' not many demons like to do because they believe we're all misshapen and ugly. I must tell ye, Grayson, I canna see her when she is in demon form—I canna ken what she is aboot. So I canna tell ye what a demon looks like, what it thinks, or what it will do, but I can feel her. She came once here to Vere Castle as a demon. I felt her, brimming with evil and ill will. And that's when she saw Colin.

"You felt her. How did she feel?"

Silence, then Jane thought to him: *Like a blackness sooking out all the air, and when she crept like black smoke into the castle, it was to see me, to find my weaknesses, to terrifee me, to make me flee my home. Behold what she did to my poor portrait. Aye, she is a demon, but what does it matter? There are all sorts of creatures from the pits in hell or other places like Border and Black Friar's Hole who sometimes break through to wreak havoc on us.*

Black Friar's Hole?

The air whipped up around him, making the bushes rustle, and a scrawny little apple fall from King Fergus's lower branch. Then it was quiet again.

"Don't go, Jane. You wanted to speak to me, so that's what you have to do. Now, tell me what you know about where she comes from—this Border."

It isna really a land, not like my beautiful Scotland. It is more a creation by forces even I dinna ken. It is beyond, it is other, it was never meant to come here, into our world. I already told ye much of that last night. Did ye not attend me?

"She sent me a strange dream last night, but I'm not sure if she was showing me Border, or if she was weaving a fantasy to terrify me. I remember breathing in the grass—it seemed poisonous to me."

What did ye see?

CHAPTER TEN

Grayson told Jane about the thick green grass, the blades so tall they waved like arms, the animals that weren't quite like earth animals, the sky that shone brightly without a sun, and the large city that perhaps was meant to look like modern London, but whoever constructed it was seeing London through fractured glass, and thus its buildings leaned this way and that, the roads and walkways sometimes twisted back on themselves. He told her how he knew he was choking to death, how Sinjun had awakened him. "Jane, do you believe she wanted to show me where she lives?"

He would swear he heard her cursing, very colorful, most words he did not understand, then, *She wants to terrifee ye, to make ye leave, like me. She doesna want ye here to protect Colin.* A pause, then, *I think she's afeart of ye.*

Afraid of him? He said, "Why didn't you want to speak to Sinjun? Why only me?"

The air quivered a bit, then her voice, soft and somehow regret-ful. *Sinjun is my wee bairn, so young she was when she first came to Vere Castle. She was sent for me, an' I kent I had to protect her, an' that meant protectin' Colin as well, since she loves him beyond reason. He is a braw*

mon, but withal all men are worthless offal. An' if Sinjun learns this demon
wants Colin, she will fly into a gang gyte—

"You mean fly into a rage?"

Aye, 'tis what I said, isna it? An' she'd do something daft. She would
try to bargain with this demon—her life for Colin's—which is what the
demon wants. But Sinjun wouldn't understand that. She would ken only
that she had to save him from the demon. Of course, the demon would agree
because it wants Sinjun deid. Demons have no honor—they lie. They are
very good at it from what I have been told.

"Who told you demons have no honor and are good at lying?"

Ye are too inquisitive, lad. Yer brain jumps from hither to yon. A kelpie
told me. His name is Barrie, and he lives in Loch Ness. Kelpies are nearly
as wicked as demons, but kelpies hate demons—why, I dinna ken. They
jeedge them—

"Jeedge? You mean they curse them?"

Aye, and that's what I said, isna it? Ye must listen to me, lad. An' demons
lie wi' great relish. We were lazing aboot one afternoon when Barrie told
me demons were evil and vicious and liars of the first order.

"You have traveled to Loch Ness?"

Aye, the first time when I was very young, before I met the bastard and
married him and he murdered me. The loch was very cold, an' the water was
nearly black, filled with peat I was told. I didna want to stick my toes in
that black water, much less my precious self, but I did, and Barrie pulled on
me toes and I yalled like a banshee. He told me what'd he done after I died.

Barrie visited me once, told me tales of the frightening monster in Loch
Ness, how she lurks beneath the waters, waitin' for fishermen to tip over
their boats, fresh meat for her bairns.

Then he was called back to Loch Ness. I haven't seen him in a very long
time, but that is what he said.

Grayson's head was swimming. He wondered if Sinjun knew all
this, if she and Jane had spent afternoons together speaking about Jane's
afterlife world. He wondered how he would make contact with the
demon Belzaria.

And she said to him without hesitation, *Go to that absurd celebration pairtie. Look at her eyes, Grayson, and because ye are who ye are, ye'll see shiny mirrors starin' back at ye because she has no real self. And the occasional flame—a demon canna keep the flames hidden. An' ye'll see and ye'll ken who she is.*

Can ye imagine spending so many groats on Donnan MacKeller's ruin of a house?

"Where did she get all the money?"

A demon can make money by skelpin' its hands. Ah, and what an idiot old Donnan MacKeller was—rutted all the time, produced so many sons, and the Sassenach killed all of them except the worst o' the lot, his firstborn. His poor wife—all her work an' she had naught left but a wastrel bairn who bargained wi' the demon for his life, an' two lassies so silly the demon let them live.

"Jane, if Donnan did make a bargain with Belzaria to keep his children and his lands safe, did his one surviving son, Calum, break the bargain? And that is why both he and his son died? And she killed all the children who ever came to live in that house?"

The air shivered around him. He felt it to his bones—Jane was afraid.

"Jane, do demons exist forever?"

I dinna ken.

So she didn't know. He started to ask if she would live forever, but instead, he said, "Jane, what is Sinjun's secret she won't tell Colin?"

He heard a huff of breath, then, *Unlike the demons, I have honor. I willna break faith wi' my sweet bairn. It is important to her that Colin doesna ken. She's afeart of what he would do, what he would think of himself. He would be powerful hurt, even now.*

"Did you know Colin saved the vicar's life in the village?"

Och, aye, it is much talked of. I believe the demon wanted to show the world that Colin was a hero. He proved himself, didna he? Now everyone hereabouts believes him to be above other men, so calm an' fast and so dismissive of praise.

Ye must stop her, Grayson. Ye must save my bairn. And Colin. The demon would take him to Border, and he would be her slave.

"How could she take him to a place that isn't really a place but rather a construction?"

Dinna mince wirds with me, sirrah! She took ye there in yer mind, didna she? And it was quite real—ye didna know that it wasn't.

"Yes, she did, my apologies, Jane."

A mon and his apologies, they flow out of yer mouth like Sinjun's smooth honey. Listen, Grayson, when Sinjun dies, as all mortals are required to do sooner or later, then I am gone as well. Philip is his father's heir. Both he an' his wifie will move into Vere Castle. His wifie is blind to me. I will have no reason to go on—I will cease to exist. I will wait and molder and wait some more. Mayhap forever.

Grayson would swear he heard her crying.

"Jane, buck up. All is not lost. Now, first things first. We must get rid of the demon, and then I will see about Philip's wife, all right? You will continue. Now, how can I defeat a demon?"

The air shimmered. A whisper. *I dinna ken.*

"Ask Barrie, and others in your realm. If I am to defeat the demon, I must know its weaknesses."

He saw her faint outline in front of him, saw her reach out her hand, lightly touch his face, but naturally he didn't feel anything.

I will try to find out.

He felt a touch of warmth on his cheek, imagined she'd kissed him, and he'd swear he felt her breath against his face.

Yer a good mon, Grayson. Mayhap even Barrie would like ye, not lay into ye wi' his claymore.

"All will be well, Jane." He added in thick Scottish, "Haste ye back."

He heard a nightingale singing, heard the rustling of an animal in the bushes. Jane was gone, and the creatures were coming back again. At least now he knew where to begin.

CHAPTER ELEVEN

"We are all magnificent specimens," Sinjun said, looking back and forth from Colin to Grayson when Colin assisted her from the Kinross coach.

Actually, Colin believed Sinjun grew more beautiful by the year. Tall, slender, her Sherbrooke hair so rich in all its colors. He leaned down, but not that far, and kissed her. "Yes, I promise I will take care around Lady Blackthorn. Dinna fash, lassie."

Of course she would worry—she always worried when something threatened him. He'd occasionally think in odd moments how blessed he'd been when she'd chanced to see him in a crowded theater lobby in her first season and told him she was an heiress and he should marry her. He smiled. So many years, so many adventures, and blessed be, the joys outweighed the sadness that life invariable dished out, no rhyme or reason.

A new adventure, and he had to admit his blood was racing in his veins, his eyes seeing more than they usually saw. He couldn't wait to meet the demon, this Belzaria. Demon? He was actually thinking a demon could possibly exist? And she wanted him, Grayson had said.

"Grayson," Sinjun said to her nephew, "I must say I hadn't realized you and Colin were of a size."

"Thankfully," Grayson said.

They turned to see a gray-haired man of noble stature standing at the head of the newly constructed marble steps to Blackthorn Manor. Sinjun and Colin didn't recognize him.

Was he a demon? Grayson did as Jane had said. He looked at the man straight in the eyes, but all he saw was a hint of boredom, swiftly followed by a hint of pleasure at the sight of Sinjun. No demon, then? He bowed low, said in a rich deep voice, "Welcome to Blackthorn Manor, my lord, my lady, Mr. Sherbrooke. I am Beaufort, the Blackthorn butler. Her ladyship desires you be brought directly to her. Follow me, if you please."

Beaufort had spoken in clipped, clear English. Yet, somehow, Grayson knew he wasn't English. Where was he from, then? Grayson looked at his straight back as they followed him into the manor.

The ceiling of the magnificent entry hall as well as the high ceiling over the immense staircase were painted stark white with dozens of gold-painted plaster cherubs hanging off the molding, staring down at them. If he touched that stark white wall, he wondered, would he feel cold? He felt his heart begin to pound fast deep strokes when he looked up to see Lady Blackthorn gracefully making her way down the stairs toward them. He had not a single doubt it was her. She was gowned like a queen in yard upon yard of pure-white brocade and silk. From a distance, she looked older, a matron, but as she moved nearer, she became young and younger still, until she didn't look above twenty-five when she stopped in front of them. Her gown was exquisitely cut, showing her small waist and her delightfully full bosom. She wore long white gloves and diamonds in her ears, around her throat, in her hair, and on her wrists and fingers. Too many diamonds, as if she had a bottomless cask filled with them and loaded on as many as she could.

She dipped a beautiful curtsy to Colin but gave only a cursory nod to Sinjun. She said in a beautiful, deep, smooth voice, "Welcome to my home, my lord. I am delighted you could join all our neighbors." Like her butler Beaufort, Grayson knew Lady Blackthorn wasn't English.

All her attention remained now on Colin. She held out her hand to him. Colin took her gloved hand and bowed over it, but he didn't kiss it.

Only then did she turn to Grayson. She was no longer twenty-five—she was at least twenty years older, and she looked like the matron he'd first seen coming down the stairs. What was going on here? He looked into her dark eyes, as Pearlin' Jane had told him to do, searching, and he saw something flicker, shine. Mirrors, he thought, mirrors flashing, and there was something more that shouldn't be there, something that smoldered hot and deadly, but it was quickly gone. He was left staring at an older woman who was staring back at him, a dark eyebrow raised in question. She was a demon. Was she Belzaria? He felt a punch of fear. At least now he was certain what this creature was, but he didn't know how powerful she was. What was he facing? He was but a man, a mere mortal man.

Like Colin, he bowed low, but he couldn't bring himself to touch her hand, *its* hand. She raised her hand and lightly tapped his cheek. "Ah, Mr. Sherbrooke, soon you will join my forty other guests in the dancing." She nodded toward the drawing room. "You do have the look of your father, Mr. Ryder Sherbrooke, and, of course, your aunt, Lady Ashburnham. The famous Sherbrooke blue eyes."

How could she possibly know that? Grayson looked toward the drawing room, saw the glitter of candlelight off the white walls, and heard the waves of laughter and voices. The laughter was louder, more raucous and unrestrained than when they'd arrived. He looked back into her face. She was tall, nearly his height. He said, his voice utterly emotionless, "How come you to be acquainted with my father?"

She gave a light laugh that sent a jab of pain into Grayson's head. It was familiar, that pain, and he shook his head.

She said, "I am fortunate to meet many people in my travels. I met your father at a soiree in London, I believe it was. But perhaps it was at a soiree in Paris? There are so many. Who can remember?"

Grayson saw Aunt Sinjun blink, open her mouth, then close it and look perplexed. He said, "You have traveled extensively then, yet you chose to move here to Loch Leven? It is not a renowned capital, my lady."

She shrugged. "I do what I wish, nothing more, and I wished to restore this particular property. Listen, Mr. Sherbrooke, my guests are laughing, enjoying themselves."

"Your guests appear to be enjoying themselves overmuch. It sounds almost as if there is madness floating in the very air itself."

She lightly touched her gloved fingers to his forearm. "What a clever thing to say, sir, but you are a writer of some renown, so I suppose you must be clever in order to impress others."

He never looked away from her. "Yes, that is very probably true. Are you impressed?"

"With you?" She looked him up and down, said again, "With you?" And nothing more. She fastened her eyes once again on Colin. He was staring at Lady Blackthorn as if mesmerized. He didn't look away from her. As for Aunt Sinjun, she was standing still as a statue beside him.

"I hear a waltz," Grayson said.

Lady Blackthorn looked back at him and laughed, and to his ears that laugh promised nothing good. He saw that she was looking back toward the massive staircase. Grayson turned to see a beautiful young girl. Surely she was a princess. She was gliding down the stairs, her step light, radiating joy and pleasure and energy—it was coming off her in waves. She skipped to their small group and lightly laid her hand on Lady Blackthorn's gloved arm. "Mama! I have met everyone but not—" She stopped and stared at Grayson.

"I am Millicent," she said, her voice demure, and gave him her hand.

Grayson bowed but didn't touch her hand. Was she Millicent or perhaps Queen Maeve? He wanted to look into her eyes, but she averted her face.

She was Belzaria's daughter? He realized she was no more English than her mother was. Ah, but her glorious blue eyes sparkled, and her smile was beautiful, showing perfect white teeth. Introductions were made, and again Grayson was drawn to the raucous noise coming from the drawing room as if all the guests were speaking at once, laughing at once.

"Your guests are enjoying themselves," Sinjun said, the first words out of her mouth. She looked vaguely surprised that she'd spoken.

Lady Blackthorn gave her a dismissive look. "I don't recall having asked your opinion."

"Forgive me," Sinjun said, and Grayson's mouth fell open. What had Belzaria done to her? Done to Colin? Why was Grayson seemingly immune?

Millicent drew close to Grayson. She tapped his arm with an exquisitely detailed oriental fan. "Mr. Sherbrooke, perhaps you would waltz with me?"

He felt the pull of her and bowed, lightly laid her gloved hand on his arm, and walked to the drawing room. Beaufort stood in the doorway, his eyes on the half dozen servants gliding through the crowd with trays of champagne. Grayson had never seen such exquisite goblets. From a distance, they appeared worked with gold.

"I'm older than I look."

He looked down into her beautiful upturned face. "You are seventeen and not fifteen?"

She laughed, tapped her fan on his arm. "No, I am nearly your age, quite of an age to be your wife, sir."

"You look young enough to be my son's older sister."

"I am lucky in my mother, sir. When I was born, you see, my mother bade all the visiting dignitaries to give me presents to carry with me into eternity. The Wizard of Spain gave me eternal youth. He said I would age very slowly, and thus I would have many husbands. All would grow old and die, and thus I would have to find another, then another."

"I have not heard of the Wizard of Spain. Who is he?"

She shrugged white shoulders. "He is a grand old pooh-bah—Uncle Alessandro, I call him. He is all bluff and good-natured, and he adores Mama, has forever. He would make the seas flood the land if it would please her. Do you recall the tidal wave in Lisbon in 1755 that destroyed the town? And what a ratty little town Lisbon was in those days. You see, the Wizard of Spain was very angry at the Portuguese bandits because they'd had the gall to rob three of his ships, and so he took his revenge. He smells of lemons, from the immense groves in Seville, where he resides. Do you like my gown?"

He stared at her, and she stared back. He looked fully into her eyes. He saw vivid deep blue, no mirrors, no tiny bursts of flame, but he knew somehow she'd managed to shield the shining mirrors and the flame. He knew she was a demon.

"I asked if you liked my gown, Mr. Sherbrooke. You are staring at me. Will you be the third of my husbands, do you think?"

He saw laughter in her eyes, and then he saw something else looking out at him that gave him a jolt. "Yes," he said, "I like your gown. It is very white."

She sighed, tapped her fan on his arm. "Mama insists upon white. Everything must be white. Myself, I prefer blue, a light blue like your eyes."

"You spin a fine tale, Miss—?"

"Blackthorn is my mama's title and a family name as well. Mama tells me we come from a long line of Scottish prelates. You have not answered me. Would you like to be my third husband? The other two, I did them no harm. They lasted their allotted time, as would you."

"Perhaps you could convince me," Grayson said. She laughed gaily and pulled him into the throng of dancers.

The waltz was fast, too fast, and too loud, as if the musicians were drunk. He saw that the dancers were hopping about, ankles showing, gentlemen sweating, weaving, and laughing, trying to keep up. He saw Lord Fergusson, the local magistrate, dancing with his plump younger wife, and his hand was rubbing her breast as her small white hand was touching the front of his breeches. There was Mr. Bellingham, the local squire, twirling his wife round and round until they were both staggering, crashing into another couple who didn't seem to mind at all. They were holding each other up and laughing, always laughing, manic laughter. The squire kissed the other woman, and her husband grabbed the squire's wife. He wouldn't be surprised if they began ripping off their clothes. He'd always wondered what a Roman orgy was like. He was seeing it now. He pulled Millicent to a stop. "What is in the champagne, Miss Blackthorn?"

CHAPTER TWELVE

She dimpled up at him, came up on her tiptoes, and whispered, "It is Mama's special mixture—more a punch, really. It is remarkably delicious and effective." A servant appeared at Grayson's elbow and handed him a glass, then gave Millicent one as well. She clinked her glass to his and said, "To our destiny, Mr. Sherbrooke."

"Yes," he said, "destiny." Grayson tapped his golden goblet to hers and pretended to take a sip. He noticed she drank deeply, smacked her lips, and leaned up to kiss him. Her mouth was warm, her breath sweet. He took a quick step back, smiled, and pointed his goblet toward an elderly man who wore immense side whiskers and was whispering something to Lady Henchcliffe even as his hand was roving over her bottom. She was a matron he'd once heard his aunt Sinjun say, who had amazing stamina in the bedchamber. "Who is that gentleman?"

When Millicent looked away, Grayson poured the punch into a potted palm tree and prayed the plant wouldn't die. She was laughing when she turned back to him, and he pretended he'd drunk all the punch. "That's Major Plintburough," she said. "He fought in the big war with Napoleon, led a charge at Waterloo. He was quite the hero— if you are English, that is."

"And you are not?"

"I? Not English? Don't I look English?"

Before he could answer, she gave a look at his empty goblet. She took it from him and tossed it to a servant, who deftly caught it and bowed to her, and she pulled him onto the dance floor. Another waltz began.

"I adore waltzing," she said, louder now, to be heard over the mad noise and the strident beat of the waltz that pounded into his head. Was she watching him closely to see if he would be affected by the champagne?

"I do too," he said, and twirled her around and around. They bumped into two other couples who exuberantly danced into their path, but there were only laughing apologies, one gentleman's eyes openly examining Millicent's breasts. The waltz grew louder, faster. Suddenly, the madly dancing couples left the dance floor. They were running toward a large table that had suddenly appeared at the other end of the drawing room, at least a dozen platters set upon it. Why hadn't he noticed the table before? Why put the supper in the drawing room? He saw guests were dipping their goblets into a huge bowl of punch in the center of the long table. Endless goblets dipped into the punch. Grayson would swear the level never changed.

"We are nearly alone," she said, smiling up at him, still moving in place as the musicians had left the narrow dais and had dashed to the punch and food behind the guests. She leaned up, pulled his earlobe lightly with her white teeth. "Do you think it is because we look so beautiful dancing together that all wish to look upon us, or because they are all *cochons*—excuse me—pigs, to the trough?"

"You aren't French."

She said in English, then in fluent French, "I am very gifted. I speak five languages. Mama insisted."

"Did a visiting wizard bestow upon you the gift for languages?"

She frowned. "Not that I know of."

"What language is spoken in Border?"

"Border? You mean the lowlands of Scotland? Please call me Millicent, and I will call you Grayson."

He twirled her around and around to the beat of the waltz that was in his head until his heart was beating hard and fast, and he knew it wasn't from exertion—it was something that simply wasn't right. She felt eager and soft. Her breath was sweet and her eyes a deep beguiling blue. Yet there was something—

"How old are you really, Millicent?"

"Ah, but Grayson, I have already told you. Surely a gentleman wouldn't request a lady's age a second time?"

"Are you also called Maeve?"

She continued to sway in his arms even though he'd stopped moving. "Maeve? Who is this Maeve?"

"She lives in Border. She told me she is Queen Maeve. I don't remember what she looked like. Are you she?"

She frowned up at him and tapped her fingers on his black sleeve. "I seem to recall one of the dignitaries my mother summoned at my birth was called Maeve. But a queen? No, I believe she was a sorceress from the Bulgar."

"How could you recall it if you were but newly birthed?"

"That was another gift, from a witch in Naples, a childhood friend of my mother's, I believe. She gifted me with absolute memory from before I was even born throughout my life."

"I wouldn't want to remember everything."

"I agree, but I am doomed to lose not a single second of my existence. I will remember each word, each nuance of this, our first meeting."

"And what did the sorceress Maeve give to you?"

"My beautiful white teeth with the promise that no matter how many years I gained, they would never fall out."

"A very fine gift indeed. Tell me, Millicent, who is your mother that she was able to garner all these favors from sorceresses and wizards?"

Millicent smiled up at him, still swaying. "Look into her eyes, Mr. Sherbrooke, and you will know. But you already have, have you not? Come, let us go back to your aunt and uncle. If I am not mistaken, your uncle is already in love with my mama. She has but to look at a man and he would kill to have her."

Grayson felt a pounding behind his left temple. This was madness—a mad illusion, a mad play with mad players. For a moment, he was back in that tower room, with the rat and Queen Maeve. Why couldn't he remember what she looked like?

Millicent grabbed another goblet of champagne punch from a hovering servant and handed it to him. He simply held the priceless gold-worked goblet. The huge drawing room was now stifling, the guests all speaking over each other, fondling each other, feeding each other. So much discordant noise and it filled his head, and the pounding behind his temple grew, making him nauseated. Did the drawing room seem larger now? Did it look more like a ballroom than a simple drawing room? Were there more candles in the ornate chandeliers, flames dancing, all glowing madly? He looked at the gigantic punch bowl in the middle of the large table, and he'd swear it was still full with the punch, magic punch, drugged punch. He saw one guest drink deeply, throw back his head and laugh loudly, then throw his goblet to a lady in a dark green gown. She caught it, saluted him, and joined him in laughter. Then she hurled the priceless goblet against the wall. The goblet didn't shatter— it seemed to float slowly to lie on the floor.

The pain in his head grew. His eyes hurt.

He heard her voice as if from a great distance. "Drink the champagne, Grayson. It will make you feel wonderful. I know—I snuck a sip when Mama wasn't looking."

Grayson didn't look at her. He walked straight out of the vast drawing room to see Aunt Sinjun, Uncle Colin, and Lady Blackthorn standing exactly where he'd left them, at the base of the ornate stairs, the golden plaster cherubs smirking down upon them, as if they hadn't moved or as if no time had passed at all. They presented a frozen tableau. No, that wasn't right. Lady Blackthorn had moved closer to Uncle Colin, too close, and Aunt Sinjun standing quietly beside him, the expression on her face curiously blank. Each of them held a goblet of the champagne punch in their hands. Had they drunk any of the punch? Neither of them seemed to be really here, only shadows of themselves. Grayson looked at the wide graceful staircase, followed the dozens of steps upward, but oddly, he couldn't see the top—the stairs simply faded into shadows.

Lady Blackthorn was leaning up now, her fingers lightly touching Colin's cheek, and he was smiling down at her, and now he'd raised his hand to cup her chin, raising her cupped chin so he could kiss her, and Aunt Sinjun only stood there, unseeing, unheeding.

Grayson shouted, "Uncle Colin, Aunt Sinjun, I fear I am grown unwell! We must leave before I am ill."

Nothing happened.

He ran to his uncle and grabbed his arm and jerked him away. Sinjun blinked, shook out her skirts, look confused, and Colin was staring down at Lady Blackthorn. Grayson shook his arm again. "Uncle Colin! We must leave!" Colin quickly stepped back, his look uncertain.

Grayson stood between them, gripped both of their arms. "Lady Blackthorn, I fear we must leave. Miss Blackthorn, a pleasure." He pulled them away, aware that the butler, Beaufort, was suddenly in front of them, walking smoothly toward the cherub-carved dead-white door, opening it. Grayson turned, took one last look. Lady Blackthorn was standing perfectly still, looking after them, Millicent at her side, smiling, showing off her perfect white teeth, and she raised a slender hand and waved at him and mouthed, "Marry me."

Beaufort said, "I have, of course, summoned your carriage, my lord."

Grayson wondered how the butler had known to do that. He gestured them outside to stand on the top marble step. He stood behind them in the open doorway, stately and in charge, watching them, the too-loud music and laughter loud roiling behind him. And suddenly there was Frazier, the coachman, holding the horses still and nodding to them. Liam, the tiger, was placing the steps in front of the open carriage door.

Outside in the chill clean air, Grayson's head cleared, and the pounding lessened, then disappeared. In the next instant, he saw himself lying on a stone floor, and he was so cold, and there was a rat staring at him. The image disappeared.

Grayson nearly shoved his aunt and uncle into the carriage. He closed the door. He looked up at the Ashburnham coachman he'd known since he was a boy. "When did the butler summon you, Frazier?"

Frazier scratched his whiskers, looked momentarily confused, and then his brow cleared. "Oh, aye, 'twere nay more than ten minutes ago, Mr. Sherbrooke. Aye, aboot ten minutes ago. Me and Liam were close by, ye ken, in a special place, we were told. Mr. Beaufort was kind. He sent me a flagon of ale."

Of course the ale had been drugged.

CHAPTER THIRTEEN

"What a lovely ball." Sinjun sighed as she nestled against Colin's side in the carriage. "How very charming Lady Blackthorn is, and the manor house—do you not believe she has made it splendid, Colin?"

Colin was staring out the window into the night, silent. Slowly, he turned to his wife. "You don't remember? She kissed me, Sinjun, and I would have kissed her back if Grayson hadn't shouted at us. But my mind didn't seem to be in my control. And you, Sinjun, you weren't there. It was as if you were a shadow of yourself, an impression, but no, you weren't there. And you still aren't. How do I get you back to me?"

Sinjun blinked. "Lady Blackthorn kissed you, my dear? But surely you must be mistaken."

Grayson was sitting on the seat facing them. He leaned forward, interrupting. "You remember that, Uncle Colin?"

"Yes, but I didn't remember until we stepped outside."

Sinjun grabbed his arm. "What are you talking about, Colin? You wanted to kiss that woman? I don't remember that. We laughed and talked and—" Her voice fell off the cliff. She stared at her husband, then at Grayson, and finally she shook her head, whispered, "Now I remember, some of it anyway." She shuddered. "It's like a nightmare."

Grayson said, "Do you remember what you talked about, Aunt Sinjun?"

She looked thoughtful, then frightened. "I don't know. I don't remember talking about anything."

"The champagne punch was drugged," Grayson said matter-of-factly. "I imagine you don't even remember drinking it. But it's over now that you're out of that house, away from her." He saw Sinjun wanted to say something, but then she shook her head at herself and stared out the carriage window.

He said, "Do you remember that the laughter was too loud? The music in the drawing room too exuberant?"

Colin was very still. "You said the punch was drugged. I remember now that a servant handed each of us a goblet of the stuff. It was a beautiful goblet, gold, and the handle was gilded, I'm sure of it. Sinjun, you were thirsty, I remember, and you took only a small sip, but like me, you didn't like the taste. All this confusion, Grayson, and we only drank small amounts of the stuff?" He shook his head. "Odd, I don't remember what I did with the goblet."

"Evidently one sip was enough," Grayson said. "All your neighbors, they drank goblet after goblet. I wonder what they will remember tomorrow morning?"

Sinjun asked, "What do you mean by that?"

"I realized it must have been like one of those Roman orgies you read about. You would not have recognized your neighbors, Aunt Sinjun. I hope they won't remember anything. One thing I'm sure of—they will all be praising Lady Blackthorn—both ladies and gentlemen—and all the talk will be of her splendid party. She will become, overnight, the gracious hostess, a lady to be admired and welcomed into the neighborhood."

Sinjun was fretting with her reticule. "But I only drank a sip of it, and yet I don't remember that hussy kissing Colin."

Colin hugged her to him. "We are free of her now. I think you will eventually remember, Sinjun. And I agree with you, Grayson, all the other guests—our neighbors—they will never remember, will they?"

"I strongly doubt it." Grayson grabbed the strap to steady himself over a rough stretch of road. "It wouldn't serve her for any of them to remember that they behaved like out-of-control Oxford students with no boundaries, no rules."

Sinjun looked over at Grayson. "You told us what Jane said, that Belzaria wanted Colin, that she wanted to take him to Border and make him her slave."

Grayson said, "I'd hoped Jane was being overly dramatic, but evidently not. And that means we must all take great care. Now, how old do you think Lady Blackthorn's daughter Millicent is?"

Sinjun said, "Sixteen, perhaps?"

Colin said nearly at the same time, "Older, at least thirty, I should say, but now that I think about it, Lady Blackthorn—the mother, she looked no older than her daughter."

They stared at each other, then looked at Grayson. "What is going on here?" Colin asked, his voice not quite steady. "Do you know how old she is?"

Grayson felt the threads weave themselves together. "I don't think either of them has an age," he said slowly. "I think their ages are what they want you to see. But I think Lady Blackthorn is indeed Belzaria, and that means we're in deep trouble."

"Because of Colin?"

"Yes, Aunt Sinjun, because Belzaria wants Colin."

"But you are younger, Grayson. Why wouldn't she want you?"

Colin stared at his nephew in the dim light. "I think whoever or whatever these two women are, they're afraid of Grayson."

When they reached Vere Castle, Hobbs handed each of them a lit candle, locked and bolted the great front doors, and said in his pinched voice, "It isna late ye come home, my lord. The party wasn't to yer liking?"

It was Sinjun who said, "I believe we were the first guests who left, but still, I remember being there a very long time. Pray, Hobbs, what time is it?"

"A pinch after eleven o'clock, my lady, only a pinch."

They'd been gone less than two hours. They looked at each other, but nothing was said.

Grayson followed his aunt and uncle up the stairs, heard her say quietly, "I will not leave your side, Colin. If this—demon, or whatever she is—wants you for whatever reason, she will have both of us to deal with."

Colin leaned down and kissed her, but he said nothing.

CHAPTER FOURTEEN

Grayson waited. He wasn't surprised to feel the air itself shift almost instantly, as if something unseen parted it to come through. She shimmered at the foot of his bed, her pearls glowing in the soft candlelight. Slowly she became clear, and he saw her face was as pale as her pearls, but then it always was. She was tugging on her pearls.

I took back my pearl, she said clearly in his mind, and she held up one of the loops, her fingers around one pearl.

He wondered how a ghost could pick up a pearl that had been too real, how she could have possibly restrung it onto one of the loops. He started to ask her, but he heard her voice clearly. *Ye saw her, didna ye, Grayson? Ye saw Belzaria, the demon?*

He settled his head against his arms. "I saw both Belzaria and another, named Millicent, supposedly her daughter." He told Jane about the drugged champagne punch, the bizarre drunken behavior of all the guests, ladies included, and how Colin and Sinjun had only taken a sip of the drugged punch, but still Colin would have kissed Lady Blackthorn if Grayson hadn't stopped him.

I would have liked to drink some of that lovely champagne punch, but like ye said, the demon poisoned it. An' all those idjits, those gowkies, the lot of them laughin' too loud an' dancin' aboot like dafties. Ah, Grayson, but there was so much fuid—it all looked so very good.

Grayson would swear he heard her sigh. "I didn't know you were at the party, Jane. You should have stopped me."

Oh nay, to hear it from yer lips, 'tis different. Ye have senses I canna remember. Aye, I knew soon enough she'd poisoned that champagne, an' so I made it taste nestie to Sinjun and Colin. But he sipped it, jes' like a mon, always doin' what he isna supposed to do, an' he nearly pree the lips wi' that demon. An' my poor Sinjun, she took only a tiny sip—but the demon had put a spell on her.

I told ye, I told ye, now didna I, that the demon wants Colin and ye canna let the bitch take him. That canna happen.

"No, we will not let that happen, Jane. Did you speak to your kelpie friend, Barrie, at Loch Ness?"

Och, aye, Barrie tried to hide from me, nestled he was in amongst the yellow heather, but I saw his bare foot sticking out and grabbed it and pulled. He yaffed, jes' like a wee lassie an' so I told him. He said he couldna help me, that he had to find a nice big goat for the monster. Her bairns were hungry, and no fishers had ventured out—they were scairt feardies because a fisher had seen her.

I told him I'd tie him up with my pearls and feed him to the monster's bairns unless he told me how to kill a demon. He hemmed and hawed, as kelpies do, forever trying to slither off, like weasely snakes, but I didn't let go of his foot. This is what he told me, Grayson: A demon loves French sweet breid and will eat the French sweet breid until it falls asleep. Then ye must strangle it, if ye can find its craig.

"Craig? You mean its neck, Jane?"

Aye, that is what I said!

"Do you believe Barrie? Sweet breid—cake, Jane? That doesn't sound like something that would make a demon fall asleep."

That is what Barrie said. Sweet breid, French sweet breid. An' he said it like I was a looby and ignorant, that everyone should ken how to kill a demon.

"What sort of cake is French sweet breid?"

The air heaved and shimmered with impatience. *French sweet breid, 'tis naught but fruit and berries in pastry. Sinjun's cook, she'll ken how to make it.*

Jane shimmered in the air, faded away, and then came back, fully formed, swaying in front of him, playing with her pearls, making one loop longer, then shorter, preening, something he imagined her doing most of the time. And that was a question: Did she see herself in a mirror? And what was time to a ghost?

She paused, and he would swear she stiffened, turned about quickly, then he saw the fear on her face, and she was gone, simply gone. He heard her voice frantic in his head: *The demon is close. Ye must kill it, Grayson, afore it kills me and Sinjun and takes Colin.*

Grayson pinched out the candle and lay on his back staring up at the dark ceiling. He heard a floorboard creak and wondered if Belzaria was here. When he fell asleep, he saw Millicent's young face, and he saw himself pulling her back against his chest in the circular tower room. In Border. And she'd told him she was Queen Maeve and Belzaria was close. The two faces mixed in his brain and changed from young to old and toothless, and he was spinning from one to the other, seeing neither of their faces.

When he woke up at the rooster's loud crow, close, right outside his window, he remembered all of it.

CHAPTER FIFTEEN

Day Three

Grayson drank a cup of Mrs. Keith's splendid black Indian tea at the big servants' table in the kitchen. Everything sparkled, not a single white dot of flour, not a single sign of Jane's mad visit the previous afternoon.

Mrs. Keith said, "Ye say ye wish me to bake a French sweet breid?"

"Yes, Mrs. Keith. I have asked my aunt Sinjun to invite Lady Blackthorn and her daughter to tea, and I understand this is their favorite cake. Do you know how to make it?"

Mrs. Keith said, "I remember my mither showing me the ancient recipe when I was a bairn, goes back ever so long, even my mither didn't know where it came from. It was a special sort of French breid, she told me. I will try, Mr. Sherbrooke."

Grayson left the kitchen, his head bowed in thought. Sinjun had already written a note to Lady Blackthorn, sent Liam with it to Blackthorn Manor. She would come. He knew she would come. And she would bring Millicent. But what he didn't know was if one could believe a kelpie named Barrie who lived at Loch Ness who'd told this to Pearlin' Jane under duress. How could a certain sort of cake put a demon to sleep?

He knew he'd better have something else in mind, just in case, and it took him an hour to figure out what he needed.

At precisely three o'clock that afternoon, a very modern, very expensive carriage pulled up in front of Vere Castle. And because Grayson had awoken to remember everything that had happened to him, he recognized it immediately. It was the same carriage that had pulled up beside him that lost day. He stood at the window and watched the coachman, a handsome young man dressed in blue-and-gold livery, hand the reins to the small tiger, then he himself placed the step at the carriage door. He opened the door, bowed, and held out his hand to assist Lady Blackthorn to alight.

Her face blurred. Grayson shook his head, staring hard at her, but somehow he couldn't seem to bring her face into focus. Then Millicent stepped down onto the step, and she was waving at no one in particular, laughing as she gave her hand to the coachman. When she stood beside her mother, he realized that he couldn't clearly make out her face either. It was if they were wearing veils, only they weren't. What was going on here? Their gowns were exquisite, identical, both a dark forest green, the pokes of their bonnets high, streaming green ribbons of the same dark shade. From his vantage point, they looked like twins, very rich twins. One of the chestnut horses neighed. Even the horses looked perfectly matched.

He turned to face his aunt and uncle, his voice low. "We will end this today," he said, "or else I fear what would happen to you, Uncle Colin, to all of us. I know you do not wish to believe in ghosts, in demons, in the advice the Loch Ness kelpie Barrie gave Pearlin' Jane, but we have no choice. Listen, neither of you should show anything but remembered pleasure of last night. You are grateful for being invited to her splendid party, all right?"

Colin looked stiff all over. He was torn, truth be told. The events of the previous evening were blurred in his brain, and he simply couldn't be certain what Grayson had told him had indeed happened. Neither did Sinjun, but she believed Grayson implicitly, not a doubt in her beautiful head. But French sweet breid?

To Grayson's surprise and dismay, another carriage pulled to a stop behind Lady Blackthorn's. This one was much smaller, much older, bordering on shabby. The vicar alighted, nodded to his coachman, and walked quickly to greet Lady Blackthorn and her daughter. He was giving the ladies formal bows, talking all the while. Grayson didn't remember seeing him at Lady Blackthorn's party last night.

The three of them were met by Hobbs at the front doors of the castle and shown promptly into the drawing room.

Greetings were made, all offered a seat.

Vicar Gordon was effusive. "I always so enjoy coming here," he said to Lady Blackthorn, then turned to smile at Sinjun. "The past lives in this room, ah, and the Kinross plaid, its reds and greens so bright, and furnishings to revere our worthy ancestors." He was fully capable of continuing indefinitely. Sinjun and Colin had heard enough of his sermons to know only a blow to the head or a cup of tea would shut him up.

Sinjun nodded thankfully to Hobbs when he came into the drawing room bearing an old silver tray. Upon it sat a beautiful Georgian teapot, Meissen cups and saucers, and beneath a domed plate, Grayson devoutly prayed sat the French sweet breid.

Vicar Gordon turned to Lady Blackthorn. "I understand from my parishioners that you gave a splendid party last night, my lady. A pity I was unable to leave my wife, what with her putrid throat that came upon her so quickly. She is better today. I am so pleased to find you here." And he gave her a big toothy grin.

Grayson cleared his throat, well aware that the demon hadn't said a single word, which was difficult at best, his aunt Sinjun had told him, when the vicar was around. She looked quite complacent, sitting upright, her beautiful green skirts spread around her. Millicent looked somehow dimmed beside her, somehow overshadowed by her . . . what—her mother? In the next moment, he finally saw their faces clearly; one was older, one younger. Mother and daughter. They seemed to be exactly what they appeared to be. Only they weren't.

When everyone had been served tea, the vicar continued with his monologue. Lady Blackthorn took a sip of her tea, looked at the vicar, gave him a nod, and in the next moment, he leaned his head back against the settee and was snoring lightly.

She smiled at them all. "Ah, he has talked himself out, I see."

The power, Grayson thought, the absolute power. At least she hadn't killed the vicar. He smiled at her. "Lady Blackthorn, I have wondered why your daughter's last name is also Blackthorn. Has she not been married before?"

"Ah, as to that, it was her father's name. A fine man, a holy man, a man who was more than a man. Her previous husbands were naught but middling fools. But they were rich, and surely that was something in their favor."

"I was told Blackthorn was a Scottish prelate's name from the twelfth century."

The demon laughed. "Surely there have been many Blackthorns over the centuries, Mr. Sherbrooke, many prelates by that name. And why is that important to you?"

"It is of interest, don't you think?" Grayson rose, went to the marquetry table, lifted the dome, and saw the large cake with apricot preserves flowing over its sides. He picked up the knife and sliced the French sweet breid.

Grayson saw both heads snap up, watched both noses sniff the air.

"What is that?" The demon was leaning forward, nearly tipping off the settee.

Grayson merely smiled and handed it a large slice of the cake. He looked at the demon daughter—Queen Maeve—yes, he remembered her as the young girl who had come to him in that tower room. But what would this demon have done to him? "Would you care for a slice? I believe it's French sweet breid."

The daughter nodded as well, her eyes never leaving her mother's slice. Her mother didn't wait for everyone to be served. She immediately cut a big piece with her fork and crammed it into her mouth.

Grayson handed Queen Maeve a slice and watched her gobble it down.

The two demons sat as human beings in a Scottish drawing room, chewing, swallowing, making sounds of pleasure, ignoring Sinjun, Colin, and Grayson.

They silently watched the demons devour another slice of the French sweet breid.

After a third slice, Lady Blackthorn paused, licked her lips, and nodded. "Excellent. I cannot remember the last time I enjoyed such excellent French sweet breid. Your cook—I fancy I will take her to Blackthorn Manor. Perhaps another slice would suit me," and held out its plate.

Grayson served each of them a fourth large slice. How many slices would it take before they fell asleep and he could kill them? They both still appeared alert—and hungry. Had cook not known all the ingredients? Was a critical one missing? What would happen if he ran out of the French sweet breid and they wanted more?

CHAPTER SIXTEEN

Grayson saw Colin staring fixedly at Lady Blackthorn as she stuffed the fourth slice of French sweet breid into her mouth. Was he remembering what had happened, and more importantly, was he accepting it, accepting that she was not a human, rather a demon?

Grayson felt the air change right behind him and knew it was Pearlin' Jane. She was hidden behind him, watching. Could the demons see her? Perhaps sense her presence?

The demon raised her head and sniffed the air. Grayson didn't feel Jane now—she'd left. She was fast. The demon turned to smile at Colin. "Your wife is really quite old and ugly, my lord," she said, even as she forked another bite of cake into her mouth. "I am here to remove her from your sight. I will erase her, as if she never existed to torment you. I shall take her place. You and I will travel to lands you have never imagined, my lord, lands that will thrill your blood."

Colin felt the pull of her, remembered that same pull last night, and he knew he was in trouble. He felt the derringer in his pocket. He wouldn't have fed this creature the ridiculous French breid. He'd have shot her—it—between the eyes. Maybe he would still need to.

Sinjun laughed. "Really, ma'am. Me, ugly? Have you not gazed into my beautiful Sherbrooke blue eyes? Admired my beautiful smile, heard my mellow voice, like bells, my husband is always telling me? It is you who are an abomination. Who would want to see other lands in your company? You are an ancient evil. How old are you? Older than the dirt in my garden? At least, I should say—just look at you."

Millicent said, her voice sharp, vicious, "How dare you speak to her like that? She is a princess, nay, a queen, more than a queen. She is the undisputed sovereign over lands you cannot begin to imagine. For her to select this man, it is a gift, to all of you." She turned to Grayson, and she was no longer sixteen. Her face was setting into hard lines, older lines.

"And you, sirrah, we tried to stop you. We both recognized what you were, the threat you were to us, and I knew you would fight to come back, and so you did.

"I was your prisoner in Border, in that tower room. Why did you let me go?"

Belzaria said, "We wanted to see you, examine you. My Maeve talked me out of killing you. She felt it would be more amusing to watch you try to best us, you with your reputation for dealing with our kind, and your silly novels about ghosts and beasts of the otherworld. But you are common, withal, despite your hardy spirit, your fine human brain, and your seeming immunity to my power. I will admit that you have a strong will. And here you are, trying to save your precious uncle from me, a beautiful queen of lands he can only begin to imagine."

Maeve said, "The earl does not need to be saved from my precious mother, do you hear me? He will be a prince, even a king, if he pleases her, and if she becomes convinced he isn't weak like the others, that he will accept all that is offered to him. He doesn't need this worthless bitch. He will thrive with my mother." She eyed the French breid. It seemed to Grayson that she had to force herself to look away, to look at him, and she shrugged. "Yes, I wanted to let you go. I wanted to see what you would do. You've done nothing but talk, talk, talk, like all worthless humans."

Grayson said, "Are you Queen Maeve? And if you are indeed she, how can she be your mother? Wouldn't that make her the queen of Border? Not you?"

"It is all of a sameness," Belzaria said, staring at the French breid. "You would not understand. Your minds are too narrow, too feeble, to see anything as it really is. She is Queen Maeve—she is whatever she wishes to be, just as I am Belzaria."

"More cake?" Grayson asked, even as he cut two more slices of the French sweet breid.

Both demons' eyes were fastened on those two slices.

Colin said, "Why do you think I wouldn't be as weak as the others, Lady Blackthorn? Belzaria? Did you marry many other men before you found me? Tell me, how many have preceded me? Did you divorce them all? Did you kill them?"

"Bah," the demon said even as it let the fork fall to the carpet. It was eating the fat slice Grayson had put on the plate with its fingers, as fast as it could. It chewed, eyes closed in bliss. It was the same with Maeve. Both demons were eating their fifth slice.

There were only two slices left. Would they finally fall asleep? Belzaria took the last bite, but didn't fall over, it opened its eyes, said to Colin, "You are a handsome man, you are an earl, and you are known even where I live much of the time. Your land, it constricts me. I do not like it here even with the splendid house that languished because I could find no more boy children to kill."

Grayson said, "What do you mean, Belzaria, you have no boy children to give it to kill? The house?"

Belzaria laughed. "So you know me. Aye, of course the house, you brainless man. Donnan MacKeller, what a fool he was, so greedy, willing to make a bargain with a demon, and then the idiot thought to cheat me. Me! Aye, we'd made a bargain, his life and lands saved from the English soldiers in return for his giving me the ancient Celtic cross he'd hidden, a cross my grandmother gave as a gift to one of his ancestors, a rickety old sot she occasionally bedded. And so I saved him, saved his lands, his family, and what did the deceitful fool do? He told me he could not find the cross, that his father had hidden it again, not showing him the hiding place. I knew he was lying. And so I cursed all the male children who would ever live in that house." It paused, popped the last piece of cake into its mouth, chewed, swallowed. "I looked and looked but could not find the cross. I do not wish to remain here. I must give up hope, and it sorely tries me. I will leave once I have Colin." The demon wiped its mouth with the back of its hand. It looked toward Sinjun. "You are a bothersome bitch. You have no worth, no value, and you are old and ugly, as I said. Colin will want to come with me—he'll beg to come with me. Shall I kill you?"

The demon leaned over and grabbed the rest of the cake slice off Maeve's plate. Grayson would swear he heard Maeve hiss. He was quick to hand each of them the two final slices, neither of them very big. The demon had killed all those innocent boy children? It chilled him to the bone. But he couldn't let them see it. He shot his aunt Sinjun a quick look to keep her still, then said, smiling, "Your wit was remarked upon by many of your guests last night, my lady. All thought you vastly amusing. Surely you are jesting now. Surely you would not wish to divide this man and woman. They are devoted to each other. Colin would not be happy without his wife."

"He will forget her in an instant." She snapped her fingers. "You saw him last night. He knew he belonged to me." The demon gave him a frown. "When I let you go, I didn't realize you were immune to us, and that is bothersome, but in the end it won't matter. You don't matter— you're naught but a garden slug, slow and stupid."

"But Mama, he is giving us French breid. He is nice now, isn't he? But this is the last slice. Isn't there any more? I will be very angry if there isn't more French breid."

Grayson felt the knotted string in his pocket, enough to garrote both of them. Why didn't they fall over? "To prove how nice I am, shall I call for more cake?"

Both demons nodded.

But there was no more cake. Grayson said quickly, "Tell me, what language is spoken in Border?"

Both demons stared at him, momentarily distracted. Finally, Belzaria said, "I must revise my thinking. I have decided that you are not a common garden slug. You are a bright lad. I shall kill you swiftly, not draw out your death as would usually please me. Did you enjoy your brief stay in my lovely Warwick Castle?"

He nodded, why not? Anything to keep it talking. Why didn't the demons fall over?

"All of you—you are so very tedious, your minds so limited. I have had enough of humans to last me one of your pitiful lifetimes. Save for Colin, who will amuse me for a time. I ask you, who would ever wish to wear a ridiculous corset?" The demon licked its fingers, rose, said to Colin, "Sir, prepare to enjoy my magnificent self. For how long? We shall see. And you, my lady, you have outlived your usefulness." It raised its hand.

Grayson said quickly, "Wait, there is something I do not understand. When I was in your tower room at Warwick Castle, I remember Queen Maeve told me she wanted to save me from you. She said she was there to rescue me. She said she was the hereditary queen of Border." He looked from one to the other. "If she is the hereditary queen of Border, then who are you?"

Belzaria threw back her head and laughed, and her thick lustrous wig fell off. She looked dispassionately at the wig on the carpet at her feet. "Ah, that feels better. My Maeve here adores to spin better tales than you write, sirrah. Now, as for you, Colin, it's time for you to visit my land and learn what it is like to serve me, your queen."

The cake hadn't worked. Neither of the demons was asleep.

"As for you, pathetic cow, say good-bye to this benighted earth."

The air split apart, and Pearlin' Jane shimmered in front of them. She jerked off her pearls and began hurling them at the demon. Belzaria shrieked when a pearl hit its face and stuck for a moment, burning, leaving a black pockmark. It howled, slapped a hand to its cheek, and disappeared. The expensive green gown lay empty on the floor. But Jane continued to hurl the pearls at the spot where the demon had stood. A flash of bright light appeared, and arms of light slapped away at the pearls, but there was a noise, a moaning, a shriek, low cries, and Jane kept throwing pearls.

Pearls struck the demon Maeve and it too disappeared, the second green gown tumbling to the floor. Jane was still hurling her pearls. She could still see the demons?

They heard the demons shrieking in unison now, an unearthly noise. But Jane was running out of pearls. How had she known her pearls would hurt the demons? A guess? It didn't matter. They owed her their lives.

Grayson shouted, "Come back, I have more French breid for you."

CHAPTER SEVENTEEN

The pearls stopped, the shrieking stopped. The air itself seemed to freeze, and then he saw a hand, only it wasn't really a human hand, it was withered, three long fingers, a yellowish-brown, and those fingers grabbed his wrist. Then other fingers shot out and grabbed his other wrist, shook it. When would the demons realize there was no more cake? Grayson prayed.

Time froze.

His wrists were released. There were two thumps, as if something substantial had hit the floor. And the demons appeared again, once more dressed in their gowns, but their faces were changing, growing older and older still, and they were making a humming noise, and finally, both were asleep—two ancient women lying on the floor, cake crumbs still on their vein-backed hands, and smeared on their mouths.

Grayson didn't wait—he pulled the knotted string from his coat and looped it around Belzaria's ancient wrinkled throat and pulled with all his might. The demon didn't move. Then its eyes popped open and it whispered in a strange guttural language, and strangely, he understood it. "I am Belzaria, I rule all I wish to rule," and its eyes closed and the demon was dead. He quickly looped the garrote around Maeve's neck and jerked tight, held it.

Nothing. Deep heavy breathing, then Maeve's eyes opened. "You think to kill me, you puling little human?"

"Yes, you ate the cake, and you're helpless. I am strangling you."

"I will turn you into filthy muck. I will grind your guts and make you eat them. I will—"

He jerked the garrote tighter, pulled with all his might, his knee against a chest that wasn't a human chest to gain more leverage. Fingered claws went around his throat, trying to choke him. The demon was stronger than he could imagine. So the daughter was younger and stronger than the demon mother. He knew he was going to lose, and when he did, all of them would die.

Jane was beside him. She was stuffing pearls down the demon's throat, a half dozen, a full dozen, and the demon was trying to spit them out, choking, heaving against the garrote around its neck, but Jane kept gathering up the pearls from the carpet, one pearl after the other, shoving them down the demon's throat.

Finally the demon died, its mouth open, ancient parchment cheeks that weren't human cheeks, bulging with pearls. Grayson slowly stood, looked down at them, Jane beside him, and he'd swear she was panting with exertion. *"Ye kilt them, Grayson, ye kilt them!"*

"We kilt them, Jane. Thank you." He watched as the demons slowly seemed to shrink and fade, and soon there was nothing left, not even the gowns. It was as if they'd never been there.

Except for a rancid smell Grayson knew had once been violets and roses.

He looked at the empty cake plate, at all of Jane's pearls scattered on the carpet. He heard her say, *Me pearls kilt that young demon – ooh what a fine thing it was, a verra fine thing.* He looked over to see Sinjun and Colin sitting perfectly still, not looking at him, not looking at anything in particular. It was if they weren't there.

Grayson walked to them, lightly shook their arms.

Sinjun opened her beautiful Sherbrooke eyes. "Grayson, what happened? I simply fell asleep—Colin!" She shook his arm, and he jerked awake. "What happened? Grayson, you are all right? Those demons, what happened?"

"They're dead." Having them not aware of what had happened surprised him. He eyed them, said, "What is the last thing you remember?"

Colin said slowly, "Lady Blackthorn—a demon? I can't believe that, I can't. But—" He drew a deep breath. "I knew she was, whatever she was, she was going to kill Sinjun, but I couldn't seem to move, and then—" He shook his head. "Sinjun?"

"No, I don't remember anything. Where are they, Grayson?"

"They're gone. Dead, I hope. What the kelpie Barrie told Jane, it worked, but I couldn't have killed them without Jane's help. She hurled her pearls at them, stuffed them into the younger demon's mouth. It finished it off. How, I have no idea."

Sinjun stared at him blank-faced. "Really? The demons simply disappeared?"

Grayson nodded. "Yes, they're gone. Maybe Border will change now that they're gone. However, we have a problem." And he pointed toward the piles of white pearls scattered all over the floor.

The air shimmered.

Sinjun stilled, and then she smiled. "Jane believes they're dead. She said she's going to Loch Ness to see if Barrie would like to drink champagne with her. And she wants to ask him more about how the pearls helped kill them." Sinjun looked blank a moment, then threw back her head and laughed.

Colin stared at the pearls. "How can a ghost have real pearls? How can a ghost throw something? It is difficult for a man to accept."

Sinjun patted his arm. "I know. Now it's up to us to restring them for her."

Grayson said to the still air, "Thank you, Jane, really, thank you."

Vicar Gordon, forgotten until this moment, jerked awake, blinked furiously, and turned bright red with embarrassment. "Oh dear, I fell asleep, how very rude of me, my lady, my lord. Was I sleeping a long time?"

"We let you enjoy your nap, Vicar," Colin said, giving him his hand to pull him up. "Perhaps you would care for a cup of tea to revive yourself?"

"Oh yes, that would be excellent, my lord. And perhaps a piece of that cake? I seemed to smell something extraordinary in my dreams, and I knew it was a cake, a special cake."

"Alas, we consumed every single slice," Grayson said. "I will have Mrs. Keith send your cook the recipe. It's called French sweet breid."

CHAPTER EIGHTEEN

Day Four

The next day, Grayson returned from Kinross village to tell his aunt and uncle about the endless gossip and consternation at the sudden disappearance of beneficent Lady Blackthorn, her glorious daughter, Millicent, the stately butler, Beaufort, and all the staff. It appeared everyone had simply left during the previous night, leaving all their fine clothing behind, all the beautiful furnishings. All that was found was one empty champagne bottle in the huge drawing room. But how could that be possible? It was soon whispered that they'd been borne away by the curse of the MacKellers. Soon, Grayson knew the story would be repeated so many times that in the years to come it would be accepted as one of the strange truths in the neighborhood.

It was a day for surprises. Within the hour, Philip Kinross, eldest son of Colin, the Earl of Ashburnham, arrived with his wife and two children, Colin and Tessa, ages seven and four, a surprise visit, only Grayson knew it wasn't. He knew Pearlin' Jane had brought them, and he knew what he had to do, what she hoped he could do.

There was laughter in the house again, the sounds of children racing about, enjoying themselves immensely.

All the staff had searched for Pearlin' Jane's pearls and found one hundred and seven. One pearl was missing. And so was Pearlin' Jane. She was too embarrassed to be seen without all of her pearls. Grayson smiled as he fingered that last pearl he'd slipped into his pocket.

The morning after Philip's and his family's arrival, Grayson was eating his porridge, alone for the moment, and he felt her behind his chair.

I canna find my missing pearl!

"I know, Jane. I fear one of the demons swallowed it. And they're long gone now."

A huffing silence, a begrudging, *Miserable demon bitch, eating one of me pearls! Maybe she spit it out, left it somewhere. I'll ask Barrie.*

"Don't worry about it. Trust me, Jane, all right? I wish to thank you again. That was a brilliant idea, throwing your pearls at them. Did you ask Barrie why it hurt them?"

I tell you, Grayson, the first pearl simply leapt out of my hand, hurled itself at Belzaria. And how would a pearl know how to hurt a demon? The young one was stronger than her mither, that wicked Belzaria. It was hard to stuff my pearls down that one's throat. Och, but both demons were old, so very old, from ancient times, and we kilt them, Grayson, we kilt them! An' my pearls!

"Yes, we did. About your missing pearl—"

"Who are you talking to, Grayson?"

Grayson turned to see Elise, Philip's wife, coming into the dining room, smiling at him. She was small and plump and quite pretty, only a year older than he was. He rose, said matter-of-factly, "I was speaking to Pearlin' Jane. She was very helpful to me, eliminating a very big problem."

A perfectly arched dark eyebrow went up. "Ah, you are jesting, Grayson. Pearlin' Jane? The ghost my mama-in-law swears to me has lived here at Vere Castle for more than a hundred years now, her friend and confidant? Come, sir, really. I have told Tessa and Colin how you make up ghost stories, and they are clamoring to have you scare them. But I do not need them, particularly before my breakfast."

Grayson looked at the patent disbelief on her lovely face, the indulgent smile, so like Colin's. "Elise, if I were to tell you Pearlin' Jane and I were discussing the events of the past week, what would you say?"

"I would say you have imbibed a very strong beverage with your porridge."

"Did you see the pile of perfect white pearls in Aunt Sinjun's basket?" He wouldn't tell her about the demons—she'd doubtless petition to commit him to Bedlam.

"They are magnificent. She didn't say where they'd come from, just that they needed to be restrung. Why?" She paused. "Ah, you're going to tell me they belong to this ghost, this Pearlin' Jane, and that's how she got her name? They are real pearls, Grayson, not ghostly pearls that don't really exist."

He only smiled, pulled back her chair, and waited for her to settle herself. He handed her a cup of tea. "Will you perform an experiment for me, Elise?"

She gave him a suspicious look as she picked up a piece of toast.

"If I give you a pearl, will you take it to the tower room, by yourself, sit in front of the window, remain silent, and simply wait?"

"You think the ghost, Pearlin' Jane, will come to me?"

"She might. She would want to know what you are doing with one of her precious pearls."

Grayson reached into his pocket and pulled out the last pearl he'd kept and handed it to her.

He could swear he heard a low laugh.

That evening, before everyone met in the drawing room before dinner, Grayson walked in to see Elise standing by the window. She looked at him when he stepped beside her. For a moment both of them stared out toward Loch Leven.

She said, "This is a magnificent view, but I find that now I prefer the view from my papa-in-law's tower room. When I went up there, Andrew the cat was sleeping on the small settee that faced the window.

He and I sat there together, I petting him with one hand and holding the single pearl tightly in my other hand."

She turned to face Grayson. "She didn't speak to me, yet I heard her say clearly, *What are you doing with my pearl?*

"Andrew looked up and began purring loudly, then he ducked his head and I would swear to you a hand was petting him.

"I was so shocked I was mute. I held out my hand, and then the pearl was gone and her voice was again clear in my head. *Thank you. I am Pearlin' Jane, but you may call me Jane. Welcome to my house.*"

EPILOGUE

When Grayson mounted Astor the following Monday morning, he knew he would arrive back at Belhaven with Pip on the morrow. He knew there would be no strange carriages stopping him, whisking him to Border. No, all was right with the world again, at least his small part of the world. He reached into his pocket and pulled out a single white pearl.

Take it, Grayson, it's my gift to you. It's now your talisman—it will keep you safe.

He felt the soft summer air, filled with the scent of heather and jasmine, and he felt a whisper of good-bye against his face.

The Ancient Spirits of Sedgwick House

THE THIRD NOVELLA
IN THE GRAYSON SHERBROOKE OTHERWORLDLY
ADVENTURES SERIES

CHAPTER ONE

I'm being watched. Eyes are following my every step. Grayson stopped in his tracks and looked around Lord Lyle's large treasure room filled with artifacts from ancient Egypt. Of course there were eyes, painted eyes of long-ago Egyptian gods and goddesses, staring but not seeing, watching. Still, he'd learned never to ignore when he felt something strange touch his senses, something that could harm him.

Was that a soft heartbeat he heard? Grayson laughed aloud at himself. His writer's brain was working hard to scare him to death. He breathed in the heavy still air and looked into the black eyes of the jackal-headed Anubis, protector of the dead. He felt a skitter of gooseflesh on his arms. He'd always felt uneasy whenever he saw a status of this particular Egyptian god. Even saying his name—Anubis—made his heart speed up. He reached out and touched the raised arm, looking at the black jackal head, the white, blue, and gold of his headdress and cloth skirt all looking as if they were painted yesterday, not over three thousand years ago. Anubis was a foot-tall statue, carved millennia ago, as threatening as a doorstop, yet it still made him uncomfortable. He looked more closely. It looked as if Lord Lyle had placed Anubis to hover over the blood-red velvet-draped stands displaying Egyptian jewelry. There were gold arm cuffs, some studded with malachite and jasper, others plain gold, necklaces of turquoise and serpentine, delicate earrings, and bracelets twisted in intricate loops and coils. He realized then that Anubis wasn't watching over all the jewelry; no, his black painted eyes were fixed upon a plain gold arm cuff set alone on its own velvet-covered stand. Why? And this particular arm cuff? And why was it set away from the other jewelry, by itself?

He picked up the cuff and felt immediate warmth. He lightly ran his fingers over the smooth gold, and he would swear it pulsed gently in his hands. Then he saw her, right in front of him, warm, breathing, alive. He felt the shock of it, the slap of fear, then got a grip on himself, accepted that he was somehow seeing a glimpse the long-distant past. He studied her. She was very young, only fourteen, fifteen, glowing with health and a girl's fresh beauty. Her long straight hair, black as a moonless night sky, fell down her back over her white linen robe belted with a golden sash. Her skin was a dusky cream, so very soft looking, and her kohl-lined eyes were black as her hair, alight with intelligence, and deep, holding secrets close. Secrets? How could this young girl have secrets?

He watched her caress the plain golden cuff circling her arm, the same cuff displayed on the red velvet stand, guarded, it seemed to Grayson, by the god Anubis, the same gold cuff he now held in his hands.

She turned to look out over the water, and he heard her thoughts. They were crystal clear in his mind.

It's such a fine gift, this beautiful cuff, and I shall wear it always. Imagine an old priest telling Jabari it is special, timeless, both in and of our time and world, and of others as well. I will ask Jabari what the old priest meant when we walk by the water reeds and breathe in the scent of the sweet pomegranates. Shall I tell him? No, I cannot, but still, he must know it cannot be.

Then, like wind whisking away smoke, she was gone, simply gone. All that remained was her name clear in his mind—Nefret—and sadness. What couldn't be? What didn't she want to tell Jabari? Who were they? Grayson shook his head. He was asking the sorts of questions his fictional hero would ask when weaving his way through a baffling fictional conundrum. As for Grayson himself, it was true he'd had the occasional vision, even dealt with strange beings, but nothing compared to his fictional counterpart, Thomas Straithmore, who battled spirits and ghosts and demons from other realms, in other times. Thomas always stepped up and stopped whatever malevolent creature from bedeviling the modern man or woman.

Grayson drew in a deep, steadying breath. It didn't matter now what had happened millennia ago. It was today, here and now—his world, not hers, the modern world. Nefret and Jabari were far in the past, long dead, long forgotten.

Grayson set the gold cuff back on its red velvet and stepped back, but still his brain was working madly. What had the old priest meant— the cuff was timeless? Both in this world and in others as well?

Who was she? And Jabari? Were they lovers? So long ago, he thought, so very long ago. Timeless, he thought, the cuff was timeless. Had the vision of her been somehow embedded in that gold cuff, and something about him had set it in motion? Had she appeared to others? Grayson couldn't help himself. He reached out and lightly touched his fingertips to the golden cuff. He felt warmth flood through him, felt her soft sweet breath against his face, smelled the faint scent of jasmine, and heard the whisper of a thought.

Every day is as every other day. Pain then, pain now, joy then, joy now. It is all of a piece.

His pulled back his hand, forced himself to look away from the golden arm cuff. *Pain then, pain now.* Had she thought it to him? He shook his head. No, surely not, but the fact was he'd never had that particular thought in his life. He would not touch the arm cuff again. He didn't want to be hurled into another vision from long-ago Egypt. He was here, now, in Bowness-on-Windemere, with beautiful Miranda Wolffe, her daughter, P.C., Barnaby, once an orphaned stable boy whose status continued to be in limbo, and his own small son, Pip. They'd accepted Lord Lyle's invitation to spend a month at Sedgwick House. They were here for pleasure, not for ancient spirits. It was a precious time to relax and enjoy, not to write, not to worry about what had happened in ancient Egypt. He turned away, forced himself to walk to where a dozen Egyptian gods and goddesses, many of them he couldn't identify, were displayed on beautiful velvet-draped stands. Of course he recognized the three statues of Amun-Ra, the king of the gods, the sun god, supposedly the first pharaoh of Egypt. The first statue presented him as a man wearing a double-plumed crown; the second, a snow-white ram; and the last one, oddly, Amun-Ra was a goose. Each statue was a foot tall, each painted with still-vibrant colors in exquisite detail, down to the placid look on the goose's face that made Grayson smile and lightly touch his fingertips to the smooth surface. Luckily, the goose didn't look at him or say anything.

A voice came from the doorway. "It always seemed strange to me that Amun-Ra would choose to present himself as a goose, but his name— Amun—means 'hidden one' or 'mysterious of form.' So aside from enjoying species ambiguity, I suppose Amun-Ra didn't want anyone to know who he was when he strolled about through Egypt—or waddled. I wonder if anyone was fooled?"

CHAPTER TWO

Grayson turned to his host, Vivien Hastings, Lord Lyle, a friend of his father's. Lord Lyle was an Egyptologist of some renown with enough money to plunder tombs with enthusiastic abandon and bring his booty back to England. Grayson said, "If they didn't recognize the goose as Amun-Ra, he could have ended up in a family's cook pot."

He'd tried for a jest, but Lord Lyle said in all seriousness, "I've wondered the same thing myself, but I suppose that as the god of everything, Amun-Ra would squawk or wave a wing, and the family would fall prostrate at his webbed feet. Your father told me that in addition to being a popular author of otherworldly adventures—and yes, I have read several of your novels and enjoyed them immensely, scared me half to death—ah, where was I?"

"My father, sir?"

"Oh yes, your father told me your interests are far-ranging, Mr. Sherbrooke, as evidenced by your success as an author. He assured me you are not an ignoramus in Egyptology."

Well, not quite an ignoramus. Grayson pictured the small statue of the god Horus—a man's body with its hawk head, the son of Osiris and Isis, protector of kings—given to him by his father on his ninth birthday. "When I was very young," he said, "my father took me to visit Lord Ingelthorpe in Norwich, who'd returned from Luxor with a score of stone tablets covered with pictures and hieroglyphs. Since we couldn't read the hieroglyphs, my father and I studied the drawings of the men and women, and I made up stories of what the people were thinking, doing, what they would say to each other. Some were recognizable as farmers, weavers, beer makers. As I recall, there were always demons and other malevolent creatures involved, hovering, ever close."

"Ah, even then you were a weaver of tales."

"Not very good ones, I'm afraid," Grayson said, but he remembered how his child's ghost stories had scared his cousins witless. Then again, ten-year-olds were not a terribly critical audience. "Later, I was fortunate because my don at Oxford was an Egyptian enthusiast. His pride and joy were two small statues of Isis and Anubis."

Lord Lyle wrapped his hands around the statue of Anubis, the one Grayson knew guarded Nefret's gold arm cuff. "Ah, Anubis," Lord Lyle said, his voice filled with affection. "How I love his name. It flows off the tongue. You know Isis was his aunt. Anubis shepherded the dead to the hall of judgment. I shouldn't have wanted Anubis's job, for if the dead person's heart failed to balance Ma'at's ostrich feather of truth, Anubis handed him over to Ammut, the devourer of the dead." He paused. "I've wondered if my heart would balance Ma'at's feather of truth or be dragged off by Ammut to be thrown to a crocodile. I find it strange the Egyptians believed paradise was lazing about by the Nile, sipping barley beer." He shook his head. "On the other hand, the Nile is rightfully regarded as the giver of life."

"So their afterlife mimicked life itself."

Lord Lyle grinned. "Just as our heaven does, I suppose. Imagine if you failed Ma'at's feather test. An ostrich feather determining your afterlife fate? It fair to makes my blood curdle."

Grayson wondered if his heart, which also contained his soul, would balance the feather of truth. Would his good deeds outweigh his rotten deeds?

He watched Lord Lyle gently pick up the golden arm cuff from its red velvet bed. It didn't appear Lord Lyle was affected by the cuff at all. He stared at it a moment and set it back on its stand.

Grayson pointed to a small sarcophagus set apart from three other large sarcophagi, a shining gold beacon studded with silver, lapis lazuli, jasper, and garnets. Beside the small sarcophagus sat its outside larger granite coffin, open, covered with carved hieroglyphs, the artists' renderings of gods and goddesses and the workers and servants who accompanied the deceased to aid him in the afterlife—several women wearing white robes to their knees, making wheat into bread or weaving the flax into linen for clothing.

He pointed to the hieroglyphs on the granite coffin. "I see no name of the child who is inside."

Lord Lyle gaped at him. "What is this? You can read the hieroglyphs, Mr. Sherbrooke?"

"I assure you, sir, my knowledge is rudimentary. I was fortunate that Champollion was translating the hieroglyphs when I was at Oxford, and I was a member of the Christ Church Hieroglyph Club. I've many times wondered if the Rosetta Stone had never been found, would we still not realize hieroglyphs are a language."

"Man is many times an embarrassment, a violent one at that, Mr. Sherbrooke, in his ignorance, in his assumptions. He is also endlessly curious, always seeking, wanting to know everything. I believe we would have come to the truth, with or without the Rosetta Stone. How? I don't know. You're right about the boy in the gold sarcophagus—there is no name." Lord Lyle pointed to hieroglyphs carved into the empty granite coffin beside it and read aloud, *"I pass to the world of the dead with no name. I beg Osiris, oh mighty god of judgment, to grant me mercy."* Lord Lyle ran a finger down the side. "It is exquisite, is it not? A coffin fit for a prince. It is not pure gold, of course, but plaster covered with gilt. Look at the crook and flail he holds tightly over his chest, and his headdress—incredible detail and covered with gold, turquoise and lapis. It bespeaks wealth, mayhap royalty. But if so, why has he no name? It makes no sense to me. Inside I would expect to find his mummy surrounded by *ushabti*. Do you know what *ushabti* are, Mr. Sherbrooke?"

Grayson nodded. "Funerary figurines—manual laborers, hoes on their shoulders, baskets on their backs, ready to do any physical labor in the afterlife. Aren't there any *ushabti* in the sarcophagus?"

"Alas, I do not know—I will never know. When the sarcophagus was moved, I did hear something move inside. Perhaps *ushabti*, but I don't know, mayhap something much larger. I would like to know, of course, but I was warned if I opened the sarcophagus my family would die painful deaths. One would usually take such a nonsensical curse with a grain of salt, but if you read the hieroglyphs on the side of the granite coffin, you will take it as seriously as I do. Come, look, Mr. Sherbrooke."

Grayson looked and read the inscription.

> *Open this keeper of my spirit*
> *and know the agony of a thousand burning spears.*
> *See your children disappear into the stygian blackness,*
> *shrieking their pain and hatred of you.*
> *Attend me or you will know mortal agony without end.*

Grayson hadn't realized he'd read the curse aloud, in English, fluently, without pause.

CHAPTER THREE

Lord Lyle looked shocked. He whispered, "Young sir, you amaze me. Your ability is far beyond rudimentary."

Grayson's heartbeat had kicked up, but he managed to say easily enough, "The curse is straightforward and simply transcribed." He realized Lord Lyle was still staring at him, so he quickly added, "Why the curse, I wonder? I grant it is a meaty one, but if an unknown boy lies within, royal or not, who would care? Or is the curse simply to frighten tomb robbers away?"

Lord Lyle said, "I don't know. Look beneath the curse. These are the only drawings of the boy, if it is indeed he."

Grayson went down on his haunches and studied the panels. The boy, about Barnaby's age, prepared to throw a silver disc to a running young man, looking over his shoulder at the boy, his hand raised to catch it. But the boy didn't throw it to the young man; he hurled the disc into the fast-moving waters of the Nile. The disc didn't sink. It hovered over the water before coming to settle atop a small wave, floating light as a feather. The boy raced after it. The next painting showed the same small boy lying on his back on a narrow bed, wearing only a loincloth, his arms crossed over his thin chest, his eyes closed. He looked dead. He was alone. There were no more drawings.

Lord Lyle said, "I have studied the final drawing, as have those I consider experts. All agree since there are no visible wounds, mayhap he caught a deadly fever or drowned. But if he did not die by natural causes, then why would the scribe beg Osiris for mercy?" Lord Lyle paused and drew himself up. "I have concluded the boy was poisoned. By whom? If he was royalty, it was to remove him from the path of succession."

Grayson nodded. "You have found nothing about the boy, who he was or who his family was? About what the disc means? His hurling it into the river—the Nile, I assume?—and watching it float away?"

Lord Lyle traced his fingers over the hieroglyphs. "No one can explain it. The Nile, yes. Some agree with me, some do not. I even wrote to Monsieur Champollion, but he never deigned to reply. He's French, of course."

Suddenly Lord Lyle yelled, his hand out, "No! Mr. Sherbrooke, do not touch the boy's face!"

His warning came too late. Grayson had lightly touched his finger-tip to the gilded boy's nose. As if he'd touched a flame, burning heat seared into his flesh. He jerked his hand back and rubbed the finger. As quickly as it had struck, the stab of heat was gone, simply gone as if it had never happened. He stared down at the stylized mask of the boy's face. Thankfully, he hadn't been drawn into a vision. What would have happened?

Lord Lyle rushed to him, looking distressed. "Bloody hell, sir, forgive me. I should have warned you immediately. Are you all right? Is the pain unbearable? Oh dear, I myself touched the boy's nose once—only once—and nearly jumped to the ceiling the pain was so great. Nothing would alleviate it, not the physician's potions, not any of my dear Lucy's creams. It was as if my finger had been flayed open. Raw and pulsing and putrid matter oozed out of it. The physician believed he would have to amputate my finger, for he claimed a poison was inside me, but I wouldn't let him. My Lucy agreed with me and dismissed the physician.

"Then, as if by magic, after exactly twenty-four hours, the pain stopped and my finger looked as if nothing had ever happened. I'm sorry, sir, but now you must suffer for a full day. Is it dreadful?" Lord Lyle made no move to examine Grayson's finger. With the description he'd just been given, Grayson didn't blame him.

Grayson said carefully, "Exactly a full day?"

"Yes. It was as if whatever it was that had attacked my finger knew when the clock struck the twenty-fourth hour and left. No more pain. My finger was once again whole, no sign of a burn, no sign of rot or pus, no sign there was ever a wound. Shall I ask Lucy to examine your finger, Mr. Sherbrooke? Are you in terrible agony? Is your finger raw and red?"

Grayson quickly pulled a handkerchief from his pocket and wrapped it around his finger. "Do not worry, sir. I will deal with my finger myself."

Lord Lyle studied the young man a moment, marveling at his fortitude, for surely the pain should be making him scream, but no, he looked to be in no distress at all. He said, staring at the wrapped finger, "I had of course touched the sarcophagus both before and after I'd bought it, and nothing ever happened. It was always warm to the touch, nothing more. Then I remembered there'd been a golden guard molded over the nose, for protection, I came to realize. It was evidently lost during the journey to England. More like stolen by one of the sailors because it was pure gold." His eyes fastened again on the stylized boy's face. "It was the sheerest happenstance I chanced to touch the nose—only the nose—and I was blighted. I look at you, Mr. Sherbrooke, and I am amazed, sir."

Grayson ducked his head, said nothing, and pretended to study the panels of the boy's coffin.

Lord Lyle said, "I have come to believe that touching the boy's nose is a warning of the curse's potency. It certainly gives evidence of a long-lived curse. Perhaps a preview of what would happen if one were tempted to open the sarcophagus." He paused a moment, looked uncomfortable, and plowed ahead. "Mr. Sherbrooke, I know of your reputation. I have read your novels about otherworldly beings—ghosts, demons, wicked spirits, all dispatched by your hero, Thomas Straithmore. And I have wondered: are your stories based on your own experiences? Are they fact rather than fiction? I have read your new book, *The Resident Evil at*

Blackthorn Manor is about vicious demons in Scotland and how Thomas Straithmore destroyed them. A pity it won't be published for six more months as your books both amuse and terrify. I was told you spoke of Loch Leven in this book. I know you have an aunt and uncle who live in Vere Castle, on the shores of the loch. So will the experiences be fact?"

Yes, he had written the real name—Loch Leven. Well, he'd have to be more careful in the future. But Grayson was well used to this question, and so he repeated what he always said when asked: "It is all fiction, my lord, all fiction. I used Loch Leven for the simple reason it is well known to me, and my direct knowledge added verisimilitude. Nothing more than that."

CHAPTER FOUR

Lord Lyle studied Grayson's face for a moment and sighed. He appeared philosophic. "I can usually tell when a person is lying to me, but you, sir, are quite excellent at it. A lie? I cannot be sure."

Lord Lyle sighed again. "Oh well, I suppose what is inside the coffin will remain a mystery for all time. I hope you and your family will enjoy yourselves here at Sedgwick House. My man, Manu, is not accompanying me this time to Egypt. He tells me he gets bilious onboard ship, and he no longer wants to roast in the interminable heat in Egypt. He will see to your needs. Manu once asked me to call him George, said it made him feel more acceptable in this sodden foreign land, which he has come to love. I told him I could not, he was not a George. If you hear him refer to himself as George, simply disregard it and call him Manu.

"Now, if there is one single month in the year when you won't perhaps be soaked to your bones by continuous rain, it is the end of August through September. Come, Mr. Sherbrooke."

Grayson gave one last look at Anubis, standing still and tall in his guardian's place hovering over the golden arm cuff, Nefret's arm cuff.

Lord Lyle carefully locked the door, turned back to Grayson, and pressed the key and a small book into his hand. "It is my journal, sir. I ask you to read it. I hope you will find it enlightening. Perhaps it will make you curious. Ah, if you feel so inclined, perhaps you can discover who or what is in the small gold coffin. I know there is something inside—there is weight, something heavier than the expected *ushabti*. It moves about when you lift the coffin. Is it the unknown boy's mummy? Or something else?

"Let me caution you not to allow your children into the room. I venture to say it might not be healthy for them to wander amongst the marvels."

Grayson nodded. He wasn't about to let any of them cross the threshold.

Lord Lyle looked to where his lachrymose wife—twenty years his junior and nearly blind as a bat—stood in the long, wide entry hall, speaking with Miranda, Pip, P.C., and Barnaby, all three children, for once, standing still and quiet beside Miranda, staring up at the very pretty lady who couldn't see them clearly.

He said low to Grayson, "Lucy hides it well, but truth is, without her glasses, I have to lead her around. Even with her glasses it isn't much better, but my Lucy has a fine inner-eye. It was she who convinced me that paying five hundred pounds for that boy's sarcophagus was a bargain." He leaned in close. "She knows when something ancient is real or fake. She assured me the sarcophagus is quite real. When I told her you and your family were coming, she smiled and patted my arm and told me you wouldn't be able to resist a mystery needing to be solved." He paused, frowned. "Your finger, Mr. Sherbrooke. I do not understand. You do not appear to be suffering as you should, as I did."

Grayson was prepared this time. "Perhaps I didn't touch the nose in precisely the cursed spot."

Lord Lyle nodded. "Yes, yes, that must be it. Otherwise, you would be bellowing with the agony of it. Do you know, my beloved wife did not tell me I shouldn't touch the nose? Ah, I suppose an inner-eye cannot see everything, but who knows when—" Lord Lyle shook his hand, bowed to Miranda, gave a nervous look to the three children, and shepherded his wife, in mid-sentence, to the waiting carriage.

"Papa, we want to go to the treasure room!"

Did all children have bat ears?

"Yes, sir, please, we will not touch anything," P.C. said, giving him her best pitiful orphan look, which would have smote him not long before, but not now. Barnaby tried to look as pitiful as P.C., but he couldn't manage it since he was bouncing on his feet, his blue eyes blazing with excitement.

Grayson said in his sternest parent voice, "Listen to me carefully, all of you. I have the only key, so no one will go into that room. I want all of you to promise me you won't try to pick the lock on the door."

He gave each of them a hard look and said again, "Promise me."

Slowly, unwillingly, P.C. and Barnaby nodded, but Pip was made of stern stuff. "Why, Papa? Mrs. Moon told us it was a 'bunch of nasty foreign gods,' and who cared?"

"That's right, sir," P.C. said. "She said paying good English money for godless statues was foolish, probably wasn't right."

Pip said, "I want to see the foreign gods. I've only seen your statue of Anubis. You can go with us. Please, Papa?"

"No, Pip. And that is final. Do not ask me again."

Miranda cocked her head at him in question. She was wondering, of course, at his extreme reaction. Thankfully, she kept her own voice stern. "P.C., Barnaby, you will obey Grayson. You will not ask again."

"But—"

"No, Pip," Grayson said, "and that's an end to it." He left the entrance hall quickly to avoid more pleas, and walked into the drawing room, long and narrow, with windows giving onto the beautifully scythed lawn that sloped down to Lake Windemere. He unwrapped his handkerchief from around his finger. He felt no searing agony, saw no sign of rot, no pus, no sign that anything harmful had happened. He knew Lord Lyle hadn't invented the story of the twenty-four hours of agony. He'd seen the remembered pain clearly in his eyes when he'd spoken of it. Grayson was left with questions: Why hadn't the curse struck him the same way? Or was his simply a warning rather than—what? Punishment? Why? Did it have anything to do with Nefret? Jabari?

His knowledge of hieroglyphs was indeed rudimentary—he hadn't lied to Lord Lyle. So how had he been able to read the curse so easily? And what of the young girl and Jabari and smelling pomegranates? He felt the familiar rush of excitement. It was the unknown calling.

He heard the children arguing in the entrance hall, heard Miranda's soothing voice and the magic words—*lemonade* and *cakes*—then running feet toward the kitchen at the back of Sedgwick House.

He looked down at his finger and wondered.

CHAPTER FIVE

The next morning was sunny and warm, and thankfully dry. A stroke of good fortune, or more like a miracle, Mrs. Moon, the housekeeper, had said, shaking her tightly curled gray head.

Grayson sat cross-legged beneath an oak tree on the bank of Lake Windemere, Lord Lyle's journal in one hand, an apple in the other. He read:

Khufu is a wily old man whose entire village of Tiye has robbed tombs for centuries, he proudly told me, and they live well off the proceeds. Khufu is their representative, their mayor of sorts and leader of the village, who assigns tasks. I told him I wanted something special, something I could donate to the British Museum after my death and be known forever.

Ah, he said, and Khufu and his three sons settled me onto a donkey, who liked to bare his big teeth at me. After leaving Lucy to drink lemonade in the shade of a mulberry tree with villagers hovering about her offering her dates and figs, we rode to the Valley of the Kings, a vast royal burial site across the Nile from Luxor and Karnak, once known as Thebes, the capital city of Egypt. I remember being astounded to learn that at its height, eighty thousand people lived in Thebes. I was told this was possible because the inundations had never failed in living memory. Inundations are the yearly flooding of the Nile that cover the surrounding lands with rich and fertile mud to grow barley, wheat, and flax. But I digress.

Khufu had disguised the tomb entrance with piles of rocks and spiny shrubs. I was grateful for my high thick leather boots because scorpions and venomous snakes abounded. I followed Khufu and his three sons into a hot, fetid, low-ceilinged tunnel, their torches providing the only light. It smelled vile, like ancient death and rot. We walked for what seemed an hour before Khufu stopped beside a wall, pressed a rock, and a large stone section slid open. He said one of his sons had accidentally shoved on the wall in that exact spot, and it had swung back. We passed into a small chamber, empty save for a small golden sarcophagus lying on a granite slab, and beside it another granite coffin in which the small golden one had rested. The lid was gone and it was quite empty, which was to be expected. Khufu told me there had been nothing else in this small hidden room, no ornaments, no statuary, no treasures, no artists' rendering of gods and goddesses and workers and servants. I stood there mesmerized by the boy's features, as stylized as any I'd seen, yet there was something more realistic about his face than other sarcophagi. His vivid black eyes were lined deeply with kohl, the amazing headdress studded with turquoise, lapis lazuli, and hematite, as bright today as millennia ago. Surely he was the child of a very wealthy family, even a royal prince, since he held the crook and flail over his chest. I was drawn again to the boy's face, and it was then I saw the molded piece of gold covering his nose. Khufu didn't know what it meant, but he urged me to leave it in place, and I saw he was glancing furtively about the small chamber, as if that ancient devourer of souls, Ammut, would leap out and drag him away. I must admit, I felt something in that still, dead air that made me shudder.

As suddenly as the fear had hit me, it was gone. The sarcophagus beckoned to me, not with unknown ancient words ringing in my head to frighten me, but the air around it seemed to pulse, to draw me in, make me want to touch it, more, to protect it, and I knew I was meant to have the sarcophagus. I am not a superstitious man, not a man prone to fancies from the Other Side, nor am I a stupid man, but oddly, I did not haggle with Khufu. I told him immediately that I wanted to buy it.

Khufu drew me aside from his three sons and said that before I bought the sarcophagus he had to tell me the warning. The village priest—an ancient specimen whose eyes were covered with white veils and who sat on palm leaves all day, seeing nothing and everything, so it was said—had warned Khufu the sarcophagus was never to be opened, that what was inside would destroy him and his family, mayhap even the entire village, mayhap all the world, mayhap even Amun-Ra and Osiris in the underworld. He said he would be blasted if he did not tell me. How he could possibly know this, I do not know, but I believe Khufu told me the truth only because the old priest ordered him to, and I saw clearly Khufu was afraid. Of course Khufu told me he'd only agreed to sell it to me because all knew of my respect and reverence for the gods and goddesses of Egypt, and thus he knew the sarcophagus was meant for such as me, that I would honor it, keep it safe. He was right about that. He added slyly it was very likely a pharaoh's son, didn't I agree? I mean, the gold, the crook and flail, the exquisite gemstones inside in the gold?

Five hundred pounds Khufu demanded.

Like many others, I studied the carved hieroglyphs with no success until Jean-François Champollion announced in 1822 that hieroglyphs were an actual language, and he'd gleaned this understanding from the Rosetta Stone with its three languages saying the same thing. At last, at last, I would be able to make out most of the hieroglyphs on the granite coffin. I found myself wondering if the sarcophagus held the mummy of the boy king, Tutankhamun, for I'd heard his name whispered in the village among the old men, *but perhaps their hints that this could be Tutankhamun were meant simply to convince me to part with five hundred pounds. In Egypt, I could only trust my own brain, my experience, and my wife, Lucy.*

I remember when I placed the boy's coffin in my treasure room, Lucy rested her palm on its chest, then withdrew it. She said only that she wondered if what was within the coffin had journeyed to the Land of the Reeds—the Egyptian afterlife for those who'd passed the feather test, a reference, of course, to the banks of the Nile, which brought life to all the inhabitants.

And then she said, "I wonder if what is within was placed there by the mighty Seti, father of Ramses II, or perhaps by Amun-Ra himself. But I do know, husband, whatever is inside must remain locked away."

Amun-Ra, the most powerful god of all that vast Egyptian lot of deities? He was the Egyptian Zeus and Jupiter—not just one of the gods, he was The God.

Then Lucy whispered, "To open the sarcophagus will invite havoc. Do not be tempted to do it, my husband."

"What sort of havoc?" I asked her, but she didn't know, said she saw a veil and it lifted for just an instant, and she beheld chaos, screaming, wailing, blackness. I asked Manu, my faithful servant, a native, and utterly loyal to me, about a veil and chaos. You see, Manu had told me he descended from a long line of priests who had special knowledge, all the way back to Ramses II. Manu leaned in close and whispered that demons and spirits preferred a child's sarcophagus. They liked to snuggle with each other around and into the small mummy and make their plans. What plans? Manu didn't know. It was simply knowledge buried deep with him and all those priests before him. I asked him why he was a servant and not a priest like his ancestors, and he merely shook his head and would not reply. But I remember he gave me a long look I could not decipher.

Khufu had said he'd refused to sell it to others, only to me.

That was a lie, clean and simple. Five hundred pounds. Of course no one had bought it.

Lucy reminded me I was paying Manu such a low wage, and he as loyal to me as a tick, willing to do anything I asked of him, that it quite offset the five hundred pounds for the sarcophagus. Yes, she told me, it was a bargain—in the long run. And so I paid the five hundred pounds and brought the unknown boy's sarcophagus to England.

Grayson thought, *And you continue to pay Manu a low wage?* But he didn't say it aloud.

"Papa, Miranda said we're going to feed the swans, and she sent me to invite you to come."

Grayson looked up to see Pip standing over him, his precious face so like his mother, Lorelei, except for his Sherbrooke blue eyes and stubborn jaw. He would be tall like the Sherbrooke men when he gained years, and he was sturdy, thankfully as healthy as a stoat, again like the Sherbrookes. Pip grabbed his hand and began tugging. "Come on, Papa, the swans are hungry. We must hurry or they'll chew on Miranda's fingers."

Grayson closed the journal, slipped it into his jacket pocket, and walked toward the dock, where at least a dozen swans were circling Miranda, Barnaby, and P.C. as they walked toward him, all three of them laughing, Miranda and P.C. flapping their skirts to keep them back, Barnaby yelling at a nipping swan. Grayson realized in that moment the five of them had become a family, his family, and such a short time it had been. Beautiful Miranda, a widow he'd met such a short time ago; her precocious eight-year-old daughter, P.C., whose real name she refused to say aloud; and Barnaby, who had no last name, a babe left on the steps of the village church and brought to Wolffe Hall by Miranda's father-in-law, Lord Wolffe, known far and wide as "The Great," and become a stable boy, a boy who'd always seemed somehow familiar to Grayson. And his own small son, Pip. They'd all come together after the strange adventure at Wolffe Hall.

Grayson breathed in the sweet warm air as he watched them.

A month of rest and exploration and play with the children here in Bowness-on-Windermere. No writing, he'd promised Miranda. Then, unbidden, he thought of what Lucy, Lady Lyle, had said about the sarcophagus: *"I wonder if what is within was placed there by the mighty Seti, father of Ramses II, or perhaps by Amun-Ra himself. Whatever is inside must remain locked away."*

Grayson once again felt the familiar leap of excitement.

CHAPTER SIX

"Papa, you won't forget, will you?"

Grayson looked down at his boy's dirty face and muddy clothes. "No, Pip, I won't forget. Ah, forget what, exactly?"

"Papa, in four weeks and three days it's my birthday. I'll be five—I counted. I'll be a grown-up boy, and you won't need to hold my hand anymore."

Grayson strongly doubted when Pip attained his fifth year he would magically no longer want to run headlong into Lake Windemere, both P.C. and Barnaby racing behind him, screaming for him to hurry before anyone could stop them. Then he saw himself between his father and his uncle Douglas, and each held one of his small hands, and they were racing over the beach, naked and shouting, running full-tilt into the Channel, yelling and cursing as they splashed into the frigid water. What a wonderful day that had been. How old had he been? Pip's age? Lake Windemere wasn't as cold as the English Channel, so maybe—

He looked up when he heard Barnaby give a loud whistle. Again, Grayson felt a tug of familiarity looking at the boy. He must ask the vicar if he knew anything at all about Barnaby's origins. Barnaby was ten years old, red-headed, but during the summer months his hair had begun to lighten to blondish-brown. He was a handsome boy who liked being called a barn cat, proud of it he was. He continued to refuse to move into Wolffe Hall, content to live in the stable and help take care of the horses, despite P.C.'s arguments and rants. "Sir," P.C. had told him the day before, "Barnaby needs a last name. If we are to marry in the distant future when we are old like you and Mama, he must have a proper last name." And he'd promised to provide a list for her perusal. He did not doubt P.C. would make the decision since it would be her last name as well.

"Let's meet Miranda halfway," Grayson said to Pip, and off they went, Pip kicking pebbles with his toe as he skipped beside his father. "Manu said it doesn't stop raining even in the summer because the gods in the lake don't like foreign bodies swimming in their kitchen."

Grayson said slowly, "You mean like us?"

"Oh no, not us, Papa. We're special. Manu said we were supposed to come here. He said it was divined, whatever that means. I promised him we wouldn't swim in their kitchen."

"Pip, did Manu tell you why we were supposed to come to Bowness-on-Windemere? Why it was divined?"

"No, Papa, but I could tell he really believed it."

Grayson swallowed a laugh at the serious look on his son's face. They were supposed to come to Sedgwick Hall? Somehow they'd been meant to come?

Pip said, "Manu said most of the gods aren't here in September because they go on holiday. That's why there's not as much rain."

"Did he tell you where they go on holiday?"

"To London, to see where all the people got their heads chopped off at the Tower of London."

The lake gods sounded like a bloodthirsty lot. He said, "All right, Pip, now you must attend me. There are no gods in Lake Windemere." He saw this didn't go over well, so he added, "All right, say there are a few gods still hanging about now. Maybe they didn't want to go to London. How does Manu know it's their kitchen and not their drawing room or their water closet, which seems the most likely to me?"

Pip's face screwed up. "I don't know, Papa. All Manu wanted to talk about was all the rain here. It never stops, he said."

Grayson said, "But no rain today, Pip. Have you ever seen a brighter morning sun?"

Pip gave this due consideration. "It hasn't rained for two days. Manu said I must be magic." He preened.

You are magic, Grayson wanted to tell him.

"Manu says water is special where he comes from. That's Egypt, Papa, a place very far away. There's a lot of sand, and you can dig your toes in. I don't want to swim in a water closet."

Grayson laughed. "I don't either." Grayson couldn't begin to guess Manu's age, anywhere from forty to one hundred. He spoke perfect English and was watchful. To make certain they didn't filch the silver? Grayson was quickly learning Manu was a master at avoiding answering a question. And Lord Lyle was right—he'd heard Manu refer to himself as Mr. George.

Pip pulled away from his father and shouted, "P.C., Barnaby! Mr. Manu said after we feed the swans, we have to try to find a god in the lake. He said there may be enough gods for all of us, but probably not since most of them are in London."

Grayson rolled his eyes. Gods in Lake Windermere or in London. Oh well, why not? He saw Miranda Wolffe waving an umbrella at him. She'd told him, "I was duly warned by Lord Lyle's housekeeper, Mrs. Moon, never to trust a sun-filled sky." He saw her beautiful white-toothed smile as he came near. How was it, he wondered, that she became more beautiful every time he saw her? She threw her head back and breathed in deeply. "Smell the air, Grayson. It's sweet, like apples ready to be picked."

The air was sweet, but not with the smell of apples. No, it was jasmine. There were miles of the stuff, draped over stone fences, climbing up the sides of houses, some even twined around the oldest gravestones in the church cemetery. He looked at the children laughing and shouting at the honking swans swarming around them. Miranda gave the children chunks of bread and told them, "Don't forget, only a little bit at a time so every swan gets some, all right?"

The children began to run away from the swans, throwing the bread behind them, the swans soon in furious pursuit, white wings flapping.

Grayson shouted, "Do not go beyond that stone wall!" He turned back to Miranda, lifted a hank of hair, and put it behind her ear, beautiful thick stuff, the color of rich Somerset honey. "I spent two days in close quarters with Barnaby on our trip here. Do you agree his hair isn't as red, more brown and blond?"

"I hadn't noticed, but I think you're right. He will be eleven soon, according to the vicar. Only a month now I've been giving him lessons. Soon he will read and write as well as a little Etonian, so smart he is."

"You're an excellent teacher. Those blue eyes of his, Miranda, I'm sure I know him from somewhere. I'll think I've grasped it, but then it's gone. Even some of his mannerisms—the way he cocks his head to one side and stares at you, expecting you to divulge the secrets of the universe?"

"I know that look well. If he's upset and curses up a storm, he gives it to me. It works, most of the time."

"I've heard him spout out animal body parts I've never considered," Grayson said, and they both laughed.

Miranda heard her daughter shout, and turned to see P.C. running away from three swans, laughing like a hyena. She said, "I must give most of the credit to P.C. She smacks him whenever he falls back into stable cant or curses, then counsels him to keep his goal in mind, namely her as his wife, and she can't marry a boy who talks like a barn cat. Yes, yes, I'm coming to accept my precious daughter one day marrying an orphan with no family who calls himself a barn cat." She gave him a crooked smile.

He took her fine-boned white hand with its long, graceful fingers and lightly squeezed. "I would like to kiss you, but I fear P.C. would attack me with a broom."

Miranda patted his cheek, laughed again, and skipped away. She was pulling more bread out of another skirt pocket.

Grayson stood watching her play with the children, all of them throwing bread to the dozen swans honking and flapping around them. In that moment, he thought the air did smell like apples and another smell he couldn't identify. Pomegranates?

CHAPTER SEVEN

It was Sunday morning, and it wasn't raining. It was pouring.

"I told the mistress," Manu said in his soft, precise monotone as he poured Grayson his coffee, "the few remaining lake gods, those not on holiday in London, are angry. They have pumped themselves up and are pouring buckets of tears on us."

"But why would they cry if they're angry?" Pip asked Manu as Grayson buttered his toast. "Why wouldn't they spit on us? Or raise their leg like Otis?" He added, "Otis is our housekeeper's dog."

"The gods do not spit," Manu said. "They weep or smite you dead." He turned and left the entrance hall, a tall straight-shouldered man with a narrow band of white hair around an otherwise perfectly bald head. He always wore a white jacket over black trousers. Lord Lyle had told Grayson he could trust Manu implicitly. Manu could solve any problem, deal with any tradesman. As for the other servants—the cook, Mrs. Minor; the housekeeper, Mrs. Moon; and two housemaids, Glynis and Marigold—they all appeared to be a jolly lot and not at all put out by an invasion of two adults and three children. Grayson saw they treated Manu with great deference.

After breakfast, P.C. suffered her mother tucking her braids beneath a wide-brimmed bonnet. "Mr. Manu doesn't make any sense, Mama. I think he likes to speak in riddles. I'd smite him if I were one of his weeping lake gods."

Barnaby said, "When Mr. Manu shook me awake this morning he crossed himself. Mr. Manu's not Catholic, he's a heathen, so why would he do that? No, ma'am, don't blight me. I heard Lord Lyle say he was a heathen. Since Mr. Manu lives with Lord Lyle, he must know what he is." He leaned up and whispered, "Mr. Manu said me and P.C. and Pip had to be careful or we'd be washed away, dead and gone, and taken to the underworld where Anubis would bring us to this bloke Osiris to see if me and P.C. were worthy of passing on to the good place. I told Mr. Manu I didn't want to pass to any place, good or nasty, until I was old and wrinkled and didn't have any teeth."

"*I*, not *me*," Miranda said automatically. "I know it sounds funny when you put yourself first, Barnaby—'P.C. and Pip and I.' Now doesn't that sound better?"

Barnaby would have rolled his eyes, but he wasn't stupid. "Yes, ma'am."

P.C. punched him on his bony arm. "You hear, you looby? Listen to Mama. She knows everything."

The five of them, each with a black umbrella, walked from where Manu had stopped the carriage across the road from Saint Martin's church on Farfallow Road. They went through the open gate with a score of other worshipers and got into the long line of black umbrellas on the stone path weaving through the cemetery to the old church door.

Grayson saw Barnaby wave around at the headstones, heard him whisper to P.C., "I don't like this, P.C. Cozying up to moldy skeletons while you sing hymns? It bain't right."

And since it was Sunday and they were on the very steps of the church door, P.C. didn't smack him, merely whispered, "*Isn't* right, Barnaby, *isn't*. I don't like it either." She gave a little shudder.

It seemed the swans and ducks had their territories, the swans by Lake Windemere and the ducks in town. The town ducks accompanied the worshippers all the way from the road to the church door, then fanned out around them, oddly silent, waiting. There was a sign on the church door: *Ducks Do Not Enter God's House.*

Miranda whispered to Grayson, "Do you think there should be a comma after *Ducks*?"

A lady at Miranda's elbow smiled. "I have wondered the same thing, but no one, including Reverend Masters, knows the answer. Did you know the ducks are rewarded for their good behavior after services?"

Reverend John Masters, Church of England, rector of Saint Martin's, no older than fifty, was tall and straight, looked vigorous, and was blessed with a rich baritone that reached every pew clearly over the pounding rain on the roof. His rich head of gold hair shone under the spear of sun that somehow magically beamed into the church for three seconds during his homily involving sin in general and exhortations to the ladies present to honor and obey their husbands.

Grayson patted Miranda's hand and gave her a solemn nod. She whispered, "I wonder what Reverend Masters's wife has to say about this admonition? Ha, I say."

The three children occupied themselves with looking for leaks in the high wooden roof overhead, hopeful since the rain continued to pound hard. But they couldn't find any leaks, so they were soon squirming in their seats, poking each other.

Miranda breathed a sigh of relief when Reverend Masters gave his final blessing to the worshippers and announced the final hymn, "Now the Shining Day Is Past." Grayson wondered if Reverend Masters was indulging in irony. The congregation flung their hearts into the hymn, gave their all to sing louder than the hammering rain.

At the end of the service, Reverend Masters stood in the vestibule and introduced Grayson to the local gentry in attendance, saying with every introduction, "Mr. Sherbrooke is, of course, one of the Sherbrookes, the nephew of the Earl of Northcliffe." He didn't mention Grayson was a noted novelist, considering that métier, Grayson supposed, unworthy of a nephew of a peer of the realm. As for Miranda and the children, Reverend Masters was all smiles and welcome since they were, after all, guests of

Lord Lyle, a local philanthropist who kept the church coffers filled, when he remembered, and more, the blessed man had promised a new organ, a promise he would keep if reminded often enough. Reverend Masters knew some believed Lord Lyle eccentric, which he probably was, and some believed him dangerous, which Reverend Masters doubted, even with all his heathen statuary from faraway Egypt he kept in that special room of his, a room always locked, it was said in a whisper, mayhap to keep the malevolent spirits within.

If Reverend Masters wondered, in whispered conversation with his dutiful wife, Joanna, under the bedcovers at night, if Miranda was Grayson's mistress, the three children bastards, the whispers never left his bedchamber. The Sherbrooke family cast a large, very long shadow, and he considered it an honor he and his obedient Joanna were invited to dine at Sedgwick House the following Wednesday.

CHAPTER EIGHT

Once Miranda and Grayson were settled into the carriage opposite the children, the drenched umbrellas at their respective feet, rain slashing at the closed windows, the children had their heads together, whispering and laughing. Miranda said to Grayson, "We knew when I accepted your kind invitation to spend a month here in Bowness-on-Windemere there could be talk about my position in the household, particularly since I'm not chaperoned, even though I'm a widow of long-standing and no longer a young miss with a reputation to guard."

Grayson laughed at her. "That's you, long in the tooth, an affliction on the eyes, so ancient you've lost most of your teeth. Come on, Miranda, you know the rules. It's a pity your mother-in-law did not want to be separated from Alphonse."

"She told me Alphonse pined for her when she was gone for very long, and a month simply wasn't possible."

He gave her a crooked grin, thinking about how Miranda's mother-in-law adored Alphonse, a sixteenth-century gentleman who resided in a painting at Wolffe Hall. "I wonder how a man in a painting could pine? No, never mind. When I first met P.C., she told me your mother-in-law was a floater, and I discovered I agreed with her. She does sort of float, as if her small feet don't touch the ground."

P.C. called out, "I crawled behind Grandmama once without her knowing I was there, and I raised her skirt. Her slippers were on the ground. I was disappointed." She turned immediately back to Pip, who was tugging on her sleeve.

Miranda lowered her voice to a near whisper. "Remember how you reassured me we would be accepted, what with Lord Lyle's patronage and your illustrious antecedents? And still I doubted, people being what they are, particularly in a village. Today in church was the test." She gave him a huge grin. "We passed."

Barnaby called out, "Everybody smiled at us. Nobody thinks we're from the other side of the blanket."

"What blanket?" Pip asked.

P.C. poked Barnaby and said to Pip, "Barnaby is making a jest, which isn't at all funny. Barnaby, I told you no one would think we weren't proper. We're with Mr. Thomas Straithmore, a hero." She shot a look at Grayson. "Why didn't Reverend Masters tell everyone you are a hero, sir?"

Grayson smiled. "My dear P.C., my antecedents are far more impressive than my heroism."

"What's *antecedent* mean?" the three children asked at once.

"You all know my uncle is the Earl of Northcliffe. He is a very important fellow, a peer of the realm, renowned even amongst other very important fellows. The good reverend is far too smart to insult a Sherbrooke. I suspect most will follow his lead. My uncle is an excellent antecedent, and that means he was born before me and I carry his blood."

"I don't have no antecedents," Barnaby said. "I guess I don't have blood from anybody."

"I don't have *any* antecedents, not *no* antecedents. Of course you have blood from someone," P.C. said. "Remember when I punched you in the nose and you gushed out blood?"

"I smeared some on your face," Barnaby said with satisfaction.

"Yes, you did, and I hurt you, didn't I? But, Barnaby, we'll find out whose blood you have. We'll find out who your antecedents are." She looked over at Grayson. "Mr. Straithmore will find out, won't you, sir?"

Grayson said, "Yes, we will discover your antecedents, Barnaby." He wondered as he did often, *Who are you, Barnaby? Why are you familiar to me?*

Miranda leaned close and whispered, "I will do my part too, Grayson, to bolster our good names. A certain Lady Chivers and Mrs. Thurgood are evidently two of the local society mavens here in Bowness-on-Windemere, and they always have tea at Tilly's Tea Shop promptly at two o'clock on Saturdays. We met them briefly after Reverend Masters's service, do you remember?"

Grayson nodded, vaguely recalling two ladies of middle years, dressed lavishly in pink and lavender, huge straw hats on their crimped curls with plumes waving in their respective faces, the plumes slightly damp.

"The Great assured me their opinions are the ones that count, and so I plan to take my well-dressed, very demure, and proper ladylike self to the tea shop next Saturday and enjoy a comfortable prose with the two doyennes."

An eyebrow went up. "You didn't tell me."

"Well, no, no need." She paused, realizing P.C. was staring at her, and deftly changed the subject until the children were huddled together again, making plans. Oh dear, for what?

She said, one eye on P.C., "The Great told me Lady Chivers's mother, Clarice, had shared a brief flirtation with him around the turn of the century. I will assure them I am a respectable widow, you are a gentleman of great renown, and our children are well-behaved and really quite brilliant." She lowered her voice. "I will lie clean about Barnaby, tell the ladies he's a neighbor's son, a favorite of P.C.'s. I must tell you too, the five-pound note you put in the collection plate will be discussed by every family over dinner tonight, you can be sure of that."

"It was ten pounds."

She laughed and punched his arm, like P.C. did Barnaby. Grayson thought about Miranda's grandfather-in-law, called "The Great" by all those in the vicinity who cared about keeping their eardrums and hides intact, and about Major Charles Houston, his long-lost heir who now lived at Wolffe Hall, much to the delight of all the local unmarried ladies. The Great was a wily old man, and Grayson quite liked him.

Back at Sedgwick, they shared a luncheon of herbed potatoes, peas from the garden, baked pike fresh from Lake Windemere, and a delicious blancmange. Conversation was sometimes difficult, what with the rain pounding so heavily on the roof. Afterward, Grayson intended to visit the treasure room to study the unknown boy's coffin. But it was not to be. The rain trapped the children indoors, and that meant to keep the three of them from killing each other, and their parents from killing them, both Miranda and Grayson were required to play game after game of loo and hearts and old maid. Even Marigold and Glynis bravely volunteered themselves to amuse the children. Marigold won every game of old maid. She wasn't more than fifteen years old, a laughing girl with shiny brown hair. Pip, Grayson saw, had sidled up to stand beside her, to help her pick the right cards, he told everyone, and Marigold had laughed and hugged him.

CHAPTER NINE

MONDAY MORNING

Grayson couldn't believe it. He woke up to blue skies and warm, dry air. He regarded the bright sun as nothing short of a miracle, but Manu and Mrs. Moon only smiled and nodded. He confessed to Manu he'd been close to ordering up an ark the previous day. Manu said only, "No tears from the gods today." Whatever that meant.

The swans were out in force to greet the townsfolk, their honks filling the air, and life once again blossomed outdoors.

Grayson, Miranda, and the three children walked through the lovely hilly town, greeting people they'd met at church the day before, stopping at each of the long line of shops, buying ices for the children, a piece of jewelry for Miranda, and a pipe for The Great, although he didn't smoke. Grayson was pleased to see Miranda was right—everyone not only knew about them, everyone was pleasant, particularly, he thought cynically, since they were freely spending groats. Evidently, they were considered a nice addition to the town.

Until they reached the small leather shop just off the main street. Grayson decided he was in need of a new belt, and giving the local leather master, Mr. Samuel Philpot—an old curmudgeon he'd heard him described by Mrs. Allenby, the local seamstress—his custom seemed prudent. They walked into the dimly lit interior that smelled of linseed oil, leather, and jasmine from the trailing vines outside the shop. There were no customers within, only Mr. Philpot, a monk's tonsure of thick gray hair circling his head, his face seamed and dry, looking as leathery as his goods. His hands were gnarled, his fingers arthritic. He stood behind a table efficiently threading a square silver buckle through a narrow black leather belt. He looked up at them and stilled.

Grayson stepped forward. "Good day, Mr. Philpot, I'm—"

He got no further. Mr. Philpot interrupted him, his voice rough and sharp, sounding as if from the bottom of a deep well. "Aye, I figured ye'd come, sooner or later. Linin' everyone's pockets, I hear, ingratiatin' yerself. Not stupid, are ye? An' everyone believin' yer so nice, but I know the truth. Ye, sir, ye can't be the father to all three o' the brats—ye're too young. And that older one wi' the hint of wicked red hair, gives him the look of a monkey wot gone awry. Here, young'un, can ye speak, or will ye spout gibberish? Will ye swing from the leather saddles hanging from the ceiling?"

Barnaby was so stunned, he could only stare at Mr. Philpot, his blue eyes wide, his mouth agape. P.C., however, stepped smartly forward. "See here, Mr. Philpot, his name is Barnaby, and he is my future husband. If you wish to call him a monkey, you must inquire whether or not I approve. I do not. You are not a nice man."

The old man laughed, showing three remaining teeth that didn't look long for his mouth. "Smart mouth on ye, little miss. I see ye haf the look o' yer mither. Will ye be like 'er when ye grows up?"

"I hope so, Mr. Philpot. Mama's beautiful and ever so smart and kind."

"Now she'd haf to be beautiful, wouldn't she?" And he leered at Grayson, a look thankfully lost on the children.

Grayson was ready to pick the old man up with a leather belt around his neck. He could practically see smoke coming from Miranda's ears, saw her open her mouth to blast him, but it was Pip who cocked his head to one side and said, "What do you mean, sir?"

"I means yer mither 'as to look beautiful, else what nob would want 'er? Then she'd be in a ditch, now wouldn't she, ye little blighters wit' her?"

Pip didn't understand, but Grayson did. Before he could grab his son, Pip stepped forward, his small hands on his hips. "See here, sir, my mother is in heaven with the angels. You will be nice to Miranda or my papa will kick your chops."

Grayson felt a burst of pride, but enough was enough, and he didn't want any of them to leap upon this nasty old man and pound him. He set Pip aside and said very quietly, "I do not understand your rudeness, sir. I believe we should adjourn outside your shop, away from my family, and discuss what—"

Mr. Philpot's eyes rolled back in his head and he fell in a heap to the floor on his side, then flipped to his back, the long leather belt curling over his chest like a snake.

Miranda went down on her hands and knees and lightly slapped his face. "Mr. Philpot, wake up!" She slapped him again, and he moaned, opened his eyes, and looked up, beyond Miranda, to Grayson.

"Let me out, let me out, let me out." He repeated it over and over, not sharp and clear, but slurred, thick with a foreign smear. Then he closed his eyes and began to snore.

Miranda rose slowly to her feet. She was trembling, but she wasn't about to let the children see it. "It appears, Grayson, if you still want to order a belt, you will have to return. Mr. Philpot is enjoying a nap. Come along, children."

P.C. tugged on her mother's hand. "But, Mama, what did he mean, *Let me out, let me out?*"

"Nothing," Grayson said, herding them out of the shop. "He didn't mean anything."

"I ain't no awry monkey," Barnaby said. "Miserable old bounder."

P.C. stared at him. "You said a lot there, Barnaby, and most of it wrong. You sounded like a barn cat again. Mama, should I clout him?"

CHAPTER TEN

A hot wind ruffled his hair and blew against his face, drying the sweat on his brow. The brutal sun beat down, but he was used to that. He stood on the banks of the Nile amid the waving long-armed reeds that grew in profusion along the shore. He wore a simple linen wrap belted by a plain twist of leather. He looked down at his sandals, made for him of leather, covered with the stoutest papyrus. They fit his feet well.

He admitted he was pleased and anxious, both balled together in his belly. He was an architect, and he was to meet with Vizier Merti about the pharaoh's new project, a pleasure garden with a huge lake in the middle, golden bridges crossing it. Afterward he would see Nefret. Perhaps they could—

He heard the footsteps before he saw a man running at him, a knife held up, ready to stab downward, into his heart. It was Sadek the magician, evil to his core, he knew it, and Sadek hated him because of Nefret. He felt fury and blood roar through him. He pulled his ivory-handled knife his father had given him from his belt and began to circle the panting man.

Sadek yelled at him, "You won't have her, do you hear me,

you puling young scoundrel? I will kill you now, and you will be gone forever."

He shouted, "Sadek, why do you not blight me into dust with a wave of your hand? How is it you dare to attack me yourself? You are suddenly brave?"

Sadek's face was contorted with raw hatred. "I want to see the blood gush out of your heart. I want to feel it wet on my hands." Sadek was running at him like an enraged bull, slashing out with his knife, chanting, "I saw the cuff. She could speak of nothing else. Of course I heard about it, and I knew it was you who gave it to her. She's mine, do you hear me? I will kill you, kill you."

"Grayson! Wake up, you're having a nightmare!" Miranda shook his shoulders and slapped his face once, then again. She'd heard him cry out through the thin bedchamber wall and had come running. He was twisting in the covers, moaning. On the third slap, harder this time, Grayson grabbed her wrist and twisted. She cried out in pain. "Grayson! Stop!"

"Nefret? You struck me?" His voice sounded harsh, slurred as a drunkard's, and oddly, he sounded foreign. He pulled her down on top of him, only he wasn't himself, he wasn't Grayson, he was Jabari, and he'd loved Nefret since the first time he'd seen her laughing with friends on the edge of the Nile, a small wooden boat in her hands, ready for a competition. He wanted her, wanted her—

Miranda was too stunned to move. She felt the long length of him beneath her, knew he was naked beneath the single blanket, felt the beat of his heart through the thin lawn of her nightgown. He was squeezing her tightly against him, as if she were his lifeline, as if he wanted to consume her. He was breathing hard, still locked in the nightmare. Miranda didn't fight him. She managed to get her arm loose and touched her palm to his cheek. "Grayson, look at me. It's Miranda. You're all right. It was a nightmare, a bad one, but you're back now."

"He was going to stab me in the heart. He wanted my blood on his hands, and that's why he didn't smite me dead with a curse. I did not know if I could stop him." Grayson felt the hot breeze, the wild pumping of his heart, the blackness of Sadek's rage, his hatred, jealousy. And now he had his beautiful Nefret in his arms, against him, his beautiful girl, she was his, only his. "Nefret." He knew he would die if he didn't have her. Grayson lurched up, grabbed her face between his hands, and began kissing her, hard, thrusting his tongue into her mouth, his hands on her breasts, kneading her, caressing her frantically.

Miranda was stunned at the wild surge of lust that flooded her. She knew what it was, what it meant, and she knew she had to pull away, had to get away from him before she ripped off her white lawn nightgown and attacked him. She tried to jerk away, but he wouldn't let her go.

He was saying into her mouth, "Nefret, why do you fight me?" He was mad with lust, his hands wild on her hips, pulling her against him, molding her bottom against him, wanting, wanting. He would die if she didn't open to him.

Miranda knew he was still beyond her, without control, now caught up in a long-ago lust for a woman named Nefret. His hands were under her nightgown, racing up her legs to her hips, inward, to touch her. She felt the hardness of him and responded, couldn't help herself. She'd wanted him since the first time she'd met him. But she wanted Grayson to want her, Miranda, not this Nefret. And she wanted Grayson, not this man he believed he was in his nightmare. Were they Egyptian? Because of Lord Lyle's treasure room, he'd dreamed he was in long-ago Egypt? With this Nefret?

She couldn't let this continue, though she loved the feel of him, his mad passion, ah, and his hands, big hands, knowing hands. But he didn't want her, Miranda, he wanted this Nefret. She had to stop this, had to. She managed to free her arm and twisted his ear hard between her fingers.

Grayson gasped in pain, released her instantly, and grabbed his ear, and Miranda rolled off to stand beside him, pulling her nightgown back down. Her heart was pounding, not with fear, but with those magical feelings she'd rarely felt before in her adult life, and those long-ago feelings had been so momentary, so ephemeral, she'd forgotten they'd even happened. But she knew very well what she felt now was lust, and those amazing urges—no, demands—were wonderful and she wanted them again. *Stop it, stop it.*

Grayson was lying still now, his eyes closed, the single cover coming only to his waist—his bare waist—his chest still heaving, his breath hard and heavy. Miranda couldn't help herself; she stared. He was really quite beautiful, all hard planes, lean, taut belly. No, she had to stop it. He moaned, and she got herself together. She leaned down and lightly rubbed his earlobe. "Grayson, wake up, you can do it. Come back to me. I'm sorry I hurt your poor ear."

"Mama? What's wrong?" Miranda jerked around to see P.C. standing in the dim pre-dawn light of the open doorway, her white nightgown floating around her small bare feet, her beautiful honey-colored hair in night braids, Miranda called them, rubbing her eyes. She looked scared. Of all the individuals in the world Miranda didn't want to see at this moment, her precious daughter headed the list.

P.C. said, "I heard Mr. Straithmore yelling, Mama. I thought some-one was trying to kill him. I wanted to save him. And you were here. Is he all right?"

Miranda drew a deep, steadying breath. *Distract her.* "P.C., you really must call him by his real name, not his fictional hero's name, Thomas Straithmore, remember? Now, I came because Grayson had a bad nightmare. He's coming out of it. He'll be all right now. You may go back to bed. Don't worry."

"But, Mama, I know Mr. Straithmore performs daring deeds. He doesn't only write about them. Grandmama said what he did at Wolffe Hall made him a gift from the gods. She said Alphonse had even blessed him from the afterlife."

"P.C., Mr. Sherbrooke isn't Mr. Straithmore. Come, you know that. Mr. Straithmore is made up. He exists in Mr. Sherbrooke's brain and on the pages of his novels. I've told you this several times and so has Grayson."

P.C. still looked uncertain.

"All right, it is true Grayson has performed remarkable deeds. But he is real, with us, and Mr. Straithmore isn't. Now, sweeting, go back to bed, and I'll come kiss you good night when I'm certain Grayson is settled."

But P.C. ran to the bed and climbed up. She scooted next to Grayson and came up on her knees to look down at him. She lightly patted his cheek. "Mr. Strath—sir—Mr. Grayson—it's all right, I'm here now. I'll take care of you. Mama will help me."

CHAPTER ELEVEN

Grayson opened his eyes to see P.C.'s precious little face leaning over him, her nose an inch from his, one small hand lightly patting his cheek. The earth righted itself, and his brain planted itself firmly once again in the present. He realized the room was a soft gray, nearly dawn. When he spoke, his voice sounded scratchy, sounded like another man's voice. It even felt somehow different. He cleared his throat. "P.C., may I have a glass of water? On the table by the bed. In the carafe."

P.C. cocked her head at him. "You sound strange, Mr. Strath—What shall I call you? Mr. Sherbrooke?"

Grayson said without thought, "That's because I was someone else, someone who lived a very long time ago. His name was Jabari, and he was an architect." He cleared his throat again. "Call me Grayson."

Miranda said, "Call him Mr. Grayson, P.C."

P.C. patted his cheek again, said, "Mr. Grayson," and repeated it, as if tasting his name on her tongue. She considered him a moment. "I sometimes dream about long ago too, more often when I was so small I could scarcely reach Mama's waist. Mama, please fill up the glass with water, Mr. Strath—Mr. Grayson—needs it. Hand it to me, please. I'll help him drink it."

Miranda smiled and dutifully fetched the water.

P.C. leaned closer and said very precisely, "Mr. Grayson, I am going to put my arm beneath your head and lift you so you may drink." And she did.

Grayson sipped at the water and sighed. *A flash of a knife, slashing toward him, the punch of fear—* Then he was back, in the present, P.C.'s small hand now stroking his arm, his bare arm. He realized he was naked. Slowly, he reached down and pulled the blanket from his waist up to his shoulders.

"Papa, why is P.C. feeding you water? Are you sick?"

Pip's voice brought him back, completely back, hearing the fear in his son's voice. "No, Pip, I'm fine, don't worry. Go back to bed. Both of you."

P.C. frowned down at him as she tucked the cover in around his shoulders. In the next instant, Pip clambered up onto the bed and pressed against P.C. Grayson shot a look at Miranda, still standing beside his bed, now grinning like a sinner, her glorious hair tangled around her face, so much of the stuff, thick, rich honey colors.

P.C. said, "I saw you holding Mama on top of you, and then she gave you the ear pinch and climbed off. You must have done something really bad to get the ear pinch. It hurts frightfully when she does it to me, but she only does it when she's really upset. I think the last time I got the ear pinch was in April. It was Barnaby's fault. He wouldn't let me harness him up like Mama's mare, Violet, and I threw a bucket of water on him. Why did she give you the ear pinch?"

I had my tongue down her throat. Grayson's brains fell out of his head.

Miranda said quickly, "No, you misunderstood, P.C. It was the only way I knew to bring him completely out of the nightmare. It worked."

"Yes," Grayson said, "it did indeed." Nefret, it had been Nefret, but then she'd become Miranda, *his* Miranda. That drew him up short. *His* Miranda? It was true he'd hadn't known her for that long a time, but now, in the still of the night, it didn't seem to matter. He concentrated on getting his wits back and drank the rest of the water. P.C. took the glass out of his hand and handed it to her mother.

Grayson felt Pip's small hand pat his whiskered cheek. "Did you hurt someone in your nightmare, Papa?"

P.C. went back on her knees beside him and scrutinized him closely. "No, Pip, someone was going to hurt him."

Grayson asked, "Why do you say that, P.C.?"

She lightly touched her small palm to his chest. "Your heart is still beating fast, Mr. Grayson. I think you were angry, maybe fighting with someone? To the death, like the knights in battle?" She sat back on her heels and frowned. "Well, like most gentlemen still do, like my father did."

"P.C.," her mother said, "your father didn't fight. He believed in causes. Any injustice made him very angry, but he didn't fight if he could avoid it."

Both Miranda and Grayson saw P.C. would clearly prefer blood and guts strewing the dream landscape, not some vague notion like injustice. Grayson said, "Yes, I was going to fight an enemy." P.C. perked right up. Pip did a little bounce beside her. "You wouldn't lose a fight, Papa. You're strong. You can carry me under your arm, and I'm a big boy."

P.C. gave him a considering look, and he knew she wanted to know all about this enemy. He wanted to know more about Jabari as well. Instead, she took Pip's hand and pulled him off Grayson's bed. "Mama, take care of Mr. Strath—Mr. Sherbrooke—Mr. Grayson. I'll take Pip back to bed."

"'Ey, wot's all this about?"

P.C. turned on him, hands on her hips. "Barnaby, you will be quiet until you can speak proper English."

Barnaby was standing in the open doorway, his nightshirt not quite covering his bony knees. "I thinks I wants to say, what is happening here now, in this bedchamber, sir?"

"Excellent," P.C. said, and lightly tapped her fingers to his cheek. "Mr. Grayson had a nightmare, Barnaby. Now that Mama and I have taken care of him, we can all go back to bed. Mama, you may see to Mr. Grayson now. Come along."

"But I want to stay with Papa." Pip wasn't usually a whiner, but he was now.

P.C. said patiently, "Mrs. Minor told me she would make us nutty buns for breakfast, but not before seven o'clock. She said Mr. Grayson gave her the Sherbrooke family recipe. If you're asleep, Pip, the time will go faster."

Grayson and Miranda watched the three children troop out the door, Barnaby looking back over his shoulder.

"The little general," Miranda said, and shook her head. "Isn't she perfectly splendid, Grayson? Ah, Mr. Grayson?"

"She is. I do wonder how many more years will pass before Barnaby attempts to take the reins from her."

"The Great thinks about seven years, when Barnaby is a young man." She made the mistake of looking down at him. That look of hers brought him fully to life.

She licked her lips. "Oh dear."

It nearly killed him, but Grayson said, "Go back to bed, Miranda. Now. Trust me, you must leave me now. Go back to sleep. Dream of nutty buns that will make you swoon. You want to be well rested to enjoy them fully."

She paused a moment and stared down at him. "I'm not Nefret, Grayson. Tell me who she was tomorrow morning, all right?"

CHAPTER TWELVE

Grayson waited until the house was quiet again, Miranda and the flock hopefully settled in their beds. He felt frustrated, the memory of Sadek's attack still vivid. Who was Sadek? He pushed back the blanket, pulled on his dressing gown, and fetched the key to Lord Lyle's treasure room from the top drawer of his dresser, beneath his cravats, washed and well starched by Marigold just that morning. He lit a candle and walked barefoot as silent as a ghost downstairs, unlocked the treasure room door, and pushed it open. Soft gray dawn light filled the room. *I've stepped into doom. The air itself is pulsing. I hear a hundred faint beating hearts at rest, waiting.*

He tried to laugh at himself in the absolute stillness, and he did, but his laugh sounded strangely hollow to his own ears, as if from somewhere else, sometime else, like the laugh of another. He was making himself mad, becoming Gothic, something he couldn't abide. He was in the blasted treasure room filled with artifacts, ancient, to be sure, but nothing more.

But he knew there was something more, knew it to his bones. And it involved Nefret. He raised the candle and found himself looking at Anubis's jackal head, directly into the god's dead black eyes. He felt a skitter of something strange, something not of this world, something dangerous, coming close, closer. He wanted to turn and leave this room, lock it, and leave it locked.

Instead, he raised the candle high. Even in the early morning light, shadows roiled and pulsed toward him from the dark corners. He walked directly to Nefret's golden arm cuff displayed on its red velvet stand. *It is special, timeless, both in and of our time and world, and other worlds as well.* He couldn't believe he'd remembered exactly what Nefret had thought to him. He didn't question it, simply picked up the cuff. It felt warm, warmer than it had been when he'd held it two days before. It seemed to pulse in the air around him. He felt no malevolence from it, nothing to make his blood freeze. He set down the candle and cupped the cuff in the palms of his hands, held it tight. Did he feel a faint beating heart? Was that soft breathing? Close, not a foot behind him? He didn't move, stood quietly, holding the cuff. Waiting. For what? Then the air seemed to blur as if a veil had dropped in front of his eyes, and he heard the faint heartbeat become stronger, louder, closer.

The veil lifted. He was standing in a magnificent room, walls of flowers and interwoven vines painted in vivid colors. The floor was a golden marble with inlaid mosaics of sea creatures. In the center of the room was a raised dais, a large square marble bathing tub at its center filled with scented water, jasmine—he could smell the lovely fragrance from where he stood. He watched a graceful thread of steam rising off the water. Behind the bathing pool on a deep ledge stood a gold statue of a colossal female figure, wearing a golden robe, her arms outstretched, a protector.

The girl in the bath was humming softly, sponging herself with fragrant soap. It was Nefret. He recognized her instantly. A young serving girl stood silently a few feet away, watching, waiting, a drying cloth in her arms. Or was she humming as well?

His heart pounded. What was going on here? There was magic in the cuff, meant, evidently, only for him, an ancient magic able to transport him thousands of years in the past. *It is special, timeless, both in and of our time and world.* No, that was impossible. The cuff hadn't transported him; the cuff had drawn him into a vision of the distant past.

He watched Nefret rise and stretch, then squeeze the wet sponge one last time over her face, her breasts, her arms. He watched her breathe in deeply. She was still no older than fifteen, a beautiful girl, her exotic sloe eyes dark as a midnight pool, her black hair bound atop her head, her young body lithe, graceful, well shaped, but not quite a woman's full shape. But what shocked him was the realization he actually knew what she was feeling. It was coming off her in waves—dread, fear, so much fear, swirling madly in her. He watched the servant girl hand her a drying cloth, then help her to step out of the bathing pool and walk down the three steps to the golden marble floor. Nefret spoke to the girl as she dried herself, but Grayson couldn't make out her words. He watched the servant unbind Nefret's long hair and pull it free, thick and lustrous, to fall straight down her back to her hips.

He said, "Nefret."

To Grayson's astonishment, she started, looked up, and stared straight at him, then jerked the drying cloth in front of her, her eyes never leaving his face.

"Who are you? Why are you here? How are you here?"

She didn't sound frightened, merely surprised at his sudden presence. He knew she was speaking ancient Egyptian, yet he'd understood her easily, just as he'd easily read the curse on the unnamed boy's coffin. When she looked at him, what did she see? A shadow, an actual man, or did she hear only his voice? No, she was looking directly at him. He held up his hand. "I am not here to hurt you. My name is Grayson, and I believe your golden cuff brought me here. I'm a visitor, from a faraway land to the north, a land you have never heard of."

"What is this land?"

"It's called England."

She seemed to taste the strange word, but she did not repeat it aloud.

"You want me to tell you why I am here. I really do not know, but your cuff obviously wanted to bring me here. Actually, I really am not here at all."

"Why do you speak nonsense, spout riddles? Of course you are here, in my bathing chamber. I see you quite clearly. You say you are a visitor? From a land I don't know? To the north? It is called Eng-land?"

"Yes. You must travel through many other lands to reach mine. England is an island, you see. It is not set in the middle of a desert."

She pursed her lips, considering this, then said, "It is absurd what you said—one of my cuffs brought you here? You must be a magician, a powerful one, more powerful, even, than Sadek."

"I'm not lying." Grayson held out the golden cuff.

She was shaking her head back and forth. "This is not possible. You cannot have my cuff. I removed it only before I bathed." And she stared over at her dressing table. He did as well. He didn't see a golden cuff.

He looked down at the cuff glowing softly on the palm of his hand. He held it out for her to see.

She walked to him and reached out her hand, drew it back. She stared at the cuff and whispered, "It is my cuff, the one Jabari gave me, the timeless cuff, he told me. But how come you to have it? Did you sneak past Raia and take it from my dressing table? And neither of us saw you? You are a magician."

Grayson shook his head. "No, I am not a magician. As I said, your cuff brought me here to your bathing chamber."

Nefret took several steps back away from him, drew herself up, and now her voice was arrogant, haughty. "My cuff has nothing to do with your being here. It is only a piece of jewelry, no matter what Jabari told me. No, I believe you are a stranger here to visit the pharaoh and you happened to come in here. Since I cannot believe no one stopped you, you must be a magician. Somehow you took the cuff from my dressing table without my seeing you." Her voice trailed off. He was aware she was studying him now, her look uncertain, a bit of fear in her voice. "Look at you, wearing an odd robe that goes to your feet. I have never seen that material before nor that color. It looks strange, mayhap not of this world, and you are very white." Her voice dropped to a whisper. "If you are not a magician, then are you a god? Are you Ammut disguised as a man? You made yourself invisible so you could kill me? Or did you wish to rape me?"

"No, no, I mean you no harm. I am not Ammut. I am not a demon.

As I said, your gold cuff brought me to you. You must believe me, for it is true."

Grayson realized the servant girl was standing still as a stone, her arms clasped around herself, obviously terrified, watching her mistress speak to someone who, to her, he supposed, wasn't there. She cried out, turned, and ran out of the chamber, covering her face in her hands.

Nefret looked after her and said, her voice emotionless, "Raia will not say anything about me speaking to you. I do not believe she even saw you. All would believe her mad. You said your name is Gray-son. What sort of strange name is that? You say you are not a god, you are not a demon, and you claim you are not a magician, but my cuff—how could it bring you here? How could you be holding it in your hand? Explain this to me."

"I imagine my name does sound strange to you. Your name sounds strange to me as well. Listen, Nefret, I do not know how much time I have here with you. I arrived here with no warning, so I could leave as quickly." Suddenly the cuff flared, and warmth streaked through him, and knowledge. He knew exactly what he must do. He said simply, "Please tell me about the unknown boy in the sarcophagus. There are paintings of him throwing a disc to a man, but then the boy flings the disc into the Nile and it floats away, hovering above the waves. What happened to him? Who was—is he? What is the disc? Who is the other man?"

She stared at him, shaking her head back and forth, and then tears filled her eyes as she shook her head. "How can you know this? No, you are a god, you have to be to know this—"

Before she could continue, Grayson repeated without hesitation:

> *Open this keeper of my spirit*
> *and know the agony of a thousand burning spears.*
> *See your children disappear into the stygian blackness,*
> *shrieking their pain and hatred of you.*
> *Attend me or you will know mortal agony without end.*

She looked terrified. She splayed her hands in front of her to keep him away from her. "No, no, it is impossible. How can you possibly know the curse? Only the pharaoh knew it, and Amenken, the scribe who carved it into the stone as it was recited to him by Sadek, and, of course Sadek himself. Sadek is the pharaoh's magician. He claimed if buried deep, hidden, the coffin would remain concealed for all time, for all eternity, so all would be safe. But how can you have seen the coffin? How is it possible you found it, and so quickly? The sarcophagus with the coffin within was secreted away only three years ago. You of the strange name and strange land? You who are holding my cuff."

Grayson said, his voice steady, "It was much longer ago than three years, Nefret."

She cocked her head at him. "No, only three years, I remember clearly that day—at dusk the sky was golden, clouds sifting through the air, and a cool wind blew off the Nile. It was dusk because Sadek said it was the time he was counseled by the black smoke to remove the coffin, to hide it, so all would be safe forever. He and his men took it away. Why are you lying to me?"

What to tell her? He said, "Nefret, explain this to me. Sadek's curse— it was meant to keep us safe from a boy? Or isn't a boy buried the coffin? But if not, then why the painted scenes of him on the sides throwing the disc?" He paused, studied her face. "Who is inside the coffin, Nefret?"

She stared at him. "But how can you know about the coffin? And the curse? How?"

He said simply, "I have the sarcophagus. I read the curse carved on the side. How do you know the curse, Nefret? You said only the pharaoh, Amenken, and Sadek knew."

She moistened her tongue over her mouth. "I've never told the pharaoh or anyone else, because I knew they'd believe me mad, but I dreamed the curse, night after night, for many nights. I could not escape it. Then slowly it began to fade away as I grew older until one night it was simply gone. I have never forgotten it; I cannot forget it. It is terrifying. The drawings you said you saw on the sides of the coffin—you are certain they show a boy chasing the disc?"

"Yes, I am certain. Do you know the name of the unknown boy?"

"There is no unknown boy. It should have been Kiya, my younger brother, son of the pharaoh, but Sadek swore Kiya was not buried in the coffin—" She shook her head. "No, what Sadek really said was that Kiya, my brother, the pharaoh's eldest son, beloved by all, was not in the coffin."

"But how can that be? What did this magician Sadek mean?"

"When Kiya disappeared, the pharaoh sent Sadek to Nubia to discover what any knew of Kiya. The king of Nubia told Sadek that Kiya had indeed appeared in Nubia, but he had died a short time after he came to court. The king told Sadek that his own priests had warned him that what was sealed inside wasn't Kiya that he had become something else entirely. Kiya was no longer a boy, no longer the pharaoh's son—he was now a demon. The king of Nubia said his priests counseled him that the coffin must never be opened, that what was imprisoned within was a demon of unspeakable malevolence and power, and he must be hidden forever. When Sadek returned and told the pharaoh, he was distraught, inconsolable. He didn't understand how this could happen, not to his beloved son. But he believed Sadek, for Sadek had proven his worth and his loyalty over the years, and so the pharaoh oversaw the inscribing of the curse and bade Sadek to hide the coffin. And then he withdrew into himself."

She whispered, her voice thin and scared, "I ask you again, Gray-son, how did you find the coffin so quickly? You said it was longer than three years. That is not possible. Three years ago, Sadek took the coffin away, at dusk. I remember it well.

"I believe you must be a sorcerer, bringing magic from this land called Eng-land. And the golden cuff Jabari gave me helped you?" Her terror was a palpable thing, but she didn't run screaming away from him. She had courage in the face of an unknown phantom, namely him, who'd suddenly invaded her bath and somehow had the cursed sarcophagus.

"I am not a sorcerer, not a magician. Believe me, I am not lying."

He held out her cuff. She hesitated, then grabbed it out of his hand. "I heard your thoughts, Nefret, that day Jabari gave you the cuff and told you it was special, timeless, both in and out of our time and world and other worlds as well. That is what I heard you thinking."

CHAPTER THIRTEEN

Her expressions went from disbelief to fear to a desperate hope. She moistened her tongue over her lips. "It cannot be possible, can it? You saw me, heard my thoughts? You heard me thinking of Jabari? But no one knows of Jabari."

"Sadek did. He tried to kill him. He attacked him with a knife. I dreamed it, Nefret."

She grew very still. She was trembling. He stayed silent. In truth, he didn't know what to say.

She said finally, "He tried to kill him. He nicked his arm, but I used a healing cream and bandaged it for him."

"Where is Jabari?"

She shook her head, then whispered, "I was told he drowned. I myself spoke to his men. They told me he drank his barely beer, then grabbed his throat and fell over the side of his boat into the Nile. None could swim and save him. It was only thirteen days after he gave me the cuff." She straightened, pulled her shoulders back. "I miss him. I will always miss him, but he is gone. I do know that his heart weighed true and he is in the afterlife."

"When I heard your thoughts you were worried. You did not want to tell Jabari something. You did not think what it was to me."

"What you say, it cannot be true. You are a spirit here to torment me."

"No, do not be afraid. I am not evil, I promise you. I am no magician. I told you, your cuff brought me here to you. So now it is you who must help me understand. Keep your secrets about Jabari; there is no need for you to tell me about him."

He drew in a deep breath. "What I really must know is how your brother Kiya became a demon as the king of Nubia told Sadek. Please, I swear I mean you no harm."

She was pale, but calmer. Now she was studying him, assessing him. He stood perfectly still, waiting, and then he heard her clearly in his mind: *It is too much. I must show him, but how? I have not the power.*

Your cuff will make it happen, he thought clearly back to her.

Slowly, she nodded. This young girl was both real and unreal, pulsing with life in front of him, and long dead. She could speak and think her thoughts to him, and he could understand her. And now she trusted him enough to believe he could show her. "Hold the cuff closely, Nefret."

She held it against her breast. "It beats with the beat of my heart. It is so very warm." She licked her lips. "How can this be, Gray-son? I never felt this before."

"I honestly do not know, but I do know that somehow the cuff will allow you to show me."

"Yes," she said. "Yes." She put her fingers to her lips, turned, and dropped her bathing cloth, uncaring she was naked. She pulled on a white robe and belted it with a narrow golden belt. She leaned down and slipped her feet into papyrus sandals. Grayson didn't know how he knew, but he accepted that this time so far in the past, so alien to him and his world, was somehow letting him enter. Then she walked quickly from the bathing room, her cuff still held against her heart, and beckoned him to follow her. She took his hand, and they walked silently down long, ornately decorated corridors—marble, painted plaster, rich benches, statues of Egyptian gods. They passed both closed and open doors, and he heard people speaking, saw the occasional flash of a white robe, a jeweled hand. Why were there no people in this long corridor?

Finally they came upon two older ladies dressed in fine linen and jewels, their eyes lined in kohl, their hair elaborately fashioned atop their heads in rich loops and coils. One was speaking in a low voice; it seemed she was sharing a confidence with the other. He saw the other woman slowly nod. She looked very grave. To his relief and surprise, they hadn't seen either him or Nefret. Evidently, since Nefret held the cuff, she had become part of this strange vision. But Nefret's serving girl, Raia, had still seen her mistress speaking to him, hadn't she? But she'd seen only her mistress. He didn't understand, but he would worry about it when he returned to Sedgwick House—if he ever returned to Sedgwick House. But knew he wouldn't be trapped in this vision of long ago, knew that whatever the cuff was, it had meant for him to come, to understand, and return to the present. To do what? He knew he'd find out.

The cuff still held against her breast, Nefret eventually led him through an open door at the end of the long corridor. They stepped onto a stone-covered walkway that wound its way through a magnificent garden. He saw a large pond, with lotus blossoms floating on top and the flash of colorful fish. Around the pond were rows of trees—sycamores, palms, and others he didn't recognize, rows of them, alternating with brilliantly blooming flower beds. The stone paths wove among an orchard of date palms, and fig, olive, and peach trees, and others he didn't recognize. He saw walls and pergolas covered with grape vines, shading benches beneath. He paused and breathed in the fragrant air. It was so very real he forgot for a moment he was a visitor in a magical place, out of time and place. He watched Nefret close her eyes, hug the cuff tightly, then slowly nod.

Another veil lifted, he thought as he watched the beautiful garden disappear. Now they stood beside the banks of a wide, swiftly flowing river. He felt shock, a punch of fear, then settled himself. He had to accept that here, now, in this ancient land, both he and Nefret had become magical with the cuff. Or was it possible Nefret's brother Kiya had somehow brought them together to the banks of the Nile using the cuff? To show Grayson something important? Would he come to understand what he was meant to do with the sarcophagus in the present?

He looked at the wide river, smelled the water, heard it roiling and tumbling, knew if he touched it his fingers would be wet. Was he really seeing the Nile from three thousand years ago? Longer? He didn't know.

Nefret stood stiffly beside him, clutching the cuff to her breast. Grayson saw the actual boy painted on the side of the coffin. He looked to be Barnaby's age, perhaps a bit older, but he was well made, a handsome child, small, laughing, and he was hurling a silver disc to a man. Like the boy, the man was dark, black-haired, his black eyes lined with kohl, wearing a white linen wrap belted at his lean waist by a gold belt. He wore a cloth headdress and a narrow collar. The boy's father? No, he seemed too young, but who knew in this ancient culture with its strange customs and mores? The boy turned back and stared directly at him and Nefret, only now his face was utterly blank of expression, as if he was in a trance, and he moved as a puppet moved, controlled by the hands of the master. The boy turned away from Grayson, away from Nefret, back to the man, but he didn't throw him the strange silver disc, he hurled it into the Nile. It floated away, dancing just above the waves. Then the boy broke into a run after it.

Nefret yelled, "Menhet! Stop him, please. Don't let Kiya get away!"

But the boy was running fast through thick water reeds along the shore, chasing the silver disc, Menhet shouting after him, running to catch him.

The air stilled. Time stilled. Nefret stood silent, looking out over the Nile, her breathing too fast, too loud. "Of course Menhet could not stop Kiya. He said Kiya simply disappeared. He led searches, many men led searches, but Kiya was never found. As I told you, the pharaoh received word from the king of Nubia that Kiya was dead. He sent Sadek to Nubia to fetch him home."

"Nefret, why do you call your father the pharaoh?"

She cocked her head at him, her look bewildered. "But of course he is the pharaoh. He is a god, he is a ruler. It is what he is."

She held the cuff still pressed against her heart. "No matter who or what you are, Gray-son, what happened cannot be undone. You and I saw it, somehow, I know not how, only that you made it possible for us to see it. My timeless cuff. My magical cuff. To see Kiya one more time, it brought me great joy." She lifted the cuff and kissed it, then stood on her tiptoes and kissed his cheek. "Thank you for appearing in my bath."

He smiled. "I really had no choice." He lightly touched his hand to the cuff. It still glowed warm. He said, "Nefret, the pharaoh withdrew into himself? What happened?"

She shaded her eyes with her hand against the brilliant sun, and her voice sounded broken. She raised her dark eyes to his face. "When Sadek returned from Nubia, he told the pharaoh that he had consulted the black smoke and was bidden to tell him the whole truth. Sadek said Ammut, the devourer of the dead, had fashioned the silver disc and entranced Kiya so he had no choice but to follow it. Sadek said the disc led him into Nubia, where Ammut put his brother demons on him and they turned him into one of them. He promised the pharaoh that Kiya had nothing to do with this, he was a victim of the demons, that his goodness hadn't been enough to overcome Ammut and his plans." She closed her eyes and remembered, and thought to him:

"But why," the pharaoh asked him.

Sadek bowed his head and whispered, "Ammut hated Kiya, knew he and his demon brothers would suffer greatly in the future when he became pharaoh. They wanted to destroy him and thus entranced Kiya and the disc.

"What the demons made of him, sire, Kiya was no longer your son. I saw it in the sacred black smoke. He became something else entirely, like the other demons, evil and malignant. You must believe me, sire, Kiya remained good. It is one of the Others who is imprisoned, a demon of great power, and thus I fashioned the curse."

She opened her eyes and looked at him squarely. "That happened three years ago, Gray-son. I have shown you what my cuff allowed us to see of what happened to Kiya. Can you tell me if Sadek told the truth? Did Ammut and his brother demons change Kiya, make him into one of them? And the king of Nubia knew of this?"

"I do not know, Nefret." He hated to say it, but it was the truth.

"It matters not now. The pharaoh has accepted what Sadek told him. But when I think of Kiya, I remember innocence and happiness. And so much goodness. His goodness was the reason the demons wanted to destroy him? If it is so, if demons can destroy the son of the pharaoh, himself a god, then there is no order in the world, there is only capriciousness and unchained wickedness."

She cocked her head at him. "Gray-son, you recited the curse, which means you must indeed have the coffin, and thus I am forced to believe you can do anything."

"No," he said. "I am sorry I am not myself magic, Nefret. I wish I were so I could tell you about Kiya, but I cannot." He stilled, realizing he did understand things, even accept other creatures such as the demons he'd killed at Vere Castle. As to what was happening now? Something about him must have triggered the vision when he touched the cuff.

When they walked through the opulent corridors once more, empty of people, Grayson said, "Tell me more about the magician Sadek."

"I believe he poisoned Jabari's beer, and that is why he fell overboard. You are the first I have told of this. There was no other to share my confidence. As for Sadek, he is the pharaoh's confidant, his seer. He gives him prophecies from his black smoke, and many times what he has predicted has come to pass. Gray-son, I do not want to believe what he said about Kiya and what happened to him. And I wonder if Kiya is indeed inside the coffin, placed there by Sadek himself, the curse meant to make people believe what he said, make the pharaoh believe it. I suppose I will never know."

"Nefret, Kiya's face when we saw him—there was no expression, as if he were indeed entranced."

She nodded.

"Do you believe Kiya is buried in the coffin?"

"As I said, I do not know." She lightly placed her hand on his arm. "I do not know how much longer than three years the coffin has existed, but I am willing to believe you now." She paused, and he saw a tear streak down her cheek.

"What is it? What is the matter?"

"The pharaoh has no heir. He announced I was to wed Sadek in seven days. I have told him, begged him, but he will not listen to me. I am afraid, Gray-son."

A small frightened voice sounded loud in his ear.

"Papa? Why are you in here? Why are you speaking to that bracelet?"

Grayson dropped the cuff, but he managed to catch it before it hit the floor. He quickly set it back upon its velvet cushion. His fingers tingled. He was breathing fast, his heart racing. He was here, now, back in the present, in Lord Lyle's treasure room, and curse him, he hadn't locked the door.

He got himself together and turned to see Pip in his nightshirt, his small feet bare, looking scared.

"Papa? Are you all right?"

CHAPTER FOURTEEN

Grayson couldn't believe it. The treasure room was a pearly gray, exactly how it had been when he'd first come in. Had no time passed during his vision? Evidently not. What to say? "Pip, is it raining?"

His son stared at him and slowly shook his head. "I looked outside when I woke up again. But there are lots of dark clouds. It doesn't look good. I'm cold, Papa."

Grayson breathed in deeply. He was here, in Bowness-on-Windemere, Lord Lyle's houseguest, and it was now 1841, not in ancient Egypt, in an Egyptian garden, not standing on the banks of the Nile. Not with Nefret.

"Good morning, Pip. Cold, are you? Come here." Pip ran to him and Grayson leaned down to catch him up in his arms. He kissed him soundly and closed his warm hands around his small feet. "This is the second time you've come in on me unexpectedly. Why are you here?"

Pip pulled back in his father's arms, then leaned close again and whispered against Grayson's ear. "I heard something, Papa, and I was afraid something escaped from your nightmare. You weren't in bed, so I looked for you." His son regarded him, his brown hair standing straight up, his head cocked to one side, mirroring how Grayson did it. Pip kissed his whiskered cheek. "Why did you come in here, Papa? This is the treasure room. Why were you holding that bracelet?"

Grayson looked at the gold cuff, shining bright in the dim light. He fumbled, then said, "I couldn't sleep after my nightmare, Pip, and came down here."

"What is that gold thing you're holding, Papa?"

"It's jewelry. It's called a cuff. You slide it up your arm until it's snug."

Pip stuck out his arm. "Will it fit me?"

Grayson didn't want the cuff anywhere near Pip. Then, he wondered: *What could happen?* He slipped the cuff up to the top of Pip's small arm.

"It's pretty, isn't it? It was worn by a princess a very long time ago."

"You mean Aunt Alex? When she was young?"

Grayson laughed, couldn't help it. "No, your aunt Alex is a countess, not a princess. This particular princess lived a much longer time ago. Her name was Nefret. Do you remember I told you stories about the Vikings and the Romans?"

Pip cocked his head to one side. "You showed me pictures. They wore togas and talked funny." He paused, frowned. "They were always fighting and eating—and other things you wouldn't talk about."

"That's right, mostly. The princess who wore this gold cuff on her arm lived much farther back than even the Romans."

Pip frowned at this, stared at the gold cuff, and moved it up and down his arm. "It's heavy. I don't like it."

Grayson was relieved Pip had felt nothing else and saw nothing else, like Nefret rising from her bath. He quickly slid the cuff off Pip's arm and set it back on its velvet stand. He manufactured a yawn. "Let's go back to bed. No one is up and about yet."

"Marigold is," Pip said. "I heard her humming. She was setting a fire in Barnaby's bedchamber. And I heard Mrs. Minor in the kitchen. Papa, that big gold box over there—why is it glowing?"

Grayson's heart stopped. He turned slowly. The small coffin wasn't glowing, thank the good Lord. No, it stood stark and alone in the dim dawn light. "You think it's glowing, Pip? What do you mean?"

Pip yawned and tucked his head against his father's neck. "A little glow. Oh, it stopped. I'm cold, Papa."

Pip began sucking on his fingers, something he hadn't done for nearly a year now.

"If Mrs. Minor is in the kitchen, she'll make us tea."

He locked the treasure room door and carried Pip to the nether regions, to the big kitchen with its row of three large windows that gave onto a garden, a hill behind it, sheltering it.

The kitchen was blessedly warm. It was nearly full-on morning now, and sure enough, there was Mrs. Minor, stretching as she poured water into a pan. She turned and gave them a big smile. "Ah, Mr. Sherbrooke and young Pip, a good morning to you. Tea you'll be wantin'. A small moment. Sit down and I'll slice you some bread."

Grayson wasn't surprised when Barnaby and P.C. soon appeared, both in their nightshirts, slippers on their feet. They weren't papyrus, not like those Nefret was wearing. He shook his head at himself and listened to Pip telling them about a gold cuff in the treasure room that had belonged to a princess who lived even before the Romans, a huge long time ago, and a big box that glowed. Grayson wasn't about to correct his son, to tell him it was really a coffin. Had it really glowed? He didn't want to think about that.

He didn't stop Pip from telling P.C. and Barnaby about the sarcophagus since the result would likely be ghoulish delight. Pip's involved recital gained some interest, but Grayson soon realized neither P.C. nor Barnaby believed Pip. They thought he'd dreamed it—no wonder, after Mr. Grayson's nightmare.

Grayson sat back, watching the children laugh, drink their tea, and cram down Mrs. Minor's bread and butter with her special huckleberry jam, telling each other it wouldn't rain, ignoring the black clouds gathering outside the kitchen windows, making plans to feed the swans down at the water's edge, then go exploring. That wouldn't happen, not without him or Miranda.

He listened to Mrs. Minor tsk and shake her head sadly as she looked out the window. She said, "No more toast for you, my pets. I'm making you nutty buns for breakfast."

Pip gave a shout, then told Barnaby and P.C. his grandmama loved nutty buns, and he kept bouncing up and down.

"Indeed she does," Grayson said. "Now, children, go back to your bedchambers, bathe, and dress. P.C., you're in charge. Clean hands and faces or no nutty buns."

The three children raced out of the kitchen, shouting at the top of their lungs. Grayson didn't move. He continued to sip his tea, inhaling the smell of the cinnamon Mrs. Minor was sprinkling on the nutty bun dough. He pictured young Nefret, the strange walk through the empty palace corridors, out into the magnificent garden—and then, suddenly, he and Nefret saw Kiya as Grayson had seen him painted on the side of the sarcophagus. It had seemed real, so very real, but it was really a vision, a magic vision, it simply had to be.

He watched Mrs. Minor knead the dough and wondered if Nefret had indeed married Sadek the magician.

He wondered how he could discover if Sadek had become pharaoh, Nefret his queen. Of course her tomb had been plundered, and her golden arm cuff had woven itself through the vast number of centuries, ending up in Lord Lyle's treasure room. He once again saw Nefret rising from the elaborate sunken bath in that sumptuous bathing chamber and compared it the bathroom upstairs with its simple bathing tub.

What had happened to Jabari? How could the small sarcophagus have possibly glowed?

CHAPTER FIFTEEN

"Grayson, what is wrong with you? The black clouds have disappeared. Magic, Mrs. Moon called it, and Manu nodded solemnly. The day is sunny and warm, and the nutty buns Mrs. Minor made for our breakfast were delicious, yet you're sitting there, staring out over the lake, ignoring the swans, the children, and me."

He turned to smile at Miranda. They were sitting on a blanket Manu had given them, simply enjoying the warm day, the lovely lake. What to tell her? How much to tell her? Would she believe him ready for Bedlam? She knew what had happened at Wolffe Hall—she'd lived through it all. He'd also told her the truth about what had happened at Vere Castle in Scotland. He doubted she really believed him, even though she hadn't rolled her eyes. He had to admit, what had happened with the golden cuff did sound like one of his novels. He studied her face, a precious face, really quite beautiful with her high cheekbones and clear soft skin. But now she looked worried about him, and that moved him, deep inside where things counted. He realized no one had really worried about him in a very long time. Well, parents always worried, but that was different, and now, with Pip, he understood that worry would never leave him until he himself left this world. He picked up her hand

and held it between his. And always, always, both of them had half an eye on the children, shouting, racing along the shore, the swans chasing them, squawking. Their closest neighbor, Mrs. Braymore, the local furrier's wife, was standing at the top of the slope watching the children, her own boy and girl now part of their group.

Miranda said at his continued silence, "It's the nightmare, isn't it? Your dream about this Nefret. All right, Grayson, Pip told me he found you in the treasure room, holding a golden cuff. Was it Nefret's? P.C. told me Pip had talked about a large box glowing, but it stopped glowing. Was it a sarcophagus? Don't you think it's time you told me what's happening?"

He gave it up and began talking, beginning with the unknown boy's sarcophagus and the curse, then Nefret. He left nothing out. Miranda didn't say a word, even when he told her about him and Nefret standing on the banks of the Nile, three thousand or more years ago. He ended and shrugged. "Did Nefret marry Sadek? Did Sadek become pharaoh? What does it matter now after millennia have passed? I do wonder, though, if the young prince, Kiya, is really buried in that sarcophagus, or something else entirely, a demon, as Sadek said."

Grayson came to attention and shouted, "P.C., grab Pip!"

She did, laughing, scolding, pulling him out of a bevy of swans rapidly closing in on him.

He turned back to Miranda. "There is nothing I can do. I can only know what Nefret, through her golden cuff, shows me, what she says to me, what she thinks to me. There is no more reason for me to go into the treasure room. It is all rather futile."

Miranda was silent a moment, then lifted his hand and held it between hers. "Remember Mr. Philpot? How very nasty he was? And then he cried out, 'Let me out, let me out, let me out.' You know that had to be a part of this, Grayson, you know it." She looked away from him, out at Lake Windemere, then up at the bright sun. She smiled, remembering Manu had warned them it would rain after luncheon. And why should she believe him?

Grayson said aloud, *"Let me out, let me out, let me out."*

Miranda said, "I believe the only way to resolve this is to open the sarcophagus."

Grayson felt a spear of cold right to his gut. He was shaking his head, back and forth. "It is too dangerous, Miranda. That curse was written on the coffin for a reason. No, I will leave the treasure room locked. It's beautiful here, and we have no obligations, no concerns, only our family here, all together, in this special place that perhaps rains a bit too much." She laughed. He'd thought but days before how quickly they'd become a family, Miranda and the three children, his and hers, all of them here in a special place, together. It was time to break away from the magic held in the treasure room of a long-ago time and place. It was time to stay in the present and enjoy his family. He rather hoped Nefret and Jabari had not been mummified. He knew he'd rather be dust blowing in the desert wind than end up a hideous creature for a future man to gaze upon and be repelled.

He stood and gave Miranda his hand. "Would you care to stroll with me down by the water? Do not forget your umbrella."

Let me out, let me out, let me out. Mr. Philpot's words sounded over and over in his mind. He knew whatever was in the sarcophagus was so powerful, even after millennia, it could take over an old man in a village in England. No, he was not going back into that treasure room.

CHAPTER SIXTEEN

TUESDAY NIGHT

Grayson desperately wanted Miranda to come to him. It was her choice—it had to be her choice. After they'd tucked in the children, he'd walked her to her door, and he'd kissed her in front of that closed door with all the pent-up need in him, shown her how much he wanted her, his hands in her glorious hair, cupping her face, kissing her eyebrows, her nose, and her soft mouth. And she'd kissed him, her tongue touching his, making him shake. He didn't think she'd wanted him to leave, but he knew he had to.

Did she love him? He knew he felt great caring for her—and lust, limitless lust. Did she feel lust for him? If they married, he would become P.C.'s stepfather. And Barnaby? Yes, he would raise Barnaby too, watch him leave his "barn cat" days behind and become a polished young gentleman, a prerequisite if P.C. was determined to marry him. And Pip adored Miranda—no, he wasn't ready to deal with all the myriad consequences, the endless considerations if he and Miranda were to wed.

He thought of Lorelei, his beloved wife for such a short time, only two years when she'd drowned in her own small pleasure boat given to her by her parents when a sudden storm had blown up. She'd been a good swimmer, but she hadn't managed to get to shore. He hadn't been there, hadn't heard her cries for help. He said her name quietly in the stillness of his bedchamber. It was a magical name. Like Nefret, Lorelei was gone forever, a sweet lingering memory. Sometimes he still found himself speaking to her about Pip, a problem, a question about what he should or shouldn't do. Did he occasionally imagine she answered him? But he hadn't spoken to her about Nefret; he'd spoken to Miranda.

Grayson remembered showing Pip his mother's portrait. He'd commissioned David Benedict to paint her only months after their marriage. He clearly remembered saying to Pip, "This is your mama, Pip. She loved you very much. And she loved me as well." And he repeated his mantra over and over.

Suddenly, a deep echoing voice screamed in his head: *Let me out, let me out, let me out.* He clapped his hands against his ears, but the voice only screamed louder: *Let me out, let me out, let me out.*

Grayson slowly got out of bed, belted on his dressing gown, pulled slippers on his feet, and took his lighted candle downstairs. He unlocked the treasure room and walked not to Nefret's golden cuff, but to the small sarcophagus. He knelt beside it and studied the paintings of the boy throwing the disc to the man, to Menhet, Nefret's cousin. He read the curse yet again, a meaty curse, one to scare a man to his soul.

Not a scream this time, no, a low throbbing voice, neither male nor female: *Let me out, let me out, let me out.*

Grayson studied every inch of the sarcophagus. He tried to move it and was surprised when it tilted. He gently rocked it back and forth on its base and heard something move within. *Ushabti?* Only the small figures of workers to accompany the dead to the afterlife to take care of him? That was what Lord Lyle believed. But why put *ushabti* inside a coffin with demons within?

Grayson rose and studied the coffin. He watched his hand gently feel around the seam between the coffin bed and the lid. He jumped back, his heart pounding hard. The lid had moved, only a bit, but it had moved at his touch. Why? He would swear his fingers tingled.

Let me out, let me out, let me out.

He stared down at the coffin, knowing, simply knowing, that

whatever was saying those words over and over was there, waiting, waiting for him to raise the lid.

Grayson heard movement and turned to see Miranda standing in the doorway. She was wearing a pale-blue dressing gown he'd seen before, her beautiful hair long and waving down her back. She looked afraid. "I was thinking about you when suddenly I heard Mr. Philpot saying again, *Let me out, let me out, let me out.* I went to your room, but you were not there. Then I knew you'd be here. Is that the coffin with the curse? What are you doing?"

He looked down at the coffin, at his hand hovering over the lid. "*Let me out*—it comes from here, Miranda. I think I'm going to open it."

"No," she said, running lightly to him. "No, Grayson, I do not think that's a good idea." Then she pulled up short. She looked closely at the boy's golden face, at the vivid lapis lazuli, the turquoise of his headdress. "It's beautiful." She reached out her hand and lightly laid her fingers on the nose. "He's beautiful. Do you think the boy Kiya is within? Not demons? Mayhap he is the one who wants out?"

"Miranda, you are touching his nose. Do you feel anything?"

She nodded. "A warmth. It feels welcoming, which sounds strange, but it's true. The warmth, it makes me feel good."

She looked up into his face, never lifting her fingers from the nose. There was something different about her, something he couldn't begin to explain. She smiled at him, then turned and shoved hard at the lid of the sarcophagus. It sailed three feet and landed on the floor, not hard, a sort of settling motion. Grayson couldn't believe it.

They stood together over the open coffin, saying nothing, looking inside. There wasn't a mummy; there were only scattered bones and shreds of dark cloth.

"The bones are large," she whispered. "They aren't a boy's bones, Grayson."

Did a demon have bones? They watched as a black shadow slowly began to sift up through the bones, weaving in and out, as if trying to bring them together. The shadow thickened, drew together, became a sort of smoke that enveloped the bones, covering them entirely. It looked oily and smelled, strangely, of coriander. Suddenly the black smoke coalesced and whooshed upward, into their faces, and they heard the bones rattle as if trying to come together and rise with the black smoke. The smoke roiled and hissed, kept dipping back over the bones, as if willing them to knit themselves together into a whole.

Silence. The black smoke hovered a moment, then lifted straight up, and they saw the outline of a man wearing only a ragged loincloth. They watched the smoke go into his gaping mouth, fill him, then spiral out, only to funnel back into his mouth until the smoke seemed a part of him, as if he was breathing it in and using it to keep himself upright.

The man rose straight up in the coffin, the black smoke now wreathing him, framing him, and he opened black eyes lined in thick kohl and stared at them. Then he opened his mouth. But words didn't come out, only threads of black smoke. Then he raised a nearly fleshless arm and looked at it, appeared to study it. He threw back his head and shrieked. And they heard a gravelly voice come from deep within the smoke, sharp as rusty shard of metal striking on glass, a voice that hadn't spoken for millennia. "*No.* It cannot be. I must be whole." Then his arm dropped and the smoke enveloped him completely until they couldn't see him.

Suddenly the smoke flew out of the coffin, carrying the nearly fleshless creature with it, and swirled through the air around them.

The smoke faded, and there stood the man. One of his legs was only bones, and flesh hung off the other leg. He howled and shrieked, and then he turned to Miranda and Grayson. He screamed, "You!" and he was lifted by the black smoke and was flying toward them, screaming words neither Miranda nor Grayson understood.

Then, "At last you opened my prison, freed me. At last I am of this earth again. But look at me! I am no longer a man. I am no longer whole and able to move about. I must have my black smoke." He shook a skeletal arm at them. "Look at me! I am a monster! It is your fault. I know you for what you are—a sorcerer. You heeded my cry to release me, but all along you meant to destroy me." And he was coming toward them, threads of black smoke dripping from his mouth like black blood.

Grayson raced to the stand and grabbed Nefret's golden cuff. He shouted, "You were entombed with a curse to hold you forever. You are not Kiya, you cannot be. You are indeed a demon. Who are you? What are you?"

The voice shrieked, "I am Sadek the magician! Nothing could hold me, nothing. But why am I not whole? Why am I—" No more words came out of that gaping mouth, only black oily smoke, but it seemed to be hurling itself at them.

Grayson held up the cuff like a shield. "It is Nefret's cuff, come whole through the millennia."

Grayson hadn't thought it would work, but to his relief, seeing the cuff made Sadek pull back into the smoke, hovering there, and they could hear a heart beating, coming through the smoke, loud and louder still, and then a loud moaning cry. "I will not die! That arrogant little girl will not end me!"

Grayson began to walk toward the writhing man, only bones occasionally clear through the thick smoke, the cuff held in front of him.

"No!"

Miranda moved to stand beside him. "I know you made me open your sarcophagus. I let you out, but it will do you no good. You are nothing now but bones and smoke. There is nothing you can make me do now."

Grayson said, "You are thousands of years beyond death, Sadek. I know you murdered Nefret's brother, the boy, Kiya. You enchanted the disc, and you paid an artist to paint the panels on the side of his coffin, to immortalize what you had done, but no one else would ever guess. Your tale about demons taking Kiya, changing him into one of them, it was nonsense, just as your curse was nonsense. But something happened. You did not marry Nefret, and you did not become pharaoh. You were cast into a cursed tomb forever, not Kiya. Who overcame your magic? Who imprisoned you? Who laughed at the curse you wrote because now it will hold you forever?"

Sadek's voice was a whisper now. "Give me the cuff, and I will let you live. Give it to me now, or I will take the boy. I will take your son."

"You will not touch my son. You already tried to kill Kiya, but you failed. You are nothing now, nothing except black smoke to blow into dead air. You are nothing at all, Sadek."

He held up the cuff, and Miranda closed her hand over his. Together they walked directly into the smoke, into that hideous creature. The black smoke heaved and twisted, and Sadek howled.

There was a great shriek. Slowly, so very slowly, the black smoke shrank, tightened into a ball that swirled through Sadek, and moved to hover over the coffin. "No!"

They watched the smoke sink back into the sarcophagus, watched the lid lift from the floor and fly to land gently on top of the coffin.

"Grayson." Miranda licked her lips. She wasn't about to let go of the golden cuff. "Is he gone? Sadek?"

"Yes." He turned and lightly stroked his hand through Miranda's hair. "Here, you hold Nefret's cuff. Tell me what you feel. What you see."

He watched her hold the cuff tightly and close her eyes. She became perfectly still. Finally, he watched her draw a deep breath. He watched her smile. She opened her eyes and gave him back the cuff. "It is now your turn."

He saw Nefret, an older Nefret, perhaps twenty years old. She was lying on her side on a magnificent chaise, a servant holding out a tray to her, laden with fruit. She was heavy with child. Her black hair hung long and lustrous down her back, held off her forehead with a golden circlet. He watched her select a date and slowly chew on it. Then she turned to smile at him. No, not at him, at a young man coming into the room.

Grayson knew it was Kiya, now a man, and as was the custom among royalty at the time in Egypt, brother and sister had married.

Nefret thought to him, *The king of Nubia protected Kiya so Sadek couldn't kill him. He gave Sadek a coffin with the body of a dead old man within. It was Sadek who returned to tell the pharaoh about how demons had taken Kiya and made him one of them.*

Kiya remained in Nubia, a favorite of the king, until he was twelve years old, old enough to lead the king's men to fight Sadek. And so he came back with soldiers and they captured Sadek. The pharaoh made him disclose where he'd taken Kiya's sarcophagus, and when it was brought before him,

Kiya killed Sadek the day he was to wed with me. Sadek's body was broken apart and stuffed into the sarcophagus, the same sarcophagus he himself had brought back from Nubia, the same sarcophagus upon which he'd had the panels of Kiya chasing the disc painted and the curse inscribed, the same sarcophagus he'd had buried deep in a cave.

But Sadek was strong, able to sense your magic and come through to you.

Nefret looked from Grayson to Miranda. *You and the strange-looking woman standing next to you—thank you.* She nodded to them and took the hand of the young man who was smiling down at her. Slowly, she seemed to fade until she was no more.

The cuff was cool to the touch. Grayson knew it would now remain cool, no matter who touched it. He looked over at the sarcophagus. He doubted Pip would see it glow again. Sadek was finally gone.

Grayson set the cuff back on its velvet-covered stand. He took Miranda's hand, and together they walked back to the small sarcophagus. "Did you see she was wearing the cuff?"

"Yes," Miranda said, "I saw."

"Shall I tell Lord Lyle there is no more curse?"

Miranda lightly touched the lid. "No, I think not. A mystery, leave it all a mystery, Grayson, and a riddle, to pass into the future. I believe it is something Lord Lyle will relish telling all his progeny. Does he have any progeny?"

EPILOGUE

The two carriages rolled away from Sedgwick House, away from Bowness-on-Windemere, the children hanging out the carriage windows, waving to Manu, Mrs. Moon, and Mrs. Minor, who stood waving back at them from the wide front steps.

Oddly, since that singular night when Miranda and Grayson had managed to destroy Sadek using Nefret's golden cuff, it hadn't rained a single day. It was as if Manu's lake gods had recognized their achievement and rewarded them. Manu had given Grayson a long look that morning and slowly nodded his head. "Thank you, Mr. Grayson." Nothing more, nothing less, and Grayson was afraid to ask him exactly what he meant.

Their final three weeks at Sedgwick House had passed quickly, too quickly for the children. They were brown, healthy as stoats, now chattering like magpies, Barnaby slipping now only rarely into cant since Miranda corrected him, and P.C. punched him.

As Bowness-on-Windemere disappeared behind a bend, he thought again of Nefret and Kiya. He prayed both brother and sister had lived long healthy lives. Imagine, marrying your sister and it was the done thing. Who cared? It was so long ago. Grayson also prayed Kiya had ruled Egypt wisely. He smiled as he lightly touched his fingertips to the sleeve of his white linen shirt, the same linen worn by Nefret millennia before. He picked up Miranda's hand. He knew they would stand together now, hand in hand, and look into a future not quite clear as yet.

He felt Miranda's breath warm on his cheek. "This, my dear, has been a month to remember."

"That's true," Barnaby sang out. "No rain for three whole weeks."

"It's my birthday in seven days," Pip said. "I know what I want for my birthday, Papa."

Grayson thought of a King Charles puppy soon to be born to a neighbor.

Pip poked P.C. and Barnaby, then gave Miranda a big smile.

The Virgin Bride of Northcliffe Hall

THE FOURTH NOVELLA
IN THE GRAYSON SHERBROOKE OTHERWORLDLY
ADVENTURES SERIES

CHAPTER ONE

NORTHCLIFFE HALL, HOME OF DOUGLAS AND
ALEXANDRA SHERBROOKE, EARL AND COUNTESS OF NORTHCLIFFE
NEAR EASTBOURNE, ENGLAND, OCTOBER 1841, NEAR MIDNIGHT

The first time Grayson Sherbrooke saw the huge black stallion, he was on his knees looking down at a flirtatious goldfish in the ornamental pond in the western Northcliffe gardens. It was near to midnight. Grayson hadn't been able to sleep and had decided a walk was just the thing to tire him out and slow down his brain, which was always busy teasing out another Thomas Straithmore story. As for Thomas's most recent otherworldly adventure, *The Ancient Spirits of Sedgwick House*, it was going on sale in the new year.

Grayson breathed in deeply. The night was cool, the air still, the moon nearly full, lighting up the gardens, so he'd pinched out his candle and left it just inside the side door of Northcliffe Hall. A clear, perfect night was an amazing occurrence, a special treat for an Englishman.

Grayson looked beyond the gardens to the home wood—filled with maples and oaks and deer and foxes and who knew what else. He'd spent many hours in the home wood as a boy, visiting his cousins, and he knew it stretched to the narrow, rutted country road that meandered through small hamlets to the larger fishing village of Eastbourne on the southern coast. The massive white limestone cliffs drew visitors from all around, even Frenchies, which made the locals snort in their ale.

A black stallion suddenly burst from the wood and pranced to the pond. Grayson held himself still and watched the magnificent animal gracefully lower his head. Grayson didn't think he made a sound, but suddenly the stallion's head whipped up and he stared directly at Grayson. Time seemed to freeze. Neither moved. He was wearing an ornamental silver bridle, a red stone set at the forehead. Then the stallion nickered softly. Grayson said, "Who are you, boy? You're beautiful, you know that? Where is your rider?" The stallion snorted and reared up, his hooves flailing the air. He gave Grayson another long look, tossed his head, and galloped back into the trees.

Grayson got slowly to his feet. He didn't wonder who the stallion belonged to, didn't even wonder why he was drinking in the Sherbrooke ornamental pond at midnight. No, what he wondered was why the stallion had looked at him with intelligence—and recognition—and why he wore a beautiful silver bridle that looked to be very old. He'd greeted him too, hadn't he? Again, he wondered how such an animal could have come to him. Grayson shook his head—his writer's brain was working overtime. A horse was just a horse. He rose and dusted off his breeches and walked back to the hall, turning to look every couple of steps toward the home wood, but there was no sign of the magnificent black stallion.

He didn't detour to the walled-in eastern garden with all the naked marble statues of men and women in various sexual positions (brought from Italy by a long-ago earl), but he would visit before the end of his stay. He imagined his five-year-old son, Pip, staring up at the naked statues, mesmerized, eager, asking questions that would leave him blank-brained, and shuddered. Thankfully, none of the children were old enough to sneak into the garden and gawk and giggle and point. Give them another four, five years.

He picked up the candle he'd left in the small entranceway, touched a lucifer to the wick, and made his way back up the massive front staircase to the western wing to his bedchamber, designated as his for years now. He found himself walking past his chamber to the nursery. He quietly opened the door and looked in. Moonlight flowed through the three large windows, bathing the long rectangular room in soft light. It didn't look much different than it had when he'd been a boy—scores of maps, mostly old, but some newer ones as well, and oil paintings of horses covered the walls. He saw Napoleon's troops on a shelf, the soldiers, horses, and the cannons in disarray, obviously defeated. Wellington's army sat in splendid formations on the shelf above, soldiers on horseback, the cannons at their backs. Thankfully there'd been no wars since the last battle between Wellington and Napoleon at Waterloo that long-ago June of 1815. But revolution was in the air in Europe, and that meant violence was coming. Would England be involved? He prayed not. He glanced at the other shelves filled with bows and arrows, several wooden foils, and ancient, thankfully unloaded, dueling pistols. A rocking horse set on three wheels stood in a corner. It was a little boys' nursery, nary a doll or a ruffle to be seen.

There were four doors off the main room, each opening into a small bedchamber. He walked to Pip's door, quietly opened it, and cupped the candle flame with his hand so not to awaken him. Pip lay on his back on the small bed, his arms over his head, needful, he'd told his father, to protect him from fire-breathing dragons that came at night. A fine solution, Grayson had said. He looked down at this precious being, always marveling, then he quietly left his room to check on Barnaby. Barnaby's hands were crossed over his chest, making him look quite dead. Where had that pose come from?

Grayson looked in on P.C. too. She was smiling in her sleep. Dreaming about Barnaby? Would he be her stepfather perhaps this year? Next year? One of her hands was closed around a small wooden pistol her grandfather, known as the Great, had given her for her last birthday. If the young Sherbrooke twins, Douglas and Everett, were here—instead of being in London with their parents, James and Corrie—he knew they wouldn't dare torment her. She'd show no mercy and clout them without hesitation. P.C. looked more like her mother, beautiful Miranda, every day, her hair the same rich honey color, her eyes as blue as a Sherbrooke's. He didn't doubt she'd break hearts when she grew up, and wasn't that a thought. Time, he was realizing, kept moving forward, sweeping away youth, making a father into a grandfather at breakneck speed. He thought of the earl, his uncle Douglas, still tall, straight, hair thick and white as snow. Grayson couldn't imagine him ever leaving this earth. Had he stood in the nursery years ago just as Grayson was doing, watching his own sons, Jason and James, sleeping?

When Grayson finally fell asleep, he dreamed the magnificent black stallion was standing silent, watching him. With recognition, wearing that ancient silver bridle. What was that red stone? He wasn't surprised in his dream when the stallion walked to him, nodded, blew into his hand, and Grayson swung himself up on his back. He rode the stallion until he awoke with a start as the stallion jumped an impossibly high fence. He realized his heart was beating fast with excitement. He felt quite well rested—wonderful, in fact. He also realized he missed Miranda and wished she hadn't had to remain at Wolffe Hall to tend her sick mother-in-law. At least he'd brought P.C. and Barnaby with him, a treat for the children as well as for him since their antics never ceased to amaze and amuse him.

CHAPTER TWO

Grayson's aunt Alex, the Countess of Northcliffe, smiled at him across the breakfast table the next morning. The sun pouring in through the long window made her red hair gleam like the most brilliant ruby, and any white hairs were discreetly tucked under the vivid red. She whispered as she handed him the muffin basket, "Cook made nutty buns to welcome you, Grayson. Your uncle Douglas will be back from the stables any minute, and he will try to nab them. Quickly, take two. Hide one under your napkin. Hurry." Alex took her own advice and grabbed two nutty buns out of the basket, hid one and bit into the other, and chewed. She looked ready to fall unconscious with pleasure. After one bite, Grayson was in a near swoon himself.

He said, "I got an icebox."

Alex stopped her chewing. "Does the ice melt and leak all over the floor?"

"Yes, but not so much as Mr. Moore's earlier ones, so I'm told. This one was made by a Mr. Hubalto Custer of York, sawdust stuffed in the sides to keep it cold. It's a marvel, Aunt Alex. My cook complains about slipping in the puddles and breaking her leg, but her food stays cold, so she shakes her head and says, 'The Lord giveth, and the Lord taketh away.'"

Grayson's uncle Douglas, the Earl of Northcliffe, said from the breakfast room doorway, "Cook informed me she won't have one of those ugly heathen boxes in her kitchen."

Grayson said without pause, "The champagne stays perfectly chilled."

Douglas grinned. "Perhaps another conversation with Cook is in order." He grabbed the basket, sat down, and ate a nutty bun in two bites. Alex deftly pulled the basket in front of her. The breakfast room was warm, the air smelling of cinnamon. Grayson felt very good indeed. He hadn't seen his aunt and uncle in too long a time, and in his youth, Northcliffe had been his second home. They spoke of his father, Ryder Sherbrooke, who'd rescued children since he'd been a very young man. Douglas said, "In Ryder's last letter, he said there are now fourteen children living at Brandon House, the newest addition a little boy, around five years old, Ryder thinks. Max is his name. He prevented the boy's sale to a brothel."

The countess cocked her head. "Goodness, why a brothel? What would a little boy do in a brothel? Run errands? Clean boots?"

Douglas cleared his throat, opened and shut his mouth. Grayson said immediately, "Yes, he would be a boot boy," and he took the last bite of his first nutty bun. "What do you suggest I do with the children today?"

As a distraction, it served. Alex said, "Take them to see the white cliffs at Eastbourne and go down to the beach. I know the water is always cold—"

Douglas said, "It's cold enough to freeze your parts off, Grayson. The children? They'll scream and splash each other and have a magnificent time. If you remember, all you boys always did. And they'll try to drown you, so be on your guard."

"Oh, I remember. When Mr. Ramsey brings them down after their breakfast"—Grayson checked his pocket watch—"in about fifteen minutes, I'll ask them. Thank you, sir, for letting the children ride the twins' ponies. Should I ask Mr. Ramsey to come with us? He seemed to like P.C. especially, said something about having a little girl around was a pleasure after noisy little boys, and P.C. told him smartly she was just as noisy. I'm only sorry James and Corrie and the twins are in London.

He scrawled me a quick note, told me he'd been invited to speak at the Royal Astronomical Society. He said it was possible Prince Albert would be there. He was very excited."

Alex nodded. "Yes, he's presenting his paper on one of the rings of Saturn. As for Corrie, she promised the twins a visit to the Tower. I believe she hired a guide to tell them all the bloodthirsty details of all the royal beheadings over the centuries. I was surprised when the twins' tutor, Mr. Ramsey, asked to remain here at Northcliffe. He said he didn't like London, said it made him physically ill. He did not elaborate, so there's a question. He then offered to look after the children we told him you were bringing with you. James and Corrie are planning on coming home next Wednesday to see you and Pip. Then, my dear, you're going to be dragged around to visit every single relative in the area. The last count, I believe, is about twenty."

Grayson took another bite of his nutty bun as he listened to Aunt Alex talk about her gardens, how people still stopped to look and explore. Uncle Douglas grunted. "One of these days I'm going to look out the window and see a face staring back at me."

Alex laughed. "I've been wondering if we should charge an admission fee. What do you think, Grayson?"

Grayson shook his head. "Let people bless you for allowing them to see the splendor of your gardens without lightening their pockets. Your beneficence will spread far and wide."

"That will mean we'll have hoards of visitors coming here," Uncle Douglas said. "Of course, the twins would love that. I can see them offering to guide people around—for a small fee." They spoke about James and Corrie's twin boys, Douglas and Everett, brilliant, both of them, naturally.

When Alex paused to chew another bite of nutty bun, Grayson said, "I couldn't sleep last night, so I went walking around your beautiful gardens, Aunt Alex. I saw a magnificent black stallion come out of the home wood to drink out of your ornamental pond. Is he one of your horses? A neighbor's?"

His uncle Douglas frowned. "A black stallion, you say, here on

Northcliffe property? At the ornamental pond? I have two blacks, but they're not let loose at night, too dangerous. A pity Corrie isn't here— she knows every animal within five miles of Northcliffe."

Only one nutty bun left. Three hands went toward the basket. Alex was the fastest. She laughed, paused. "You are our guest, Grayson, but—" She took a big bite. "Sorry. Tell us more about the stallion."

Grayson took a sip of strong black oolong tea, only a dollop of milk, just as he liked it, and said slowly, "It was odd, but I don't think the black stallion belongs to anyone. Actually, he looked like he was his own master." He shrugged. "Like he was also something else altogether."

His uncle reached over and punched his arm. "Come on, Grayson, don't romanticize a horse or turn him into a character for one of your stories. What was so unusual about the animal?"

"Silver reins and bridle, an odd, ornamental affair. It looked very old.

Alex leaned forward. "That is unusual. Do you think he threw his rider? But what would anyone be doing in our home wood?"

No time for more discussion about the black stallion. They heard the children's excited voices, a babble of words, laughter, arguments, a couple of kid-snarls between P.C. and Barnaby. "Ah, my troops have arrived."

There was a knock on the door, and Mr. Ramsey stuck his head in. "My lord, my lady, Master Grayson. I have the children. They are, ah, rather insistent to be gone."

"They always are," Grayson said, tossed down his napkin, and rose. "Pip, P.C., Barnaby, come and bid a polite good morning to his lordship and her ladyship."

Barnaby made a credible bow and confided to Douglas, "I want to be a lordship when I grows up."

P.C. punched his arm. "*Grow* up, not *grows*. And you can't be a lordship, Barnaby. Everyone knows you have to be born a lordship or it's all over. However, you will be my husband, and that is every bit as fine as a lordship, isn't it, sir?"

Douglas studied the small boy—ten years old or thereabouts, Grayson had told him—the dark-red curly hair, the bright blue eyes.

He said to P.C., his voice deep and serious, "Being your husband would make him a king, P.C."

P.C. poked Barnaby's arm again as she beamed at the earl. "That is what I tell him, sir. If he ever disagrees, which he sometimes does because he's an ignorant boy, I smash him."

Pip said to her, "Your mama says Barnaby speaks the King's English like a little Etonian, whatever that means. But don't we have a queen, Papa?"

Grayson nodded, waited for more.

Pip said, "I tell P.C. Barnaby's too big for her to smash. Aunt Alex, Barnaby has red hair and blue eyes, like you."

Alex smiled. "Indeed he does."

"Do you think he could belong to you?"

Once the children were out the door, Douglas called out, "Grayson, a moment, please."

Grayson turned, his head cocked to the side.

"The little boy, Barnaby—he looks familiar to me, but you said he was an orphan, left on the church steps as a baby and taken in by the Wolffe family. So why, I wonder, could he possibly look familiar?"

"He looks familiar to me as well, sir. I've thought and thought, but no name comes to mind. I hope you have better luck, Uncle Douglas. Now, I'm off to the white cliffs. Thanks for letting me ride Garth. He's splendid."

"Take care he doesn't toss you over his head. It's one of his favorite tricks. That, and whipping his head around and taking a bite of your knee. Enjoy freezing your parts off."

CHAPTER THREE

Grayson was blessedly tired after a full day herding three excited children on the beach below the white cliffs. Mr. Ramsey didn't find the water cold, which was astounding, and the children did indeed try to drown the both of them, as Uncle Douglas had said. Still, he wasn't about to let himself go to sleep, not yet. She would come—she always did. He spun story ideas, wondering what new demon or spirit his manly hero Thomas Straithmore would overcome in his next adventure.

Between one breath and the next, there she was, the resident Northcliffe ghost, the Virgin Bride. As always, she made no sound, simply appeared, hovering at the end of his bed. Her young face was as pale as alabaster, smooth and soft looking, just as beautiful and unchanging as it had been when he'd been a boy visiting his cousins so many years before. Her long pale hair hung loose down her back—beautiful hair, thick, like spun summer clouds. She floated, simply floated, shimmering like nearly colorless veils. She didn't speak—she was dead, after all— but she thought her words. It was Uncle Douglas's gospel that she never visited a Sherbrooke male, only suggestible, weak-minded ladies. But she'd come to him and to his cousins as well from their earliest memories, and what to make of that? The Virgin Bride was the Sherbrooke ladies' protector, Aunt Alex said, to which Uncle Douglas snorted and muttered, "Female hysterics."

"Hello," Grayson said, pulling himself up against his pillows. "I'm glad to see you. When you didn't come to welcome me last night, I worried something had happened to you." Although, what could happen to a ghost he couldn't imagine. He wished again he knew her name, but she'd never told him, and he'd asked her. He almost asked her if she'd been well, then realized it was a stupid question.

She thought to him, *I was visiting your aunt Sinjun and uncle Colin and Pearlin' Jane in Scotland. She has added flesh, and so I told her— not Sinjun, but Jane. I asked her how she could float about properly in her ridiculous pearls with the added flesh, and she threw one of her pearls at me. Grayson, I must tell you, there is something about Olafar Ramsey, the twins' tutor. He is not what he seems.*

He was still thinking about Pearlin' Jane gaining flesh, wondering how the devil a ghost could gain flesh. She didn't eat, so— "What do you mean? Have you seen him act strangely? Have you seen him mistreat the children?"

She swayed a bit, leaned closer. *Oh no, Olafar loves children as much as I do. Ah, P.C., what a smart little nubbin she is. And Barnaby, he's a beautiful child, so full of life. I know I have seen someone who resembles him. My little Pip tells me ghost stories, just like you did, Grayson. No, it is not that at all. Olafar is different. He is not a demon, at least I do not think he is, but he is not quite human like you either. I am not certain what he is. His heart, it beats very loudly, but perhaps he was simply frightened when I appeared to him and I am wrong. But I do not think so. I asked him who he was, and he told me readily enough. When I asked him what he was, he said he was himself, nothing more. And what does that mean?*

I am worried, Grayson. You must find out who he is, what he is. I expect you to see to it. I must admit I like him. He is shy, but—

There was a light knock on his door. As it opened, the Virgin Bride simply disappeared. Grayson whispered to the blank air, "Wait, what about Barnaby's father? Who is he? What about Olafar not being like me?" But she was gone. Pip ran full tilt to the bed and leaped up. Grayson scooped him into his arms, held him. "What is wrong? Is someone ill?"

Pip hiccupped against his father's neck. "No, no, a nightmare, Papa. P.C. woke me up, told me to stop being a baby, that there weren't any dragons in the room, but there were, Papa, there were, but they left. Then she whispered in my ear she'd heard you talking to someone, and how could that be when you weren't close by the nursery? So we came." Pip craned his head around. "I told P.C. you were probably talking to the Virgin Bride. Where is she, Papa? She hasn't visited me yet."

P.C. hovered a moment in the doorway, then raced to the bed to jump up and snuggle next to him and Pip. "I heard you talking, sir, and I knew someone must be talking back to you, but I couldn't hear her. Pip told me it was a girl ghost from before people spoke English properly, but of course I didn't believe him."

Grayson hugged her. "You heard me speaking? But how is that possible, P.C.?"

"I don't know, but I did, and I knew it was a female. Yes, it was a she, and I thought of my mama and knew she might shoot you if there was a lady in your room, and since she isn't here, I knew I had to take care of it myself. A ghost? That is absurd, despite what Pip says." Still, P.C. looked about, but the room was dark and she couldn't see very far. "Where is the lady, sir? In the armoire? I don't see her. And why do you have a lady in your bedchamber? What gall."

"I tried to tell her, Papa, you were speaking to the Virgin Bride, but she said I was a loony and to shut my trap and stop trying to scare her, that only Thomas Straithmore speaks to ghosts and demons and spirits. Well, and her grandmama speaks to Alphonse all the time, but he's not a ghost, he's a picture."

Grayson wanted to laugh, but he held it in. He himself had spoken to Alphonse once, a courtier in Queen Bess's court in the late sixteenth century. A powerful presence was Alphonse, both during his life and after his death. Grayson said, "Pip's right, I was speaking to the Virgin Bride, P.C. She lives here at Northcliffe. She died a very long time ago.

I imagine she'll visit you, just as she visits Pip and his cousins, Douglas and Everett. Perhaps Barnaby too. She loves children."

P.C. came up on her knees and crossed her arms over her white nightshirt. "That won't do, sir, although as an excuse it might fool Pip. No, my mama will say I made it up to protect you, and mayhap she'll swat me. She won't like this at all. Where is she, sir? Where is this so-called ghost lady?" P.C. called out, "I know you're here. Come out and show yourself. Promise me you are not trying to steal Mr. Sherbrooke's attentions from my mama."

CHAPTER FOUR

Grayson grinned at her beloved little face. "No one is trying to steal my affections, P.C. In fact, your mama knows I'm going to tell the Virgin Bride all about her, but I imagine she already knows. I don't know how she does it, but she does. She is the protector of the Sherbrooke ladies. You must never be afraid of her. She isn't hiding in the armoire, P.C."

"I really tried to tell her about the Virgin Bride, Papa," Pip said again. "But she's a girl and thinks she knows everything," he added over his shoulder to P.C., and she poked him in the arm, gave him a little push, and plastered herself to Grayson's side. He made room for both children.

Grayson said, "P.C., the Virgin Bride was born during the reign of Good Queen Bess in the sixteenth century. She was only sixteen when she died, on her wedding night, she told me. She was welcoming me to Northcliffe Hall. I'm sure she'll visit you soon."

Pip said, "Douglas and Everett told me last year she likes to play guessing games with them, sort of like a tutor."

P.C. frowned at Pip. This was new. "What kind of guessing games?"

Pip said, "Well, she asked them what would happen if they fell off the earth, since it's flat."

"The world isn't flat, and so I shall tell her," P.C. said, then she fell quiet. Grayson could practically hear her thinking. What an amazing child she was. She said, "I have decided I will not believe in this Virgin Bride until she comes to me." She raised her voice. "If you are really here, Virgin Bride, come and say hello to me."

To Grayson's surprise, the Virgin Bride shimmered at the foot of the bed, lighting the chamber. Pip said, "Here she is. Hello, Mathilde."

Mathilde? "How do you know her name, Pip? She's never told me."

"I asked her, Papa."

P.C. stared at the apparition, not at all frightened, and slowly nodded. "I am P.C. If my mama continues to love Mr. Sherbrooke, he might be my step-papa. I'm older than Pip. You can tell me things he wouldn't understand. Do you like being a ghost?"

Mathilde thought to all of them, *No one gave me a choice. I was dead and then I was here.* If a ghost could sigh, Mathilde did. *I was named after William the Conqueror's wife, Mathilde, a lady my mother much admired. I miss my little dog. His name is Arthur. Grayson, Olafar wants Arthur. I heard him muttering about Arthur, how to get to him. Does he want my little dog, or another Arthur? Of course I welcomed him. But still—* She broke off, then, *Your uncle Douglas's joints are paining him. I must go wake Alex so she can apply the cream.* And she was gone.

"How could she leave? I have so many questions." P.C. was quiet a moment, then, "A ghost, a real live ghost. Hello, Barnaby. Come in. You are too late to meet Mathilde."

"Mathilde? Another girl? Where is she? What is she doing in Mr. Sherbrooke's bedroom? Your mama wouldn't like that, P.C."

"She's a ghost, clothbrain. She's called the Virgin Bride. Her name is Mathilde."

Barnaby climbed up on the bed and snuggled next to Pip. "There ain't any such things as ghosts, P.C., leastwise there shouldn't be. I bet you're trying to impress Mr. Grayson, making up ghost tales to scare him."

P.C. reached over and punched him. "Mama would scold you if she heard you say *ain't*. It's *aren't*, you saphead—there *aren't* any such things. Don't forget. Mind your grammar. And yes, since I have met a ghost right here at the foot of the bed, I declare there are ghosts." She said to Grayson, "Barnaby still forgets proper English when something unexpected happens, like a ghost popping up. It's all right, Barnaby. The Virgin Bride will like you, maybe even correct your grammar." She frowned, said to Grayson, "If she's been dead a long time, shouldn't she speak funny, like everyone did in the olden days?" P.C. paused, considered. "I know—I'll ask her when Barnaby and I will get married."

Barnaby whimpered.

Grayson started to say even a ghost couldn't know the future, then he paused, wondered. Grayson snuggled in with the three small warm bodies and marveled at what life and the afterlife served up. It was a pity that in another year or so, none of the three children would dream of cuddling with him in the middle of the night. He savored the moment as he fell to sleep, feeling three heartbeats, three warm breaths against his neck, his arms. His last thought: What was Olafar Ramsey? Was he really after Arthur, the Virgin Bride's dog? No, that was ridiculous. The only other Arthur Grayson knew about was King Arthur, but he was even longer dead than the Virgin Bride's little dog. No, the Virgin Bride's name was Mathilde, a very pretty name.

CHAPTER FIVE

Late the following morning, the adults were in the drawing room, waiting for Olafar Ramsey to come down with the children for the promised visit to Clangston-Abbott, a nearby village boasting a certain Mrs. Whimsey's special scones and Devonshire cream. Grayson turned to his uncle. "How did you sleep, Uncle Douglas?"

Douglas blinked at him. "Splendidly, of course," he said.

Alex said to Grayson, "The Virgin Bride told me his finger joints were causing him discomfort, so I smoothed them with the special cream. He never really woke up, but I know his sleep eased."

"Special cream, Aunt Alex?"

She nodded. "The Virgin Bride gave me the recipe. That is, of course, she thought it to me. It was fashioned by her great-aunt Meg, said to be a witch and a healer. It works."

Douglas grunted.

The Sherbrooke butler, Maximus—tall, strapping, perfect white teeth, and hair black as the stallion Grayson had seen—strode in his stately manner into the drawing room, cleared his throat, and announced in a ringing deep voice, "My lord, my lady, the Smythe-Ambrosios are here."

"This is unexpected," Alex said, rising slowly. "Grayson, the

Smythe-Ambrosios are newcomers to the neighborhood, here for only nine years. They have three sons, seven grandchildren. I was told by Lady Marsdon that their niece, a Miss Elphinstone, is currently visiting them from Antwerp, Belgium. A surprise visit, she told me."

Grayson and Uncle Douglas rose as an older couple—both very short and plump, both dressed to the nines—came into the drawing room, both wearing big smiles. In their wake came a young lady dressed in a deep forest-green gown and a high-plumed hat, a green ribbon the same shade as her gown tied beneath her chin. She towered over them, looking for the world like she was herding them. Miss Elphinstone, Grayson assumed. She looked to be in her midtwenties. Her hair was a soft brown, her eyes a darker brown. Her skin was as white and smooth as a new snowfall. She was quite pretty, an unusual small dent in her chin to add even more charm. After greetings and introductions, she gave both Alex and Douglas a lovely curtsey. As for Grayson, she simply gave him a long look, then a slow smile. She gave him her hand, and he kissed her wrist.

Grayson was established quickly as a nephew of the earl, a widower, and thus of great interest, it seemed to him when Mrs. Smythe-Ambrosio eyed him speculatively and began praising his ever-so-exciting novels. As for Miss Elphinstone, when asked, she replied she had not, unfortunately, read any of Mr. Sherbrooke's surely splendid novels. Finally came the reason for the visit. The Smythe-Ambrosios were here to extend an invitation to a small dinner party with some dancing perhaps, on Friday evening. Impromptu, don't you know, for their beloved niece. Naturally, the invitation was accepted.

Grayson heard the children's voices, and he rose. He said all that was proper and excused himself. To his surprise, Miss Elphinstone rose as well. She said, "I would like to meet your children, Mr. Sherbrooke."

"Only one of them is mine, the youngest one, Pip. Children, come meet Miss Elphinstone. Where is Mr. Ramsey?"

Pip, P.C., and Barnaby were huddled together, talking in whispers. Grayson—a father—knew they were planning an adventure, undoubtedly one he wouldn't like. It was obvious they were anxious to leave, but manners were manners, drummed into them since they could walk, with the exception of Barnaby, but he was learning fast.

Grayson introduced the children to Miss Elphinstone. Greetings were exchanged. The children were polite, even though their feet were tapping to be gone. Grayson looked around, asked again, "Where is Mr. Ramsey?"

Barnaby, who was staring at Miss Elphinstone, said, "Mr. Ramsey said he would meet us at the stables, sir, and we were to go along with you." Barnaby added without pause to Miss Elphinstone, "You're awfully pretty, ma'am." She immediately bent down and looked Barnaby in his bright blue eyes. P.C. moved closer, not about to allow a female poacher near her future husband. Not a fool, Barnaby added quickly, "I mean, you're not as pretty as P.C. or her mama, Miss Miranda, but still—"

Miss Elphinstone laughed and lightly touched her fingertips to Barnaby's face. "And you, Barnaby, who are your parents?"

"I don't have parents, ma'am. I was found on the church steps, and then the Great brought me to Wolffe Hall and made me a barn cat. Been a barn cat all me life."

"He was the finest barn cat in the neighborhood," P.C. said and moved closer, trying to squeeze in between this too-lovely lady and Barnaby. "He has left his barn cat days behind him because he will be my future husband. He lives in the hall now, in his own bedchamber, and my mama is teaching him the Queen's English so he won't embarrass her when he's her son-in-law."

Miss Elphinstone looked enchanted by these confidences. She said, "You look familiar to me, Barnaby, and that is odd since I am from Belgium. Hmm. No idea who his family is?" She looked up at Grayson.

"No, and the Wolffe family has looked for many years now, but no luck. You know, he looks familiar to me as well. I've also been trying to find out who his parents are and why he was left on the church steps in our village."

Miss Elphinstone lightly patted Barnaby's face, then turned to take P.C.'s small hand between hers. She leaned closer, whispered, "What does P.C. stand for?"

P.C., all prim and proper, said, "I regret I cannot tell you, ma'am. It is a lifelong secret."

Miss Elphinstone said, "I have a name I did not like either. Like you, I did something about it. I'm R.M. Do you know what that stands for?"

P.C., all her attention now on the tall lady, said, "Perhaps Roberta Mary?"

"Oh no, that is much too pretty. Hmm, P.C. Is your name Pertinella Constanza?"

"No, ma'am, it's much worse." She went up on her tiptoes and whispered against Miss Elphinstone's lovely white ear, "I will go to my grave before I tell a single soul." Then she stared a moment at Miss Elphinstone and came even closer. She whispered something none of them heard and straightened, smiling up at Miss Elphinstone.

Miss Elphinstone threw back her head and laughed deeply. The children stared at her, and then they began laughing even though they didn't know why.

Grayson said, "P.C., what did you tell Miss Elphinstone?"

P.C. looked sly and shook her head. "It is a confidence between ladies, sir. I cannot tell you. Miss Elphinstone, would you like to go with us to Clangston-Abbott to eat scones and Devonshire cream? Mr. Straithmore—well, it's really Mr. Sherbrooke—he's promised we would visit Mrs. Whimsey's shop."

Grayson couldn't believe his ears. P.C. was actually inviting another lady to accompany them? Usually, P.C. was fiercely protective of her mother, always had an eagle eye out for any possible poacher. What was going on here?

As it turned out, Miss Elphinstone was unable to accompany them, much to P.C.'s sorrow. When pressed by P.C., however, she said she would be delighted to ride with them on the morrow, if she was able to leave her aunt and uncle. "I wish my beautiful snow-white mare was here, but alas, she is at home." She smiled at P.C. "Her name is S.W." Of course the children wanted to know what the initials stood for, but Miss Elphinstone only shook her head. "I promised never to tell."

Pip asked, "You promised your horse never to tell? But didn't you name her?"

"Actually, my uncle Smythe-Ambrosio named her when he was there on a visit at her birth. She was not pleased, but there was little I could do except shorten it to S.W. She swore me to secrecy." She made a small *X* over her chest. "One should never break an oath to a horse." She saw Mr. Ramsey coming down the stairs and rose. She smiled down at each of the children, turned, and walked without a backward glance back into the drawing room.

Miss Elphinstone was all the children could talk about, what her initials stood for, what her mare's initials stood for. As they stuffed themselves with scones, P.C. said, "Miss Elphinstone liked you, mayhap too much, Barnaby. I must think about this. Should I tell her you are too young for her? Should you give me an engagement ring to ward her off?"

Grayson held in a laugh and said, his voice serious, "P.C., your fingers are going to grow with you. I think it's too soon for Barnaby to give you a ring."

P.C. thought about this, nodded. "All right. But, Barnaby, I will be watching her, even though I think she is marvelous," P.C. said. She turned to Grayson, frowned. "And you, sir, you belong to my mama, so do not look at Miss Elphinstone with any stronger emotion than polite friendship."

Pip, who had no interest in marital sorts of things, announced he wanted to ride in the home wood when they returned to Northcliffe. This was agreed upon. "Without adults," Pip added, his voice firm. "I promise we will be careful, Papa. You will not worry about us. You don't have to worry about us either, Mr. Ramsey."

Olafar slowly nodded. "I think they will be safe, Mr. Sherbrooke. There are clearly marked trails. There are no tigers or lions to eat them."

The children found this hilarious and could talk of nothing else as they walked through the small village, visited the old Norman church, and joined a ragged old man who told them they could help him chant for the sun to chase away the blackening clouds and coming rain.

The children chanted their hearts out, but the black clouds remained. However, it didn't rain.

During their ride back to Northcliffe Hall, Grayson reined in Garth next to Mr. Ramsey's gelding. "Have you yet met the Virgin Bride? My son tells me her name is Mathilde and she misses her little dog, Arthur."

Olafar Ramsey jerked on the gelding's reins, and he pranced to the side. He leaned down and spoke to the gelding as he stroked his neck. Battle snorted, calmed. Ramsey nodded, stroked his neck again. "She came to me the second night of my employment at Northcliffe Hall. She told me who she was and that she would protect the children with her life—rather, with her death, however that would be. I suspect she wanted to be certain I would not harm them. I did not know her name, and I asked her. Mathilde, you said?"

Grayson nodded. "She never told me her name either—why, I don't know. Maybe because we're adults, but how does that make sense? But she told my son Pip. I've been told it's unusual for her to visit any males in the house, but I never believed it. I'm pleased she came to welcome you."

"As I said, I think she's suspicious of me. But I believe I relieved her mind because she came to me again three nights later, told me—well, she thought to me—that she would believe, for the moment at least, that I loved the twins. She also liked my name, Olafar. She thought it over and over and thought to me that she'd never heard such a wonderful name before. She is very beautiful."

"Were you afraid when she suddenly appeared the first time?"

Olafar cocked his head at Grayson, surprise in his dark eyes. "Why, no. Well, that is to say, I was taken aback, but she seemed very gentle, very shy, really. I made the error of asking his lordship about her the following day, and I believed he would choke on his brandy. He looked at me like I was an idiot, told me it was likely Cook's turnips that did me in." A pause. "Of course I didn't believe him. The Virgin Bride—Mathilde—has visited him as well. She told me she had. She said his lordship refused to accept anything not firmly planted on the earth. I believe I heard a smile in her voice."

Grayson said, "You've been with the twins for four months now. Does she visit you often? And the twins?"

Olafar nodded. "Yes, nearly every night. We've spoken of many things. I asked her if she liked to ride. Still, I am not sure she trusts me entirely." The words were no sooner out of his mouth, when he turned his head away and coughed, called out, "Barnaby, don't sing to Pickle. He isn't a music lover, and he's liable to kick you. When you dismount, you can walk away, and sing your heart out." Sure enough, Pickle, the small dun pony, had flattened his ears and was swishing his tail. Barnaby immediately stopped singing in Pickle's ear. The pony's tail went back up, and his ears pricked forward.

They spoke of Oxford, where Mr. Ramsey had been in Trinity College, Grayson in St. John's College, several years before him. Mr. Ramsey said, "My father wanted me to open a stud. He is horse mad, you see." He flushed and changed the subject to one of Grayson's more hair-raising Thomas Straithmore adventures. "It fair to curdled my blood."

Grayson said, "It is always my aim to curdle a reader's blood, Mr. Ramsey. Tell me, are you horse mad as well? Like your father?"

Mr. Ramsey nodded but said nothing.

Grayson said easily, "I happened to see a beautiful black stallion at midnight my first night at Northcliffe, racing out of the home wood to drink in the pond. Have you seen the horse? Do you know who he belongs to?"

"I haven't the faintest idea, Mr. Sherbrooke," Olafar said and continued to look between his horse's ears. "I haven't seen such a horse."

"My uncle told me this beautiful bay gelding you're riding wasn't broken, that he was supposedly vicious and everyone called him Battle. Yet, I was told, you petted him, spoke to him, and he blew, butted your shoulder. He said all the stable lads were astonished when you mounted with no trouble, and Battle actually pranced about the stable yard."

Mr. Ramsey said easily, "I suppose I inherited my father's way with horses." Olafar ran long fingers down his neck. "Battle is a splendid lad. Actually, he is peace-loving. He was only afraid when he first arrived at Northcliffe. He soon realized all the stable boys saw his fear as aggression. He likes that." Grayson would swear the gelding nearly purred.

How, Grayson wondered, did Mr. Olafar Ramsey know the pony Pickle didn't like music?

CHAPTER SIX

When the small cavalcade returned to Northcliffe Hall, the sun was shining brightly again, much to the amazement of the adults. The children saw the sun as a sign. "Sir, please, let us ride for another hour. Only an hour, we promise. We'll be good. We'll keep our ponies on the trails. Please."

Who could withstand P.C., with Barnaby and Pip singing a nonstop accompaniment, like a Greek chorus? Grayson looked to Mr. Ramsey, who nodded. "If Mr. Sherbrooke agrees, I will agree as well. No more than an hour, though, children. Then you must come back for your dinner. Cook worries, you know."

Promises were made. Both Olafar and Grayson watched from the western garden as Barnaby, P.C., and Pip rode sedately into the home wood.

An hour later, Pip and P.C. came running into the drawing room, out of breath. "Sir!"

"Papa! Barnaby's gone."

Grayson roared to his feet, as did the earl and countess. P.C. told them Pip wanted to play find-me-if-you-can, one of his favorite games. True enough. Pip always ran to hide somewhere in the house or on the grounds at home.

P.C. said, "It was Barnaby's turn to hide, but we couldn't find him, sir. He wasn't *anywhere*. Pip and I were at the edge of the home wood when Pickle came running out, but he didn't have Barnaby." Her voice caught on a sob. "We must find him, sir, we must, or I will die a spinster, alone and unloved, and everyone will blame me forever for losing Barnaby, and I will have to take the blame because it is my fault. Please don't blame Pip—he's only a little sprat and doesn't have a brain that works well yet. Please, sir, please, we must find Barnaby." And P.C. burst into tears.

Alex pulled her close and comforted her while the earl and Grayson gathered six men and rode into the home wood.

It was growing dark, the thick end-of-summer maple and oak leaves still canopying, cutting most of the sun, casting shadows on the floor of the wood. They spread out, each man taking a separate trail, each man with a gun to fire if he found Barnaby. Grayson was surprised to see Olafar dismount and lead Pickle, Barnaby's pony.

Olafar said only, "Mr. Sherbrooke, Pickle knows where Barnaby is. He's a smart pony." Grayson watched Mr. Ramsey and Pickle fork to the far-left trail. He heard Pickle snort.

Not five minutes later, a gunshot rang out. Birds flew out of trees and bushes. Grayson knew, without even thinking about it, that Mr. Ramsey had fired the shot. He'd found Barnaby. He said a quick prayer of thanks and rode to the east.

Henry, a stable lad, rode beside him. "Mr. Sherbrooke, I remember now—there be a small gully twenty yards that way. I think—" But he didn't finish. He was suddenly thinking of what they could find, namely a dead Barnaby.

They met at the top of the gully, dismounted, and looked down, but it was nearly dark now and hard to see. No one had thought to bring lanterns. "I'm down here," Olafar shouted. "Barnaby was unconscious, but he's coming around."

Barnaby felt hands lightly stroking his head, heard Mr. Ramsey's voice, gentle and soft, repeating his name over and over. He opened his eyes to see Mr. Ramsey leaning over him. "Good, you're awake. Now, Barnaby, I know your head must hurt badly. Do not move until you can talk to me without your head pounding. I have you now. Pickle brought me to you. He loves you and was worried."

Olafar called up, "He's awake now. I'll need a stout rope to bring him up."

Grayson called down, "Gem is riding back to get one. Tell Barnaby it won't be long now."

Barnaby's head hurt worse than when P.C. once put out her foot and he stumbled into a briar patch. He felt nausea swim in his belly. No, he wouldn't throw up. He wouldn't. He opened his mouth, but only a whisper came out. "Mr. Ramsey, you're here. Thank you, sir."

"As I said, Pickle brought me here straightaway." He held the boy against him and began repeating words over and over, the same words, like a chant. Barnaby didn't understand, but soon his head no longer felt like it would jump off his neck and roll away. He no longer wanted to throw up his innards.

Slowly, with Mr. Ramsey's help, Barnaby managed to pull himself onto his knees. He cleared his throat and gave it his all. "I'm all right, sir." Pause, then he burst out, "Sir, it was a branch, and it whacked me right in the head, tossed me over Pickle's rear parts, and I fell and started rolling, down and down, and then I guess I hit a rock. Will I live, sir?"

"Oh yes, Barnaby, I daresay you will live to be a hundred. Don't worry now. We'll have you home and in bed in a trice."

And it wasn't an hour later the group returned with Barnaby, held close in Grayson's arms, Pickle walking beside Battle, who didn't seem to mind the small pony periodically poking his nose against his neck.

P.C. burst out of the hall, running down the front steps, her skirts hiked up above her knees, Pip on her heels. "Barnaby! Are you all right? Where did you hide, you looby? You will not die. I won't allow it. Think of the future, our future."

Barnaby groaned. "She sounds all worried, Mr. Sherbrooke, but I know when I'm all right again, I won't want to live after P.C.'s done with me."

"Don't worry, Barnaby. If she yells at you, tell her you feel faint and for her to stroke your brow with rose water. She'll forget she wants to pound you, all right?"

CHAPTER SEVEN

Grayson knew, as did every other Englishman, that in England, if you predicted rain, it was rare you'd be wrong. He stood at the large window in his bedchamber, staring at the rain slashing against the glass. He thought of the panic all the adults had felt when Barnaby had gone missing, thought about Mr. Ramsey and how he'd walked with Pickle, Barnaby's pony, how he'd seemed to know exactly what to do. Well, it was over. Barnaby had spent a restful night, with Aunt Alex's dose of laudanum, and he was quite fine this morning. P.C. had sat beside him, stroking his forehead, and Pip had offered to play guessing games with him so his brain would keep working. All was well. Still, the bone-deep fear remained.

He stared at the cascading rain. It was just as well. He didn't want to take any chances with Barnaby. Better he stay quiet today. He'd still worried, wondered if they should fetch the Sherbrooke doctor, until the Virgin Bride had assured him Barnaby was fine. He believed she'd spent the night hovering over him.

His uncle Douglas's valet, Mortimer, was assisting him, which he appreciated. Ponsonby, his own rheumy-eyed valet—who was always telling him he planned to retire to the seaside, even though he was reminded he already lived near the sea coast—hadn't come with them, since walking up and down stairs pained him. After Mortimer assisted Grayson into his coat, Grayson thanked him and took himself to the nursery. He paused. No sound of children shouting, arguing, laughing. He heard nothing at all. He felt immediate alarm and opened the schoolroom door. Mr. Ramsey was reading at his desk. He looked up to see Grayson, nodded in welcome. He said in a quiet voice, "Barnaby is fine, even ate a large breakfast with P.C. and Pip. I offered to help Barnaby dress, but he wouldn't hear of it. They'll be out in a moment." He paused, smiled. "I believe Pip told him and P.C. ghost stories, the same stories you'd told him when he was young, which he isn't now because he's five."

Grayson laughed. "Yes, my son, the old man." Grayson turned and quietly opened Pip's door. He was seated on the side of his small bed, pulling on his boots. Grayson leaned down to straighten his collar and kissed him. "Barnaby is fine, so no more worrying. I'll be going down to breakfast, Pip. I'll see you soon."

When he went back into the schoolroom, he said to Mr. Ramsey, "When the children are ready for polite company, please let me know. I believe it best Barnaby rest today. I know a word game they might enjoy playing. I imagine my aunt Alex knows more games to keep them from driving all of us mad." He added, looking toward the rain splashing against the schoolroom windows, "I'm glad it's raining. Otherwise, we could have a riot on our hands."

"I fancy the rain won't last much longer," Olafar said matter-of-factly. "The Virgin Bride assured me Barnaby would be fine. We are not to worry."

Grayson wondered why she hadn't come and thought it to him. After all, he'd known her all his life. He said, "Miss Elphinstone was supposed to go riding with us today—" Grayson shrugged. "We'll see." He left the schoolroom and went down the wide front staircase to the dim entrance hall. Maximus wasn't to be seen. However, to his surprise, when he walked into the small dining room, Miss Elphinstone was enjoying breakfast with his aunt and uncle. She didn't look at all wet, and she was smiling at him.

His uncle Douglas called out, "How is Barnaby after his adventure?"

"He is fine, sir. He said if he appears weak, and places a hand against his head, it is his defense to keep P.C. from smacking him for being careless."

Both Aunt Alex and Uncle Douglas laughed. He said, "My boy, do join us. Miss Elphinstone arrived for the promised visit to Sir Thomas Bowlin's stud farm, but alas, I doubt it will come to pass now. She has been telling us she feeds carrot juice to her horses at her home in Antwerp."

"That's right, my lord. I have found horses are mad for carrot juice, all except for my own sweet mare S.W. She spits it out, looks at me like I'm trying to poison her."

"So what do you give her to drink?" Alex asked, waving her slice of toast loaded with blueberry jam.

Miss Elphinstone laughed. "She likes goat milk, nice and warm, fresh from the goat. And to eat, you'll not believe it, but S.W. loves to chew on licorice. Ah, good morning, Mr. Sherbrooke."

"Good morning, Miss Elphinstone."

"Do call me R.M. My aunt and uncle send their felicitations. They are quite in a dither about their party for me tomorrow night, the sweet dears. I am pleased Barnaby survived his adventure."

Grayson said, "If you tell me what R.M. stands for, I might tell you what P.C. stands for."

"I do not like 'mights,' Mr. Sherbrooke. Will you tell me?"

Grayson grinned. "On second thought, I fear P.C. would throttle me in my sleep were I to do so." He began spooning scrambled eggs onto his plate.

When he turned to the table to sit down, Miss Elphinstone said, "I would too."

Douglas laughed. "All these initials. Wait, would you look at this—it was storming, thunder booming, but now the rain has stopped. Is that a speck of sunlight coming through those dark clouds?" He shook his head in wonderment. "I've never seen English weather cooperate like this before. You must be magic, Miss Elphinstone."

They heard the children in the entrance hall, voices high and excited, even Barnaby's.

Douglas's voice boomed out, "Children, come here."

Pip immediately ran to his father. "I forgot to tell you, Papa. When Mr. Ramsey woke us up, he told us we were going to visit a stud farm today, if Barnaby felt all right, and Barnaby swears he's in the pink. What's a stud farm, Papa?"

After a beat of silence, Miss Elphinstone said, "It's a lovely place where boy horses meet girl horses and perhaps they get married."

Barnaby frowned, turned to Grayson. "But horses don't get married, do they, sir?"

"I understand there is the occasional ceremony. Let's ask Miss Elphinstone if horses get married in Belgium. Ah, where is your tutor?"

"Not exactly in the way we humans get married, Barnaby, but horses fall in love and they have children—colts and fillies. You'll see beautiful horses today at Bowlin's stud farm. Sir Thomas is renowned for his, ah, horse facilities."

Barnaby said, "Sir, Mr. Ramsey will be down in a moment." He paused, frowned. "I ain't niver seen no happily married horses, have you, P.C.?"

P.C. scowled at him. She was seated too far away from him to punch him for his bad grammar. She also realized, Grayson saw, she couldn't very well hit him because she might hurt him.

Barnaby cleared his throat, said slowly, with great precision, "Forgive me. I have never seen a happily married stallion. In my barn, they sometimes bite each other." He shot P.C. a look. She beamed at him.

Miss Elphinstone cocked her head at him. "Your barn, Barnaby?"

"Yes, ma'am. I was a barn cat, but P.C. does not like that since she will leg-shackle me." He raised his chin, and Grayson saw the bruise on his forehead. "It's still my barn."

They turned when Mr. Ramsey came into the room, bowed to the earl and countess, and said, "Children, we will go to the stables and give the horses carrots until Mr. Sherbrooke is ready." Before they all trooped out, he looked toward Miss Elphinstone, who now stood facing the fireplace.

CHAPTER EIGHT

Grayson was on the edge of sleep when the Virgin Bride appeared at the foot of his bed. He was aware of her even before he awoke. He heard her voice, quite loud in his head.

Grayson, I told you Mr. Ramsey isn't what he seems. He is lovely to me, but he will not tell me the truth, and I know there is a truth he is not telling. What have you found out?

That was to the point, after a fashion. "I haven't found out anything, Mathilde. To me, he seems exactly what he is, a young man finely educated, born into a good family."

He wants Arthur, but not Arthur my little dog. Now I know it is the other Arthur, the king who lived so long ago. I visited Tintagel when he spoke of the Round Table to the children. It was in ruins then as it is now, and there were no piskies there to talk to me, not even ancient Aeron, the leader of the piskies, said to have been at the famous Round Table. He loves to talk, but he was visiting Paris, I was told. Grayson, have you dealt with piskies? With Aeron?

Grayson said, "I know they're a Celtic fairy race, settled in Cornwall and Devon, a very long time ago. I believe I saw one once when I visited a friend in St. Ives. He was a shriveled old man wearing a coat that looked like green lichen. Oh yes, he had a huge crop of bright-red hair on his head. He didn't speak to me, only stared at me from a hedgerow. Then he nodded and disappeared. I called to him, but he didn't come back. Is it true, Mathilde, piskies hate Englishmen and bedevil them whenever they can?"

Was that a laugh he heard? She thought to him, *Oh yes, indeed. Piskies like to steal their horses and give them terrifying dreams. But you're an Englishman, Grayson, and yet they did nothing to you.*

Suddenly, the white veils seemed to fade, then brighten again, and there was movement.

"Mathilde, what is wrong? You are distressed. Talk to me."

She fluttered, agitated, he could tell, and then she settled again. *I believe Olafar took the children somewhere. Not their bodies, but he took their spirits. He must need them somehow, but I do not know why. If he is doing this, is it dangerous? I do not know.*

Grayson's heart sped up, and a flash of fear hit deep. "What do you mean, he took their spirits? You believe Olafar is some kind of otherworldly being, Mathilde? But how could he use the children's spirits? How could he take their spirits anywhere, Mathilde?"

I do not know, but I know he is. I do not think he would hurt them, but still— You must do something.

I visited Pearlin' Jane today. Aye, your aunt Sinjun and uncle Colin are healthy as stoats. Do not worry about them. I told her about Olafar, told her I was worried about the children at night. Jane said if I never again told her she had gained flesh, she would speak to Barrie, her kelpie friend at Loch Ness, see if Barrie could help me. I feel something, Grayson. It is the children.

She was gone. Grayson threw back the covers, pulled on his dressing gown, lit a candle, and ran to the schoolroom. He quietly opened the door and listened. All was quiet. He went to Pip's small chamber, looked in. Pip was on his stomach, one arm dangling over the side of the bed. Grayson walked to him, set the candle on the floor, and gently turned him over. "Pip," he whispered against his cheek as he lightly rubbed his arms.

Pip didn't respond. His breathing was smooth and even, but he didn't awaken. Grayson was so scared he couldn't get spit in his mouth. "Pip, wake up. Now, Pip." Grayson lightly shook him.

Pip's eyes flew open. "Papa? What's the matter? What's wrong? Is Barnaby all right?"

He pulled Pip into his arms, rocked him, and whispered against his ear, "Nothing's wrong. Everything's all right. Barnaby is all right. I'm sorry I woke you, Pip. I was worried about you."

Pip yawned and nestled against his father's chest. "I'm all right, but I had a strange dream, Papa."

Grayson felt his heart begin to pound. He knew he had to keep calm, but it was difficult. "What did you dream, Pip?"

"I was riding, Papa, on a big beautiful black horse, but I wasn't scared. We were galloping so fast, and his black mane was flying, and I could hear him breathing. Then, Papa, he stopped and turned his big head to me. Papa, I could tell he was excited."

Grayson's heart was pounding harder, but he knew he had to keep calm, not let Pip see his fear. "Did he speak to you, Pip?"

Pip yawned and snuggled close. "He said we were nearly where he wanted to go, and then—I was here with you." Grayson kissed him, aware Pip's head lolled against his arm. He drew in a deep breath and kissed his son's soft cheek again. "Go back to sleep, Pip."

Grayson looked in on Barnaby and P.C., heard their easy breathing. Then he went to Olafar Ramsey's chamber. It was much larger than the children's small rooms, nicely furnished with a sofa and a comfortable chair, a desk, and bookshelves. The bed was behind a curtain. Grayson slowly walked to that curtain, his hand cupping the candle. He pulled it back.

CHAPTER NINE

Olafar shook off his silver reins and bridle, and once again he was a human man. He was here, finally, he was here at Camelot. Camelot, how the very name sang on his tongue. Would he be able to remain here this time and not be whisked back in but moments from now? No, he would stay. He knew Pip's spirit was extraordinary. Pip's spirit would tether him here until he was ready to return. He quickly stuffed his reins and bridle into his jacket pocket and walked to the huge double wooden gates. Wait—where were the soldiers ready to fire arrows down on him? Where were the people and animals and children? Where was the porter demanding his name? If, that is, the porter could see him. After all, he was a man over a thousand years in the past. The gates weren't even closed. What was going on? Maybe it wasn't Camelot. Maybe he'd failed, yet again.

No, he wouldn't, couldn't believe that. Pip's spirit was so strong, so pure. Olafar pushed the heavy gate open and walked slowly inside to a huge inner courtyard. It was empty, quiet as a tomb, not even a hint of a breeze to ruffle the leaves of the apple trees in the small orchard across the courtyard. He walked across the vast empty expanse toward a center wooden tower, rising at least forty feet above him, the sound of his boots loud in the unnatural quiet. He climbed the wooden steps leading to a single massive door, leaned his palm against it—the door was warm, and that was curious—and slowly it swung inward.

He stepped into a large central hall, as empty of people as the courtyard. There were scores of long wooden tables with benches, all empty, all shoved against the wooden walls. He breathed in the silence, praying for the sound of voices, but felt only the air still and warm on his face. Where was everyone? He'd always imagined Camelot to be bursting with people, loud talk, proud valiant knights striding in to join their friends at Arthur's Round Table. And children, he'd pictured scores of children racing about the courtyard. But there were no children. What he saw were vivid tapestries covering the wooden walls, a dozen unlit wall rushes. It should be dark in this vast chamber, but it wasn't. He could see perfectly, and that made no sense. Oddly, it didn't bother him. He was too excited to finally be here. But was he really here? At Camelot? He walked toward the windows and looked out. He saw only darkness. When had night fallen? True, he'd come at night, but in the past, he'd always arrived during daylight, but only remained for short periods of time. But now, with Pip's spirit—he prayed.

Olafar stood in the middle of the great empty hall and looked about. It looked as if everyone had simply stood up and left. And gone where? He walked slowly down a central path toward a magnificent throne set high on a dais. There was a smaller chair set beside it. For the queen? For Guinevere?

Suddenly, he smelled roasting meat and followed his nose. Beside the dais was a smaller door. He opened it and stepped into a blazing, vibrant, noisy kitchen, filled with people working—stirring huge pots with long-handled spoons, kneading bread, shoveling loaves into a great open oven. No one paid him any attention. It was as if no one saw him. Olafar felt as though he were in the middle of an ancient painting suddenly come to life around him. He walked to a big man swathed in a huge white apron, cutting long strips of beef. "Excuse me," he said and lightly touched the man's arm.

The man turned and looked at him, through him, really. He said in very odd English, "Be ye a ghost wot stands beside me? Be ye an important ghost to tell me future, or are ye a wandering ghost of little account?"

"No, I am not a ghost. I am a visitor come to pledge my fealty to King Arthur. But there are no knights or soldiers—that is, no one at all. No one except all of you in the kitchen."

"So ye be a visiting ghost. Heed me now, ghost. We must make the banquet. Not much time now or we'll lose our heads. Aye, Lord Thayne, the noxious swine, will wield the axe himself. But ye canna lose yer head, bein' yer a visiting ghost."

Olafar felt fear curdle his belly. "But King Arthur can't be dead. It isn't his time. There was no Saxon warrior called Thayne. Tell me the truth. Where is everyone?"

"Be ye daft, ghost? All the knights and soldiers, all the people and their families gathered their belongings and fled when Arthur breathed his last, for all knew Thayne and his soldiers would come to Camelot and lay waste and rejoice, the Saxon dogs."

"What about Guinevere?"

"Oh aye, the queen left too with her ladies, all her jewels stuffed in a sack."

For a moment, Olafar could only stare at the fat man, who was humming again, paying him no more attention. Olafar said, "Why didn't you and your people leave? Are you not afraid this Thayne will kill you?"

The man turned, curled his lip. "No one kills the cook, ghost. We are making enough food for a hundred soldiers, but only one is important, and that is Thayne." He lowered his voice. "Since ye be a ghost, I'll tell ye. I am going to poison the sauce on his boar steak. The witch Morgan gave me the poison to feed to him. She said he would suffer more than Arthur suffered when Thayne drove his sword through Arthur's chest. She said I would not be blamed, that Thayne's death would look like a mighty seizure."

Olafar watched him pour liquid from a small bottle into a beautiful carved wooden mug and stir it with his finger. Olafar couldn't accept that Arthur was dead, that Guinevere and all the people had fled. Camelot couldn't be taken over by the Saxons. That hadn't happened. It was then

Olafar realized he'd traveled to another Camelot in another time, another place. Voyaging backward, his father had told him many times, willing time to unfold into the past you wanted to visit, was never a certain thing, especially if the spirits you chose to aid you weren't strong enough. Time currents were fickle, his father had told him, tossed you hither and yon. Nothing was ever certain when you traveled back to where you didn't belong, to a time that wasn't yours. His father was right—this couldn't be his Camelot, where honor and bravery and splendor reigned. And this warrior, Thayne, had killed Arthur? No, impossible. But here, at this Camelot, Arthur was indeed dead, and Guinevere was gone, as were all his people and soldiers.

He watched the cook continue to stir the liquid in the carved mug with his finger. He was humming.

Suddenly, Olafar smelled lavender, old, sweet, and close, and then he felt her close, the Virgin Bride, Mathilde. Odd how he sensed her even before she appeared to him. He basked in her scent, for how long he didn't know. Then someone was shaking him. Olafar's eyes flew open, and he stared up at Grayson Sherbrooke, standing over him, holding a candle. For a moment the ancient past and the present blurred together, and Olafar didn't know where he was. Where was his bridle? He had to escape this place. He had to gallop away. Then everything righted itself. He was Olafar Ramsey. He was a tutor in the Earl of Northcliffe's great house. He whispered, "Mr. Sherbrooke, what is wrong? Is Barnaby all right?"

Grayson saw confusion when he looked into his eyes and felt—strangeness, otherness. He said quietly, "Where were you, Olafar?"

It didn't occur to him to lie. He said, "I was at Camelot, but no one was there. It was deserted except for the cook and his minions. So it wasn't the right Camelot. The time currents flung me to another place, another Camelot."

"Why was the cook there?"

"He planned to poison the Saxon warrior Thayne, who'd murdered Arthur and come to take his place to rule over Britain. But it cannot be. There was no Saxon warrior Thayne. It was the vile Mordred who murdered Arthur and destroyed Camelot.

"The other Camelot, the one I visited, it wasn't real. But I was at one Camelot, in one time, in one place, so it was not a complete failure." Olafar realized what had come out of his mouth. He stared up into the young man's shadowed face, his eyes glittering in the flickering candlelight. Olafar had known from that first night there was something different about this Sherbrooke male, and he'd felt a brief yearning to understand his differentness. What to do?

Olafar said very quietly, "How did you know to ask me where I'd been?"

CHAPTER TEN

Grayson said, "The Virgin Bride—Mathilde—came to me. She said you were using the children to help you, but she didn't understand what you needed them to do for you. I came to the schoolroom. I was frightened when I couldn't immediately wake up Pip. But when he opened his eyes, he told me about his strange dream. He was riding a huge black stallion. The stallion spoke to him, told him they were close to where he, the stallion, wanted to go. Pip wasn't at all afraid. Why did you want to go to Camelot, Olafar?"

Olafar slowly sat up and swung his legs over the side of his narrow bed. He pulled a blanket around himself and rose. He poured a mug of water and drank deeply. He said to himself, not to Grayson, "But it wasn't the right Camelot. Still, I did manage to get there and stay there for a little while."

Olafar gave a small laugh. "Olafar was also my uncle's name. My father said my uncle Olafar should not have died, but he blundered, and his life was forfeit. I was in his image, so my father said his name was now mine, and I was to take heed to make no blunders."

"Olafar, are you the black stallion I saw at the ornamental pond?"

"Yes, I am he. I saw you, knew you were somehow different from other men, and I wondered what sort of man you were. You were never afraid of me. You wanted to understand me."

Grayson nodded. "What are you?"

"I am a kelpie. Well, I am a half kelpie. My father's family hails from Shetland. They belonged to an old noggle tribe who protected the few human families living there. But my father wanted to see the Loch Ness monster, and so he moved near Urquhart Castle on the western side of the loch. He told me he did meet the monster, and she scared him half to death. He shape-shifted into a giant sea snake and surprised her enough to escape being dinner for her children.

"When he shifted into human form, he liked to drink at a pub near Inverness. He met my mother there. One night when he became a stallion and was galloping on the moors, he saw her standing by a yew bush. She told him she was waiting for him. She rode him, laughing, shouting to the heavens. When it rained, he carried her to an abandoned shack and became a human man. They married. He didn't know she was a witch until their wedding night, when she flew them into the heavens, singing at the top of her lungs. I was conceived that night, so my father told me." Olafar paused a moment, then shook his head. "I am human, but I am also other, just as my father is other, just as his father was other before him. I am different because I also carry my mother's witch blood."

Grayson said slowly, "I know of only one kelpie. His name is Barrie, and he lives near Loch Ness. Perhaps your father knows him."

"I will ask, although asking me if I know this Barrie is like my asking you if you know a man named Phillip in London. But it is possible since we live a very long time, unless we blunder, like my uncle. How do you know of this Barrie?"

"A ghost named Pearlin' Jane told me. She resides in Scotland. They are friends, she said." Grayson looked straight into Olafar's dark eyes. "I also read kelpies are a vicious race. You revel in destruction, in tormenting men."

Olafar laughed. "I venture to say most kelpies are too lazy to do much tormenting, but they enjoy having this fine reputation. No, kelpies are usually content to lie about in a loch and tell stories to each other of long-past adventures. They live in peace, for the most part. They have an affinity, I suppose you would call it, for the lochs and the Scottish air. My father, Corinth, owns a racing stud near Newmarket. To all those who know him, he is a human, nothing more, nothing different, yet still, he runs with his horses at night. He is very content to be who and what he is. Just as no one knows who or what my mother is. They are popular with other humans, comfortable with them. My witch mother's name is Arkadie, but they tell humans her name is Mary."

"Does he wear an old silver bridle when he becomes a horse as you did when I first saw you?"

"Yes, all kelpies must wear their silver bridle, or they cannot become men again. My mother told me one night it fell off him when he was racing another stallion. Thankfully, she found it and slipped it over his head again. She still rides him at night. I believe one time it came to rain and they returned to the abandoned shack. She smiled."

Grayson sometimes reflected how very different his life occasionally was from other men's. Here he was in the middle of the night, speaking to a half kelpie, half witch, who'd traveled back to Camelot, only it was the wrong Camelot. He said, "Does my uncle Douglas know your father? Corinth Ramsey?"

"Yes, certainly. Your uncle's stallion, Garth, comes from my father's stud. Perhaps it is best not to tell your uncle that Garth's former owner is a half kelpie."

Grayson said without pause, "Perhaps not. Olafar, does my cousin James and his wife, Corrie, know who and what you are?"

Olafar shook his head. "I do not feel it would benefit them to know a half kelpie was their twins' tutor. Their minds are not flexible like yours. Actually, I've never before met a human mind like yours. Oh aye, of course they accept the Virgin Bride's visits and her presence, but otherwise? They are firmly tied to the rules that govern the human world."

Grayson supposed that was true enough. But James had lived with the Virgin Bride, very much a ghost, all his life. Didn't that make him flexible as well? Didn't it make him wonder what else was there in this world? He said, "Why didn't you wish to follow in your father's foot-steps?"

"Ah, you wonder why I'm a simple tutor, not rich like my father with all his horses." Olafar realized he was desperately thirsty. He shrugged into a worn dressing gown and belted it. He walked to his desk and lit his own candle and poured himself another mug of water. "Please, Mr. Sherbrooke, sit down." He drank more water, wiped his hand across his mouth. "I know I shall very likely pay for speaking so frankly to you, even though you are an extraordinary human, but the truth is I have been lonely. When I am Bonaduce—the black stallion you saw—I search out other horses, and we gallop together. I was alone that night I saw you. You were not afraid of me. I believe now that you guessed I was different?"

CHAPTER ELEVEN

Grayson said slowly, "It was the Virgin Bride who told me you were something else. She was concerned. Tell me, Olafar, do you like keeping the human form?"

He nodded. "I know nothing else. When I was a boy, I spent my days as a human and many nights as Bonaduce. My father taught me the perils of our kind. My witch mother taught me the world's calamitous history and potions. I have a small amount of her talent. I was sent to school at Eton, like other boys of my class, then Oxford, and I discovered I was a scholar. I sang ditties at the pub and downed ale, but I had few friends."

"Why?"

Olafar shrugged and sat forward in his chair. "Even as a boy, I never learned what to say to others to make them like me, so I was always quiet, and no one ever paid me any attention. I watched, but I never got the human knack of friendship."

No wonder he was lonely. "But your father is different?"

"Everyone my father meets likes him. All his horses are like his children. They worship him. My father tried diligently to teach me to be more at ease with the human form I presented to the world, but I did not succeed. I finally accepted I was different from my father." He shrugged. "So I am alone, except at night when I am Bonaduce and I chance to meet other horses. They are wary at first, but it soon passes, and we hold competitions. Still, I fancy I will die alone, sooner rather than later if I chance to blunder like my uncle Olafar." He was quiet a moment, pulling at a thread from his dressing gown sleeve. Then he raised glowing eyes to Grayson's face. "But then a miracle happened. I heard one of my father's friends speak about the Sherbrookes searching for a tutor for small twin boys. A tutor. My heart sang, my future spread out bright in front of me. Surely children would accept me, wish to be with me, and so I came to Northcliffe Hall." He gave Grayson a radiant smile. "The twins have given me joy. They do not see me as different, as odd. They are smart and lively and keep the loneliness at bay." He paused a moment. "They hug me good night. And I know they would hug the Virgin Bride if they could."

"Will you age?"

"Slowly, very slowly, unless I blunder like my uncle Olafar. When the twins go off to school, I shall have to leave. But now I know my life has meaning and happiness as a tutor."

"You have not found a human woman or a witch to be your wife?"

Olafar shook his head. "No. I am not at ease around women."

"You need to explain yourself to Mathilde—the Virgin Bride. She is concerned. Speak to her, Olafar, assure her you mean no harm to the twins or to any child. She will show you more mysteries in our world."

Olafar said, "I have told her I mean no harm. I tell her I love the twins and would protect them with my life. I respect the Sherbrooke family. Many times I know she is near but she does not show herself. And I speak to her in the quiet of the night, asking her over and over to trust me."

"I will tell her you are not to be feared. I will tell her your mother is a witch. It should fascinate her."

Olafar said, "Did she tell you to come to me tonight?"

Grayson nodded, looked in the candle flame. Was it glowing more brightly? "She said you were using the children to get what you wanted, namely King Arthur."

A light shone again in Olafar's eyes. Enthusiasm billowed out of him. "Oh yes. What a proud and glorious ruler was King Arthur, perhaps the greatest ruler in humans' benighted history. He shines with bravery and goodness, but he was killed by evil. He was betrayed."

"Olafar, you are a scholar, a learned man. You know King Arthur's very existence is still questioned, as is Camelot and the Round Table, and yet you were there, so I must now accept Camelot did exist. Arthur killed by Mordred, who destroyed the unity of Arthur's Round Table, and led to his usurping the throne—it is all fiction, made up by Sir Thomas Malory in the fifteenth century. It is also from him we learn Guinevere broke her faith with Arthur and fled with Lancelot."

"*Le Morte d'Arthur*, yes, I have read it many times. But listen, Mr. Sherbrooke. It has been passed down through my family for hundreds of years that Malory had kelpie blood. Yes, that's right. Not only that, he also was blessed with visions, and many of them were of King Arthur, his court, his Round Table, his wife, Guinevere. He simply wrote what he saw in one of these visions. However, I have come to believe absolutely that these visions of Guinevere and Lancelot were not real, that Malory's vision was distorted. His vision was wrong." He paused a moment. "Or, I suppose it is possible Malory was offered a great deal of money to spin a tale of romance and betrayal and tragedy. And so I have wanted to go back to Camelot and see for myself what truly happened." He drew in a deep breath. "Tonight, I was able to fly there. Tonight, the time flux presented a Camelot, only it was not the real one."

Grayson said slowly, "So you are able to travel back in time?"

Olafar nodded. "Yes. Physically? When I arrived at Camelot, it felt to me that I was a flesh-and-blood man, but the cook believed I was a ghost. But still, he saw me. But Camelot was a very long time ago. Perhaps it was my spirit that visited Camelot, Mr. Sherbrooke, but then again, when you woke me, I was here, in my bed. Was my physical self there? I do not know."

"You can send yourself back to anywhere, to any time?"

"Yes, and as I said, this was the first time I actually arrived at Camelot, not the real Camelot, but to another Camelot in a different place, in a different time, or maybe simply a chimera whipped up by the time flux. But still, this time I was closer than I've ever been before.

"Until now, wherever I've visited in the past, I am unable to stay. I am whisked back very quickly. But this time, Mr. Sherbrooke—"

"Please, call me Grayson."

"Very well, Grayson. It is your son, Pip, who enabled me to stay. Pip has an amazing spirit. I recognized it immediately. It is because he is your son, of your blood, I suppose. I took his spirit with me. Even though it wasn't the right Camelot, he got me there, and as I said, I stayed until you woke me. I can see you would like to behead me for taking your son, but please understand, I would never harm Pip or any other child. Never." He stopped when he saw the father's fear for his child on Grayson's face. "Grayson, let me reassure you about the children. When my father told me I could stay where I traveled when I journeyed back in time, he told me I needed a child's spirit to tether me, and not just any child. I would have to find a special child. He assured me there was no danger to the child. I was only using his purity of spirit and adding it to my own so I could travel back and remain as long as I wished. He said the child would have a wonderful dream of riding a huge black stallion, and the dream would be forgotten by morning. The child would perhaps be tired the following day, but nothing more."

Olafar waited a moment, then said, "I swear to you I would never harm Pip. His spirit, it's as pure, shining bright as a star. Being with him enabled me to remain at this alternate Camelot. Otherwise, as I said, I am tossed back into the present. You wonder how it works. I cannot tell you. I know only that a special child's spirit is necessary for me to stay." Again, he studied Grayson's face. "Pip is the key to my finding the real Camelot, I know it."

Grayson nodded slowly. "All right. Tell me about this different Camelot you visited before I awakened you."

"Once I touched Pip's hand as he slept, within seconds, I stood in front of a vast wooden fortress. It was empty of soldiers and people both inside and out. I went into a great hall, and again, no people, no soldiers. Then I went through a door and into a kitchen, and here were many people preparing a feast. The cook believed me a ghost and spoke to me freely. He told me a mighty Saxon warrior called Thayne had killed King Arthur, and Guinevere had left with all the other people from Camelot. Thayne would come shortly to take Arthur's place as king of the Britons. The cook said he was going to poison his boar steak. I watched him stir poison into a mug. Then you woke me up. Will Pip's spirit with mine be able to set things aright and take me to the real Camelot? I do not know. But given what happened, given how close we were, I know with Pip I can go to the real Camelot."

Grayson wondered briefly what his hero Thomas Straithmore would do now. He said, "As I told you, when I awakened Pip, he told me he was riding a big black stallion. He wasn't afraid. He was thrilled, and that is why I wasn't afraid for him."

"If it's all right with you, I want to try again."

"How would that work if you used all the children's spirits together?"

"They would all ride on my back, but not at the same time, slips of time apart." He looked frustrated. "It is difficult to explain. If I took more than one child, all would be with me, yet each of them would be alone with me—with the black stallion, with Bonaduce. But I do not need P.C. or Barnaby. Pip is magic."

CHAPTER TWELVE

Grayson studied the candle flame, now burning low, then looked closely at Olafar's shadowed face. "I've always believed Camelot existed, a real place, a magical place, idealized, of course, and ruled by Arthur Pendragon, King Arthur. Arthur and his knights defined honor in that long-ago dark and savage Britain. Malory's addition of romantic betrayal, all human frailties shown in full bloom, in such a vastly quixotic, mystical place called Camelot, has moved me, as it has so many others."

Olafar sat forward. "Oh yes, Arthur was the epitome of strength and honor, always a shining presence, an ideal for a man to aspire to. And all the pure knights were presented as examples of chivalry and honor and idealized love."

Olafar paused, then said, "You do understand it is up to me to go back and discover the truth. Was Malory's vision true? Did Guinevere and Lancelot betray Arthur? Did Mordred really kill him and destroy Camelot?" His eyes burned with an intense light. "Next time, with Pip, I will find my way to the real Camelot, not this chimera tossed at me by a strange time flux. I want to right the wrongs, discredit Malory's story that is now viewed as history. I pray I discover Guinevere did not betray Arthur, that she and Lancelot remained loyal and true."

Grayson slowly nodded. "I believe it would be helpful if you explained to Pip what you and he were going to try to accomplish. He is only five years old, but he is smart. He sees people and things clearly for so young a—human." Grayson rose. "Let me know what you decide. Until tomorrow, Olafar."

Grayson looked in on all three children before he returned to his bedchamber. All were sleeping soundly. Dreaming of galloping on the back of an incredible black stallion?

When he was back in his bedchamber, on his back in the soft bed, the covers pulled to his neck, the Virgin Bride appeared at the foot of his bed. One moment, there was only still silence, and in the next, there was filmy light and a presence so vivid it seemed the air nearly parted for her. "Good evening, Mathilde. Did you hear my discussion with Olafar?"

She shimmered. Grayson fancied he could feel her excitement. *Oh yes, I listened in wonderment. The story about Guinevere and Lancelot's betrayal—so real, so much a part of the legend, yet it was made up hundreds of years later. It is accepted as a whole, no matter if parts of it were added at a later time. You accept all of it or none. Ah, the passion Arthur's name still evokes. I think it is like the legend of the virginity of Queen Elizabeth, which was not at all true, but now it is accepted. My mother believed the Arthur legend. She hated Guinevere for her betrayal, but not Lancelot for seducing her. Is that not strange?*

I have wandered through many human lives in my time, Grayson, seen a bit of happiness, seen immense cruelty, so many tragedies, witnessed births and deaths. I have made Sherbrooke lives easier when I could. Even though many of your ancestors, and yes, the current earl, Douglas, does not like to accept me as real even though he knows very well I am since I helped him save Alex all those years ago. Well, many years to you, but a moment in time to me. I have visited the Sherbrooke children who became men and women and moved from Northcliffe, but always, I must return here to where I first appeared so long ago.

I did not think I could ever be surprised, people being what they are, never changing through the centuries, repeating the same mistakes over and over, but still pushing on, ever on. But, Grayson, the kelpie, Olafar, he is different. I know he is brave. I know he has a burning curiosity, and he wants to right wrongs that were only created by a human man in the first place. He truly believes this Malory was part kelpie and had visions of ancient Camelot. I do not know if this is true, only it is of vital importance to him. I believe I now like Olafar. I trust him with the children. I want to help him. Will you ask him if I am able to journey back to Camelot? With him? With all of you? I know you, Grayson—you want to journey back with him and Pip, do you not? You want to see for yourself.

He grinned. "Yes, you do know me well, Mathilde. Why don't you ask him if it is possible for you to journey back? It seems to me it would not be a problem, given you can leave Northcliffe and go where you please, so why not in the past as well?"

Her hair whipped about her head in an unseen wind, and her white face seemed to glow. Her pale veils shimmered. *It makes my heart pound, Grayson, so very fast and hard. Yes, I will ask Olafar. Do you think he will let me ride him when he shifts to a black stallion? When will we leave?*

He wasn't going to mention she didn't have a beating heart. "Soon, I imagine. Perhaps tomorrow night."

I want to prove my mother wrong, prove Guinevere did not betray Arthur. But will she know it? I do not know where she is. I only hope she is nowhere near me. It was her fault I died so young.

"What happened?"

An evil man, a covetous woman, namely my mother, and a disposable child, namely me. I killed him, Grayson, on my wedding night when he would have raped me, and she killed me in a rage. So long ago, yet only a moment in time.

The Virgin Bride whisked away and left Grayson's heart pounding.

CHAPTER THIRTEEN

Grayson didn't want to go to the Smythe-Ambrosios' party. He wanted to stay with Olafar and discuss how they would all go back to Camelot tonight. He accepted there was no logic to any of it, no result he could see that would make a whit of difference. Except to Olafar. Well, if it turned out the so-called vision Malory had of Guinevere and Lancelot's betrayal wasn't true, well, then Grayson knew Thomas Straithmore would somehow prove it. Would his readers consider it simply another otherworldly tale spun from his imagination? He had a frightening thought: What if Camelot hadn't really existed? What if King Arthur was nothing more than the imaginings of another long-ago writer, like himself, spinning a story to entertain?

Grayson thought about the twelfth-century French poet Chrétien de Troyes. He'd been the one to invent Lancelot in his work *Lancelot, or The Knight of the Cart*. Logic dictated Malory had only loaded on, making Lancelot and Guinevere lovers. He realized he was getting a headache trying to weave his way through fiction, visions, and what really transpired in a place called Camelot, a place not every scholar even agreed existed.

He wondered if he could conveniently claim illness when Maximus informed him Miss Elphinstone was riding her white mare, S.W., up the long drive. But no, he was a gentleman. He walked out of the house to see her turn her mare into the west gardens. He followed her, without much hope of getting out of attending her aunt and uncle's soiree. He saw her dismount and walk to where his aunt Alex was discussing her roses with a group of visitors who'd been making themselves at home in her gardens. She immediately joined in. When she saw him, she excused herself from a voluble older lady accompanied by her maid, and called out, "Mr. Sherbrooke, I was hinting to anyone who would listen that her ladyship employs Cornish elves to keep her gardens in fine fettle."

"They're not elves—they're piskies in Cornwall," Grayson said.

A lovely eyebrow shot up. "Just so, Mr. Sherbrooke. Now, I am here to ensure all of you are coming this evening to Blandish Manor."

Grayson nodded, no choice in the matter. His aunt Alex, on the other hand, was looking forward to the evening. She said, "It has been too long a time since we have visited with all our neighbors in one place."

After more pleasantries, and too many looks from Miss Elphinstone, she whistled and her beautiful mare, tail high, came prancing to her side. "Until tonight," she sang out, leaned down and said something to her mare, and off they went. Grayson and Alex stood watching her ride down the long drive. "It is odd," Alex said, "but two days ago I did not believe her beautiful. Indeed, I believed her barely passable. But today, watching her speak to the visitors, I found her quite charmingly lovely." She cocked a dark-red eyebrow at him. "Best take care, Grayson. She was looking at you with a bit too much interest, like you're a desired dessert, mayhap even a nutty bun. What do you think?"

"I think if she wants P.C. to continue being friendly, she will stop eyeing me like a blancmange."

And so it was that Grayson, Uncle Douglas, and Aunt Alex arrived at Blandish Manor at eight o'clock on a surprisingly clear and warm Friday evening, dressed to show their good taste and each with a large swig of brandy from Uncle Douglas's flask to shine at social conversation.

There were fourteen guests to dinner in the charming Queen Anne dining room, all close neighbors, all ready to enjoy themselves. Grayson saw the gleam in Mrs. Smythe-Ambrosio's dark eyes when he realized he was seated between her niece and a rheumy old gentleman whose claim to fame was an inherited fortune and surviving Waterloo. On Miss Elphinstone's other side was a young man who appeared mightily interested in her. Grayson wished him luck.

Before he raised a spoon to his turtle soup, Miss Elphinstone leaned close. "Please call me R.M., Mr. Sherbrooke. May I call you Grayson?"

"You may, but I will not call you R.M. You must tell me your actual name, or you will have to remain Miss Elphinstone."

She took a bite of a soft dinner roll, swallowed, and said, "I lied to the children. I wanted to keep in the spirit of their fun. No, I am not R.M., I am Delyth. It is a common enough Welsh name. My father, however, called me his nemesis."

"Why?"

"Ah, Mr. Sherbrooke, I fear I must know you better before I tell you. Will you ride with me tomorrow? Are you free?"

Luckily, he wasn't, or he wouldn't be, once he'd spoken to his uncle Douglas.

By the end of the elaborate meal flowing with excellent champagne from Smythe-Ambrosio's cellar, the gentlemen remained in the dining room to drink port and talk politics, which interested Grayson not one whit. He and his uncle Douglas were among the first to join the ladies in the drawing room. Grayson wasn't surprised when Miss Elphinstone played Welsh ballads on the piano and sang in a lovely soprano.

Upon their departure, Delyth took his hand, eased close. "If I cannot see you tomorrow, then I shall see you on Sunday. At church. And then, who knows what will happen?"

Alex said as their carriage rolled onto the country road back to Northcliffe Hall, "A splendid evening. All our neighbors seem to become more intelligent with champagne, don't you find that true?"

"Only if you have also become more intelligent with champagne, Alex."

She grinned at him. "Just so. However, Douglas, I am concerned Miss Elphinstone wants Grayson. She is not subtle."

Grayson sighed. "What should I do, Aunt Alex? Should I simply be honest and tell her about Miranda? Of course, if she isn't interested in me, I would be offending her and embarrassing myself."

She leaned forward to pat his knee. "Trust me, Grayson, she is interested. Go ahead, tell her you are involved with another lady, but I do not believe it will discourage Miss Elphinstone."

"Her name is Welsh. Delyth. It is a beautiful name." Was Aunt Alex right? But if so, why him in particular? This trip had dished up so many unexpected things, including Miss Elphinstone. He itched to see Olafar. Perhaps tonight they could travel to Camelot. What an odd thought that was, but no odder, he decided, than the two vicious demons he'd dealt with in Scotland.

Douglas frowned. "I'm not so certain Miss Elphinstone is enamored with Grayson, Alex. I agree she wants to stay close, but to entice him? I'm thinking it's something else entirely." He shook his head.

CHAPTER FOURTEEN

It was well past midnight, the children soundly sleeping, when Grayson met Olafar in the schoolroom. To his surprise, the Virgin Bride was hovering behind Olafar's left shoulder. She looked as she always looked—flowing, soft white veils, her magnificent hair hanging loose to her waist, like spun gold. No, there was a difference. It seemed to him she was somehow brighter, more *present*, she glowed with such excitement. Grayson smiled at her, and she seemed to glow even brighter.

He said to Olafar, "Do we awaken Pip?"

"No," Olafar said. "I will connect to his spirit using a simple kelpie chant. As for you, Grayson, and you, Mathilde, I am not sure. This is new to me. What will happen? Will you come with me, or will you remain here, only your spirits, like Pip's, sustaining me, and not actually with me? I do not know. However, I do know that you, Grayson, should lie next to Pip, very close."

He turned to Mathilde. She shimmered, flowed closer, and thought to both of them, *Olafar, I can simply flow into you, become one with you, at least temporarily. Do you believe that will work?*

Olafar beamed at her, and in his mind, he heard her laughing, a girl's high, sweet laugh of excitement.

Grayson lay wide awake, lying on his side, Pip hugged close to him. Why didn't something happen? Where was Olafar? Where was Mathilde?

Suddenly, from one instant to the next, he was astride the beautiful black stallion, Bonaduce. Pip wasn't with him. He panicked. "Where is Pip? I was holding him next to me in his bed."

But Olafar was now Bonaduce and couldn't answer him. Pip's spirit, he thought, only his spirit was here. Was Grayson really here or, like Pip, only his spirit? Was this all a dream spun by a kelpie? But Grayson felt wide awake, wildly alive, his heart pumping with excitement.

Where was Mathilde?

He felt her warm against his cheek, as if fingers touched him lightly. *I am here, Grayson. Yes, Pip is asleep in his bed at Northcliffe, and dreaming a glorious dream. Ah, Grayson, I have enjoyed many adventures but none so fine as this. This is magnificent. You and I, we are actually here! Riding a horse. I had forgotten—*

Bonaduce soared upward, and Grayson heard himself shout with pleasure, heard Mathilde whoosh out a breath. How could she have a breath? He wasn't going to worry about it. Nothing happening was logical; nothing was real. Or was it? Where were they? Why was he flying higher into the heavens? Grayson didn't know.

Bonaduce trumpeted a whinny, and suddenly they were on the ground again in the middle of a forest, oak trees crowding in on them, lush in their summer green, with moonlight filtering through, fingers of light parting the leaves. Grayson saw they were on a rutted path. Bonaduce slewed his big head around, and in the next instant, he was human again.

It was amazing to watch. More amazing to him, Grayson didn't simply fall to the ground once Bonaduce became a man. No, one instant he was on Bonaduce's broad back, and the next he was standing in the middle of an oak forest. Olafar said, "You wondered why you were with me and Pip wasn't. In his dream, he is, Grayson. Trust me, he is enjoying himself. Does he see you? I do not know."

Grayson wondered aloud, "But am I really here, or like Pip, is it only my spirit? And my spirit can talk to you? Or am I as solid a human here as I was back at Northcliffe? It is all very strange, Olafar, even to me, and believe me when I tell you I have experienced many inexplicable things in my life."

Olafar smiled. "Yes, I imagine so if your Thomas Straithmore novels are based on your own otherworldly adventures. You know this is new to me as well, Grayson. I see you, yes, and we both appear to be here. I know your spirit is strong, Grayson, and your mind is open, always wondering and wandering, seeking out creatures who shouldn't exist, but do. You have abilities ordinary mortals do not have. Are you really here with me?" He shrugged. "As I told you, I have no experience with another adult human. I have always traveled alone before, sometimes with a child's spirit to tether me at my destination, mostly not." He looked thoughtful a moment, then said, "An experiment—" He hit Grayson on the arm with his fist.

Grayson felt a punch of pain. "Given my arm hurts, I will rule I am here—somehow." But was he, really? He didn't know. "Where is Mathilde?"

Olafar called out, "Mathilde, are you here as well?"

I will be here soon, Olafar. I must reassemble myself. Ah, what excitement. I swear I could feel the wind whipping through my hair as if—as if I were young and alive again.

Both he and Olafar turned, looking, waiting. Olafar said, "Mathilde, I can see you sort of fluttering. How do you feel?"

She thought to them, *How do I feel? What an odd question to hear. I am dead, Olafar. Am I supposed to feel something now?* She paused, then, *Oh my, I feel happy. I feel excited. I want to dance. By all the saints my evil mother denounced, I feel alive, or nearly. What is happening?*

They watched as the white veils, instead of growing brighter, seemed to grow fainter, fading into nothing. Then they felt a shift in the air, a sort of shivering, as if the air itself was parting and a shape was forming, a young girl's shape. Grayson's mouth went dry. "Olafar, what do you see?"

Olafar had Bonaduce's reins and bridle in his hands, weaving them through his fingers. He said simply, "I see a beautiful young girl, a budding rose, nearly a woman grown. Mathilde, you are smiling at me. You are breathing like I am breathing. And your hair—" Olafar's breath hitched. He shook his head as if to clear his vision.

Mathilde was no longer wearing shimmering veils and fluttering about. She was wearing an old-fashioned gown of green wool with a high neck and long sleeves, a narrow gold belt around her waist. Not clothing from her time, the sixteenth century. No. Was it a gown from long ago, the time of King Arthur? Her glorious blond hair was held back from her face with a strip of matching green wool.

Grayson said, "Hello, Mathilde. I am glad you are here, but how can it be?"

Olafar said slowly, his eyes never leaving her face, "If we are indeed back at ancient Camelot, you were not born yet, not for hundreds of years. You had not died yet."

Grayson said, unable to take his eyes off her, "So does that mean coming to another time, a time before you died, you could become human again and, well, alive?"

Instead of thinking to him, Mathilde said in the king's pure English, "I have no notion, but I do know I am here with you and Olafar. I breathe. I feel. I never want to leave this place or this time. How very odd—I am speaking. I can hear the words coming from my mouth." She began twirling about, skirts flying, her magnificent hair streaming around her head. Grayson couldn't believe it. It couldn't be real. But she was here, and he was here, both because of a half kelpie who wanted to prove Sir Thomas Malory's vision about Guinevere's betrayal had been wrong. And Pip was sleeping back in the present.

In the past, with other spirits, other creatures, Grayson had simply let his brain accept where he was. And so he gave it up. He was here, hopefully at long-ago Camelot.

Olafar held up his hand. "Mathilde, I will dance with you later. Come now, we can talk more about all these questions again, but I do not know how long we will be able to remain here, in the distant past. I'm hoping with the two of you, and with Pip's strong spirit, we can be here for as long as we like, but who knows? Now, it's time to see if the time flux has brought us to the real Camelot."

"I am at Camelot," Mathilde sang out.

CHAPTER FIFTEEN

Mathilde skipped, she turned in circles, and she danced, holding her skirts high. Then she started singing, a sweet clear melody, a song neither of them recognized.

Olafar laughed. "Come, we must go to Camelot."

Mathilde continued to sing softly as she skipped beside them, so excited she was.

They walked out of the oak forest to see an immense wooden fortress at the end of a long expanse of barren ground. It was a knights' practice field. In the distance was a small town, and behind the town, the sea lay beyond, calm and deep blue in the bright sunlight. The Irish Sea? Were they in Tintagel? Grayson said, "Olafar, does this look familiar to you?"

"Oh yes, it surely does." He took Mathilde's very human white hand and pulled her along, faster now. "I don't know why, but I feel we must hurry. What if we are too late? No, no, but something is going to happen, and we must be there to stop it."

The three of them ran to the huge wooden fortress, stopped, and looked about. Olafar said, "It is like before. There are no soldiers about. I fear the time flux has again sent me to the right place but the wrong Camelot. Come, let's see if the gate is open."

The gate swung open with only a light push, and they walked into an immense courtyard. It wasn't empty. There were scores of men, women, children, animals, and soldiers all mixed together. But they weren't moving. They seemed to be frozen, as in a tableau or a painting.

"I do not understand," Olafar said, staring about. "So many people, but there is no life. Or life has simply stopped. Why? What is going on here?"

Mathilde said quietly, "You wonder why all the people aren't going about their lives. I think they are a representation of what Camelot was or could have been. Listen, Olafar, accept you are not here to see the people of Camelot. Your focus is on seeing King Arthur and Queen Guinevere, so mayhap this time flux you spoke of brought you here only to see them. Let us go inside."

Olafar looked around and slowly nodded. "Perhaps. Perhaps you are right."

Mathilde grabbed both their hands and ran lightly through the people who were really only the images of people, no substance to them, across the courtyard and up the dozen wide steps, through the wide wooden doors and into the vast central hall. It was again filled with people, many dressed finely, many soldiers with axes and swords, again, a tableau, just like their counterparts outside.

On the dais at the end of the hall were two thrones. On the large one sat a young man, sun-darkened hands on the carved throne arms. His dark hair was pulled back from a strong granite-carved face and bound in a club at the back of his neck. He looked like he would not hesitate to destroy anyone who threatened him, or perhaps disagreed with him. He wore a beautiful golden-threaded long tunic over black leggings with fine black leather boots cross-gartered up to his knees. A beautiful silver sword was fastened to a wide leather belt at his lean waist. Excalibur? A gold crown set with what looked to be rubies sat on his head. He wore a thick golden chain around his neck. At the end of the chain was a blackened disk covered with deeply etched figures and characters. He wasn't paying any attention to the frozen people in front of him, nor did he appear to see them. He was turned slightly on his throne, speaking toward the vivid red curtains at the edge of the dais. He said clearly in English they understood, and wasn't that strange, "Guinevere, come here. Lord Thayne will be here soon."

The red velvet curtains parted, and a woman slipped through. And not just any woman—it was the Guinevere of legend, so beautiful a man would stutter just looking at her soft white skin, her thick golden hair pulled back by golden combs, showing a face surely fashioned by the gods. Behind her came a young man, golden as the sun, his face fashioned by the same gods as Guinevere's, tall and fit, and he was smiling at Arthur. He looked noble, a warrior, a man fashioned for great deeds, yet there was something in that smile, something sly, something that perhaps bespoke duplicity.

"Where were you?" Arthur asked his queen, his voice clipped and sharp.

Guinevere said, "One of my stockings went astray, and my lady had to fetch me another. Lancelot joined me outside our chamber, and we hurried here to await Lord Thayne."

"Come sit in your place. Thayne will be here soon." He spared a look at Lancelot, nodded and smiled, but his eyes were watchful, distrusting. Lancelot bowed and stepped off the dais. Suddenly, he stopped and became as frozen as were all the other people in the great hall.

Arthur said to Guinevere, "I have been told by one of my spies that Thayne is here to kill me. I have told all my knights to be ready. There are many men like Thayne who pretend to friendship and honor but have none."

Guinevere nodded, walked to her throne, and sat gracefully down on an elaborate green embroidered cushion. Arthur said between seamed lips, not looking at her, "I am sending Lancelot to Londinium. I want him to meet with soldiers I have heard are searching for a master. If he finds them able, he will bring them here."

She seemed to stiffen, yet her graceful white hands lay quiescent in her lap. "Will it be dangerous?"

Arthur turned to look at his queen and said sharply, "There is always danger, no matter who or where you are. We ourselves are awaiting danger right here in Camelot. Why would you be concerned? He is my man. He will do as I tell him to do."

"But surely you must need Lancelot here—"

Suddenly, there was a loud shout. The doors of the great hall flew open, and armed men flooded in, yelling, their swords drawn. King Arthur leapt from his throne, drew Excalibur, and jumped from the dais and into the battle. They saw a warrior leap at him while he was fighting another, his sword held high, and he was bringing it down into Arthur's back. And then—

Olafar, Grayson, and Mathilde once again stood outside the giant wooden gates of the fortress.

Mathilde grabbed Olafar's hand. "What happened?"

"I do not know. It was as if we were simply plucked out—by what? What power could do that?"

Grayson said slowly, "You spoke of the time flux taking you to the wrong Camelot. It appears it brought you back to the wrong Camelot again and jerked us out just before Lord Thayne murdered Arthur, and, one supposes, Guinevere ran away with Lancelot."

Olafar looked up at the empty ramparts and searched for soldiers, but didn't see any, and listened for any noise that did not come. He said slowly, "It is odd, but I feel something, a differentness. Perhaps the time flux has shifted again, perhaps because I am with you and Mathilde and together, with Pip's spirit, we are now strong enough to bring us to the right Camelot, the one of history."

Grayson said, "Only one way to find out. Let us go to the great hall."

Mathilde said, "Guinevere, she was more beautiful than any woman I have ever seen or dreamed of."

Olafar nodded. "She was so beautiful it made my teeth ache to look at her."

Grayson couldn't disagree.

CHAPTER SIXTEEN

The great hall was as it had been but moments before—filled with people, courtiers, and soldiers, but again, they were only images, *representations* Mathilde had called them, frozen in time, nothing more substantial than people in an old painting.

On the large gilded throne sat a strong-looking middle-aged man, his thick dark hair mixed with silver strands, and like the young Arthur, it was pulled back from his face and bound in a club. It was King Arthur. He was dressed more elaborately than his younger counterpart, his tunic fine gold-spun linen, the same thick golden chain around his neck with its black etched disk. He wore Excalibur fastened at his side on a fine black leather belt. Beautiful boots covered his feet, bound by supple leather cross garters to his knees. He was tapping his strong, blunt fingers against the throne arm. He turned and called out, again, in English they could understand, "Guinevere, hurry, love. I wish you to be here when Lord Thayne arrives. I want to keep you safe."

The red velvet curtain parted, and a woman slipped onto the dais. It wasn't the Guinevere of legend, the Guinevere they'd just seen, a temptress so beautiful a man's lust rose fast and hard. Although this Guinevere's face was lovely, the fact was she was short and plump, middle-aged, like

Arthur. Her hair wasn't the spun gold of a man's dreams, lustrous and thick. Like Arthur's, her hair was threaded with white, and it was bound in netting pulled back from her face. She wore a gown of soft green linen, a thin golden chain around her waist. She looked like a settled matron, perhaps a mother of grown children, just as King Arthur looked older and more settled. She had a bit of a double chin. They watched her smile at her husband, a sweet smile that held no guile. "My lord, one of my stockings went astray, and my lady had to fetch me another." She leaned down, not very far, and kissed the tip of his nose. She lightly stroked her palm over his cheek. "Do you feel better? I did not like that cough during the night."

Arthur grabbed her hand and pulled her onto his lap. Her feet dangled. She laughed, a lovely sound, light and carefree. He said, "I am well. Worry you not, sweeting. The cream you rubbed on my chest cured me. I have determined I married a witch, and I am glad of it." And he kissed her again and set her on her feet. She settled beside him on the smaller throne. He said, "If my spy is right, Thayne has come to kill me instead of offering peace. Be alert. When he enters, what he plans will be clear soon enough."

Guinevere raised a white hand from the folds of her gown. In it, she held a knife. "We will protect each other."

They heard loud voices coming from outside the great hall. Suddenly, the frozen tableau came alive. People were shouting, running, men pulling their swords, women jumping onto the dais to protect Guinevere. King Arthur jumped up, pulled Excalibur from its scabbard, and leaped down from the dais and plunged into the battle.

It was as if they were spectators, watching a battle in front of them, but they weren't really there, weren't really a part of it. But it was real—they saw blood spurt from heads and bodies, saw an arm cleaved to fall on the wooden floor, flinging blood everywhere, heard swords clashing together, heard death yells. As suddenly as it had started, it stopped, and once again, it was a tableau.

Only Arthur moved. He stood panting over a man, blood covering his chest, moaning, staring up at him. Arthur spat on him. "You announced you wanted peace, yet I knew you only wanted my death, the destruction of my kingdom." He raised Excalibur and with both hands struck downward, sending the mighty sword deep into the man's chest.

The man didn't make a sound.

Guinevere appeared at his side, panting, clutching at his arm, her knife tight in her hand. Arthur pulled out Excalibur, wiped off the blood on Lord Thayne's tunic, and slid it back into its scabbard. He called out, "Lancelot? Where are you?"

A heavy middle-aged man with faded golden hair, flecked with white, came striding up, nodded to Guinevere, and bowed to Arthur. "We were ready. His men are dispatched, my lord. All is well." He kicked the dead body at Arthur's feet. "It is as your spy told us. Thayne was a treacherous swine."

They watched Arthur, Guinevere, and Lancelot walk back to the dais, Lancelot smiling, nodding as Arthur sat himself again on his throne. "Ah, a lovely fight, but so quickly done. I fear my bones grow old, my lord. I fear I have strained my back."

"All of us grow old, my friend," Arthur said. "But we were still strong and powerful when we needed to be. Thayne, he was a young man, and yet he was no match for us. Guinevere also told me she suspected Thayne. I believed her more than my spy. Thank you." He leaned over and clasped Guinevere's hand.

Grayson, Olafar, and Mathilde stood silently, watching, barely breathing.

Grayson said quietly, even though he knew the three people on the dais couldn't hear him, probably didn't even see them or know they were there, "I believe you have your answer, Olafar. At least, I hope the time flux brought us to the right Camelot. And thus, Sir Thomas Malory's vision was a fiction."

Olafar nodded. "I believe I understand. Malory didn't have a vision. He had enough kelpie blood to travel back. He was caught in a time flux the first time. Yes, both of us were taken to the wrong Camelot. But he believed it, no reason not to, and it became his truth. After all, he'd seen the betrayal with his own eyes. And his truth became, unfortunately, the world's truth." He grinned and rubbed his hands together. "Yes, I know it to my bones this is the correct Camelot. It feels right. It feels real. The three of them together throughout their lives—yes, that's as it really was. Let us go home now."

Mathilde suddenly looked like she was going to cry, but she nodded, slowly. Of course she didn't want to go back. Understandable, since she would be dead and become a ghost again. If only there were some way to let her remain alive, but of course there wasn't. She'd been born in her time and died in her time. The three of them walked through the great fortress, walked across the practice field and back into the oak forest. Olafar walked directly to the same spot they'd first appeared. He pulled the reins and bridle out of his shirt and held them high. In the next instant, Bonaduce was flying high above the ground, Grayson on his back. Mathilde, still human, clutched Bonaduce's black mane, her glorious blond hair whipping out behind her.

Would she simply fade away when they returned to the present? How could it be otherwise? Grayson sighed. Sometimes life—and death—wasn't fair.

CHAPTER SEVENTEEN

Alex Sherbrooke waved a letter at the breakfast table and said to her husband and Grayson, "A letter from James. He, Corrie, and the twins are coming home early. They want to visit with you, Grayson—and Pip, of course. Evidently the twins have been talking nonstop, wanting to hear a ghost story from you."

Grayson nodded, smiled. "And I do have a wonderful story to tell them." He rose. "Please excuse me. I must see to fulfilling a promise."

"What promise?" his uncle Douglas asked, a white brow raised. "To whom?"

"It's not really a promise, but it's something I've thought about a lot, and now I want to act."

He left his aunt and uncle staring after him and went to the third floor to the schoolroom. Olafar was reading while the children finished their breakfast. Pip, P.C., and Barnaby were laughing, arguing, who knew about what. At least they weren't throwing food at each other. Pip looked up, smiled at his father, and then turned back to P.C. It didn't appear Pip remembered his ride on Bonaduce's back. Had he remembered the first time because Grayson had pulled him out of the dream and it hadn't yet faded? Evidently so.

"Grayson." Olafar closed his book and rose. "How are you feeling this very fine morning?"

"I feel as fine as the beautiful morning. It is not raining, a wondrous thing. May I speak to you, Olafar?"

They walked to the far end of the schoolroom, out of the children's hearing. Grayson said, "The Virgin Bride, Mathilde, she was as real as you and I were at Camelot."

"Yes, yes, she was." He shook his head. "And how real was that, exactly? We seemed real enough to each other, but we were only observers to all the people at Camelot. I do not know how to explain any of it, Grayson."

Grayson said, "It seems like a dream, a distant but still very finely detailed dream. Mathilde didn't want to leave, Olafar. She didn't want to be a ghost again."

Olafar nodded. "I know. When we returned, she didn't say anything. She simply disappeared. I haven't yet seen her today. I've given it a lot of thought, Grayson, and I have an idea."

Grayson smiled. "Mayhap it is the same idea I have."

Both Olafar and Grayson called to her, but Mathilde did not appear. Grayson rode with the children, took them to the neighboring village of Porthe, and bought them ice cream.

That afternoon he walked in the eastern gardens, thinking, hoping what he and Olafar wished would be possible. He heard her, knew who it was, and turned to see Delyth beautifully gowned in a dark-blue riding habit, a pert hat set atop her head. She held a riding crop against her skirts. "Is there something I may do for you, Delyth?"

She eyed him, then sighed. "I have already seen Olafar. Now it is time for you to know the truth. You believe I am Belgian, but that is not true. I simply took the shape of Mrs. Smythe-Ambrosio's niece, here to surprise my aunt and uncle. They welcomed me gladly, and I made up grand stories for them about the family in Antwerp.

"You also believed I was flirting with you, Mr. Sherbrooke. I was, but it was for a reason."

Grayson arched an eyebrow.

Slowly, she pulled a beautiful silver bridle from a pocket in her gown. "My name is Delyth Ramsey. I am Olafar's sister. I am also half kelpie, half witch. I've been careful he hasn't seen me up close, else he would know who I am. I did not want him to know I came because I knew I had to protect him, and believe me, he would be insulted. And so I've watched from afar.

"You know our mother is a witch, but she is not just any witch. She is very powerful. She sees things, knows things. She told my father and me that you are a man who sees things other men don't, a man who has experienced many strange and wondrous things, a man who's dispatched demons and evil spirits from long ago. She said this differentness made her afraid for Olafar because she couldn't see clearly into your mind to assess how you would deal with him. Would you see him as a demon? See him as being dangerous to your son and the other children? An abomination to be destroyed? So I volunteered to come."

Grayson could only stare at her in amazement. "Of course I would not kill Olafar."

She smiled at him. "Forgive her. She's a mother, and she worries. No, I realized soon enough you would never harm Olafar, which is why I'm telling you the truth now. Olafar is happy. He loves the twins and travels with their spirits. He told me you accompanied him to ancient Camelot."

"Yes, last night. Olafar is now content. Did your mother also know about Mathilde, the Virgin Bride? She is the resident Sherbrooke ghost, a young lady who died in the sixteenth century. She is the protector of the Sherbrooke ladies. Olafar told you she traveled back with us?"

At her nod, Grayson said, "It was miraculous. She was human, but back here in the present, she was once again a ghost."

"Olafar told me he needed to speak to her. About what, he did not tell me. But I know, I know." She shook her head. "My mother, never shall I doubt her again. She not only is a powerful witch, but she is also blessed with the second sight. That is, she sees things no one else can see, feels things no one else can feel. And she was right. I was with my parents last night, and she told me she saw Olafar with a beautiful young woman with long, glorious blond hair, and the young woman was laughing and dancing and singing. She told me Olafar was going to marry her."

Grayson could only stare at her. "But that is not possible. She is a ghost."

Delyth leaned forward and kissed his cheek. "Ah, but she wasn't at Camelot, was she? I fancy Mathilde and Olafar will travel back and forth many times in the coming years, visit many places, perhaps even go back to Rome in the time of the great Caesar. Will she have children in another time? Will she grow older? I'll ask my mother. Perhaps she can see their future."

She lightly touched her fingers to his arm. "You are a fine man, Mr. Sherbrooke, and very kind. I thank you. My mother also said to tell you Barnaby's father is George Nathan Cox, eighth Baron Worsley. His main country residence is in Hartlepool, not far south of where you live. Barnaby is not illegitimate. He was stolen by a jealous woman and left on the church steps in your village. Barnaby's mother died shortly after his disappearance—from grief, my mother said. Baron Worsley searched and searched for his son. You will bring him great joy when you return Barnaby to him, Grayson. Oh yes, there will be no doubts. Barnaby is the picture of Baron Worsley. Both have bright-red hair and eyes as blue as a summer sky." She paused a moment, leaned forward, and kissed him. She stepped back and pulled the silver reins and bridle from her gown pocket and held them high. In the next instant, Grayson stared at a beautiful palomino mare. She butted her head against his shoulder, then kicked up her hind legs and galloped out of the eastern garden.

EPILOGUE

"Papa?"

Grayson smiled at his son, now looking up from his eggs, a slice of toast in his small hand.

"Yes, Pip?"

"Last night Mathilde came to kiss me goodbye. She told me she and Mr. Ramsey were going to China. I asked her where China was, but she didn't know. She doesn't really talk, but you know what she's saying anyway. I asked her how she could do that, and she laughed. I felt her kiss me, Papa, and I heard her still laughing, and she hummed. Then she was just gone."

"China," Grayson repeated, and smiled. The Virgin Bride would remain, yet she wouldn't, not really, not in her world, but in long-past worlds. "It's a marvelous place, Pip, very far away and very different from England. She will like it there."

As Grayson watched his son finish his breakfast, he thought about Olafar. He knew Olafar would speak to Uncle Douglas this morning and tell him a family matter was forcing him to leave his employ. Grayson knew, of course, Olafar had no choice. He had plans, grand plans, and he had to be free to carry them out.

Grayson smiled as he thought of Barnaby. When they returned home, he would ride to Hartlepool to meet Baron Worsley and tell him about his son. When Delyth had said his name, of course Grayson remembered where he'd known the baron. He'd been at Oxford, perhaps five years before Grayson. He'd been plain George Cox then, the bane of the dons, always in trouble, and Grayson had heard some of the fantastic stories of his exploits. What would P.C. have to say about Barnaby's newfound father—a baron—and his future title? She'd preen, he knew it. And what would Baron Worsley think of P.C.? Grayson had no doubt the baron would be enchanted.

Grayson's writer's mind gave him the first sentence to his next book: "*The witch saw her small son's future in her scrying mirror and smiled. It was an incredible future.*"

The Red Witch of Ravenstone Folly

THE FIFTH NOVELLA
IN THE GRAYSON SHERBROOKE OTHERWORLDLY
ADVENTURES SERIES

CHAPTER ONE

BELHAVEN HOUSE, NEAR WHITBURN, NORTHERN ENGLAND

TEN DAYS BEFORE CHRISTMAS, EARLY MORNING, 1841

What would Grayson do if Pip had been stolen when he was a baby? Simply gone from his cradle one morning, no ransom demand and no clue where he was. Year after year, ten years, searching, searching, but Pip was never found. Just thinking about it made Grayson colder than the English winter. He thought of George Nathan Cox, Baron Worsley, whose baby boy had been stolen, and Grayson wondered if the pain had ever dulled, blurred over the passing years. Grayson didn't think so—it would be too deep, burrowing into his very bones.

Albert pawed the ground, flicked his tail, and neighed up at the gray sky as Grayson hitched him to his small carriage, the Queen's Phaeton. It was a gift he'd bought himself after the wild success of his first other-worldly novel, *Demons of the Dark*. He'd seen the graceful open carriage in Braverman's showroom on Titus Street in London and had fallen in love. It was a small, light, four-wheeled carriage with open sides, large graceful wheels, and a stout hood that provided some protection, but Grayson knew a two-and-a-half-day journey in an English December meant depressing dark clouds and rain, probably buckets of it, cold and heavy, a misery. No hood, however stout, could compete with the English weather. But riding in the Great's ancient carriage was impossible, not for two and a half days. He'd puke up his innards. He only hoped it wouldn't snow. This close to Christmas, though, snow was a strong possibility. He left early, feeling a moment of regret that his precocious son, Pip, wasn't there to whine and beg him to take him along wherever he was going. Didn't matter to Pip—anyplace they went promised an adventure. But Pip was at Wolffe Hall with all its denizens watching over him. Grayson didn't want to think about the mischief the three little terrors would get up to in his absence. Actually, they didn't need his absence to bring the house down. But at least Pip wouldn't be the instigator; it would be P.C., Miranda's daughter, and ten-year-old Barnaby, whose father Grayson was traveling to meet.

NEAR RAVENSTONE, HARTLEPOOL

EIGHT DAYS BEFORE CHRISTMAS

Albert loved drawing the phaeton, his steps as high as his tail. He was the king to Grayson's Queen's Phaeton. The first two days on his drive to Hartlepool had been as expected—dismal, cloudy, and cold—but thankfully there'd been no rain. But today, the third and last day of his journey, the weather gods had bestowed an early Christmas present—a warm clear day on the eastern coast of England. Grayson couldn't remember a day like this before in his life. Glorious summer had elbowed its way in for one last performance.

He walked out of the Halfwhistle Inn in Pudleigh Dale onto High Street under bright sunlight. "A Christmas miracle," the villagers were calling the fine day, rubbing their hands together, most in their shirtsleeves. Grayson decided it was a definite portent.

He arrived in Hartlepool in County Durham in the early afternoon, the warm weather still holding, the sky a brilliant blue, his coat folded on the bench beside him. Hartlepool was an old trading town with a bustling harbor on the North Sea. Fishing boats and cargo ships lined the docks, and the town smelled strongly of fish and wet ropes. Grayson drove beside the medieval seawall, through Sandwell Gate, and onto Hart Lane, filled with citizens basking in the unseasonable warmth, dogs and children dashing about. Ducks waddled around the town pond, quacking for bread from every passerby. He doubted he'd find the town as charming if he were huddled inside his greatcoat against a frigid North Sea winter storm. He stopped the phaeton to admire the magnificent St. Hilda's church, the focal point of the town.

Grayson thought briefly about staying at the Hangman's Inn, sleeping for twelve hours, and visiting Baron Worsley on the morrow in fresh clothes—but no, not on this miracle of days. He was tired and excited at the same time. Imagine, Barnaby the barn cat, a future baron. It boggled the mind.

If it was true.

The old innkeeper waved to the south with a gnarled hand and told him Ravenstone, the baron's manor house, sat atop a small hill called Stoker's Rise. Grayson also learned Baron Worsley was well liked by the townspeople, his family part of the fabric of the area for more than two hundred years. Grayson listened to the innkeeper praise the baron as he drank a pint of ale while Albert was being brushed and fed.

"Poor man, wot he's endured these past years—aye, a decade now. But soon he'll have hisself a new wife, and there'll be laughter again at the big house. Everyone knows the new bride's responsibility is to give him an heir, even the lady herself. Funny thing about the new wife, though."

What's funny about the new wife? Grayson wasn't given an answer to that question, only head shakes. He didn't have time to ask questions—it would be dark in a couple of hours. Time to get a move on.

If the baron was getting married soon, what about Barnaby? He wouldn't worry about that yet. First things first.

He didn't bother with the carriage. Once Albert was saddled, Grayson swung his leg over his broad back and settled in. His horse whipped his head about and neighed. Grayson ran his gloved hand down Albert's glossy gray neck. "I know you're tired, but we're not going far."

A scant fifteen minutes later, Grayson turned Albert onto a wide drive that curved slowly up Stoker's Rise to the top. He pulled Albert to a halt in front of a lovely three-story brick manor house with east and west wings stretching out like arms from a central block, the brick seasoned to a mellow gray, ivy twining up the outside walls. So this was Ravenstone. It looked as settled and content as the town, sitting atop Stoker's Rise amid a forest of pines and oaks. A narrow ribbon of a stream flowed at the base of the wide tended front grounds, connecting, he'd been told, to the river Tees, which emptied into the North Sea. Grayson handed the reins to a boy of about twelve and listened to him tell Albert what a lovely big lad he was and now it was time for a good brushing and some fine carrots, not more than a week old from Mrs. Pritchert's garden.

He climbed the ten deep-set front steps and gave the elephant-head door knocker a single bang. The thick door was immediately opened by a middle-aged man of small stature, slim as a sapling, and beautifully dressed in black, his shirt white as new snow. As for his head, it show-cased more hair than Grayson's horse—an abundance of hair, thick and dark brown, dusted with only a bit of white at the temples and pomaded to a high shine. He said in a deep, mellifluous voice, "You are Mr. Sher-brooke, sir? Oh yes, I recognize you from the drawing on the back of one of your novels, *The Demon's Spawn from Castle Highcliff.* Welcome, sir, welcome. This is such a pleasure. I am Frobisher, sir, and I will do my best to scatter any pebbles you might find in your path."

Grayson smiled. "Thank you."

Frobisher stepped back and bowed him into a dim, dark, wood-paneled entrance hall. "The baron is all atwitter wondering why you wanted to see him. Sir, allow me to say, not only do I enjoy your novels, but so do my seven children. All of them sit on the floor in front of the fire, listening to me terrify them before they scatter to their beds, the boys shrieking. But not my girls—not a faint heart among them. My blessed wife, alas, is of a timorous nature and cannot abide the fright. If you will please follow me, the baron is in the drawing room."

"Thank you, Frobisher. I cannot imagine a woman who has borne seven children being afraid of anything."

Frobisher paused, cocked his head. "It is a mystery, sir, one I have tried to solve, without success."

He opened the double doors and announced, "Mr. Grayson Sherbrooke, my lord."

Grayson stepped into a large room dominated by an ancient fireplace and an alcove looking onto the front grounds, with three tall, skinny windows. The faded gold draperies were open to welcome in the sun. The paneled walls were painted a light blue, making the room look bright. The furnishings appeared to be from various past eras and come to rest in the drawing room, from a heavy mahogany seventeenth-century Spanish table to four Regency Egyptian claw-footed chairs. A gold-and-white Louis XIV marquetry table stood by a love seat that looked vaguely Dutch to Grayson. There were scattered old rugs on the wide-planed oak floor. A dozen paintings, mostly of horses, lined the walls. It was a wonderful room, cozy, friendly, meant to be filled with children and laughter with no concern for a spill or cat claws in sofa arms.

Barnaby would love this room. So would P.C. and Pip. Grayson frowned. He felt something, a sort of push against his consciousness, perhaps a query, a seeking—he wasn't sure. He shook his head at himself. He was too deep in his latest novel, and it was making him imagine things that weren't there. Or was his brain alerting him to something unseen here in Ravenstone?

A man stepped from the shadow of a large old German cabinet, one panel drawer open to show dozens of old rolled parchments. Maps? Was the baron a cartographer? Grayson's first look at Baron Worsley made him stop in his tracks and stare. He saw Barnaby in twenty-five years. George Nathan Cox, eighth Baron Worsley, was a fine-looking man in his middle thirties, tall, slender, his eyes as blue as Barnaby's, his hair the exact same shade of dark red, with a bit of a curl. Did his hair become blonder in the summer as Barnaby's did? He saw a light sprinkling of freckles across a nose a bit longer than his son's, but the shape of his mouth was identical. When he walked gracefully to Grayson, his hand outstretched, Grayson saw the lines beside his eyes. His mouth was solemn and looked like it hadn't shared a smile in a long time. Grayson's pulse kicked up, his heart thumped, and he whispered blessed thanks to the Almighty. A wild smile split his mouth.

The baron said in a pleasant baritone, a hint of a question in his voice, "Mr. Sherbrooke? I believe you were behind me some five or six years at Oxford. You were in Christ Church?"

Grayson once again found himself marveling at the serendipity of meeting a half kelpie, whose mother was a witch, who'd told him who Barnaby's father was. He knew he was grinning like a fool. "Yes, I was. Your exploits were legendary. I could never figure out how you managed to jump from building to building without falling and breaking your neck."

George Nathan Cox blinked. He looked like he might laugh, but he didn't. "I'd forgotten that idiotic fiasco. Ah, as I recall, that harebrained episode involved two flasks of rum and a very pretty girl named Felicity. I would have been sent down if my don hadn't known my father, the two of them great admirers of William the Conqueror's Battle of Hastings." He waved a hand toward the open cabinet door. "Those are copies of the Bayeux Tapestry." He paused and cocked his head again, so much like Barnaby. "Frobisher has talked my ear off about the famous Mr. Sherbrooke coming here, actually here, to Ravenstone. I have not seen him so excited since the birth of his fourth son last summer."

Grayson simply couldn't hold it back. "Sir, I have your son. There is no doubt—he is your image."

CHAPTER TWO

Baron Worsley froze. He looked like he'd been hit with a rock. He slowly began shaking his head, and Grayson saw terrible pain in his eyes, deep and abiding. He said in an agonized whisper, "Wh—what did you say? You have my son? No, it isn't possible. Brady has been gone since he was a baby, taken on September second. He would have been eleven soon on January second. I don't know what this is all about, but—it's not possible. I've looked and looked but never could find him. I offered rewards, searched until I had to accept he was dead." He choked. "His kidnapping, it killed his mother." His voice fell off a cliff, and he stood still and alone, a man drawn into himself, into his familiar pain, and he swallowed.

Grayson kept his voice low, very calm. "I know this is a shock to you, but I do have him. I am very sorry about your wife, but you are alive, and your son will once again be reunited with his father."

The baron took a step toward Grayson, naked hunger on his lean face, and desperate hope. "You have really found Brady?"

Grayson took the baron's cold hands between his and squeezed. "More to the point, I've found *you*. His name is Barnaby. He calls himself a barn cat because that's where he's insisted on living since he couldn't bear all the females in the Wolffe household hovering over him all the time."

"I—I don't understand."

Grayson smiled. "He was found by the vicar on the steps of St. Gregory's church in Cowpen Dale, near Whitburn, two and a half days north of Hartlepool, on the coast. The vicar brought him to the Wolffe family at Wolffe Hall. He's spent the first ten years of his life there, tending horses primarily. Indeed, he's magic with them, and he will very likely marry the daughter of the house, P.C., who is eight. That's what she calls herself, because her name is rather outlandish. P.C.'s mother, Miranda, is teaching Barnaby to speak the Queen's English so no one can refuse to allow Barnaby and P.C. to wed when they grow up." Grayson stopped to take a breath. The baron's eyes were fastened on Grayson's face as if he wanted to pull words out of his mouth.

"Brady is a barn cat?"

Grayson laughed. "That's what he likes to call himself. He is very proud of it. He's a marvelous little boy. Let me assure you he's never been mistreated. He is loved and is an integral part of the Wolffe family. The head of the Wolffe family is Baron Cudlow. Barnaby—Brady—is also popular among all the neighbors and much liked in Cowpen Dale."

The baron still looked dazed. He opened his mouth, closed it. *My son. Bradford. I called him Brady when he first looked up at me when he was nursing at his mother's breast. He's alive, he's well, and he's a barn cat?*

"Please, tell me more. Tell me everything."

"I have told only Miranda, Mrs. Wolffe, about finding you, no one else. I had to make sure what sort of man you were before I did. And to verify, of course, that you are indeed his father."

The baron stared helplessly at Grayson and shook his head, a man coming out of a stupor. "I—I still can't believe it, can't accept it can possibly be true, not after all this time. It's been a decade. Finally, I knew I had to give it up, had to accept Brady was dead. I knew I had to marry to produce an heir to the barony. Indeed, I plan to wed in January, but—" He trailed off and simply stood in front of Grayson. His face was no longer pale as death, but flushed, nearly as dark red as his hair. "I'm afraid to believe it. You wouldn't lie to me? He is really here? You brought him?"

"No, I didn't bring him with me. I had to meet you first, make certain you are his father."

"Yes, yes, of course. My manners—please sit down. I must know everything. How did you find out?"

But neither man sat. Grayson said, "Two months ago I took my son, Pip, P.C., and Barnaby to visit my aunt and uncle, the Earl and Countess of Northcliffe, near Eastbourne."

"Yes, James and Jason's father, Douglas Sherbrooke. Yes. But what happened? How . . . ?"

Grayson wasn't about to tell the baron just yet a half witch, half kelpie had relayed to him the identity of Barnaby's father, as told to her by her witch mother. "A visitor to Northcliffe Hall saw Barnaby and remarked she knew a gentleman who resembled him mightily. It was incredible serendipity," Grayson said. "Because I am very fond of Barnaby—Brady—I inquired of my father, Ryder Sherbrooke, what he knew about you. My father knows everyone and everything about them."

"Yes, I know your father. He's a splendid man, though some in the Commons believe him a trifle eccentric in his constant demands to change the child labor laws . . . And, well, please tell me."

Grayson smiled. "My father wrote you are a good man, solid, trustworthy. He wrote he remembered when your son disappeared with his nurse, neither of them ever found, and soon thereafter your wife died, that all were touched by your tragedy and your search for your son for the past decade. He wrote you'd retired to your country home, Ravenstone, and were more or less a recluse until you appeared this past spring in London, your goal to find a wife since you knew you had to sire an heir for the barony.

"Then I wrote to you. Understand, I had to make these inquiries to be certain Barnaby—Brady—is your son and that you are a good man." Grayson gave him a big smile. "But in my gut I knew it was true, and so I wrote to you. I found your invitation cordial and smiled at your very polite, very well-bred probe as to the nature of my visit. I left immediately to come to you."

The baron's face was incandescent. His eyes seemed an even lighter blue. He looked ready to rise to the ceiling. He paced to the three tall windows and back, suddenly stopped, and whirled back around. "I can't believe it. A week before Christmas and I will have my son returned to me! A Christmas miracle, Mr. Sherbrooke, thanks to you. God has blessed me more than I could ever deserve." He shouted, "Frobisher! Champagne, now! My son is found! Brady is alive! He is a barn cat!" And the baron threw back his head and laughed. That laugh of his sounded scratchy, like it had been packed in mothballs for too long a time, but it was full and filled with joy. He grabbed Grayson's hand and shook it up and down.

Frobisher stood in the doorway, tears in his eyes. "My lord, such glorious news. I'm off as fast as Benton's rocket!" He turned back. "Three glasses, my lord?"

"Yes, of course. Go! And bring Mrs. Clendenning!" He said to Grayson, "I'm George—please call me George."

"And I'm Grayson. I moved from London to Cowpen Dale earlier this year. When I met Barnaby, I knew he looked familiar, but I couldn't pin it down."

"The person who told you—I must have his or her name. I wish to thank them."

Grayson eyed him. He'd known George would ask. Well, time to tell him the truth. "George, tell me, do you believe in strange sorts of otherworldly things?"

"You mean like the demons and spirits in your novels?"

"Yes."

"No, of course not. It is fiction you write, Grayson."

Again, Grayson was aware of something at the edge of his consciousness, questioning, seeking. But what? He didn't know. Whatever it was, the baron wasn't aware of it. Grayson said, "Well, then, perhaps you are about to become a believer in otherworldly possibilities. I was actually told your identity by a witch's daughter. It's a tale for when we travel back to Cowpen Dale."

George arched a dark-red eyebrow. "A witch's daughter? Come now—" He shook his head and grinned, showing teeth as straight and white as his son's. "I want to hear all about this witch and her daughter who knew I was Brady's father. You said two and a half days' journey from here? Please stay—we can travel together tomorrow." He paused, naked joy in his shining light-blue eyes, his son's eyes. "I can never repay you, never. I am in your debt until the day I leave this earth." He pumped Grayson's hand again. Then George Nathan Cox, eighth Baron Worsley, lowered his face into his hands and wept.

CHAPTER THREE

Grayson, Miranda, and Barnaby sat in the drawing room in front of a blazing fire. Barnaby wore new clothes, though he'd carped and complained, whined the shirt itched and the trousers cramped his parts. Grayson had only laughed. "Did I not promise you the pain of the new clothes will be worth the discomfort? Trust me."

"But, sir, why am I here at your house? With Mrs. Miranda but not P.C.? You know P.C.—she hates to be left out of anything. She's powerful upset. She was so mad she even made Pip dance with her. Not that he minded—the little nipper loves to hop around." And Pip, game for anything, had tried valiantly to waltz with P.C., with her leading, of course. Their galloping circles around the Wolffe drawing room had been a sight to behold, what with the Great enthusiastically clapping his arthritic hands, while Elaine, Miranda's mother-in-law, endeavored to play a waltz on a piano that desperately needed to be tuned.

Grayson studied Barnaby's—no, Brady's—handsome young face, the child whose life would change utterly in the next few minutes. He took Barnaby's hands in his; thankfully, they were clean because Miranda had overseen his bath. "Barnaby, Mrs. Wolffe and I need to speak to you privately."

"I knows that, sir—that is, I *know* that. If it's about a Christmas present for P.C., she dotes on Musgrave Jr., and he needs a new collar, and there's a chess set she's set her poppers on, saw it in York, all carved animals, the king a giraffe. Remember how the Great threw his king across the room when P.C. beat him and knocked off his head? Not the Great's head—the chess king's head. And Pip, he wants a bilbo catcher."

"Barnaby," Grayson said. "Thank you for your advice. Now, listen to me. This isn't about Christmas presents. Well, actually, it is. A huge Christmas present—for you." He drew a deep breath. "You know you were left as a baby on the steps of St. Gregory's church in Cowpen Dale."

"Aye—yes—and the vicar brought me to Wolffe Hall and Mrs. Miranda let me be a barn cat. Well, finally, after I fell to my knees and begged her for mercy."

Miranda's eyes twinkled. "Yes, you did, Barnaby. You complained you were getting too many kisses, and Mama-in-law squeezed you so tight it near made your ribs creak."

Grayson wanted to roll his eyes but didn't. He looked at Barnaby's winsome young face and said slowly, "Mrs. Wolffe has told me you've asked her over the years about your parents. She told me she's heard you and P.C. talking about who you could be, who your mama and papa were, and P.C. told you that you were a prince and you would grow up to save her from highwaymen, in the misty future."

Barnaby grinned. "Then she said she could save herself, but me being a prince would be a good thing, because it would impress the Great and you, Mrs. Miranda. I know it's all made-up, sir. I know I ain't— aren't—I'm *not* a prince." His chin went up, and he shrugged his scrappy, well-dressed shoulders. "Fact is, no one wanted me, and that's why they left me on the church steps. I'm not a baby, sir—I know what's what."

Grayson heard acceptance in that young voice, and it smote him. "You're not an orphan, Barnaby. You have a father, and I've found him."

For the first time since Grayson had met Barnaby, he didn't say a word, only stared up at him, his blue eyes unblinking, still as a stone, frozen just as his father had been.

Barnaby ran his tongue over his lips and whispered, "I have a father?

A father? But how is it possible? If I had a father, I'd be with him. I don't understand, sir."

Miranda took his hand. "When you, Pip, and P.C. went with Grayson to visit Mr. Sherbrooke's aunt and uncle at Northcliffe Hall, Mr. Sherbrooke discovered your lineage—that is, who your parents are."

Grayson said, "Barnaby, I traveled to Hartlepool where your father lives. I have met him. He is a splendid man. There is no doubt. You are his image."

"But why didn't he want me? Why did he throw me away?"

It was a punch to the gut. Grayson said, "He wanted you—never doubt that. You were kidnapped, with your nurse, or your nurse was part of the plot. No one knows, but both of you simply disappeared. We don't know who did it or the reason why they did it. They left you on the steps of St. Gregory's. There was never a demand for ransom. There was never again a sign of your nurse. Your father searched for you for ten years, but you were here, a great distance away."

Barnaby suddenly pulled back from Grayson, drew in on himself, and shook his head back and forth, just like his father. He whispered, "A father? I have a real father? Not some bacon-brained cove that wants me to be his barn cat?"

"Yes, you have a real live father. I've met with him. And I promise you, he's not bacon-brained. He's an excellent man. He's been miserable for ten years, Barnaby, because he didn't have you. He's thought of you every day. Your birthday is on January second. Your real name is Bradford Edward Cox. Your father's name is George Nathan Cox. He is the eighth Baron Worsley. You are his only son and heir. Someday you will be the ninth Baron Worsley."

Barnaby licked his tongue over his lips. He looked very small, very vulnerable. He whispered, "But that can't be—things like this don't happen to boys like me. Things like that are for those romantical novels Mrs. Elaine reads."

Miranda pulled him into her arms and rocked him. "I know this is all very confusing." She kissed his forehead and took his arms in her hands. "Listen to me. You are no longer a barn cat, my dear. You are now a boy with a real name and a real family. I don't know how many relatives you have, but we'll find out. And do you know what? Your father is here. He came back immediately with Mr. Sherbrooke, he was so anxious to see you. Would you like to meet him? He will call you by your real name— Brady. It's a fine name, and it suits you, don't you think?"

Barnaby burrowed against her, his body heaving. "Brady? I ain't, aren't—I'm—*not*—this Brady. I can't be—I can't. He won't like me. I'll say wrong things. I don't know him!"

Miranda met Grayson's eyes over Brady's head and kissed his clean ear. "I know you're overwhelmed. I know it's hard for you to accept suddenly having a father as being real, but it is real—your father is real. This is a joyous day for both of you." Miranda pulled out her mother's voice, underlying steel with a coating of sweetness. She gently pushed him back. "I want you to straighten up now. Pull back your shoulders and up with your chin—that's it. You are a brave, worthy boy. You're wearing a new shirt and trousers, and you look very fine. And you speak nearly perfect English. Grayson and I are so very proud of you. The life you were born to have is now returned to you."

Grayson rose and pulled Brady up to stand in front of him. "It's time to meet a man who loves you even more than we do, a man who's searched for you for ten whole years." He paused, smiled. "I do believe you have the look of a future baron. And do you know, even a baron could rescue P.C. from highwaymen." Still, Brady looked like he wanted to bolt, or crawl under the sofa. Grayson lightly held him in place. "A father, Brady. You now have your very own father who loves you very much. And I really like your name—Brady. It's a substantial name, one with charm, a name that promises a smile and countless adventures. Do you know what else you have?"

Barnaby looked agonized. He slowly shook his head.

"You have your father's smile."

"But how can he love me? He don't—*doesn't*—know me, sir. I'm just another boy to take his horse's reins and feed him carrots—the horse, not my father."

Miranda said, "You can ask him that, Barn—no, Brady. You know what else, Brady? P.C. will be so happy. She's always known you had a noble soul, and she's been proven correct. You will grow up a gentleman, Brady, just as P.C. will grow up a lady."

Grayson smiled. Miranda had said the perfect words.

Barnaby looked thoughtful. "If I'm really a lordship, then P.C. can marry me and no one can say boo and try to fry my liver."

"That's correct. Soon, you will sound like a young Etonian. Your father is going to be so happy to have you back."

Still, Brady looked worried, and Grayson, inspired, said, "Your father is a horseman. Your home is called Ravenstone, and it's also a stud. Hunters, racehorses, most of them beautiful Arabians, Brady. And he himself loves to ride and hunt. You'll be right at home."

"Sir, this isn't one of P.C.'s jests, is it? She's not trying to torture me?"

"P.C. doesn't even know, Brady."

He ran his tongue over his bottom lip. "Horses, sir? He has a stud?"

Grayson said, "Yes. I saw it with my own eyes. Do you know when P.C. finds out, it will be like Mrs. Miranda said—she'll crow and strut around, proud as a peacock." He gently massaged the boy's shoulder. "You've always been important, but now the whole world will see you as important too. The whole world will rejoice that you and your father are reunited. I'm going to get him now." He hugged the boy to him, then set him away and gripped his shoulders in his hands. "It will be all right—you'll see. Be yourself and all will be well."

Grayson walked to the drawing room door and opened it. "George, come in and meet your son."

George Nathan Cox, Baron Worsley, stepped into the drawing room and stared at the young boy who stood stiff and tall and scared. He looked ready to bolt, maybe dive through the front bow window. George looked into his own blue eyes, at his own dark-red hair, curlier than his, at the scatter of freckles across a straight nose, his nose. George thought of the long passage of years, a decade of pain and despair, and finally acceptance his son must be dead. It all fell away as he stared at the precious boy who was his son. What was important was here, standing in front of him. He strode across the room and picked up his son in his arms and whirled him about. *Jane, I hope you're looking down at your son and you're smiling.* "My boy, at last, at last." George kissed his cheek and held him tight.

Barnaby was terrified, and yet—this was his father? He pulled back in the man's arms and studied his face and the tears swimming in his blue eyes. "Am I really your son, sir? How can you be certain? I mean, we don't look anything alike."

Laughter filled the drawing room.

That night, George Nathan Cox, eighth Baron Worsley, lay on his back in bed in Grayson Sherbrooke's guest bedchamber, his son beside him, silent, scared, stiff as a board. He knew Brady hadn't wanted to stay with him, a stranger, but he'd bowed to Grayson's wishes after an hour in the drawing room with Miranda telling George stories of Brady's first ten years. George was so happy, he wouldn't be surprised if he floated right out the window.

He knew, of course, he was faced with a huge task. He had to make friends with a boy who was his son but who saw him as a stranger. Well, he was. He was the adult, and it was up to him to breach the walls. George realized now Grayson had been right to force them together tonight. Here in the darkness, lying side by side, they could begin to form a lasting bond. He prayed and said into the darkness, "Did Mr. Sherbrooke tell you I have a stud?"

"Yes, sir, he did." Was that a bit of interest he heard in his son's voice?

"Brady, have you ever heard of King Stuart?"

"Oh, aye—*yes*, sir. He won the Gold Cup at Newmarket and the Guineas at Ascot. Our vicar, Mr. Harkness, told me after church one day that King Stuart will be the next Eclipse. He had to whisper since his wife, Mrs. Vicar, er, Harkness, was standing close by, and she might clout him for being a gambling sinner. Even Mr. Tubbs, our head stable lad, thinks he's the fastest three-year-old he's ever seen. Oh, sir, have you seen him race? Have you gotten close enough to him to pat his neck?"

George laughed, enchanted by this monologue. He realized the laugh had just popped right out of his mouth. It felt very good. He felt lighter; he now saw endless possibilities in this amazing new world. He slowly turned onto his side to face his son, who'd come up on his elbow, so excited he was nearly bouncing on the mattress. George wished he could see his face, but it was too dark. He said, drawing out the drama, "As a matter of fact, I helped his dam, Italian Princess, birth him."

There was a moment of stunned silence, then Brady gasped. "Really? You're not juddering my toe? But how could you be in a stable in the muck, you being a lordship and all?"

"Of course I was there, because, you see, Brady"—pause—"I own King Stuart."

Brady gaped at him, afraid to believe those incredible words. "But how is that possible? I mean, you're a lordship, but you're not a fancy duke. I thought only the prince or a duke could own such a horse. You really own King Stuart?"

"I bred his mother, Italian Princess, to Xavier, a great racer in Ireland. King Stuart's trainer is an Irishman named Sullivan. I'm told you're magic with horses, Brady. So is Sullivan. Horses do whatever he says. You'll like him. He'll teach you. You will go with me to the races to watch all our horses run. It's very exciting."

Barnaby was so overwhelmed he couldn't speak, then words burst out of his mouth, fast, tumbling over each other. "I ain't never been— no, no, I have *not ever been* to the races. The Great wouldn't allow it, agreed with Mrs. Vicar, said it leads to gambling and that makes you lose all your money and fall into a ditch. The Wolffe ladies don't care either, and the Great's heir is an American and he doesn't know horses, only rides them. I can get near King Stuart, maybe even pat his neck, maybe even feed him a carrot out of my own hand?"

"Yes. If all goes well, King Stuart will race three or four more years, then I'll put him out to stud. Ah, the colts and fillies he'll sire." George reached out his hand and touched his son's shoulder. "And now King Stuart is ours, Brady. Yours and mine."

Barnaby—no, he couldn't think of himself any longer as Barnaby.

He was a proper boy now, with an actual father, and he even had three names. He was Bradford Edward Cox. He heard his father—his father!—whisper more magic words. "I have a new pony, an Arabian, sired by the great Regent himself. His name is Pepper Pot. He's fast as the wind, Brady. And he is yours."

CHAPTER FOUR

WOLFFE HALL

THREE DAYS BEFORE CHRISTMAS

Everyone gathered around the candlelit spruce fir tree in Wolffe Hall's drawing room. Josiah Wolffe, Baron Cudlow, was called the Great by all those who didn't wish to be struck with his wolf-head walking stick. He presided over the company in his massive chair, a lucifer at the ready in case an errant wind blew out one of the candles—quite unlikely since all the draperies were pulled over tightly closed windows. A full bucket of water sat beside the tree in case one of the candles caught a branch on fire.

Miranda sat beside Grayson, watching P.C. and Barnaby—no, Brady—huddled in the corner, their heads together. Was she telling him her wedding plans now that he was a boy with a real name, and a baron's son—unbelievable to her since he was such a coddle-brain. Was she telling him where he was going to take her for their honeymoon? Miranda's smile was close to crazed—imagine having a son-in-law in ten or so years. She looked over at Baron Worsley—no, George—listening with grave attention to the Great expound, probably about his finally finding his precious heir, even though Major Houston was still more bloody American than a solid, reliable Brit, and wasn't that enough to make his hair grow even higher on his head? So unexpected he'd been, and now he was an integral part of the Wolffe family. It was a pity Captain Houston was in London spending Christmas with his new fiancée's family.

Pip was speaking to Elaine, Miranda's mama-in-law. Miranda recognized the look on that small, precious face. He was so serious, using his hands, probably trying to coax out of her what she'd gotten him for Christmas. There were more presents this year than last, all arranged next to the tree on a special table brought into the drawing room each year. Most were wrapped in strong brown paper with sturdy twine, some wrapped lovingly in silver tissue. She knew Brady's father had very nearly cleaned out the stores in Cowpen Dale and Whitburn. He hadn't forgotten P.C. or Pip in his elation. George really was a splendid man, a man whose mouth was always curved in a smile now, permanently, no matter what mischief Brady got into in the future, which, she imagined, would be quite a lot. She saw him turn his head every few minutes to look at his son, and his smile would always grow wider, his blue eyes, Brady's blue eyes, bright with promise. Once she had to look away, his expression was so naked in its happiness.

Grayson's hand squeezed hers, and she turned to him. He was looking thoughtful and content, more handsome than his fictional hero Thomas Straithmore. He'd come so unexpectedly into her life, just as Baron Worsley had come unexpectedly into Brady's life, bringing magic and fun and so much gaiety she wondered she didn't burst with it. Life, Miranda thought, basking in the soft candlelight from their Christmas tree, could be sweeter than her mother-in-law's special sixteenth-century recipe for mulled wine.

P.C. called out, "Mama, Bradford Edward Cox, the future ninth Baron Worsley, tells me he is going to train racehorses and win races all over England. I told him his father, the eighth Baron Worsley, obviously isn't a mutton-headed moron, and so there is no way he will let Brady near his racehorses."

At P.C.'s voice, George turned to look at the two children, a smile on his face, of course. He looked younger, the lines beside his mouth no longer noticeable, the burden of grief lifted off his heart.

As for P.C., Grayson had been right. Once she'd been convinced

Brady was really and truly a future baron, she'd positively preened and strutted around, announcing it was because of her he no longer spoke like a barn cat and even the Great would want them to marry.

Miranda called back to P.C., "Brady will learn to train the horses, P.C. His father and Mr. Sullivan, his trainer, will teach him."

P.C. gave this some thought, nodded. "Then I will be taught too. Bradford Edward Cox and I will read the *Racing Calendar* together. That's what it's called, Mama. And we will study the *Racing Book* so we will know every racehorse since the Great was on the ark. Very soon I will be able to teach Mr. Sullivan better ways to train the horses. I will wear beautiful hats to the races, Mama."

Barnaby punched her in the arm. "I will train the horses, P.C., and buy your hats for you."

"I shall be a baroness, Bradford, so if you are to buy my hats, you must learn good taste. Mama says you are born with it. Or not."

"I gots the best taste—"

She punched him. "It's not *gots*—it is *have*."

Brady said without pause, "I have the best taste. You'll see, P.C."

George had been trying to listen attentively to the Great tell him how his heir had suddenly appeared, just as Brady had suddenly come into George's life, both home now. In truth, though, George's attention never wavered from his son. He hadn't looked forward to Christmas, to the endless rounds of holiday parties he was duty-bound to attend, visiting his elder sisters, seeing their children tearing into their Christmas presents. But now, he felt full to bursting. Never could he have dreamed the Christmas of 1841 could bring him such complete happiness. So long he'd despaired and cursed the fates, so long he'd searched. And now he was here, not ten feet away from his son, who was talking with great animation to a precious little girl named P.C. who could be his daughter-in-law someday, and who corrected his son's grammar. It was dazzling to think of what he would teach his son—his family history, and of course there was his extended family, since George had three sisters and so many nieces and nephews, Brady's cousins, but he imagined all that was important to his son was a pony named Pepper Pot. And Brady would go to Eton. That stopped George cold. He wanted his son with him. *A tutor.* Yes, he would have a tutor until—sometime in the future.

He remembered when he'd awakened that morning and for an awful moment believed he'd dreamed he had his son back. Then he'd heard a snort and smiled into the gray dawn light. His son. Yes, it was a Christmas miracle. He began composing letters to his sisters in his head, telling them the miraculous news, canceling his regular trips to see them. No, he would spend this Christmas in Whitburn at Wolffe Hall with his precious son.

He looked at P.C.—her full name never to be spoken aloud—and yet again his smile bloomed. She took Brady's hand and skipped over to him. "Sir, I wish you a Merry Christmas and welcome you to our family. But now it's important you understand what's what. Your son is deserving of three names because he has a noble heart and a brain nearly as amazing as mine. He can plan all sorts of wicked adventures. He's not afraid of anything except me, and only occasionally, and that proves he's very smart. He loves horses and cats, particularly Musgrave Jr., the house cat, and he's mine. In short, sir, you must assure me you will be a proper father to him and polish his English until he will make a perfect husband for me."

George smiled down at the bright little girl who would be as pretty as her mother when she grew up. "Will you really marry Brady, P.C.? You are so certain? You are only seven?"

"I am eight, sir. Bradford Edward Cox is ten." P.C. paused and frowned at him. "I must admit it did disturb me that Bradford Edward Cox has gained another year without my knowledge, but Mama believes it's acceptable that he will be eleven in January because I am still smarter than he is. Well, she didn't say that exactly, but it is close. On his birthday, I will see that Cook makes him a special treat." She gave Brady a punch in the arm. "I approve of his three names. They fit him nicely. I plan to teach him until he is old enough to marry me. I have already decided our first child will be named Horatio, a noble name, and he will grow up to worship his father and his mother. Well, he'll worship his mother a bit more." P.C. moved closer. "I must ask you, sir—what will you do for him other than give him money, which he doesn't need, racehorses, and new clothes?"

George said promptly, "I will give him love, a pony named Pepper Pot, and I will correct his English when you are not present to do so."

The little girl beamed up at him and gave him a small curtsy. "Then I will accept you as my future papa-in-law. Mama, did you hear what Bradford Edward Cox's father said? I believe he will do nicely."

Brady said, "P.C., you've been tippling, haven't you? Mrs. Miranda, you must guard the champagne. She won't shut her mouth after even a little sip."

Miranda called out, "Brady, I will attend the champagne closely. P.C., we are grateful you deem Baron Worsley to be acceptable as Brady's father."

P.C. glowed. "I have to admit I was worried, Mama, but now I believe the eighth Baron Worsley will make me a fine father-in-law." She gave Brady another knock on the arm and pulled him away to look at presents.

The Great said suddenly, bringing everyone's attention back to him, where it belonged, "Miranda, one of the candles came loose from its moorings. Make sure it doesn't burn down the tree."

Miranda obligingly tightened the candle's holder to the fir branch. And because she loved him and because it was Christmas, she leaned down and kissed his forehead. "You are a blessed gentleman, Grandpapa-in-law."

The Great harrumphed, cleared his throat. "I was just on the point of telling the baron here that the queen's consort had dozens of spruce firs sent from Germany to decorate Buckingham Palace. Bah! Albert thinks himself such an innovator. Doesn't the little German princeling know Christmas trees have been around longer than I have?"

P.C. said, "Sir, I don't believe Christmas trees were even born that long ago. They wouldn't have fit on the ark and would have drowned out in the great flood."

Miranda cleared her throat over a laugh. "I know several people in the village have small trees, but candles are so expensive. They put little trinkets and paper ornaments on them. I believe, thanks to Prince Albert, Christmas trees will become quite the fashion for everyone. Can't you imagine it? Families standing around their Christmas trees singing carols? It's perfect."

The Great grunted, shook his head, his cornucopia of white hair—as impressive as Frobisher's—unmoving. "So many presents you ladies demand for Christmas. It costs me a fortune to make the lot of you happy. And now trees for everyone in England? Even Mr. Bugby the butcher will want a Christmas tree? Waste of money. Where will we grow them? We can't bring them all over from Germany. Hmm, perhaps it would be a good investment to grow the trees here, sell them, and garner enough of a profit to buy the ladies the silly little gewgaws they like so much."

Miranda smiled, wondering what the Great thought a gewgaw was and if she might want one.

Elaine, the Great's daughter-in-law, held up her hand and twirled around the diamond-and-ruby bracelet on her wrist. "Sir, do you remember? You gave me this lovely gewgaw my first Christmas here at Wolffe Hall."

"Humph," the Great said.

Brady's voice bubbled with excitement. "His lordship—er—my father is giving me a pony for Christmas." He turned to the baron. "Sir, do you like to sing Christmas songs? Everyone here does. Even Pip knows most of the words."

Pip could only nod vigorously since his mouth was full of the almond biscuit Elaine Wolffe had given him.

George said, "Yes, certainly I do. I'm a bit rusty, I fear, but the words will come back to me. I always sang at Christmas when I was your age."

P.C. said to the baron, "I must tell you, sir, Bradford Edward Cox has a pleasing voice. He sings to Musgrave Jr. about chomping on mice. Should you like to hear him sing, sir? Then we can all join him. Mama has an angel's voice."

George said, "Do you sing 'Good King Wenceslas,' Brady?"

Bradford Edward Cox, now known as Brady, except to P.C., stood tall in his new finery that cramped his parts and sang in a pure, sweet boy's voice.

Soon everyone joined in.

Grayson lifted Pip in his arms and swayed with him to the music, both of them singing along. He didn't think he would ever enjoy a more splendid Christmas holiday.

CHAPTER FIVE

Eleven-year-old Bradford Edward Cox, son and heir of the eighth Baron Worsley, was scared through his new wool socks to the soles of his feet. He was sitting beside P.C. across from his father in a crested coach—and wasn't that amazing, driving up a long, winding drive to the top of what his father told him was Stoker's Rise. It was a cold, cloudy day, and everything looked gray and heavy, the trees bare, forlorn and trembling in the wind. Brady thought it looked like the sky would collapse on them. He saw the distant house. A dark cloud settled over it, making shadows crawl over the miles of ivy. Whatever it was, it wasn't home.

Only it *was* his home now. What was he to do? P.C. took his hand and squeezed. She whispered, "This will do nicely. You and I will be happy here. Mama will plant beautiful flowers everywhere for us, and you and I will read the *Racing Calendar* and eat strawberry scones."

All right, that sounded good, maybe even perfect. He rested his forehead against hers and felt the fear begin to dissolve. He said to his father, "Sir, is Pepper Pot big enough for me to carry P.C. in front of me?"

George didn't blink, didn't pause. "I'm sorry, Brady, but Pepper Pot is only for you. But don't worry, I will provide a pony for P.C."

"And Pip? He's a bruising little rider."

"Yes, Pip will have a pony too." George did a quick mental review of his horses. No ponies appropriate for an eight-year-old girl or a five-year-old boy. He'd visit Sir Malcolm Benderwith, a local squire and master of the Durham Hunt, and borrow ponies for P.C. and Pip. If only he could, he'd keep all three children. He dreaded the day when P.C. and Pip had to leave to return to their own homes with Grayson and Miranda. He wondered if Brady had thought of it yet. It was not a day he looked forward to.

Their carriage drew to a halt in front of ten deep stone steps. George sat forward. Two centuries of pride rang out in his voice. "Brady, this is your home, Ravenstone."

Brady studied the large gray stone house with ivy growing up its sides, standing stark beneath that depressing gray sky that threatened rain at any minute. It was bigger than Wolffe Hall, he realized. He'd always believed Wolffe Hall was the grandest house in the world, certainly the grandest where he lived. Up close, Ravenstone wasn't so bad. There weren't any bars on the windows, at least.

George correctly read every expression that flitted over his son's face. "The stables are in the back of the house. You'll meet Pepper Pot as soon as you're settled in. And I'll show you Ravenstone Folly."

P.C. cocked her head at him, her lovely honey-colored hair falling over her shoulder. "What's a folly, sir?"

George smiled. "A folly is a building of some sort that costs a lot of money and isn't really good for much, like building an old medieval tower on your land. Ravenstone is the name given to the manor house by the original Cox heiress from France in the 1600s. I'll tell you about her and her strange ways later. She also had built a structure called Ravenstone Folly, which is still standing, gloomy and solitary, fit for one of Mr. Sherbrooke's novels."

The front door burst open, and Frobisher strode out, his bountiful hair brushed high and pomaded into a stiff crown in celebration of this miraculous day. Following him were two footmen, two maids, two kitchen maids with Mrs. Clyde, the cook, a white hat on her gray head and a huge white apron wrapped around her waist, and his housekeeper,

Mrs. Clendenning, silver-haired, solid, with beautiful dark eyes, towering nearly as tall as the baron, bringing up the rear. Frobisher turned and merely nodded. The staff moved quickly to stand in a straight line in front of the steps.

Frobisher then gave a sharp whistle, and two boys came running around the house, followed more slowly by Sullivan, who looked weathered and as old as God, but grinning from ear-to-ear, showing a mouthful of beautiful white teeth.

George jumped out of the carriage, lifted out P.C. and his son, and hugged both of them against him. He didn't think he'd ever been so happy, so proud in his life. He raised Brady's small hand in his. "Everyone, I would like you to meet my son, Master Brady." He leaned down and whispered in Brady's ear, "These are now your people. They are excited to meet you. Be yourself and don't worry, all right? Frobisher and Mrs. Clendenning will take care of you. Any question you may have, you ask either of them."

But it was a pale, scared little face that looked at all the people smiling at him, all marveling at his return. Brady heard words like "he's the image of his father," "it be a miracle," "thank the good Lord," and on and on it went.

Frobisher yelled, "My lord! You're home with Master Brady and this pretty little girl! It is a wonderful day, one to be recorded in the history books, to be commemorated in ballad and song, perhaps a resounding poem. What say you, Mrs. Clendenning?"

"I say *hooray*, Mr. Frobisher."

Frobisher walked forward and bowed to Brady. "Master Bradford, welcome home."

George introduced P.C., who nodded gracefully and gave her mother's smile.

Frobisher and Mrs. Clendenning stepped forward as the second carriage pulled up, disgorging Grayson, Miranda, and Pip. It was shortly followed by the third carriage, with mountains of luggage; Pip's nanny, Mary Beth; Grayson's valet, Haddock; and Miranda's maid, Meg. The three children were soon huddled together, laughing, talking, and pointing, and George heard the word *folly* and whispering voices. The adults had traded off children during the two-and-a-half-day trip to Hartlepool, so no child felt left out for too long a time and no adult went mad.

After George introduced Pip, Miranda, and Grayson, P.C. announced to the baron's staff, "All of you look ever so kind. I shall be your mistress someday, and we will have cakes and sing."

There were laughs and smiles directed at the pretty little girl with hair the color of rich honey, just like her mother's. She stood on Brady's left, Brady's father on his right, holding his hand tightly. Brady leaned over and poked P.C. in the arm.

Everyone welcomed Master Brady home, and the maids curtsied to him. *To him.* Imagine. It fair to curdled his brain. He felt as nervous as Musgrave Jr. when the Great yelled at him for spitting up a fur ball. P.C. whispered, "Do you think they'll curtsy to me when we marry?"

Brady whispered in her ear, "If you do your handsprings for them, they'll curtsy for you now. Wait, not now—you'll show your drawers since you're not wearing trousers."

George swallowed his laughter and personally ushered the children to the newly redecorated nursery on the third floor. The workmen he'd set to painting and resetting shelves and laying new floors, not to mention bringing in new furnishings, had done an excellent job. He showed Brady his bedchamber connected to the nursery, and because Brady wasn't a young child now, he called the immense room and its connecting chambers Brady's rooms. He'd had prepared two other small bedchambers for P.C. and Pip just across the hall. Mrs. Clendenning efficiently oversaw the distribution of luggage and people to their proper rooms.

That evening, George, Grayson, and Miranda sat at their ease in the drawing room. Miranda waved her hand about. "I love this room, George. It's so welcoming."

George smiled. Jane had said the same thing. He said, "My mother, I was told, couldn't make up her mind which style she preferred, so she took a bit from Germany, a bit from France, a bit from England, and a bit from Spain. My wife, Jane, loved it, didn't change a thing." George swallowed. "After she died and Brady was gone, well, I don't suppose I cared, so it hasn't been touched."

Grayson said, "I agree with the ladies. Leave it alone. I must say, George, having Sullivan tie a red ribbon in Pepper Pot's mane for Brady was a stroke of genius."

George grinned. "It was Frobisher's idea." He sat back in his high-backed Italian chair and crossed his hands over his lean belly. He said simply, "Our local hunt master, Squire Benderwith, is delivering two ponies tomorrow for Pip and P.C." He stilled, shook his head, rose, and began pacing.

Miranda said, "George, whatever is wrong?"

He stopped, splayed his hands. "I wish I could keep myself right here, in this very wonderful moment—stop time, if you will—but we all know you can't stay here forever." A dark-red eyebrow went up. "Or perhaps you two could marry and all of us could live here at Ravenstone and none of us would have to face separating those children."

Grayson said easily, "I will discuss this with Miranda, see what she thinks, but don't worry about it now, George. Let's see what unfolds."

The ponies were brought over, the children were maniacally happy, and Cook was heard singing as she made more pastries than she had in the past ten years. Laughter once again filled Ravenstone. All was going swimmingly until on the morning of the third day George Nathan Cox's fiancée arrived from Suffolk via London with her mother, younger sister, and two maids.

CHAPTER SIX

Lady Elvebak was stout, complacent, and believed every opinion issuing from her mouth was The Final Word. She loved abundant lace and flounces and purple, and scattered diamonds all over her person. Grayson devoutly hoped her daughter, Lise Marie, George's fiancée, was the opposite of her mother; otherwise, George wasn't in for a very happy life. Thankfully, unlike her bedecked mother, whose opinions reverberated to every corner of the drawing room, Lise Marie appeared soft-spoken and very polite. Even more thankfully, Lise Marie didn't look like her mother or her sister. She was tall, slender, and pretty, with dark-green eyes and a wealth of shining mahogany hair dressed in subdued ringlets around her face. Blessedly, her gown didn't sport a single flounce. It was elegant and became her. She evidently said very little when her mother was in the vicinity. She wore a simple gown of pale green, a matching green ribbon around her slender neck, and no diamonds, only an emerald engagement ring on her finger.

The younger daughter, Clarissa, all of twenty, sat next to Lady Elvebak on a footstool, an attendant to the queen. It was unfortunate she copied her mother's presentation, except for the diamonds. Grayson imagined Lady Elvebak wore every diamond she owned. Clarissa was pleasant looking, her eyes a soft brown, but she looked like she frowned more than she smiled, perhaps learned from her mother.

"As I was saying, my precious Clarissa has accepted the suit of Mr. Gregory Hawley, a fine young gentleman and the son of Viscount Eldow." She looked over at her other daughter. "As for Lise Marie, I feared she would dwindle into a spinster until the baron came up to scratch. Her ring is nothing to be remarked upon."

"Mama," Lise Marie said in an agonized whisper, "I picked out my ring. It is what I wanted."

But Lady Elvebak had already moved on. She was looking around the drawing room. "When Lise Marie is your wife, George, she will, of course, insist upon improving the condition of this room." And the old besom actually shuddered.

"Mama, please, I don't wish to make any changes," Lise Marie said, her voice utterly ineffectual, a token protest, probably one made all her life. "I love this room."

Lady Elvebak gave her a dismissive look, but she subsided, for the moment.

"I do too," George said, and he never stopped smiling at the old harridan.

"I agree with Mama," Clarissa said. "I shouldn't want to bring anyone important into this common room."

Lady Elvebak patted her young minion on her shoulder, then turned to aim her cannon at Miranda. She announced in her strident, confident voice, "I do not know who your people are or if you are worthy of my attention, Mrs. Wolffe, but I will say you aren't exactly plain. It is unfortunate you are unpolished, with no style— to be expected, since you live in a backward, undistinguished place I would never visit. London wouldn't give you any attention." She cast a sapient eye on her elder daughter. "Of course, my beautiful Lise Marie, whose very presence makes my French dressmaker sigh with pleasure, could be the epitome of style if only she didn't insist on severe lines and no pleasing accoutrements, like diamonds. But she is still young and unformed, though she is close to becoming a spinster. I daresay she will become more like her dear mama before many more years pass."

George swallowed, then smiled when he remembered Lise Marie from eleven years before had always copied her older sister, Jane, in her speech and in her dress, down to her slippers. He said, his voice only a trifle on the cool side, "I think Lise Marie and Mrs. Wolffe are both lovely, ma'am. They both admire simplicity and elegance."

"My dear Sir Lawrence showered me with diamonds. He knew they would elevate my distinction, and all people remark upon my magnificent style. So obviously you are wrong, my lord, even though it means my daughter must hear the truth."

Miranda could only stare at the old besom. Before she could open her mouth, Grayson said pleasantly, "I agree with George. Both Miss Elvebak and Mrs. Wolffe look lovely in their less flamboyant styles. Let me add Mrs. Wolffe is renowned for her beauty and her kindness. As for the northeast of England, I've found it to be far more pleasant than the filth and extravagance of London."

Lady Elvebak dismissed him. "You're a man. You know nothing. You write novels, sir, surely an absurd occupation."

George said smoothly, "Did I not mention, ma'am, that Mr. Sherbrooke is not only a renowned novelist but his uncle is the Earl of Northcliffe?"

Only a brief moment of consternation, then diamonds flashed as Lady Elvebak shook her fist at him. "You should have told me immediately, George. Very well, it is acceptable for Mr. Sherbrooke to pen his ridiculous tales since his lineage is distinguished. However, one mustn't forget that your father, Mr. Sherbrooke, isn't the earl, and he has no prospect of becoming the earl."

"I sincerely hope not, ma'am," Grayson said, wanting to laugh. Instead, he toasted her with his teacup, rather wishing it was a brandy. He wanted to escape. He looked at George, who appeared infinitely pained and accepting, both at the same time.

Grayson felt a jolt of cold, a sort of opening in the air itself. He stilled, waited. It was the questing he'd felt the first time he'd been here, only this time it wasn't a gentle pushing against his consciousness. It was more. This time there was impatience, anger. What was going on here? That last push had felt nearly physical, as if someone had punched him in the head, then nothing. The air was once again calm and warm. There was no *otherness* nearby.

"Mama, please," Lise Marie said again, her voice a gentle wave against a tsunami. "I enjoy reading Mr. Sherbrooke's books. Do you not recall I read you *The Haunting of Mr. Moses*? You liked it."

"It passed the hours on a dismal day," Lady Elvebak said and tossed her head. Up went her chin. "Unlike Mrs. Wolffe—who is not fresh and young as you are, Lise Marie—you could be a visual delight fashioned in my image, if only you would make the effort. You are just like your sister. Despite all my endless encouragement, Jane refused to present herself to advantage. Even though I forbade it, she danced in the park where everyone could see her, singing all the while, dressed like a servant. All believed she was lucky indeed to attach the dear baron." Her bird's-eye stare flickered toward George, who'd gone stiff as a board.

Grayson still couldn't believe Lise Marie was the sister of George's first wife, Jane. He judged her to be in her early twenties, which meant she'd been very young indeed when her older sister died after Brady was taken. So this was what the innkeeper in Hartlepool had meant when he'd said, "Funny thing about the new wife." He imagined all knew the baron was marrying his former sister-in-law. Had George lost his wits? He wanted Lady Elvebak as a mother-in-law—again? Once again, the presence was pushing against his mind. Was it Jane? She didn't want her sister to marry George? Why was she coming to him?

Suddenly Lise Marie jumped to her feet, shook out her skirts, and smiled at everyone before her eyes rested on George's face. "My lord, I should like to meet your son, Brady. He is my nephew, and soon he will be my stepson."

Miranda, no slouch, rose as well, seeing escape at hand. "Yes, let us visit the stables. I wish to see P.C.'s pony. George, Grayson, please come along."

Lady Elvebak said, "I suppose you must meet this child George claims is his long-lost son, though I doubt it's true. It's most irregular, George, the sudden appearance of this boy. I trust you haven't been duped. You will present him to me, and I will make the correct determination."

Grayson winked at George, who grinned.

Lady Elvebak was left with Clarissa, Frobisher hovering at their elbows with a plate of Cook's famous seedcakes. He said, "My lady, Miss Elvebak, I am told these delightful pastries go excellently with diamonds."

Lady Elvebak eyed the seedcakes, eyed Frobisher's polished mountain of hair with approval, and nodded majestically. "I will try one, perhaps two, of these seedcakes. Clarissa and I will tell you if they are acceptable."

"I will inform Cook, Mrs. Clyde, of your ladyship's approval."

"I haven't yet approved." She took a big bite, chewed slowly, swallowed, and nodded. "You may escort me to my usual chamber, Frobisher. I shall take another small one and repose myself before dinner. Clarissa, you will come with me. I wish you to bathe my forehead with rose water. I am fatigued." She paused at the doorway, looked back into the drawing room, and gave a small shudder. "This unexpected boy, Frobisher—who do you think he is?"

"He is, without a doubt, his lordship's son, my lady. I, ah, daresay you will wish to welcome him."

"Humph," said Lady Elvebak.

Frobisher bowed, placed several small seedcakes on a plate, and escorted Lady Elvebak and Miss Clarissa up the wide central staircase. Before he left the old harridan to her maid and her daughter, he heard her say, "After Lise Marie is wed to the baron, I shall see to refurbishing that dreadful drawing room."

Clarissa said, "I fear Lise Marie won't listen to you, Mama. Jane never did. She always laughed when you ever so nicely gave her your opinion."

"Lise Marie isn't her sister," Lady Elvebak said. "She is very different. You will see."

At the stable, the adults admired the ponies and watched P.C. and Pip being led about the training ring by stable lads, Brady's pony trotting along beside P.C.'s pony, Ginger. All were in high spirits, the children and the stable lads, who hadn't heard so much gaiety in all their years of service here, and marveled at it.

Grayson drew George aside and said without preamble, "Why are you marrying your wife's sister? Did you not suffer enough with her mother? She's a terror, George. Or wasn't she such a terror when you married your first wife, Jane?"

George never looked away from Brady, cantering around the ring on his own, his pony, Pepper Pot, tail high, glossy and brown with a white lightning strike on his face. "Oh yes, Lady Elvebak was always a terror. I'm convinced her husband died of an inflammation of the lungs to escape her. But I fell in love with Jane the moment I saw her singing and dancing in the park across from her London home. I quickly realized Jane couldn't wait to get away from her mother. Once we married, Jane allowed her to visit Ravenstone only twice, a week in June after the Season and a week in November. Not Christmas—neither of us could have borne her presence at that joyous time." His voice caught. "It was only for one year, though. Then Brady was born and he was taken and she died." He paused to collect himself. "But Lise Marie—she was here often. The sisters loved each other, and all of us spent a great deal of time together." He turned to look at Grayson, shrugged. "Lise Marie loved Jane, loved Brady for the short time he was with us, and she was devastated by his disappearance and her sister's death." He paused, looking toward his son on Pepper Pot's back. "When I finally accepted the fact I had to have an heir and girded my loins for a London season, I made an obligatory visit to Lady Elvebak. I hadn't seen her in nearly seven years. When I arrived, Lise Marie was no longer a young girl, but a grown woman." He shrugged. "Within two days, she told me she'd loved me since she was fourteen. She told me she'd waited for me to see her, really see her. And finally I did." Another pause, then, "Jane's portrait hangs in my study. You will see Lise Marie looks a great deal like her sister."

"You are marrying her because she looks like her sister?"

George shaded his eyes when the sun slithered through a gray cloud and shone brightly down on the paddock. He said finally, "I was honest with her, Grayson, told her I had to have an heir. She knows I do not love her. But I do like her. And now I've been worried she wouldn't like Brady, that she would see any male children she bore as more deserving of being my heir, but it appears she and Brady are going to become friends. She will become his mother in time. It will be all right."

Grayson prayed George wasn't being wildly optimistic. "You are also marrying her because it was easier for you."

George turned to face him, gave him a crooked grin. "Yes, I suppose you're right. I'm not noble like your Thomas Straithmore, Grayson. I am thirty-six years old. I view the world differently than I did a decade ago when I believed there would be the perfect woman for me and life would unfold as I wished it to. But life, as you well know, isn't like fairy tales—life rarely proceeds the way you want it to. There is joy and soul-withering sadness, and you never know which you'll face. And in my position, there is duty and obligation—namely, my responsibility to provide an heir to the barony."

George was right. Life was capricious; you never knew what was coming. But what had come to George was his long-lost son. Even though the situation was fraught, Grayson gave him a blazing smile. "And now you have Brady back with you."

"Yes, you brought me a miracle. I am in your debt until I cock up my toes."

"You've paid any debt you owe me, George. To see Brady home with his father, it is more than enough." He paused a moment, then said, "You said Lise Marie and Jane were very close, that they spent a lot of time together here at Ravenstone. Has Lise Marie mentioned feeling her sister when she's here at Ravenstone?"

George cocked his head. "What do you mean, Grayson?"

Grayson shrugged. "They were siblings, very close. Lise Marie must have many fine memories of her time with Jane here, isn't that right?"

"Well, of course. Yes. But no, she hasn't mentioned anything about Jane other than the occasional story she remembers fondly. Why do you ask?"

"Curiosity, nothing more."

Grayson left the baron to yell encouragement to the children, laughing at his son's antics on Pepper Pot's back. Grayson retired to his room to write. Thomas Straithmore, his hero, was involved with a virgin bride ghost and a kelpie tutor and King Arthur. King Arthur? Well, sometimes things happened in a book he never expected. Should he keep it close to the truth? He would see what came out of his fingers onto the paper. His characters many times took the reins out of his hands and did as they pleased.

After a dinner with Lady Elvebak in full flower over stewed oysters, baked pheasant, and a towering lemon cake for dessert, George asked Grayson to come to his study. Grayson looked up at a large portrait of a lovely young woman hanging above the elegant Italian Carrara marble fireplace. She was painted in a riding habit of rich dark-green velvet, her matching hat curved around her hair with a jaunty feather sticking up. She was in semi-profile, obviously smiling, petting the neck of an immense black stallion. He could feel the laughter in her eyes, her joy in life, and her smile was Brady's. He found himself opening, focusing his mind on the portrait. *Jane, if you want to tell me something, you can.* He waited, but there was nothing at all, only the portrait of Brady's mother, the sound of George's breathing and the warm air.

Grayson took a step back and considered. He supposed Lise Marie did have the look of her, but it was more in how she dressed her hair, her choice of styles, but not the same innate enthusiasm for life itself. Grayson said, "Has Brady seen his mother's portrait?"

"Not yet. I wanted to know what you thought. I don't want to overwhelm him."

"She's lovely, George. You're right—perhaps it's best to wait until tomorrow."

George never looked away from the portrait. He said, "It's odd, but I don't remember Lise Marie dressing so much like her sister, but it has been more than a decade and she was a young girl then." He took one last look at his long-dead wife and said, his voice pensive, "As we were saying earlier, life never unfolds as we expect. There can be so much pain you think you'll drown in it, and then, suddenly, miraculously, you're covered with rainbows." He stopped cold and shook his head. "I apologize for acting like the only person who has known tragedy. You lost your own wife when Pip was very young."

Grayson felt a flash of remembered pain before it faded into quiet memory. Lorelei had laughed with her eyes too, looked at life like a rare treat. But then she was gone. He said quietly, "After Lorelei died, I wanted to close myself off, shut out life, if you will, but I couldn't. I had Pip. As you know, time passes, as it always does, and the pain fades. I moved to Cowpen Dale and bought a new icebox and met Miranda and P.C. and Barnaby. And now a new page has turned." He smiled. "Right now, despite the noxious presence of Lady Elvebak, I think life is very fine indeed."

George nodded. "I imagine if I'd had Brady, I would have been forced outward as you were, Grayson. An icebox. I believe Cook was talking about how they actually work. You must tell me about this invention." He pulled out his watch and grinned like a child at Christmas. "It's time for me to tuck in my boy for the night. Shall I tell him a story?"

"Yes," Grayson said, "I imagine Miranda is singing to P.C., and Pip awaits me to terrify him with a tale of demons and evil spirits." But he wouldn't tell anyone about the *other* he'd felt so strongly, the *other* he knew was here at Ravenstone. Had the *other* been here all the time, or was it due to Grayson, his openness, his willingness to accept and believe?

Or was it the unexpected appearance of the long-lost son?

CHAPTER SEVEN

TWO NIGHTS LATER

Brady saw a woman walking toward him in the soft, dim light. He lay perfectly still, wondering how he could be so awake when he was dreaming. If he wasn't dreaming, then this meant he was in trouble. He felt a shaft of panic, and a yell built in his throat, but nothing came out of his mouth. It seemed he couldn't move, couldn't make a sound, could only watch and wait for the woman to reach him. He wouldn't be afraid of a lady. As he watched her, it seemed to him like every step she took was a conscious decision. As she neared, he realized she wasn't wearing a gown but scarlet scarves wound tightly around her. Her shoulders and arms were bare. He'd never seen such bountiful upper parts. Closer and closer she came, her long black hair flowing to her waist, swinging as she moved, as if moved by an unfelt wind. As young as he was, he recognized she was beautiful, and he also recognized deep inside that she was powerful. Dreaming, yes, he had to be dreaming. A dream couldn't hurt you, could it?

She called to him, her voice soft, compelling, saying his name over and over, almost a whisper, but he heard her clearly. He wanted to speak, wanted to move, but he still couldn't. He could only watch until she stood directly in front of him. She towered over him. She reached out and lightly touched her long white fingers to his face. Her fingers were warm, too warm, almost burning him, but he couldn't move away, couldn't make a sound. Her voice was low and soft. "Your skin is so smooth and white, your hair just like your father's. You are a fine little English boy. It is a pity you are so young. If you were older, it would be different. But you should not be here. I never foresaw Grayson Sherbrooke finding your father, never foresaw your coming home. What shall I do with you? What shall I do with *him*?"

Brady jerked up in bed. He was panting hard. He was alone—of course he was alone. A dream—that strange woman speaking to him. He had to stop being afraid. She'd been nothing but a dream—well, sort of a living dream. Why had he made her up? He touched his cheek where her fingers had lain against his skin. It was no longer burning, but still very warm. But how could a dream make his skin burn? Brady felt a spurt of terror, jumped out of his very comfortable bed, ran across the hall to P.C.'s bedchamber, and dived onto her bed. A bit of moonlight shone through the window. He shook her shoulder. "P.C., wake up, wake up!"

P.C.'s eyes flew open. "Barn—Brady, what's wrong? You had a bad nightmare, didn't you?" She threw back the covers and pulled him against her, covering them to their noses. "It's all right," she whispered against his ear, squeezing him hard. "What happened? What did you dream?"

Brady got hold of himself. He had to remember he wasn't a barn cat any longer. No, he was a baron's son, not some straw-chewing wrinkle-brain. He felt her warm breath against his cheek, felt himself growing calm. He hiccupped once, whispered, "Let me tell you before I forget what she said."

When he finished, P.C. was silent a moment, rubbing her hand over his arm. "Here's what we're going to do right now."

Grayson was aware of warm breaths and fast breathing and thought of Pip. He opened his eyes, ready to draw his son against him and soothe him. But it wasn't Pip. He saw P.C. and Brady on their knees, one on either side of him, each with a small hand on his shoulder, shaking him.

He wasn't alarmed. He pulled both of them against him, kissed their foreheads. "Are you two my middle-of-the-night late Christmas presents? Or have you come to tell me a story?"

Brady hiccupped, swallowed. "A story, sir, and it just happened."

Ah, a nightmare. "Tell me."

"And then she said, 'What should I do with you? What should I do with *him?*' She meant you, sir—she meant you. And something about she hadn't *foreseen*—that's the word she said—she hadn't foreseen you'd find me, that you'd bring me home. There was more, but I can't remember."

Grayson rubbed Brady's back. "You did very well. Now you said she had black hair, lots of it, tumbling all around her face and down her back?"

Brady nodded vigorously. "Yes, more hair than I've ever seen on a head, even more than Frobisher."

"Red scarves wrapped around her? But her arms and shoulders were bare?"

"Yes, sir, I ain't—I haven't ever seen anything like her. And her front lady parts were big and white."

Thankfully, this went over P.C.'s head. She lightly kissed Brady's cheek. "Good, Brady, that's very good. Tell him about how you know it wasn't a dream, how when she touched her fingers to your face it burned you." P.C. pressed her fingers against his cheek. "Sir, his cheek is still warm. Feel."

Grayson lightly laid his palm against Brady's face. He felt the outline of two fingers, pulsing with warmth, and Grayson felt a jolt of fear. No, no, how could Brady's visitor be Jane? She was his mother. Surely she'd want him to come home, live his life here the way he was meant to?

P.C. said, "You feel the heat, don't you, sir? So how could it be a nightmare?"

Brady said, "She was real, I swear it. She came to me in my sleep. She spoke to me and she touched me."

"What's going on?" Pip was running toward the bed as he spoke.

"Why didn't you get me?" He jumped on the bed and wormed his way between Brady and his father. "I heard you and P.C. running around. What's the matter? Did the Virgin Bride come?"

P.C. said, "Don't be a looby, Pip. The Virgin Bride's in someplace called China. No, Brady had a strange woman in his room, and she was touching his face and burning him. Feel his cheek."

Pip felt his cheek, then dived in to snuggle closer. "Was the lady Mrs. Miranda, Papa? She went to the wrong bedchamber?"

So much for discretion, Grayson thought, and kissed his son. "No, Pip, it wasn't Miranda. I think this is something else entirely." He knew to his bones Brady's visitor hadn't been Jane. Tightly wrapped red scarves, seductive, flowing black hair . . . Who? What? Suddenly he saw the ancient text he'd read at Oxford, penned, his don had told him, by a reclusive wizard said to inhabit a cave in the Bulgar. He'd never forgotten the crude drawing of the Red Witch, as she was called—an incredibly beautiful woman with long, wavy black hair, and it appeared she was swathed in bright-red flames. The wizard had written she'd escaped from hell, but no one knew if she could exist in other realms. The Red Witch was real? In this realm? Could she have visited Brady? But for what reason?

Grayson said, "Brady, when she came to you, was it light enough so you could see her clearly?"

"Not really, but I could still see her. It was like she brought her own light with her."

"Did you see her eyes?"

Brady's fear was easing. He was warm, and he was safe. "Dark eyes, sir, very dark, maybe black—I'm not sure. And there was black stuff drawn around her eyes."

Her eyes were lined with kohl. Grayson remembered the witch in the drawing had lined eyes. "When she touched your face, did you feel her fingernails?"

"No, her fingertips were flat against my skin and really hot. Why, sir? Do you know who she is?"

"Perhaps. Brady, do you remember anything else she said?"

Brady was silent, but P.C. said, "You told me she said something about your being a fine little English boy and how you had smooth skin and your hair was like your father's."

Brady nodded. "Yes, and I remember she said how if I was older it would be different. What would be different?"

Why would it be different? Grayson said, "Listen to me now, all of you. What happened to Brady—let's keep it a secret for now, all right? Pip, you too, all right?"

They all agreed. He hugged all three children to him and knew there was no getting them to go back to their rooms. "Now, let's all get back to sleep."

When George couldn't find his son the next morning, he was terrified. When he opened Grayson's bedchamber door, he felt the breath whoosh out of him, his relief was so profound. The three children were cuddled against Grayson, all deeply asleep. George stood in the doorway, his heart still pounding, regaining control. What had happened to make the children come to Grayson's room?

George turned to see Miranda walking swiftly down the hall. He raised his fingers to his mouth and stepped aside for her to look into Grayson's bedchamber. She said, "Probably one of them had a nightmare, got the other two, and here they are." George wished they'd come to him, but he managed a smile. It would take time; he had to be patient.

Miranda understood. She touched her hand to his arm and rubbed. "Understand, George, Grayson is also Thomas Straithmore to them, a hero who conquers monsters and demons. He is invincible."

George and Miranda turned to see Lise Marie tying her dressing gown as she hurried toward them.

George had never seen her hair loose. Beautiful hair, wild and thick, tousled around her face. She looked very pretty. He took her hands in his and smiled down at her. "Good morning, my dear. I apologize if we woke you. Come look. The children are all sleeping with Grayson."

Lise Marie cocked her head to one side, just as Jane had. "I heard running feet and was worried." Then she smiled and moved to stand beside them.

Grayson came slowly awake to the sound of whispers. He opened his eyes to see their visitors standing in the open doorway. He said quietly, "I had guests in the middle of the night. Let me see if I can crawl out without waking them."

He managed it, barely. P.C. did sit up a moment and say clearly, "Oysters aren't meant for ladies, Mama." And she fell back down. Grayson lightly touched her face with his fingers and knew she hadn't really awakened. He no longer slept naked, not with Pip occasionally coming into his room at night unannounced. He belted on his dressing gown, turned to see the three little bodies had moved and now were pressed close together. He drew the covers over them.

He said quietly, "I fancy one of them woke up and fetched the other two. I was the handy adult."

He wasn't going to say anything about Brady's nightmare or vision or visitation. It was too soon. He needed more information. The first thing was to draw a picture of the woman who'd visited Brady. Could it be the Red Witch? If it was, why was she unhappy about Brady's sudden appearance here at Ravenstone? He found himself eyeing Lise Marie. Or was one of the guests not what she seemed?

CHAPTER EIGHT

Later that morning, all three children were playing in front of the fireplace in the cozy drawing room while a heavy rain pounded against the windows. The air was sweet-smelling from the lavender Miranda had set in a bowl on the mantel. She and Lise Marie sat side by side on a green-and-white striped sofa that looked vaguely Dutch, worn and old and infinitely comfortable, keeping an eye on the children and discussing the wedding in two weeks. Lise Marie said quietly, "It's going to be a simple ceremony at St. Hilda's in Hartlepool, only Ravenstone staff and family present. I knew George would hate another grand wedding like the huge event at St. Paul's with my sister." She shook her head. "I want only sweet memories for George and me. My mother is very disappointed, as you can imagine."

More like infuriated she couldn't parade about in her diamonds. Miranda wondered how much unpleasantness Lise Marie had endured with that decision.

Grayson had come into the drawing room and overheard. He said matter-of-factly, "It will be delightful. You are very thoughtful, Lise Marie."

Lise Marie smiled. "Is George still in his estate room?"

Grayson nodded. "He said his manager believed Christmas was all well and good, but it was over now, wasn't it? George believed Mr. Lorrox would shoot him if he didn't get himself in order." He didn't see the old besom and Clarissa, and that was a relief for present company.

Grayson waited until P.C. vanquished Brady in a board game, then rose. "Brady, I need to show you something. P.C., why don't you and Pip play jacks?" Both children hopped up, excited.

"What is it, Papa? What are you going to show Brady?"

P.C. said, "Sir, Brady will need my opinion, no matter what it is you wish to show him."

Miranda gave Grayson a searching look, then turned to her daughter. "P.C., Pip, let Brady go with Grayson. I'm sure he'll tell you all about it later." There was just enough mother's steel in her voice so that both P.C. and Pip subsided. P.C. picked up the smooth stones and tossed them on the wide oak planking between two very old Turkish rugs as Pip picked up the ball.

Lise Marie, though, frowned at him. Grayson merely smiled at her, took Brady's hand, and led him out. "Let's go to the library. I want to show you a picture I drew."

As they walked down the corridor to the study, Brady said, "A drawing of Mrs. Miranda? She's ever so pretty. P.C. has her blue eyes, you know." He paused and frowned. "I guess I do too, only different, like my father's."

He'd finally called the baron his father. Grayson wanted to click up his heels. "No, it's not a picture of Miranda."

Brady looked alarmed. "You drew a picture of another lady? You didn't betray Mrs. Miranda, did you, sir, with this other lady?"

"No, I did not. Where did you hear that word, Brady?"

"The vicar, sir, Mr. Harkness. He said some queen named Jezebel betrayed her husband, and betrayal was a really bad sin and dogs ate her."

Evidently Mr. Harkness had had an argument with Mrs. Harkness. "No, I drew a picture of your hot-fingered lady. I want to know if you recognize her."

Grayson pulled out a piece of foolscap from inside the small marquetry table drawer and flattened it out on the top. He'd drawn as best he could from memory the picture of the witch who'd escaped from hell, known in the ancient text he'd read as the Red Witch. Instead of being encased in flames, as in the drawing in the text, he'd wrapped her in scarves. He was fortunate George kept colored oil pencils so he could make the scarves red. They weren't as dark a red as he'd like, but they'd do. He'd colored her hair black as sin, as Brady had described. "Is this something like her, Brady?"

Brady looked down at the drawing, sucked in his breath, and stepped back. "It's her, sir—maybe, sort of. But she was lots bigger on top—you know, her woman's parts. And her hair was thicker, all around her face, dancing around her head like it was alive."

Grayson didn't make her breasts larger, but he colored in more black hair.

"Yes, that's it."

"Look at her face. Is it close?"

Brady continued to study the drawing, then frowned. "I'm not sure, but I think she looks a little bit like Lise Marie, only more beautiful, like she was a painting."

Grayson drew back and studied his drawing. Perhaps Brady was right; he wasn't certain. Suddenly Brady froze.

Grayson immediately grabbed his arms. "What's wrong, Brady?"

Brady pointed, whispered, "Is that my mother?"

Grayson looked at the large painting of Jane Elizabeth Cox, Lady Worsley, hanging above the elegant Italian Carrara marble fireplace. Along with her son, Grayson again studied her portrait, her dark-green velvet riding habit, her hat curving around her hair, the clever feather. And he thought again, you knew she was smiling even though she was in half-profile. "Yes," he said, trying for a normal voice. "You have her smile, Brady. Do you see it?"

Brady said, "She's pretty. Is there a picture of her showing all of her face?"

"I don't think so, no."

"She's got her hand on the black stallion's neck. What happened to the stallion?"

Grayson blinked. You never knew what would come out of a child's mouth. "We'll ask your father." He paused a moment, then said, "Brady, I would ask you not to mention my drawing to anyone. Well, P.C., but make her promise not to tell any of the adults, all right?"

Brady nodded. "I doesn't—don't—even want to think about the hot-fingered lady." He swallowed and pressed against Grayson. "Do you think she'll come to me again tonight, walk right in my room and talk to me and burn my face?"

Grayson said matter-of-factly, "I think you should sleep with your father tonight, Brady. Trust me, your father will keep her away." Grayson was uncertain what to do now. He didn't want to alarm anyone, but this Red Witch, for whatever reason he had yet to fathom, was real and deadly. But why was she here at Ravenstone? Why had she focused on Brady?

Brady appeared thoughtful as he slowly nodded. "We can talk about King Stuart winning the Guineas at Newmarket." He paused, and a big smile lit up his face. "Father let me sit on King Stuart's back yesterday." Brady gulped and nearly choked up. "It was the best moment of my life."

Grayson placed the drawing back in the drawer and led Brady back to the drawing room, which turned out to be a mistake since Lady Elvebak was holding court, lecturing Pip and P.C. about their atrocious manners.

Pip raised his head when he saw his father. "Papa, what's *atro-shus* mean? Is it bad? The big lady made it sound bad."

George, who was speaking quietly to Lise Marie by the closed draperies, turned and laughed. "Lady Elvebak was only jesting, Pip. This room is meant for a happy family, a place where you can play and talk, even sing and clap your hands. Carry on." And he sent his former mother-in-law a look to freeze her blood, but Grayson didn't think it had more than a momentary salutary effect.

After a lunch of paper-thin ham slices, warm bread, cheese, and a dish of peas and carrots that weren't touched by the children, Grayson knew he couldn't let George continue in ignorance, knew he had to include Lise Marie and Miranda. If Lise Marie was somehow involved with the Red Witch, he would know—he'd see it on her face. But how could she be? None of it made any sense. He needed to visit George's library, see if any of the older books looked promising.

The four of them adjourned to the study, leaving Frobisher and Mrs. Clendenning to oversee the children's reading in the drawing room. Grayson was well aware P.C. wasn't about to let Brady out of her sight. As for Lady Elvebak, she excused herself after ten minutes, complaining that the unrestrained children's noise gave her a headache. It was true there was a lot of laughter because P.C. was reading Mary Lamb's humorous retelling of *A Midsummer Night's Dream* written for children, acting out the parts with some talent.

The children didn't notice when she made her stately exit from the drawing room. However, Clarissa didn't accompany her mother. In fact, she moved closer. After a few moments, she said, "P.C., can I read Bottom's lines?"

Mrs. Clendenning said, "Ah, Bottom, I always enjoyed him. I believe there is another copy in the library. I'll get it for you, Miss Clarissa."

CHAPTER NINE

That night Brady slept with his father, and both Pip and P.C. slept with Miranda. As for Lise Marie, she slept with her door open. Grayson made himself as comfortable as he could on a chaise pushed behind the large armoire in George's bedchamber. He lay in the dark silence listening to George whisper stories about King Stuart's past races.

Grayson had to admit he was relieved when George only raised an eyebrow at Grayson's account of the visitation of the Red Witch to his son the night before. George wasn't about to let his son know he found the so-called visitation more a fantastical nightmare. Lise Marie tried to accept what had happened to Brady, but it was obvious she believed, like George, that he'd had a nightmare—a new house, a new bed, that was her opinion. As for Miranda, she was quiet. Later, she kissed Grayson, shook her head, and remarked that no matter where he was, if there was something otherworldly hovering in the vicinity, it would find him. Grayson wondered if she had a point.

As Grayson lay there, a single blanket pulled to his chest, he asked himself yet again, *Why would the Red Witch come to Brady?* He'd had Brady repeat several more times what the Red Witch had said to him, until Grayson was satisfied. *Your skin is so smooth and white, your hair*

*just like your father's. You are a fine little English boy. It is a pity you are
so young. If you were older, it would be different. But you should not be
here. I never foresaw Grayson Sherbrooke finding your father, never foresaw
your coming home. What shall I do with you? What shall I do with him?*

It was obvious she'd believed Brady was either dead or gone for good,
believed he'd never come back to Ravenstone. Had she arranged for him
to be taken? But why? For the life of him, Grayson couldn't figure out
why she would even come here in the first place and why she would
care. *Brady, what is it about you that brought her here?*

The Red Witch didn't make an appearance that night. Grayson slept
soundly until the morning sun poured through the windows onto his
face. He quietly left the bedchamber, with a final look at Brady, asleep
with his face on his father's shoulder, both lightly snoring.

The day was fresh from yesterday's rain, but cold. Fortunately, there
was no wind. The sun continued to shine bright as a polished shilling
through the naked-branched winter trees.

There was no keeping the children inside, so all the adults—with the
exception of Lady Elvebak, who demanded Frobisher read to her and Clarissa from Mary Shelley's *Frankenstein*, which Frobisher was to say later
nearly scared the hair off his head—bundled up and headed to the stables.
The children rode their ponies, while George, with Lise Marie riding a
black mare named Lilah next to him, led them on a tour of his lands. They
stopped at every tenant farm. George introduced his son to his people,
and he was so obviously happy. His people were clapping and smiling
and calling his son—his son!—Mr. Brady. Lise Marie and George were
congratulated on their upcoming wedding. All appeared to approve of her.

Grayson overheard P.C. tell the baron, "I like the Clavers, and Mrs.
Claver's lemonade is excellent, but sir, I must tell you, Brady and I saw a
small roof leak in the kitchen. The next rain won't be good. The Clavers
didn't mention it to you because you were so happy to have Brady back
with you. Brady wanted you to know."

He stared down at his son, who was holding the little girl's hand, pulled a small notebook and pencil out of his coat pocket, and handed it to Brady. "Thank you. Now, any more repairs you see that need to be attended to, write them in the book."

"Papa," Pip said, "I must have a book too in case P.C. and Brady miss some leaks."

"You don't know how to write yet, Pip."

This was a blow. Pip sighed. "It is time I learned, Papa. Teach me next week, all right?"

It was a lovely morning. The children raced their ponies across an open field, and Pepper Pot won, Brady shouting at the top of his lungs, P.C. claiming it was all luck, and Pip cheering, not caring who won.

Lise Marie had asked Mrs. Clyde to pack a picnic lunch. At last George led them to a small old six-sided stone building, a hexagon he called it. There was no lichen or ivy covering the weathered gray stones. The door looked like a tall, arched church window. It was Ravenstone Folly, he told them, built by the Cox heiress who'd insisted the manor house be renamed Ravenstone, and this small tribute to her was to be called Ravenstone Folly. The floor was scarred wide oak planks, nothing else. The single room was just large enough to spread out the white cloth and arrange the food on it. They all gathered close together, laughing, talking, eating every morsel. No one else seemed to notice the small space didn't smell quite right, only Grayson did, and he frowned. What was that smell? Was it only age, too many years piled on top of each other and somehow trapped in here? Or was it that someone had crouched here, throwing strange ingredients into an iron pot, speaking low, singsong incantations? Grayson wanted to laugh at himself and his too-active imagination. He took a bite out of his chicken leg.

When the cold chicken, sweet local goat cheese, rolls, and jam were a memory, P.C. asked the baron, "Sir, why did the Cox heiress call this Ravenstone Folly?"

George said, "I was told by my father the Cox heiress wanted it named Witch's Haunt. Why, I don't know, but maybe this story explains it. A very long time ago, Druids lived in these parts. Actually, many of them lived in the woods near Stoker's Rise, along with witches, powerful witches, it was said, who ignored the Druids. The Druids, supposedly, were afraid of them and kept their distance. Then, a few years later, evidently the Cox heiress wanted Witch's Haunt changed to what it's called today—Ravenstone Folly. Why did she change her mind? No one knows."

P.C. moved closer to Brady, took Pip's hand, and drew him next to her. Brady said without thought, "You mean like the Red Witch, sir? Was she the queen of the witches? Do you know if she lived here?"

George didn't know what to say. He sent a look to Grayson, who smiled and said matter-of-factly, "I think the Red Witch is a good name, makes you stand up and take notice, makes you wonder at unexpected shadows and listen for strange sounds. It could fit right in one of my books, don't you think so, Pip?"

Pip gave this some serious thought. "This Red Witch, Papa, she's scary, but not as scary as your demons and spirits."

When they'd packed up their picnic and walked outside, it seemed to Grayson he could breathe more easily—he felt freer. Miranda looked around her, at the crumbling pilasters, the two chipped stone columns that fronted this strange folly. "I think it's more this looks like some sort of stage scenery they use in plays, like it's all made up so you feel a sense of darkness and doom."

P.C. nodded. "Maybe the Cox heiress was an actress and built it so she could perform her silly magic tricks here, or maybe she came for picnics, but I can't imagine that. Inside, well, it's sort of gloomy."

Brady said, "Who wants to have a picnic with a witch? She might throw you in a cauldron instead of feeding you chicken."

So everyone felt something strange and scary about Ravenstone Folly, not just him.

George said, "All good points. Now, let me tell you about Stoker's Rise, a name that goes back to the Middle Ages to Josiah Stoker, who wanted to be buried in a pyramid like those in Egypt. He spent years bringing dirt in his ancient wheelbarrow to exactly where Ravenstone stands today, slowly building it up, adding rocks and dirt and pebbles so it wouldn't wash away in the rains. Folks knew he hadn't built any chamber in his pyramid like the ancient Egyptians did, so how could he be buried inside? But Josiah only shook his head. When he finished the rise, he proclaimed he was ready to die. It's said he climbed to the top of the rise, and from one moment to the next, he was gone—he simply sank into the pyramid." By the time George finished speaking, his voice was a whisper. The children were gathered close around him, mesmerized.

Pip said, "Do you think his bones are under your house, sir?"

"I sincerely hope not, Pip," George said. "But who knows?"

Grayson looked at the children's rapt faces. *You're magic with words, George. And this Ravenstone Folly, what is it about this place that unsettles everyone?*

After lunch, they rode to the nearly overflowing banks of the stream that ribboned its way through the land to the river Tees. It wasn't all that deep, but it was wide enough, George said, to make it important to know how to swim. There was something about the calm gray water that made the children stand well back from the shore.

Brady said, "I wonder what's on the bottom."

P.C. poked him and whispered in a singsong voice, *"Sink into my depths and a monster will grab your toes and chew them off."*

There was laughter, abruptly shut up when a sudden wind blew up, a wind so vicious, so powerful it pulled pins from the ladies' hair and made their skirts whip about their legs. Suddenly Brady yelled. The wind was shoving him toward the stream. The water was no longer calm; it was roiling, bubbling up, moving fast and faster still. George reached out to grab his son, but Brady was lifted off his feet and hurled into the water.

The wind swirled around George and Grayson, pushing them back, but together they managed to get to the water's edge. It was as if there were an invisible wall in front of them. Brady's head came out of the water, and he yelled, "Papa! Help!" But neither George nor Grayson could move, no matter how hard they pushed against the unseen force. Grayson grabbed both Miranda's and Lise Marie's hands, and the three of them ran into George. He broke through the invisible barrier and jumped into the water. When he cleared the surface, he stroked fast and hard toward Brady, managed to grab him under his arms to bring his head out of the water. George tried to swim against the powerful current back to shore, but he made no headway. They were being carried downstream.

Everyone raced along the shore toward the stone bridge that arched over the stream to the other side. Miranda grabbed a stout tree branch and threw it to Grayson. He ran to the middle of the bridge, leaned down, and shouted, "Grab it, George!"

George managed to wrap his hand around the branch, holding tight as the current pulled and jerked at him. His hand slipped. Brady, one arm around his father's neck, grabbed the branch with his other hand. Lise Marie, Miranda, and Grayson pulled. Grayson shouted, "George, we're going to bring you back to the shore. You and Brady, kick as hard as you can against the current."

The adults pulled with all their strength as they staggered back across the bridge to shore, dragging Brady and George. They heard George yelling constant encouragement to his son. When at last Brady and George staggered out of the stream, George enfolded his son in his arms and rocked him back and forth. "I couldn't have held the branch without your help, Brady. You're a hero."

As suddenly as it had come up, the wind died. The water was placid once again, moving slowly downstream. It was as if nothing strange had ever happened.

All of them were panting, so grateful there were no words. As for Grayson, watching George and Brady, he knew he would admire this man until he penned his last novel.

P.C. ran to Brady, pressed herself against his back, and whispered over and over, "You saved your father. I will let you save me someday from highwaymen, I promise."

"Me too, Brady," Pip said, and squeezed in.

Grayson wanted to laugh, but there was simply no laughter in him. Both Miranda and Lise Marie were wind-whipped, their hair tumbled around their faces, their gowns askew. Both George and Brady were pale, wet, and shivering, but at least they were alive. And all knew the wind hadn't been natural. It wasn't a *who* that wanted Brady dead—it was a *what*.

CHAPTER TEN

Grayson searched out an empty part of the garden, settled himself on a bench beneath a rose arbor, cleared his mind, closed his eyes, and focused. Time passed. He held his focus. Slowly, the cold air grew warmer.

"Open your eyes, Mr. Sherbrooke. I'm here."

A beautiful woman, the image of her daughter, Delyth, was seated beside him, stylishly gowned, her fair hair wrapped in thick braids around her head. She looked to be, perhaps, the age of Delyth's older sister. He had no idea exactly how many years she'd lived in this earthly realm. She sighed and placed her white hand on his arm. "I am Arkadie Ramsey, mother of Olafar and Delyth. I can see you already recognize me. I suspected you might call to me. I did not wish to interfere unless you felt you needed me. My appearing isn't usually done, but I worried after I bade Delyth tell you the name of Brady's father. Again, my thanks to you for what you did for Olafar." She paused a moment, looking beyond him, beyond the present—where, he knew not. She said, "I knew the Red Witch had lived here at Ravenstone for a very long time now, that she had merged with Gabrielle, the only daughter of the Cox heiress, as you call her. Gabrielle was a very willing vessel and a stronger witch than her mother. She settled in, and time passed. I remember years ago I heard talk, as we of my kind do, that Gabrielle had stolen the babe of Baroness Worsley, who then herself died. Until very recently, I believed the poor lady had died of a broken heart because of her lost son, but of course it wasn't true. But the truth eluded even my scrying mirror. But now, given what's happening, it is my belief Jane refused to join with the Red Witch—or, if you like, refused to merge into her, to become one with her—and thus the Red Witch killed her. But none of it was clear, however, even in my visions. All I knew was the Red Witch in any guise, be it a baroness in modern-day England or a succubus in ancient Persia, is dangerous. Yes, she is called the Red Witch, but she is indeed a succubus, feared throughout the land in ancient days, near to forgotten today.

"It is my feeling the Red Witch believes Lisa Marie to be more accepting, more malleable, than her older sister, Jane, and thus set her in George's mind when he knew he had to wed to produce an heir. Then, unexpectedly, you entered the picture, Grayson. I granted you a favor, and you returned the baron's long-lost son to him.

"I know if she isn't stopped, the Red Witch will kill Brady, as she tried to do today. She will try to seduce Lise Marie. Will she give in, accept what the Red Witch offers her? I cannot see the truth of that—too many branches stretching off that path to follow all of them, if you will."

She rose and smoothed her lovely skirts. "Go to George's library. You will find a book lying on his desk. You will read what's important to all those here."

Grayson said, "Thank you, Mrs. Ramsey. Can you tell me how to stop her?"

"There is only one way. You must remove her vessel—that is Gabrielle."

"But Gabrielle has been dead for hundreds of years."

"Ah. Do not forget, Mr. Sherbrooke, evil never long remains unseen and unheard. It waits to slither out again and again, bringing endless pain and suffering.

"I thank you again for what you did for my beloved son, Olafar. He is the happiest of men now. If you need me again in the future, perhaps I will come, perhaps not." Arkadie Ramsey seemed to shimmer, then she slowly faded away. The air seemed to chill again, making him shiver. He said quietly, "Thank you, Mrs. Ramsey. I forgot to ask you about Olafar and Mathilde."

He heard a soft voice whisper, "Their family just moved to Rome. Olafar is a friend of the Borgias. I believe the pope plans to make Olafar a cardinal. Mathilde is very happy, and I am a grandmother, at least three centuries ago. They return once a year, Olafar to visit with our family and Mathilde to visit with the Sherbrooke twins, Jason and James."

He wondered what it was like for Mathilde to become a ghost again, only to return to a time before she was born so she could be alive. Such endless convolutions. He rose, shaking his head, and walked quickly to George's library.

An hour later, Lise Marie passed around hot cups of tea in the drawing room. No one wanted to talk about what had happened, not yet—it was simply too overwhelming—so what conversation there was came out of Lady Elvebak's mouth, and she had only one theme. She pointed a diamond-laden finger at Brady. "You shouldn't have dived into the stream—irresponsible, that's what it was. I hope you learned your lesson, young man. You nearly drowned your father. I wouldn't have been happy because dead he couldn't have married Lise Marie."

Pip looked up from his blueberry scone, a frown on his face. "I will ask Papa why the Red Witch is mad at Brady."

Lady Elvebak said, "That is quite enough. You are too young, a little parrot, nothing more, spouting whatever your father says, and all know he writes frightening novels, not real life. Red Witch? What nonsense."

Lise Marie said, this time her voice firm, even a dollop of impatience, "Mama, we have told you. Brady did not dive into the stream. There was a sudden powerful wind, not a normal wind, and it focused on Brady. It shoved him into the stream. It wanted to kill Brady. For heaven's sake, Mama, look at me and Miranda. We looked a fright when we came in. It was that wind. It knew what it was doing. It was—evil."

"Ha! That a daughter of mine could become hysterical along with the rest of you credulous—"

Grayson walked into the drawing room in that moment, a very old book under his arm. He paused, knew immediately what was going on, and wasn't at all surprised. He said easily, "Pip, may I have a scone?"

Pip jumped up, grabbed a scone, and gave it to his father. "I'm glad you're here, Papa. I don't like any of this."

"It's nearly over, don't worry." He seated himself next to his son and Miranda and took a bite of scone.

Lady Elvebak eyed him. "Just what do you mean by that, Mr. Sherbrooke, it's nearly over?"

Grayson said, his voice easy, calm, "Pip, you wonder why the Red Witch is mad at Brady and Lise Marie believes it evil?"

"It's all nonsense," said Lady Elvebak.

"It is frightening," Clarissa whispered, and shot a look at her mother, "if that's really what happened. Are you certain Brady didn't jump into the stream?"

Brady, still white as a sheet, shook his head, whispered, "Something was shoving at me, really hard, like a lot of hands or maybe a moving wall, just pushing, pushing." He fell silent, swallowed. P.C. immediately took his hand and moved even closer to him.

Clarissa said, "I wish I had been there to help you, Brady."

Lady Elvebak stared hard at Grayson. "What is that book you have?"

"This is the history of the Cox family, their genealogy, if you will, along with comments made by various past barons." He added to Pip, "Genealogy is the recording of fathers, mothers, children, births and deaths and marriages, down through the centuries so you know who your family is now and was then."

George frowned. "I'd forgotten it even existed. I can't imagine how you chanced upon it. I suppose I should bring it up to date. I know my father paid it no attention, so entries probably stop with my grandfather."

Grayson cleared his throat, looked at the children, knew there was no choice—they had to hear this as well. "That's true, George. All of you, please listen. The book begins with the first Baron Worsley, who built

Ravenstone in 1633 on land granted to him by Charles I. Bartholomew Cox. He was a banker, not a soldier, so it was financial assistance he offered to King Charles I, with the result he didn't have enough money to build a manor house worthy of his new title. So the king arranged his marriage to Henriette du Plessis, the younger daughter of the Duc de Lac, a wealthy nobleman in Normandy. All called her the Cox heiress. The union was fruitful. There were eight children; two survived to adulthood, one girl and one boy. The Cox line continues to this day, George, though all entries stopped with your grandfather.

"This is what the first Baron Worsley wrote when he was a very old man." Grayson opened to the page he'd marked with a slip of foolscap and read aloud.

She is finally dead. I never thought to outlive her, but I have. If my ancient bones would allow it, I would dance a jig. Yes, I am certain she is dead. I myself saw her laid out in her coffin in the drawing room in all her finery, her corpse rotting, for it has been hot. I relished every nasty breath I took. Still, I demanded the doctor assure me yet again that she was well dead. I myself threw the first clot of earth on her and prayed with all my might she might stay inside the special coffin I had made for her, the lid solid iron and nailed down on all sides.

So at last it is over, and I can now record what happened. Henriette was a vindictive witch of incredible power. Her father knew it, of course, and that's why he made me such a huge marriage settlement to get her out of France. She ordered my life just as she ordered everyone around her. If she was displeased with me, she gave me boils on my neck and in my armpits until I was afraid to even speak unless it was to praise her. She told me to build her Ravenstone Folly, a paean to some ancient Greek witch, and so I did. She spent a great deal of time there alone, for which I was profoundly grateful. I know not what she did during those hours she was there, probably mixed evil potions and prayed to witches past and future, and schemed.

It was not long after King Charles II was married to Catherine of Braganza that Henriette was invited to attend the queen. How she managed this, I do not know. The king enraged my wife with his brazen indifference to his wife and queen, and his unashamed debauchery, which was distressing to his poor queen, who suffered four miscarriages in her efforts to produce an heir. It is true Charles was a foolish man, albeit charming, but he was my king, a great deal better than that hypocritical monster Cromwell. I feared for him because I knew what Henriette was and what she could do. Indeed, I'd suffered under her hand for years. But I knew I had no choice. I was granted an audience with His Majesty, and I told him the truth. He was disbelieving but polite, of course. The following months, the king, I was told, suffered greatly from boils, hives, and stomach pains so great he nearly expired. Of course, this curtailed his visits to his many mistresses. I know in my heart Henriette was responsible for his suffering. She did not punish me, so I knew she had not discovered what I'd done. When the queen dismissed Henriette from court, the king's suffering stopped. It is my belief the king finally told his queen about my visit and what I'd said about my wife, and that is why she sent Henriette away.

I remember once when she was in her cups, she said over and over she was descended from the Red Witch of Fire, and the Red Witch was still here, waiting for a proper vessel, possible because fire was the most powerful of the four elements. I wondered if she herself wanted to be the vessel.

She disliked her only surviving son because he was common like me. Gabrielle, her only surviving daughter, has become more terrifying than her mother. At least she ignores me, believes me a doddering old fool not worthy of her notice. Before I die, I must get her married off to some French nobleman, a fitting turnabout, and out of England, or I know she will kill her brother, for she despises him. Is she the vessel for the Red Witch?

Grayson raised his head. "He writes no more. There is a note written by the second Baron Worsley that his father died two days after he wrote these final words. He also writes his father had been in good health one moment, and the next, he was simply dead."

Lady Elvebak half rose and shouted, "It is nonsense, utter nonsense, like one of your silly novels." She eyed George. "I fear for your issue, George, since you descend from this cloth-head. His wife, a witch! Descended from the Red Witch of Fire? It is absurd. It is all a farrago. It nauseates me that any of you could be so credulous. Lise Marie, you don't believe this, do you?"

Lise Marie held up her hand and asked Grayson, "What happened to his daughter, to Gabrielle?"

Grayson said, "There is no marriage listed, no death date, only a birth date. Her name is simply marked through. She was erased. By her brother? I think he's the most likely. Like his father, the second baron lived a long and fruitful life, so whatever happened to Gabrielle, she was unable to kill him, or he simply wasn't important enough to her to kill." *Perhaps Gabrielle didn't die at all,* he thought, but he didn't say it aloud.

Grayson paused. "I've wondered about the succeeding Cox wives. All of them have lived well into their nineties, much longer than the times would dictate. Until Jane."

Lady Elvebak rose majestically to her feet and gave them all a look of disgust. "Mr. Sherbrooke, you do everyone a grave disservice, putting these ridiculous ideas into their heads. Clarissa, come with me. I wish to have my tea in my room. Bring a plate of scones."

CHAPTER ELEVEN

That night, Grayson lay on his back in his bed. The room was quiet; the only sound he heard was his own breathing. He looked toward the large armoire in the corner, saw no movement, and closed his eyes. He waited. *What now?*

He finally fell into a twilight sleep, then suddenly he jerked awake to see her standing at the end of the bed, swathed in red scarves wrapped tightly about her. It was dark, but he saw her clearly. She seemed to glow. She appeared young, her body lush; her breasts, nearly uncovered, were milky white, a dramatic contrast to her ink-black hair, thick and vibrant, waves dancing around her pale face. Her coal-black eyes were thickly lined with kohl. Deep and hard her eyes, and they were focused on him. She was beautiful and terrifying. She wasn't of this world. It appeared she could indeed exist in other realms, at least in this one.

He slowly sat up in bed and watched her lean toward him, pressing her breasts together, the temptress. He hoped she couldn't hear his heart pounding. He said pleasantly, "You are the Red Witch, who became one with Gabrielle Cox three hundred years ago, Gabrielle the daughter of Henriette and Bartholomew Cox?"

He imagined she meant her voice to be low and musical, but to his ear she sounded like she'd newly come from hell itself. And if fire was her element, why did she send out waves of cold? "Yes, she is part of me. Gabrielle and I became one. We are still one."

"Is this because you cannot exist without a host witch here?"

The air seemed to shift around her, light colors splashed in the air, and he heard a different voice, low, musical. "I am Gabrielle. Unlike my poor mother, who tried and tried, her final potion, her final incantation, exploded her old heart. Ninety-two she was in your years, never ill in her life. All marveled at it, but not my father, accursed common creature that he was, and my equally common brother. I saw his joy when she died. And then my miserable brother removed me from mortal existence. Before I breathed my last, the Red Witch saved me, taught me how to attach myself to the afterworld and enjoy consciousness and power. As a bribe to my brother not to try to kill me, she granted him long life."

"You are her host?"

A slight pause, then, "We are one. That is all you need to know."

"So your brother erased you from the family book. How did he try to kill you?"

The red scarves shimmered and seemed to wrap more tightly around her. Her beauty was astounding. He felt the hair on the back of his neck stir.

"The oaf put a sleeping potion in my wine. He choked me with one of my mother's silk scarves, but the Red Witch saved me."

Grayson wished he'd known the second Baron Worsley, a man of his time who'd believed in evil and dealt with it. Only he hadn't—not quite.

The Red Witch said, "We know who you are, Grayson Sherbrooke. Your abilities are acknowledged among our kind—among many kinds, actually—but now it will gain you naught. You will not stop us."

"Stop you from doing what? Killing a little boy who has done you no harm?"

"One of us wanted him dead because he should not be here. It is so easy to snuff out the life of a babe, but we did not. We merely removed him from this house—our house—and he survived. We admit we were surprised when that interfering witch Arkadie Ramsey told you who his father was, but we were willing to wait and see what happened.

"But no longer. Unlike the others, we will be the ones to kill you and that little brat you brought back to our home. We do not know how you found the family book, but it doesn't matter. You cannot stop us. We own Ravenstone. It is our home and will be our home forever."

"You killed Brady's mother, Jane, didn't you?"

She laughed. The scarves glittered in the dim light, and her hair danced about her face. "Ah, Jane, we had such hopes for her. All believe she killed herself, threw herself in the stream and drowned because of her grief for her stolen babe, but none spoke it aloud out of respect for the baron. And it was repeated until, finally, it was believed."

Grayson saw movement from the corner of his eye and hurried to say, "What do you mean, you had such hopes for her?"

"For nearly two hundred years we have controlled the wives of one baron after the other, until that cursed Jane. Like the others, we came to her, offered her a long and pleasant life, a male heir to carry on the title, with us at her side, asking nothing much, really, simply content to be here in our home."

"Why?"

Gabrielle laughed again. "We promised my mother we would protect what was hers forever, see to it our line continued, see to it *we* continued. And the only way we could remain here at Ravenstone is to meld with the wife of the baron. The two of us alone weren't strong enough to combat the tides of time or the pull of hell. Two hundred years we've flourished, and Ravenstone has flourished, just as we promised. When we made ourselves known to Jane, she laughed at us—laughed!—told us she wanted nothing we could give her. She told us we were evil. She denounced us, consigned us to hell."

Grayson said, "So you shoved Jane into the stream like you did Brady today."

"We had the strength to do it. We admit, Jane surprised us. She was a strong swimmer. We had to hold her under. Then we had to bide our time for years before the baron realized he had to have an heir and wed again. We knew Lise Marie, Jane's sister, had loved him even as he'd loved her sister, and now, finally, she was old enough to wed with him. We had faith in Lise Marie, so quiet, under her mother's influence, malleable. She would welcome us and our promises once she was wed to the baron." Her hair lifted away from her face as if blown by an unseen wind. She seemed to grow more beautiful, her body more lush. "Until now, there has been no magic, no power, in any of the Cox male children. We have finally created a potion we will feed Lise Marie's son. It will make him magical. He will see us, recognize us. He will control all of you paltry earthly beings. He will not be like Jane's son, a common little boy, anchored to this earth, no wildness in his heart, no magic in his blood.

"We will make a bargain with you, Mr. Sherbrooke. We will not kill Brady if you simply remove him and return him to where we left him eleven years ago. All will be as it should be again. The baron will be happy with Lise Marie. He will watch her son rise to greatness in this human world, and we will be at his side, only he will not know it, but Lise Marie will."

Grayson said quietly, "George, it is time."

George Edward Cox, eighth Baron Worsley, stepped from behind the armoire set against the far draperies. The Red Witch whirled to face him, her scarves flying out around her, then tightening themselves again. She stared at him, shaking her head. "We did not know you were here, Baron. We wonder why we did not catch your scent. We suppose it's because we have grown too used to the scent of *otherness* on all of you. But it does not matter. So now you know the truth. You now know it is a bright future we offer you. So now you know what to do."

George said matter-of-factly, "Yes, now I know exactly what to do." He smiled at her, hard and cold. "I will not marry Lise Marie, so all your plans, your schemes, your potions, will come to naught.

I will sell Ravenstone. I will tear down that accursed folly stone by stone. I will take my son, Brady, to live elsewhere, far away from here, far from you."

An unseen wind tore at the red scarves, blew the thick black hair into tangles. "No! You cannot. You belong here. For three hundred years your family has belonged here. We belong here! We must stay here!"

"Or what?" Grayson said. "You will cease to exist? You, the Red Witch, you will be returned to hell where you belong? And you, Gabrielle, you will finally die as you were meant to so many years before?"

"No!"

It was George's cold rage that allowed him to smile dismissively at the shimmering witch whose beauty and seductiveness seemed to reach out to him, meant to stir his lust, meant to make him crave her with all his being. He said very precisely, "You murdered my wife, and you stole my son. I loved them more than my own life. Here is what I will do: if you kill either Brady or me, the Cox line will become extinct, and all properties will revert to the crown. Of course, there are many Cox relatives, but they are all women. There are no males to inherit. Did you not realize my last living male heir died six months ago? Tell me, is Grayson right? Will you, the Red Witch, be returned to hell? And you, Gabrielle, will you finally cease to exist when my line dies?"

She leapt forward, her red scarves swirling around her, her hair blowing into his face. She screamed, "You cannot leave Ravenstone! You will not! You will remain here. You will wed with Lise Marie, or we will—"

"Will what? Kill me like you did my precious Jane? Again, you know you cannot. Your threat is meaningless." He paused a moment. "When you shoved Brady into the stream, I jumped in after him. What would have happened to you if I had drowned?"

Silence.

George smiled at her. "No, you didn't know the Cox line would end with my death. If you had known, you would have been forced to save Brady as well, for I would not have let him go."

Grayson gave a huge yawn. The Red Witch whirled on him, a white hand stretched toward him, fingers curved into claws, the red scarves billowing. "This is all your fault! How did you find the book with Gabrielle's name erased from it? How did you know?" She was panting. "*You* we can kill."

Grayson said, "Don't even consider it. If you smite me dead, George will still leave Ravenstone."

George snapped his fingers. "Brady and I will leave that fast. I swear that before my son. If you dare to harm Grayson, I will not sell Ravenstone—I will burn it to the ground. Would you burn up with the house? Would the two of you be flung into hell where you belong?"

She was silent. The red scarves began to whip around her body, faster and faster. She screamed out, even as she backed away, "We will return, and we will know what to do. You will not leave. You will not! You cannot!" And she was gone.

After a moment, George walked over and sat on the edge of Grayson's bed. He dropped his head into his hands. "I wouldn't have believed such a creature—actually, two of them in one body—could exist, much less what she—they—have done over the centuries."

"You held firm, George. I wonder if she—they—will come back?" He grew thoughtful. "You know, I don't believe they will. They are somehow tethered to this specific place, to this specific house, the house of the Cox heiress, Gabrielle's mother. What will happen to them if you, the Cox descendant, leave? Will they grow weaker until they are no longer able to exist in our world? I don't know."

George raised his head. "I don't care. Do you know, the only thing I will miss about Ravenstone is my splendid stud. But I will sell the house and build elsewhere." He smiled. "I think Brady would enjoy living near P.C. and Pip. He and I can build a new stud. King Stuart will continue to win. Brady will be safe. Our lives will be our own." He looked down at his clasped hands. "I suppose I will also miss the drawing room. Jane loved that room. Maybe I can re-create it. I believe Lise Marie and I should still wed. These past days, I find I have grown very fond of her—her honesty, her strength, her goodness. What do you think, Grayson?"

"I believe I heard of a large property that's become available, not five miles from Wolffe Hall, a lovely old manor house I believe Lise Marie would like very much. The owner is in debt and must sell."

George rose and rubbed his hands together. "There is one thing I know I must do before we leave. I must destroy Ravenstone Folly."

EPILOGUE

Gabrielle, part of the Red Witch for so very long, was gone. Even the memory of her spirit had been crushed by the baron's final act, tearing down the folly, hacking away each stone. But it was Grayson Sherbrooke who'd instructed the workers to cart the stones away, separate them, and bury them deep. The women had smoothed down the dirt and planted lupines. It was as if Ravenstone Folly had never been.

When Grayson Sherbrooke had arrived, the Red Witch had known who and what he was. His reputation had spread that far and wide, and she'd counseled Gabrielle he was dangerous to them and to keep her distance from all of them, but they hadn't. Gabrielle had begged to visit the baron's newly found son, and so they had. And the brat had gone directly to Grayson Sherbrooke.

Ah, Gabrielle. The Red Witch supposed she'd enjoyed Gabrielle's sometimes witty observations as she hovered in Ravenstone Folly, her mother's sanctuary and workshop, where the old witch had stirred her potions, planning new tortures for those around her. The Red Witch had to give Gabrielle credit for perfecting the potion they'd planned to give Lise Marie's son. But now it was all for naught. She was a human witch, withal, tethered to this place, to this family. When the last stone from the folly had been smashed, she was gone.

Like Gabrielle, the Red Witch hadn't believed the baron would sell Ravenstone, his ancestral home, the home Gabrielle's mother's money had built three hundred years before, but he had. He'd packed up all the furnishings, removed the horses, and moved those servants who wanted to go with him and his son, including their extended families, even Sullivan the trainer's mother from Wexford, Ireland. Nor had he left the tenant farmers to the mercies of an unknown new owner. He'd sold only the house and grounds. The rich farms were still his and his responsibility.

She'd watched, helpless to stop the baron and his men, watched his newly found son, Brady, work as hard as anyone, always smiling now, laughing, knowing they would move close to where he'd spent his first ten years, and she wondered yet again why they hadn't murdered the brat. None of this would have happened if only they'd simply killed him. But Gabrielle's one good deed didn't matter now.

Would the baron even miss Ravenstone? Feel its loss deep in his bones? She didn't know. Finally, the house stood empty, yet even then the Red Witch didn't leave. She spent hours roaming the rooms or sitting on the smooth mound of earth at what had been Ravenstone Folly, remembering. Even though she knew she had no choice but to leave, for a chance to save herself from being sucked back into hell, part of her still wished everything could be what it had been again. Only it wasn't, and it never would be again.

Still, she lingered until the rich merchant family arrived with a score of screaming children and a pack of servants, who appeared quite a different lot. The new master, prosperous and common, and his fat wife, with her double chin and loud voice, appeared at first awestruck with her magnificent home, but then they immediately changed the name to Wyford House. She finally had to accept her home for the past three hundred years was no more.

She knew to survive she would have to find a new vessel soon. At least she knew where to go, to a young witch who was already being whispered about behind hands. Would she make her part of herself, nourish and hold her in moments of elation or fear, perform magic together, rejoice in common bonds?

The Red Witch whisked herself off to Italy, to Mantua, to the elegant Varano villa, in the Varano family since the sixteenth century. She hovered, watching the big house, splendidly elegant and graceful in a way the English would never understand, knowing that once she became one with the wife, she would regain her purpose, enhance her power, and feel again the pleasures this world offered.

She watched the twice-widowed Count de Varano, older, fashionably bewhiskered as were his contemporaries, perhaps even more debauched than his father and his father before him, and his tender young raven-haired bride, seemingly so helpless and fragile, so malleable and soft, walk through their lovely terraced gardens, weaving in and out of the long, stately line of cypress trees that bordered the Mincio River. She knew the marriage had nothing to do with mutual affection; it was about joining wealth and property to garner more power for the families.

So this fresh young innocent wife, now the Contessa de Varano, was the witch being gossiped about. None knew it but the young lady herself when she'd begun to come into her power. She'd found ancient texts in her father's library, writing of the magic in her line. The Red Witch had herself scented the magic on her and rejoiced.

Even as she watched the couple, watched the husband fondle his wife's breast, the Red Witch moved closer, her nostrils filled with the magical scent on the young contessa, a welcoming smell, an inviting smell, and she knew Lucretia would give her a new home. She would be happy here.

From the terraced garden, the young Contessa de Varano stopped and looked around her. She scented *otherness*, as if the air itself was parting and giving her something precious, meant for her alone. It was close and drawing closer. She opened herself to the marvelous sensations, the power and completeness, and welcomed it. She felt at one with the *other*, and so very strong, as if there was nothing she could not accomplish now. She realized then the *other* was the Red Witch of lore, written of in the ancient texts.

Her new husband continued to fondle her breast. She let him, feigned interest, for she was, after all, a new bride, and she knew her duty. There would be time enough to give him what he deserved.

ENGLAND

JUNE 1842

On a warm sunny day in June, King Stuart won the Guineas at Newmarket for the second year in a row. Brady and P.C. and Pip were clustered together and yelling, waving their arms, cheering wildly, just as the adults were cheering behind them. George Cox, Baron Worsley, hugged his wife, Lise Marie, close and kissed her soundly. Then he turned and gathered his son to him and whispered, "Jane, you would be so proud of our boy."